KJ BURRAGE

HERALD
TO THE
DRAGON
KING

BOOK 3
THE DRAGON'S HEIR

Paperback ISBN: 978-0-6454001-8-2

Hardcover ISBN: 978-0-6454001-9-9

Published by Valiant Heart Publications

Cover designed by MiblArt

Before You Read

This title was written with upper YA readers in mind. While Herald of the Dragon King is not particularly gory or "spicy", it does include instances and themes that are (hopefully) heartbreaking. Herald of the Dragon King includes themes and discussions including alcohol consumption, anxiety and depression, blood and corpses, death, grief, mentions of past poisoning, physical abuse slavery, violence and torture. Please note Herald of the Dragon King includes battle sequences and some characters display symptoms of PTSD.

Contents

To coffee addiction and a wild imagination. Thank you.

No, seriously, thank you to those people who believed in me.

To my first editor, my ever patient mum, Jacki Stevenson.

My first Beta reader, Janine Burger, who has been reading my stuff since she was 8.

And my mother-in-law, Kaye Burrage, for devouring everything I have written so far.

SION
SION
SILK PALACE
ARAH
THE STRONGHOLD
TORRYN
HABRON
PALLARYN
SILVERDYNE
ANDROSSAH
HABBETH
AVIAH VALLEY
PARU MOUNTAINS
KUDAH
HAVEN
BAY THRANGUL
PARUHULISE
KORKALIE
TORQUI
ADDRYN SEA
RAMA

SILK PALACE
SION
STONETHAW RANGE
TORRYN
HABRON
ARIMAC
PALLARYN
TANNRYN
LAKE OF MIRROR
SILVERDYNE
PALDERA RIVER
ANDROSSAH'
HALBETH
AVIAH VALLEY
PARŪ MOUNTAINS
HAVEN BAY
PALDERA RIVER
KUDAH
THRANGUL
PARUHULISE
KORKALIE
TORQUI

TORRYN
RSHON LAKE
THE STRONGHOLD
PALLARYN
ARELLE FOREST
Rshon Spine
DYNE
PALDERA RIVER
ADAVAN FIELDS
PALDERA RIVER
RANGUL
LAKE OF MEMORIES

CHAPTER ONE
Jodathyn

Solan's Summer House, Aviah Valley

Tornyth bucked and writhed under the pressing weight of Deovyn and reconsidered the wisdom of allowing his dragon brother to goad him into sparring. Unable to jostle his *sudunyn* off his back, he huffed at the indignity. Long blades of grass tickled his nose, and he sneezed. Smoke curled from his nostrils.

From across the field, he could hear Mandros' booming laugh. He was sure that if it were possible, his white scales would flush crimson. He sneezed again, this time igniting the grass. Reaching out a clawed hand, he extinguished the small fire.

"You need better control than that, white scales." Ignoring the chuckling of the russet dragon, Tornyth wrenched his head around to nip him. His teeth missed and hit thin air.

Deovyn's rumble deepened. "Do you surrender, *sudunyn*?"

Tornyth growled. He blinked, focusing on the humans before him. The *vehyl* seemed to be torn between the fascination of the wrestling match and the awe of the dragons that were landing among them. The vast green fields belonging to Solan's estate stretched further than the human eye could see. Lord Solan liked to keep a firm barrier between himself and the common villagers, even if he rarely visited his summer estates.

Several guardsmen had retreated, giving Mandros' league of dragons room to land and scent the air. Not Guardsman Carew. He sidled closer to Zapyr, craning his neck to take in his size. Lowering his head, Zapyr flared his nostrils, and the guardsman had the audacity to stroke the golden scales of his face.

"You're a big fellow, aren't you?"

"I would hope so," Zapyr replied. "I swear you humans get smaller with each passing century."

"Nonsense. It's your head that's swelling, Zapyr." Deovyn playfully pressed Tornyth's snout down into the dirt.

Carew tilted his head back and laughed, waving his comrades to come closer. He was a brave one, Tornyth decided. The moment the young King's Guardsman had volunteered to ride on his back into battle, he had known he was a natural dragon rider. Not all humans took to the skies well. The king's captain, Tiernan, should be proud of his second-born son.

"Do you surrender, *sudunyn*?" Deovyn's breath was pleasantly warm along his back spines.

"I am absolutely defeated, brother," Tornyth replied.

Knowing that his brother thought he had been subdued, Tornyth waited until the russet dragon roared his victory. As Deovyn celebrated, he darted forward and nipped him in that soft, vulnerable part of his neck.

"Ancient One's Talons, Tornyth!" Deovyn cried. He swayed his triangular head from side to side with a growl of pain. His large, tawny eyes narrowed, promising retribution.

"I thought you were a big, bad battle dragon. Are you going to let a little nip stop you?" Even though it had only been a minor victory, Tornyth preened.

"It burned!" Deovyn snapped. "Your bite burned!"

"Hatchling! I shall never surrender!" Tornyth replied. Across the grass he heard a few of the other dragons' amused rumblings at Deovyn's cry of indignation.

"Then prepare to have your scales knocked off!" Deovyn stalked forward.

"Careful, war worm," Nym cried. "I saw our dragon bite you! He might do so again."

"It would be my pleasure." Tornyth rose and lunged. Deovyn lowered his head, and their horns clashed.

Blinking at the power of the impact, Tornyth retreated.

"Dragon skulls are hard, brother." A sly grin split Deovyn's scaly face, which widened with the promise of revenge. He unfurled his wings, and an invisible force ripped Tornyth off balance. He tried to dig his claws into the earth, which only gouged holes in the ground as he toppled over. The wind intensified, and he tumbled nose over tail.

Dragon laughter rang in Tornyth's ears when the force relented and he could stand on his own two feet. Dizzy, he sat on his haunches and glared at his *sudunyn*.

Deovyn ignored his growled warning, turned his back and locked gazes with Et-hir and Nym, who were standing apart from the king and his men. Carvelle stood docilely at Et-hir's side, his little hand clutching hers as he looked around at the dragons in wonderment. Deovyn lifted his claws and waved. "Don't fret, ladies, your white dragon is mostly unhurt."

Et-hir's shoulders shook with her laughter. Snorting stray bits of grass from his nostrils, Tornyth took his time to study her. His defeat soured her attention. Deovyn cast him a knowing smirk, and Tornyth lunged.

Deovyn roared in shock as fangs bit down into the flesh of his neck. Annoyed and embarrassed, Tornyth squeezed his teeth together. His vision clouded over. The blood running through his veins heated and then cooled.

The abrupt change of temperature made Tornyth's body convulse. Pain erupted behind his eyes. Crystals of ice formed on the membranes of Deovyn's wings and along the scales of his face.

"Tornyth, let go," Deovyn gasped. His wings unfurled as he dug in his claws and jerked his body back.

Tornyth did not hear him. There was another voice, uninvited, speaking to him.

"Death to the son of Mandros."

A moan escaped Tornyth's lips. He braced his back legs and attempted to pull his teeth free of Deovyn's scales. He felt his teeth slice across his brother's neck, wishing he could scream in horror of what he had done.

"I killed his human in battle."

Fury and hatred that he knew did not belong to him took Tornyth's breath away. He stumbled backwards and slumped to the grass.

There were sounds all around him. Lying on the soft grass, his energy drained, Tornyth was pulled into a vision.

He saw horses screaming, their riders struggling to keep them under control. Above, he sensed the awful oppressiveness of Grey Shadows.

The scene shifted around him. One of the Grey Shadows held a King's Guardsman in its grasp, squeezing with all of his might. Tornyth shuddered involuntarily, hearing the bones crack and groan under the pressure. Orion shot at the Grey Shadow, and then he cast his bow aside. He was running towards the dreaded creature and pressed his hands against the Grey Shadow's scales. Power warmed his blood, and his hands came away burned. Even though the pain in his palms was agony, Orion took up his sword …

Tornyth came back to himself to the sight of the king's sword impaled in the ground in front of his eyes. His brother's hands tapped his snout to rouse him.

"What's wrong with him?" Kieryn's voice was tight. The king glared around at the assembled dragons. "What have you done to my brother?"

His head felt like it was stuffed full of duck down. Tornyth raised his gaze. Mandros was at his side, his reptilian body taut, ready to pounce, while Zapyr's wings were fanned out to halt the other dragons from coming closer. The scales around Deovyn's bite were burnt and blistering. At his side, Sidrah was tending to him. The teal dragon, Curarfur, was observing Tornyth's movements carefully.

It was with some shame that he took notice of Captain Tiernan holding Carvelle to his side, his free hand on the pommel of his sword. "Otherworlds," Tornyth groaned. "What happened?"

"This is what comes of harbouring dragons," a guardsman muttered. There were murmurs of agreement, and Tornyth lowered his snout in shame.

"Nonsense. He's grown dragon who hasn't been properly nurtured when he was young. You foolish humans think you can tamper with a dragon's soul and there be no consequences." The strength of Zapyr's defence surprised Tornyth. He had expected anger. "If you do not wish to support my *sudunyn*, you are free to leave."

Kieryn's fists clenched at his side. It was rather presumptuous of Zapyr to dismiss the king's men.

"Touch a shield-fire dragon at your peril, humans," snarled a dark red dragon. His scales reminded Jodathyn of the colour of Kieryn's finest wines.

"Calm down, Edisyn." Deovyn lifted his head. "No one is going to harm Tornyth."

"Ice-fire is a difficult power to control at the best of times. Tornyth will learn to better regulate the power now that he is aware it's in him." Sidrah moved away from Deovyn. Under her steely gaze, the humans shuffled. Tornyth ignored the uneasy glances.

"Aluel? What's shield-fire? Is there something wrong with me ...?" Tornyth's guilty conscience stopped him from admitting to Mandros that his thoughts had in fact been sinister in nature.

"Shield-fires are dragons who do not possess battle-fire. They often dedicate their lives to the nurturing and building up of dragon communities."

"There's something wrong ... I hurt Deovyn."

"I know. Stay quiet until we can work out a way to help you." Mandros' calm almost put Tornyth at ease.

Above him, Mandros shifted. "Is there anything else you want to tell me, *mynrell*?"

With a weary sigh, Tornyth manifested back into his human form. Kieryn gripped his elbow. It was an unnecessary movement. Jodathyn was quite capable of changing forms without losing balance. He let his brother 'help'.

"I had a vision ..."

"*Mynrell*?" Mandros inched closer.

"I heard, Your Majesty, that you sent out some of your men early this morning?" Jodathyn asked, searching Kieryn's face. "They've been, or will be, attacked by Grey Shadows."

Captain Tiernan swore. Carvelle squirmed in his grip and at the king's nod, the captain released the prince. "Are they alive?"

"One dead," Jodathyn confirmed. Carvelle ran past his father and straight into his legs, wrapping his arms around his middle.

Jodathyn glanced up, spotting Nym's pale face. She had been angry this morning; the guardsmen said it was because her brother, Theo, had run off with the king's delegation. And now he had delivered some bad news about what may have befallen him.

Carew laid a comforting hand on Nym's shoulder, leaning over to whisper in her ear. Jodathyn frowned. Hadn't they been fighting this morning? Now they seemed friendly.

"Theo did not feature in the vision, Nym. Hopefully that means he is alright. I saw a death of an older guardsman and Orion attempting to shoot the Grey Shadow ... His hands came away burned ..."

"Power almost always manifests heat," Jael said.

"Or a lack of it." Tiernan's eyes roved over Jodathyn from head to toe.

Agitated, Zapyr unfurled his wings. There was an intense anger in his hard, azure gaze. Jodathyn shifted even though he was certain that the golden dragon's ire was not aimed at him. "*Aluel*, I'll go and help the one called Orion."

Without waiting for permission from Mandros, Zapyr turned towards Kieryn. "Where did you send your *vehyl*?"

"Silverdyne," Jodathyn replied, "I'll go with you."

"No," Mandros said. "You're not yet ready to fly into unknown situations."

"I can ..."

Mandros shook his head. "We're at war, *mynrell*. It's not wise to expose an untrained dragon, no matter who he is. Or what he is capable of."

Jodathyn nodded his head. He hated to admit it, but Mandros was right. This wasn't the time to test his dragon's ability to adapt in a fight.

"I'll bring your friends back," Zapyr said. He leaped into the air and with two quick beats of his wings, he was gone.

Mandros watched and with a shake of his head, he gestured to two other dragons. "Salvea, Gylleah. Go with him."

While everyone's attention was on the departing purple and silver dragons, Carvelle tugged on Jodathyn's pant leg. "Uncle," he whispered. "You mustn't listen to the voice."

Jodathyn's mouth was dry. How did Carvelle know about the bodiless voice that had spoken to him? He repressed a shiver of revulsion. The other's presence had been suffocating, dripping with malice.

"He's gone now," Carvelle said, taking his hand. "It's safe, Uncle."

Jodathyn swallowed again, keeping his eyes along the horizon. That was the question. Was he safe? Was there a darker, deeper power within him thanks to his dragon side? He had been so relieved to taste true freedom for the first time in his life that he did not stop to question the motives of the creature within him.

Under Mandros' watchful gaze, Deovyn slunk closer. The movement caught Kieryn's eye, and the king's hand darted out for his sword. Cocking his head to the side, Deovyn dipped his head and ceased.

"Kieryn, this is Deovyn, my dragon brother," Jodathyn said. He turned his attention to the russet dragon. "Are you well?"

"Injuries happen when dragons wrestle," Deovyn replied.

"It looked like two grown dragons playing to me," Carvelle said.

"Yes, I can imagine that is what it looks like to untrained human eyes." Deovyn grinned, turning his head to look at Sidrah, who was rolling her eyes at him. He lowered his whole body to the ground, using his hind legs to shuffle his snout closer, his keen amber eyes on Kieryn. The king shifted his weight, his fingers glossing over the handle of his sword.

"You must be the famous little prince." Deovyn's nostrils flared. "You're adorable."

Cocking his head to the side, Carvelle replied, "Am not. I'm almost grown. And you're a *young* dragon."

"My apologies, my prince," Deovyn said. Spreading his wings out wide, he swept into a bow, lowering his crowned head to acknowledge Kieryn's presence. "A pleasure, Your Majesty. I am Deovyn Wind-Speaker, son of Mandros."

"Indeed, it's a pleasure to meet you, lord dragon," Kieryn replied. He inclined his head regally, keeping one eye on Carvelle as he did so.

"Before Tornyth, Deovyn was my youngest," Mandros said. "The one you named Jodathyn after."

Kieryn's eyes widened. "You were Jodathyn the Small and Mighty?"

"I'm still small and mighty." Deovyn folded his wings. He craned his neck to take another look at Carvelle.

"Uncle has the Sight," Carvelle said. "Sometimes he makes funny sounds when he's sleeping."

"That's called snoring," Deovyn replied.

"I don't snore!" Jodathyn bristled.

"You snore, little brother." Kieryn scoffed. He absently let his hand drop to his side, his gaze returning to Carvelle, who was now poking Sidrah's foreleg. It looked as if the young prince was trying to pluck out the silver specks among her black scales. Sidrah for her part looked unbothered by the attention.

"My brother is unhappy," Jodathyn projected to Mandros.

"It's only natural. He's a good papa who's not used to our presence, and his child is awfully close to an apex predator." Mandros looked his way and

then turned his face to glance over at his assembling dragons. *"He'll find his peace with us soon."*

Carvelle moved towards Mandros, tilting his head as he did so. "I like your tattoo," he said. "Uncle should cover his slave tattoos as you have. They're horrible."

A smile curled on Mandros' face. "My tattoos, young prince?"

Carvelle gestured to the space at Mandros' left-hand side. "Your human has a tattoo of a dark dragon impaled on ... is that a spear? It's a bit gory, but I guess suits the fact you were a warrior king."

"You can see the ghost of my human heart." Lowering his head, Mandros eyed Carvelle as if he was a strange curiosity. "You can see me for who I once was, can't you, little one?"

Carvelle blinked. "That's how I knew the white dragon was my uncle. I saw them together when he landed. But then Orion whacked him on the nose. Silly Orion thought he was saving me. The dragon wouldn't hurt me, but Orion wasn't listening."

Mandros' smile only grew. By now other dragons had pressed in closer, along with the King's Guard.

"What type of power is this?" asked the teal dragon, Curarfur.

"Can smell his blood from here," Sidrah murmured. "It practically sings with power."

At the mention of blood, Kieryn startled. His hand was upon his sword. Tiernan copied the action. "Lord Mandros ..."

"Not to worry, *vehyl pallu*," Mandros replied. "House Pallarus is a blessed lineage. Power runs strong in our bloodline. Even though you hold no power of your own, your blood still sings with possibility. Carvelle has inherited his power from you. It seems your son can see people and dragons as they truly are. His powers will continue to develop as he matures."

"Aluel, is he?" Jodathyn had never seen Deovyn so hopeful.

Lifting his crowned head to the sky, Mandros laughed. The sound reverberated around the fields, and the ground quaked until the green dragon quietened to chuckles. There was a fierce joy in Mandros' amber eyes when he answered. "We have the Herald of the Dragon King and the one who will be the new beginning. The Dragon King himself."

"Yes," Carvelle said. "I was born to be king, and I have a dragon. I'll be emerald one day, just like you."

To his dying day, Jodathyn would never forget the shock that crossed Kieryn's face. The king's hand groped thin air as if he could draw his errant son closer to him.

Chapter Two
Jodathyn

Solan's Summer House, Aviah Valley

"Are you sure you are well?" Jodathyn's concerned gaze swept over Deovyn. To mull over his new and potentially lethal power, he had isolated himself to be alone with his thoughts. Deovyn had sought him out and curled up at his feet. The russet dragon had been quite content to snooze in silence while Jodathyn studied the other dragons from afar.

Deovyn stretched his wings and tucked his tail under his belly. "Do you see any injury?"

Jodathyn winced, his mind going back to the ugly burns and oozing blistering on his brother's scales. "Something is not right with me. I burned you."

"Well, that's no bad thing," Deovyn replied. "Your power did exactly what it was supposed to do. Next time be careful when nipping a friendly dragon. Oh, here we go ... the first brave human."

Understandably, the humans had their reservations about having dragons in their midst. But as time passed, curiosity demanded that they creep closer to study the dragons.

"They were waiting for the humans to approach them," Tornyth whispered as Jodathyn spotted Jael striding between two dragons in order to introduce himself to Sidrah. *"It's the best course to take with frightened creatures."*

Sidrah lifted her head gracefully and peered down at Jael. The troop medic bowed to the black dragon, who turned her face to call for Curarfur. The teal dragon rolled to his feet. He slinked across the grass, careful to keep his belly close to the ground to appear nonthreatening.

"They'll be comparing notes about us," Tornyth whispered. *"Healers are always keen to learn off one another."*

"Time for *Lord Deovyn* to shine." Standing, Deovyn stretched out his wings once more, winking down at Jodathyn.

"What are you up to?"

"Wrestling with the humans has two benefits. One, a chance to hone my skills, and two, show them we're not scary, unthinking, uncaring beasts."

Deovyn lumbered forward, approaching a small group of guardsmen who had been edging closer. He lowered his head so that he was eye level with the humans. Jodathyn stifled a laugh as the russet dragon pleaded his case.

It didn't take him long to convince first Nym, then Carew to spar with him. He tried to coax Voran into playing, but Jodathyn's old personal guard gruffly rebuffed any efforts to join in and stormed towards the house.

Tiernan watched the red-haired giant and shook his head. He grasped a spear out of one of his men's hands. "Let's see what you've got, dragon."

Deovyn looked immensely pleased.

Meanwhile, Carvelle weaved in between the dragons, introducing himself and asking them about their powers. The dragons welcomed him enthusiastically. General Roane, the olive dragon that Mandros seemed to trust above all others, let Carvelle touch the supple membranes of his wings. Kieryn watched his small son intently, his arms crossed against his chest.

"It'll take some time for our vehyl brother to feel comfortable around dragons," Tornyth whispered. *"Look, there's Fydellah and Ruevyn."*

As Jodathyn approached them, Fydellah lifted her head in greeting. "I can't read them as well as humans," she complained.

Jodathyn considered the concerned look on her face. "Their humans are long gone. Dragon minds work differently. Sidrah would like to answer your questions."

Fydellah raised her eyebrows at him.

"She's the black one with the healers," Jodathyn said. He lifted his hand and pointed her out. "My dragon sister was very patient with me."

Fydellah glanced over to Sidrah and Jael, looking uncertain if she should disturb the healers. Curarfur had rolled onto his back, his belly soaking up the sun's rays. He looked to be asleep. Jael was standing, leaning up against his side.

"She won't mind?" Fydellah bit her lip.

"She'll be more than happy to speak with you. Go on. She doesn't bite." Jodathyn grinned. "Well, not humans."

Stiff-backed, Fydellah moved across the lawn towards Sidrah. For a long moment, Jodathyn watched her, then turned towards Ruevyn, who cleared his throat.

"Do you not wish to speak with the dragons, Rue?"

"The dragon I wish to spend time with is here, right beside me," Ruevyn replied.

Turning, Jodathyn smiled at his friend.

"We're on the precipice of war," Ruevyn said. "Some that we love have already paid the ultimate price."

"What are you trying to say?"

"No one is watching us. They're busy … One last run through the gardens, Joddie?"

Jodathyn snorted. "Aren't we too old for these games, Rue?"

Slapping Jodathyn's shoulder, Ruevyn turned tail and ran across the lawn. "Never! You're it!"

"He's mine!" Tornyth roared.

Breathless, Jodathyn leaned against the rough bark of the apple tree. He looked up the twisted branches and was tempted to climb her once more. His dragon had a better idea.

"The stream is overgrown," Jodathyn said. Stooping, he plucked up two apples and gestured with a nod that Ruevyn should follow him. "I want to show you a dragon trick."

Intrigued, Ruevyn followed, and Jodathyn tossed him an apple. The farmer ran his fingers over the firm, red skin. They didn't seem as rosy or healthy as the ones that were found in the King's Orchard, but Jodathyn lifted it to his lips.

"To eternal friendship!" Ruevyn solemnly saluted with his apple and took a big bite. And spat it right out again. "Argh!"

Jodathyn laughed at Ruevyn's expression, and his friend lobbed his apple at him. It missed and hit the ground with a solid thump.

"Swim?" Tornyth suggested.

Raising his eyebrows, Jodathyn tossed his own apple over his shoulder. He said nothing and led his friend to where he knew the water ran deep. The bank was shrouded with overgrowth, which would provide them with some privacy. He unlaced his shirt and let the cool autumn breeze tickle his belly.

"It's a beautiful afternoon," Ruevyn remarked, "but don't you think the water might be a tad cool for a swim?"

Jodathyn threw his shirt at Ruevyn before manifesting into his dragon form. He stretched out his reptilian head over the water and breathed. "Not for long, my friend."

Ruevyn bent down, testing the water with his fingers. "It's warm."

Jodathyn returned to his human shape as his friend eagerly tugged his shirt over his head. His stomach cramped upon seeing Ruevyn's tattoo, and his fingers rubbed at his own. Ruevyn's eyes lingered on the runes; when he caught Jodathyn's eye, he looked away.

"No longer shy, my prince?" Ruevyn asked.

"I trust you," Jodathyn replied. Ruevyn Kelvie had been at his side when he had been a vulnerable child. To break the tension, he said, "Apparently, lowborns bathe in streams with their pants on."

Ruevyn let out a bark of laughter. "How did you learn that, I wonder?"

Jodathyn waded into the warm water, letting it lap around his sore muscles. When he found a deep section, he dunked himself under the surface. "I'm not sure I want to incriminate myself."

Ruevyn followed him, staring in disbelief. "This feels amazing."

Jodathyn closed his eyes and basked in the warmth. "I love being warm. I wonder if it's the dragon in me."

"Yes," Tornyth whispered, *"I love heat. Warm is safety."*

"I've missed this," Ruevyn said, "just you and me."

"Couldn't imagine Illeanah joining me for a swim." Jodathyn chuckled sadly. "You should have met her, Rue. She was intelligent and witty and ..." Tilting his head, Jodathyn studied Ruevyn carefully. There was a strained expression on his face, as if Illeanah's name was unpleasant for him to hear. "Sorry, I shouldn't speak of it—"

"It's perfectly alright to talk about your highborn friends," Ruevyn said, stepping further into the water. "I'm not jealous."

"I always thought that she'd be the one I'd marry," Jodathyn murmured. Ruevyn had turned away. It was hard to tell if it was the right time to talk about his life. "There was no one else and then ... Et-hir ... and Illeanah is dead ... And if I think too hard on it, the guilt is crushing me."

"You never made a promise to Illeanah," Ruevyn said. His voice was tight. "Did you ever tell her you loved her? Or kiss her or even hold her in your arms?"

"No." Jodathyn sighed. "But her death hurts."

"She's gone, Jod. Nothing you can do can bring her back," Ruevyn replied. "Besides, Et-hir is a better choice of woman for you. She'll bring you joy."

"I'm sorry. You came out here for a lovely afternoon, and here I am ... feeling ..." There were no words that Jodathyn could speak to describe his confusing emotions.

"I came to spend some time with my friend," Ruevyn said. He floated on the surface of the water, his eyes shut. "Whatever he might be feeling. I've missed you more than words can say."

Jodathyn rubbed warm water into his sore muscles. As he did so, he heard voices approaching. He tilted his head, instantly recognising the deep tenor of his brother and the low rumble of Mandros.

Dunking himself deeper into the water, Jodathyn contemplated calling out to let them know he was nearby. However, he didn't want to explain to his brother what he was doing swimming in the stream like a small boy. Especially since he had a bath like a proper gentleman last night. Normally, he had Carvelle with him; playing with his nephew often gave him a reasonable excuse for some of his escapades.

He couldn't see where they were. They seemed to have paused in their walk. Waving his hand, Jodathyn hushed Ruevyn. If he strained his ears, he might hear what they were saying.

"My son, Carvelle," Jodathyn heard Kieryn say. "Twice now you have mentioned he has a bond with the white dragon."

"Yes," Mandros rumbled. "It is something I am puzzling over myself, *vehyl pallu*. The bond was created before the prince's birth ... an unusual occurrence indeed."

"I am afraid I do not understand, lord dragon."

"An act of great sacrifice is the only way a dragon can bond with an unborn."

"How is that possible?" Jodathyn heard his brother trail off. "Jodathyn was only thirteen summers when Carvelle was born. His dragon had not manifested."

"A young dragon comes into their own between eleven and fifteen summers," Mandros said. "It could be that Tornyth was trying to manifest. It's unprecedented, but I surmise the dragon may have had an influence over Jodathyn."

Jodathyn sucked in a breath. The terrible memories of his attempted poisoning of Lord Solan came unbidden to his mind. Could this be the sacrifice that Mandros had spoken of? He had nearly lost his life in saving the queen and Carvelle. He had assumed that since his Sight warned him of the plot against the queen, Tornyth had urged him into action.

"My son." Kieryn paused. "A dragon?"

"Yes, dragons will only bond with dragons," Mandros said. "When the time comes, Tornyth will naturally step in as *Rshon Aluel* for him. He doesn't know it, but he's already dragon father to the prince. Always has been. Always will be."

"Jodathyn is very close to my son."

"You will always be Carvelle's *aluel*. The first concept of dragon fathers wasn't to replace the *vehyl* fathers of vulnerable dragons."

"Jodathyn has called you *aluel*."

Mandros' answering rumble held a hint of anger. "I'll not honour your father, *vehyl*. He doesn't deserve my respect. I'm simply Jodathyn's *aluel* since his own father abandoned him."

"I never understood why ..."

"Jodathyn told me you saved his life when he was a child."

"Yes," Kieryn admitted. His voice was soft. "Now I am a father myself, I can appreciate the horror of it more. I couldn't bear to tell him the truth of the matter. At three days old, Jod, poor little mite, was taken before the king's council for judgement. He had not been fed, and they wrapped him in the sheets his mother had birthed him on. I think Father hoped he would die from neglect. He didn't. He was strong and very noisy."

"Dragon young are resilient," Mandros said. "And noisy when scared and hungry."

"I begged Father to show him mercy, and the council relented. When I strode across the room to pick him up for the first time, he opened his eyes. It wasn't the eyes of a human baby that looked at me ... I saw the dragon ... I've kept this secret. I've told no one in case the council found out and demanded to have him killed."

"I would hazard when your unborn child was in danger, Tornyth acted to repay your mercy. Dragons have extraordinary memories."

Jodathyn could hear Kieryn sigh heavily. "Tell me, dragon, how is this all possible?"

"You're asking me about the origins of dragonkind in Rama?"

"Yes."

"Dragons were ancient even in my time. To understand the value and tenacity of Ramian dragons, you need to know Artrothian history."

"*Artroth*?" Jodathyn could hear the incredulous tone in his brother's voice.

"What do you know about the natural enemy of Rama?"

"Very little," Kieryn grumbled. "Most of the histories have been lost."

"Do you not think that might be a mistake, to remain ignorant of your enemy? Never mind. While humans have forgotten their dark and ancient past, we dragons have not. When the world was young, thousands of years before I walked the earth, the Artroth islands were ruled by powerful beings called the *lyron finyr*."

"*Lyron*? As in armour?"

Kieryn may not be as adept in the ancient tongue, but his brother had a good command of the known aspects of the almost forgotten language.

"*Lyron* means scales or armour; *finyr* is overlord. *Lyron finyr* can be translated to scaled-armoured overlords. They were dragons, pure of blood. *Lyron finyr's* human forms were said to be powerful and beautiful. But they were ruthless and ruled the islands of Artroth with iron fists. They only mated with other *lyron finyr*—those born with mixed bloodlines or dragonless were killed under the rule of the Artrothian emperors," Mandros snarled. "And humans ... they considered humans either a resource to be mined and discarded.

While their society was certainly corrupt, not all *lyron finyr* sided with their emperor. Families and clans began to break away, especially those who had young that were half-blooded or dragon deficient. It is in a dragon's very nature to protect what is theirs.

Rumours of another land occupied by scattered *vehyl* and plenty of resources reached Artroth. The fleeing dragons called this land *Ramyr*, or safety. Over time and many years, it became Rama.

It infuriated the *lyron finyr* who continued to hold to the old ways. They considered those who fled a resource that belonged to them. To this day, this is how Artrothian *lyron finyr* think of Rama. Theirs for the taking.

Our great dragon mother, Glory in Green, was one of the fleeing dragons. Her brother had no dragon of his own, and so her *aluel* smuggled them to Rama. She was the first Ramian dragon to rebel against Artroth openly. She realised that humans who descend from Artrothian dragons could, in fact, manifest into dragons. The rise of the Ramian dragons began with her. We revere her. We call her Mother Dragon.

Even if Artrothian blood runs thin, the potential power of dragons remains potent. It's there in the bloodlines, waiting to emerge again. It will always be a part of Rama."

"This war … this Galgothmeg?"

"Although Ramian dragons have long left her shores, we have kept the Artrothians at bay. The fight for your kingdom has long been fought over the oceans and far-off places. Now Artroth is bringing the fight to you."

"And Jodathyn? How does Jodathyn fit with all this?"

"A white dragon in Artroth is said to be near impossible," Mandros said. There was smugness and pride in the dragon's tone. Tornyth rippled in pleasure. "Artrothians believe he is the harbinger of doom."

"Is he?" Kieryn asked. "Their doom?"

Mandros laughed; the sound seemed harsh. "He could very well be. An impossible manifestation, a strong secondary power; don't let his shield-fire fool you. Tornyth is a dangerous dragon."

Mandros and Kieryn's voices faded away, leaving Jodathyn staring at Ruevyn in disbelief. Ruevyn tilted his chin to look up at him. "Well, that's certainly Ramian history like I have never heard before."

"Our land is ancient," Jodathyn murmured. His heart fluttered in his rib cage.

In his bloodline, perhaps in many Ramian bloodlines, ran an inhuman power. He knew as he had listened to Mandros' words that they were absolute truth. He was dangerous. The question was, how dangerous?

CHAPTER THREE

Orion

The Road to Silverdyne

Orion's stomach twisted itself into knots as the two remaining Grey Shadows landed on the road. Through the soles of his boots, he could feel the ground trembling under the weight of the dragons. Peering through the dust and dirt, he could make out one of the foul beasts nudging their companion.

Thankful that his power still held the first beast paralysed, Orion glanced at Lyntton. He could feel the beginnings of panic. Lyntton's eyes flicked toward him, then pointedly to Theo, who was a trembling mass of nerves. Orion could only pray that his power continued to hold.

The Grey Shadows prowled around their helpless companion, swaying their heads back and forth in confusion. Then the larger of the pair lifted his head to stare at them with empty eyes, its lips curling into a snarl.

Sweat beaded on Orion's forehead. He could feel his power struggling to hold down the Grey Shadow. The warm tingle of his gifting became a burn, and he had a strong desire for water.

"Merciful Otherworlds!" Theo groaned, his face paling. "What if they eat Edd?"

Swallowing back bile, Orion let his eyes wander over to the corpse at their feet. Edd's body was so mangled from the crushing power of the Grey Shadow's fist that he knew it was not possible for him to have survived. With injuries like that ... a man like Edd wouldn't want to live out his days so terribly broken. The thought sickened Orion.

"We protect him. It's the best we can do," Lyntton replied. Orion could see the muscles in the older guardsman's jaw clenching and felt a little better. As experienced as he was, Lyntton was still struggling to remain composed.

Flexing his fingers, Orion turned his face away from the sight of his burned hands. Even now he could feel the heat of his power prickling his skin. Although the fresh burns made the endeavour painful, he forced his fingers to hold on to the grip of his sword. He would die with his blade in his hands. There wouldn't be much he could do against two massive grey dragons, but he would never surrender. If today was the day death greeted him, he would perish fighting.

Orion returned his eyes to the road, curious why the Grey Shadows were delaying their attack. He was by no means in a rush to engage them in a fight. Their slow response had him on guard.

Together, the Grey Shadows swayed their heads back and forth. They brought their mouths close to their paralysed friend, and rumbling spewed forth flames. The fire engulfed the helpless dragon, and it shrieked and wailed. Orion stepped back, observing with a detached horror as his power continued to hold the dragon immobile. The putrid smell of the burning dragon permeated the air.

"Oh, how merciful," Theo moaned, with a roll of his eyes.

Shielding his face from the flames with his arm, Lyntton turned towards them. "The forest! Go!"

"You jest! That's kindling!" Theo cried. Orion detected a hint of hysteria in his voice.

Quashing the feelings of dread, Orion rebuked himself. His father had trained him for difficult situations. This was his moment. Grasping the sleeve of Theo's shirt with his free hand, he gave the thief a little push. "We can't stay here! The forest is an obstacle. Go!"

One of the Grey Shadows lifted its enormous head, regarding them with empty eyes. It lurched forward, its movement disjointed and unnatural. It advanced with a gait of a predator who knew its prey had no escape.

Orion readjusted his grip on his sword again. "Theo, run to the forest. I'll give you as long as I can. Run and don't stop."

"Otherworlds!" Theo muttered. "I wanted to see the dragons of old, not monsters."

"Maysden! Shoot. I'll attack," Lyntton shouted.

Licking his lips, Orion had his sword sheathed and bow notched within a matter of seconds. He glanced at the older guardsman to see if he had any further instructions.

The Grey Shadow closest made another rumbling sound that preceded fire. Orion released his arrow. And missed.

Orion cursed. He never missed.

"Breathe," Lyntton growled. "Remember all your training. Don't let panic control you."

Squeezing his eyes shut, Orion notched another arrow.

Beside him, Theo, who still hadn't made a move for the forest, yelled and threw his sword at the Grey Shadow. It clattered uselessly on the road. If they weren't in so much peril, Orion might have laughed at the futility of the thief's action.

"Never relinquish your weapon," Orion said.

"I panicked." Theo stared at his discarded sword.

Orion kept his eyes trained on the Grey Shadow as Lyntton leaped from the ditch with a cry. He distracted the dragon with an arrow to its eye while Lyntton abruptly changed paths and swiped at the opposite foreleg.

Orion had seen Lyntton fight when he tested new recruits. Now, on the field where they were fighting for their lives, he admired the older guardsman's agility. While Lyntton teased the Grey Shadows, Orion prepared to take another shot.

He aimed for the soft places, trying to keep the dragons confused and enraged. Firing at random intervals, he hoped the dragons wouldn't be able to anticipate his next shots.

It was the whooshing of wings that heralded their salvation. A golden flash tore past the Grey Shadows, knocking one over before grabbing the second in deadly talons. Orion watched in open-mouthed wonder as the golden dragon flew higher with his prisoner.

A purple streak hit the remaining Grey Shadow while a silver dragon delicately landed in their space. Lyntton jolted at the dragon's entrance and hastily retreated. Orion noticed he didn't turn his back on the beast and kept his sword raised.

Orion didn't think he'd seen anything so marvellous as the golden dragon in all his life. He could only watch as the dragon took his prisoner higher into the sky, and without ceremony, dropped him. The Grey Shadow plummeted, but not before the gold dragon dived after him, grabbing his throat in his jaws. He snapped down, and Orion fancied he heard the crack of bones. A trail of blood and gore rained from the sky as the Grey Shadow fell.

The purple dragon battled her Grey Shadow on the ground. She pinned it down, tore its mangled wings and bit at the throat. The silver sat on her haunches, studying her claws. She reminded Orion of a bored student.

Beside him, Theo was gasping and panting with fright. He lifted his finger to point at the golden dragon circling above them. "That's more the type of dragon I wanted to see. Is that the one who looked at you as if you were dinner?"

Orion nodded. "He liked the smell of my blood."

The silver dragon chuckled. Her amber eyes were trained on Lyntton. She cocked her head to the side, and her nostrils flared as she sniffed at the guardsman. "There's not enough meat on your bones, *vehyl*, to be considered a meal."

Lyntton froze, his stance ready to battle. "Maysden ... tell it to back off."

"Erm ..." Orion didn't know how to break the news to his superior officer that he didn't quite have the power for that.

"*It*!" the silver dragon exclaimed. "Did you hear that, Salvea! *It*!"

"Oh, the audacity." The purple dragon landed nearby and stood over the corpse of a Grey Shadow. She looked distinctively bored.

"Ah, you have my apologies," Lyntton muttered. His hard gaze flicked to Orion as if begging him to do something about the dragons. "Are you friend or foe?"

Salvea, the purple dragon, blinked her large green eyes at them. "We killed Grey Shadows for you."

Lyntton and the two dragons continued to stare at each other in awkward silence. Taking a few steps forward, Orion retrieved Theo's sword, if only to do something with his nervous energy.

"I told you to run into the forest!" Orion snapped, thrusting the sword at the thief.

"I wasn't going to leave you!" Theo replied, snatching the sword from Orion's grip. He reached out with his free hand and shoved Orion. *Hard.*

Orion blinked, taken aback by Theo's annoyance. "Why not?"

"You're my friend," Theo answered, crossing his arms against his chest. "I don't know what it's like for horsemen, but there's honour among my kind. Thieves protect their friends."

"It's good to see the *vehyl* have not changed much in the last thousand years or so." The great golden dragon laughed. Orion jumped; he had been so intent on Theo that he hadn't realised the dragon had landed. He had the impression he had been watching the interaction for some time. "Orion Maysden, born of Silverdyne, we meet once again."

"You have our thanks, Lord Zapyr." Orion bent at the waist and swept into a bow. While serving Jodathyn, he had learned how to treat those of a lofty rank.

"I see your lock has changed," Zapyr said. "Your father must be proud."

Theo nudged Orion playfully. "He would be. He shot someone in the head."

"Who are your friends?" Zapyr tilted his head to peer down at Theo.

Grabbing Theo, Orion pushed him towards the dragon. "This is Theo Torkelle, born of Korkalie ... He's a stonemason by trade. And this is Lyntton ..."

"Lyntton Pressun, born of Farholm, King's Guardsman." Lyntton's smile was strained as he saluted.

"I see you have met my companions Gylleah the Lady of Justice and Salvea Water-Whisper, and I am Zapyr the Splendid."

"Is anyone hurt?" Gylleah, the silver dragon had moved on to flicking large stones across the dirt road with her claws.

"Just Edd." Orion turned, gesturing to the cooling body. "He charged the Grey Shadow. We lost him and his horse."

Theo nudged Orion none too gently. "Your hands, nitwit."

Surprised that he forgot about his own burning hands, Orion flushed and looked down at them as if they belonged to a stranger. They were red, swollen, and the skin was already peeling. His mind registered the pain now that the attack was over.

"Show me," Gylleah said.

Stepping forward, Orion showed the dragon his hands. She lowered her snout and breathed warm air on them. The skin prickled, and the pain diminished. "I'm not an accomplished healer, but your hands will not suffer any ill effects."

"Salvea, go back and report." Zapyr turned his unusual blue eyes towards the purple dragon. She nodded regally and leaped back into the air. "I was sent to help you get your message to Silverdyne."

The silver dragon snorted. "*Sent* is a bit of a strong word, don't you think? You didn't wait for the command, and one must wonder why."

Zapyr snarled and snapped. "I was *sent,* Gylleah."

Gylleah stared back at Zapyr. She blinked lazily. "We should honour your fallen, then leave this place."

Stepping off the road, Zapyr found a patch of dirt. With his great claws, he gouged a man-sized hole. He turned and lifted Edd's lifeless body. He brought the dead man close to his snout and rumbled some ancient sounding words, then delicately laid him down in the grave. Blue eyes considered the still form of Edd, and then he reached down with his claw and straightened the corpse's head. Orion flinched at the feathery thud of the dirt filling the hole as the dragon used his tail to cover the body.

"Sleep well, King's Guardsman. Your duty is finished. Peace be with you on your eternal rest."

Orion stepped onto the road and grabbed the spear that had fallen from Edd's hand. He glanced up at Lyntton and offered him the spear.

"You knew him longer," he whispered.

Unmoving, the older guardsman stared at the soft earth of Edd's grave. Orion shifted uneasily, and then Lyntton held out his hand for the spear.

"*Araae helphelwyn,*" Lyntton said, thrusting the spear into the ground.

"*Terini gorthorawyn.*" Orion murmured the echoing reply. Never had the ancient words of the King's Guard held so much meaning. Live valiantly. Die honourably. That was all any man could hope for in the mortal realm.

Orion stared unblinkingly at the grave until Lyntton clapped him on the shoulder. It seemed so unfair. His father had tried to prepare him for the day he lost a brother-in-arms, but he never thought he would bury a man on his first day. When they had ridden out this morning, he had not even thought that one of them might fall. He stole a glance at Lyntton and knew that he had known and respected the danger of their mission. He had been prepared.

"They were ancient words even in my day," Zapyr rumbled. Orion was shaken from his reverie as the golden dragon turned back and dug a second hole. He picked up the dead stallion and placed it in the grave next to his master. "Sleep well, son of field and hoof."

Orion watched in awe. In Silverdyne, it was custom to bury horses who had served with distinction rather than burning them on pyres. Watching the dragon bury the dead horse with honours, he wondered if that practice was an ancient one too. It was a way of life in Silverdyne; he had never questioned where the practice came from.

"Your horses have fled." The silver dragon offered her clawed hand, which Lyntton stared at dubiously.

Feeling helpless, Orion looked down the road. Their mounts were long gone.

"Orion's beast magic couldn't hold them and the Grey Shadow," Theo said.

"Indeed." There was a gleam in Zapyr's eyes that showed exactly how curious he was by Theo's statement. "Wonderful."

The silver dragon rolled her eyes.

"My magic doesn't help us if we don't have horses," Orion said.

Zapyr laughed and stretched out his long neck. He hummed a long and deep sound. It was a distinct sound, very different from the sounds he had previously experienced with Tornyth. The pitch was lower.

Orion was about to open his mouth to ask what was happening when he heard hooves.

But that was impossible.

Their three mounts had returned, Zoryn in the lead, galloping back like a well-behaved mount. The horses stamped and playfully charged at the golden dragon, prancing about him like they were young foals.

Zapyr lowered his snout to give each horse an affectionate nudge. "Orion Maysden isn't the only beast-talker. It's time to fly."

Looking down at Silverdyne from the back of the dragon, Orion allowed himself to feel the homesickness he had buried since leaving his hometown. Nestled between the fork of the Paldera River and wide green fields, the ancient town gave him a deep sense of pride and awe.

Silverdyne was in his blood. This was where he belonged, his home. When he left, it had been with shame. Another young horseman, Tad, had accompanied him to the citadel. He could still remember his friend's pinched expression as they rode out of the town gates. Tad hadn't expected him to return to Silverdyne.

The last time he saw his father's face still haunted Orion. He had awakened at dawn, as was his family's custom. The house was quiet. His parents had both seemed fatigued the night before and retired early. So Orion pulled on his boots without breaking his fast and left the house to begin his chores. He thought to complete both his and his father's jobs.

Orion was brushing down his favourite mare when he spotted his father stumbling towards the stables. His blood immediately froze. Looking back, Orion knew this was the moment he realised his father was doomed.

In the last few decades, Silverdyne had been periodically struck with a sweating sickness. One variant carried off his grandparents and his older siblings. It took the young and the very old. Some instances it was more aggressive, appearing suddenly and leaving devastation in its wake. Half a year ago, his parents had been one of the first in Silverdyne to contract the sickness and perish.

"Father!" Orion cried, throwing his brush, and ran to meet his father halfway.

"NO! Stay back, boy! Don't touch me" was his father's chilling reply. A great hacking cough stopped his father's words. A spittle of blood left his lips. "Your mother and I are ill ... Go to Natayn's property until it's safe."

"I can't leave you here." Orion tried to protest, but it was in vain. "Let me help you!"

"Orion, leave me ..." His father sucked in gulping breaths. "Ask Natayn to tell the others you have been with him all week helping with the new foals in his stables."

Orion watched in distress as his father fell to his knees, his skin deathly grey. He looked to be covered in a sheen of sweat. Orion took a few hesitating steps forward.

"Please, Orion," his father stammered. "I cannot lose my only child. My heart could not bear that."

"Pa. I won't get sick ... the beast magic."

His father's green eyes flashed in anger. "If you stay and don't fall ill, you'll be suspected of magic, boy. I would lose you to a worse fate."

"The horses ..."

Shaking his head, his father frowned at him. "Leave the horses ... Go now."

Orion stayed rooted to the spot, conflicted if he should obey his father or run to him to help.

"I cannot ..." Orion's father choked back on a sob. "I cannot lose you ... I need to know you're safe. Wherever you may go, whatever may happen, I'll always be with you, Orion."

It was his father's next plea that decided Orion's course of action.

"Your ma loves you so well," his father continued to weep. It was a strange sight for Orion to behold. "She's begging for her lastborn child's life. She's dying ... She needs peace, Orion. Give it to her. Flee for *her*."

It was with a tremendous effort Orion's father forced himself to stand and salute. Orion's vision was blurred with tears as he mirrored his father's action. And so, that was how Orion found himself fleeing his home, leaving his father on the soft green grass to crawl his way back to his own sick bed. It had hurt to see his warrior father brought so low. Worse still was the guilt, the regret and grief he felt every time he thought about his parents.

He should have gone to his father. He should have embraced him one last time, even taken his father's anger. Now he longed to hear his parents' voices, to feel the strong clap of his father's hand on his shoulder. Ghosts and memories were all that was left.

"You're home," Theo whispered in Orion's ear.

Tearing his eyes away from the fields he had played in as a youngster, Orion set his sights on the stone gates that were the entryway to the town proper. Beyond the town was a well-known road that led to his father's house.

"There," Orion said, pointing. "My father's house."

"It's big," Theo murmured in appreciation.

"It doesn't have the same comforts as Aviah Valley," Orion replied. "But it's home."

As they flew over the town, Orion heard the sharp bursts of the warning trumpets. They had been spotted. He cocked his head to listen and laughed. He hadn't been sure if he would hear the trumpet blasts from the air. What would poor Spearmaster Natayn think of two dragons carrying three disgruntled horses?

"We'll land in the fields near your home," Zapyr said. "We'll let the *vehyl* come to us. Landing in a town is fraught with difficulties."

The two dragons landed among the grasses and freed the horses, who snorted and pawed the ground. Theo was the first to dismount, nimbly leaping from Zapyr's back at a height. He landed on his feet with confidence.

He turned to look up at Orion. "Need a hand?"

Orion grunted and dismounted. "When did you get so graceful?"

"Thief, remember? Jumping off roofs is an occupational hazard," Theo said. "I had to learn to be quick on my feet to survive."

"Yes, very nice dismount, *vehyl*," Gylleah said.

Zapyr lay down on the grass and closed his large blue eyes. Orion quite liked his unusual colouring. The blue seemed to glow. "Quiet. I wish to warm myself in the sun before we leave."

Gylleah snorted, her warm breath startling the horses. Annoyed, Zapyr blinked and rumbled at the frightened animals, and they immediately quietened, their ears twitching at the sounds Zapyr crooned at them.

Lyntton hefted the king's standard and walked in the town's direction. Orion knew that once the riders of Silverdyne saw the banner, they wouldn't attack. He didn't wander far before the thunder of hooves announced the rapid approach of riders.

Orion felt a smile tug on his lips and unconsciously patted his horseman's lock. Theo sent him a knowing smirk.

The horsemen came into view, led by none other than the Spearmaster. Natayn had been a longstanding friend to the Maysdens, and Orion was keen to see him and his family. Orion lifted his hand in greeting and wondered what the riders would think of the snoozing dragons. Checking over his shoulder, he noticed that Zapyr and Gylleah were both lazing in the grass, basking in the sun. They seemed completely unbothered with the approach of armed men.

"We come in the name of the High King, Kieryn Pallarus," Lytton shouted.

Natayn thundered forward, leaving most of the horsemen behind him.

"Well, I'll be," Spearmaster Natayn said, his eyes upon Orion and then the dragons. The expression on his face could only be described as dumbfounded. It wasn't often Spearmaster Natayn was at a loss for words. Orion noticed he had reined in his horse at a safe distance from the dragons. "Orion Maysden has returned home, under the banner of the High King and on the back of a dragon no less."

CHAPTER FOUR

Kamoore

The Citadel of Pallaryn

After so many years lurking in the shadows, simpering and degrading himself, Kamoore had done it. Pallaryn, the shining citadel of Rama, was his. They said that the royal house of Pallarus was the most powerful dynasty in the known world. It had stood for centuries, and it was a Kamoore that had toppled it.

The glory days for house Pallarus were long over. After centuries of rule, they had grown weak and complacent. Rama deserved a ruling family that was decisive, active, and willing to do what was necessary to stretch her influence. He was the man for the job.

Born of an ancient bloodline, Kamoore's ancestors had fought alongside Arturyn the Unifier. A fact that house Pallarus liked to forget; the first great king of Rama did not fight alone. Arturyn wasn't the only mighty man of valour that bled. Instead of honouring those with prestigious descent, King Kieryn took his favourites from those who had talents that benefited him, not the realm.

Lord Hallidyn Whitoak was a self-made man. He rose to power when he formed an alliance with the king to discredit Solan. Even the king's wife was not of the great lords' preferred bloodlines. She was of northern stock, a daughter of a minor lord who rarely ventured from his lakeside manor house due to poor health.

And the way the king allowed his King's Guardsmen to talk to him. *Disgraceful*! Fighting men should submit to their masters, not have their opinions made known. A lowly born man couldn't be expected to have the same intelligence as someone with his proud lineage. A man of his calibre deserved to rule over lesser men. It was a birthright.

Twisting his favourite ring around his finger, Kamoore considered his next move. Now that he was the new master of Pallaryn, the citadel needed a new name. Names held power, and while the citadel clung to her title derived from the Pallarus dynasty, she would never truly be his. Today marked the beginning of a new era for Rama.

Kamoore curled his fingers around a golden goblet full of fragrant wine that he had taken from King Kieryn's chambers. The ridiculous boy had the hide to call him a pompous fool while he himself had quite an ostentatious collection of wines. He lifted the goblet to his lips and drank deeply.

The thought of the deposed king soured the taste of wine in his mouth. He remembered when Kieryn was a boy overshadowed by the dictatorial power of his father. When Solan removed King Hadryn from the mortal realm, he had assured him that Kieryn would be easy to manipulate.

Kamoore leered down at the goblet, which was inlaid with precious jewels and the royal family crest. He took another sip of wine, licking his lips to savour the strong tartness that the ex-king enjoyed. King Kieryn had proved stronger than Solan had anticipated.

His father's violent death only briefly shook King Kieryn. To hide his part in King Hadryn's murder, Solan denied the new boy king the right to view the body. Kieryn protested loudly, demanding his rights as a grieving son. Solan then petitioned the great lords to forego certain funeral rites to 'protect' the vulnerable king. Outvoted, Kieryn sulked in his dark chambers.

King Kieryn's breaking point had been when Solan had his men extract Jodathyn from his arms. He exploded in a fit of anger, screaming for his King's Guard. Unbelievably, the king suffered a blow when Solan's men tried to quieten him. They later executed two of them for striking the king, but the result was the same. Jodathyn was taken away. And Solan became the king's enemy for life.

Solan thought to distract the new king with hunting and feasting. But instead of shirking his duties, Kieryn was at every council meeting. He rigorously checked his correspondence and spoke for himself in diplomatic matters. For all his faults, Kieryn Pallarus was a fiercely devoted High King.

It was amusing to watch as King Kieryn thwarted Solan's plans at every turn. The king could be incredibly petty.

Where his father, King Hadryn, had ignored the Sionians to their north, Kieryn extended a hand of friendship. At first Kamoore was thrilled with the bursting trade of luxurious goods, and he took advantage of the foreign traders who the king welcomed. Then he realised what Kieryn was up to. The Sionian king and his royal family had become allies with the boy. A young king with allies was a dangerous thing indeed. He tried to warn Solan, but his pleas went unheeded.

Never mind; Solan was about to pay the price for ignoring his warnings. And the price would be high.

"My lord." A serving boy with bright flaming hair stepped into the audience chamber. His haughty green eyes stared up at the high ceiling, his lips parted in wonder.

This room was reserved for the king's council and those who had been summoned. He hoped to change that practice. This room displayed the might and glory of the ruling class. It was meant to be seen and feared.

Running his tongue along his teeth, Kamoore stared down at the boy, who lifted his chin defiantly. He tapped his fingers along the golden armrest of the throne. "I am king, boy."

The boy's knees hit the ground. "Your Majesty," he murmured. Green eyes, full of hate and mistrust, glared back at him.

"What do you want?"

"King Thylyssa wishes to speak to you, *Your Majesty.*"

Kamoore grunted, thrusting out a bony finger at the discarded goblet. "Clean that up."

His servant straightened his shoulders and obeyed. Five years ago, he had taken him from his family's estate in Garrowmyth. His father had been a minor lord, a drunkard who had owed him money. He had taken the boy as payment. The boy's maternal grandfather, an old man, had chased them on horseback until he collapsed upon the dirt road. He remembered laughing as the boy wept for him to go back to his dear grandpapa. He refused.

It wasn't the first time he had taken a son of a minor lord as payment. He enjoyed wringing out the instilled confidence from his servants. Charming young ones, who once dreamed of their own greatness, became little more than dogs to serve his every whim.

"Send him in," Kamoore barked. Looking at the serving boy, he only felt contempt. He briefly wondered if the boy remembered his name; he certainly never used it.

"Of course, Your Majesty," the boy murmured with a dip of his head. He stood and sneered. Soon it would be time to discard him and start afresh on a new lordling's son. He had proven too challenging to train.

When Thylyssa entered the chambers, he didn't bother to look around at the magnificence of the room. Proud. That was what Thylyssa was. Proud and treacherous. Kamoore was well aware that if Thylyssa was willing to turn on house Pallarus, he most certainly would turn on him as well.

"Did you send the boy to annoy me?" Kamoore demanded.

Thylyssa's bored expression didn't alter, but Kamoore caught the dangerous gleam in his eyes. "I like to throw little mice to the wolves."

Kamoore inwardly preened at the praise of being compared to a wolf. "You'll be riding south then?"

"No. I want Will Hartcurt. That damnable boy belongs to me," Thylyssa replied. "Our benefactor approaches. What do you plan on telling Solan?"

Kamoore tilted his head. "Solan doesn't need to know the details."

"Make sure it's done."

"My dear Thylyssa," Kamoore replied, a smile tugging on his lips. "Solan thinks me no more than a slug. He won't stand in our way."

"You are certainly an interesting man, Kamoore."

"No." Kamoore disagreed with a short bark of laughter. "Just a very patient one."

"Make sure you greet our benefactor." True to his nature, Thylyssa did not look at all impressed. "And subdue those pesky King's Guardsmen."

Kamoore laughed. "I'll take Solan with me to introduce him."

Thylyssa paused by the door. He traced a finger along his lips. "Farewell, Lord Kamoore."

In the evenings, the palace was filled with a strange hush. There was a certain thrill of victory to that. When the people of Pallaryn, his people, looked up to admire the ancient stronghold, they would be met with the assurance that the Pallarus family had been defeated.

He took a reluctant Solan to walk among the pikes of the dead to meet their benefactor. While the sight of those who had died because of their loyalty to Kieryn Pallarus bothered Solan, he felt a rush of power and confidence. Their benefactor would be pleased with the success of the coup.

Glancing up, Kamoore considered the head of the King's Guardsman above him. He had been a young one and had proven to be a troublemaker. When Solan had given into the young man's demands that he might comfort the wretch Illeanah Whitoak, Kamoore could have pulled out his hair in frustration. Solan, the fool, had agreed.

Even now he could recall the look of disgust the King's Guardsman gave him as Illeanah's pretty little head rolled away. It annoyed him. Even bound and about to die, the young man thought Kamoore weak and pathetic. He could see it in his dark eyes.

So Kamoore ordered Solan's men to teach him a lesson before they separated his head from his shoulders. They flogged him in front of his peers until he had no voice left in which to scream.

When it came time for him to die, he merely sighed and whispered, *"Araae helphelwyn. Terini gorthorawyn."*

Upon hearing their famous words, the other King's Guardsmen saluted as the axe was brought down upon his neck.

"What did it gain you, I wonder? You lived valiantly and died with 'honour', yet what did your famous words give you?" Even in death, the guardsman's eyes held an unyielding peace. Kamoore hated him for it.

Beside him, Solan paused and grunted. "A man like that would have been valuable on the battlefield."

"I don't plan for there to be a battlefield," Kamoore replied. He patted his red ring affectionately. His victory was near. "I have a surprise for you."

In response, Solan inclined his head, looking every inch the magnanimous overlord. He was about to learn that he wasn't in control. And he hadn't been for some time. Thinking that Kamoore was weak, Solan underestimated his patience as they plotted Kieryn Pallarus' downfall.

"I will be riding south to establish my part of the kingdom. I thought to take Androssah for my citadel."

Kamoore hummed in response. Solan's plans would not affect him. He glanced down over the wall of the palace. Most of the common people were keeping their distance. Curling his lip, Kamoore knew it was a matter of time before the Ramian people would prostrate themselves at his feet or die.

Many dynasties began with oppression until power and rule were established. There would be a short time of violence before prosperity. The streets of Pallaryn would run red with blood, and then the foundations of his kingdom would be laid. He knew he had the strength for the required brutality to establish his throne.

"Sounds like a storm." Solan paused and turned his face towards the sky. Indeed, Kamoore could hear the rumbling in the distance. He turned to see the confusion on Solan's face. "And yet, that is not thunder."

Kamoore grinned, flashing his teeth. "It's not a storm."

"I wonder what it is."

"A surprise, my friend."

Solan tore his eyes from the sky and glowered at him. Kamoore wasn't too sure if it was the annoyance of being called 'friend' or if Solan suspected him of foul play.

The rumbling came closer, along with the terrible sound of great wings. A huge silhouette flew overhead. Following the monstrous figure were several screeching, ghostly shapes. On the city streets below, the common people of the citadel screamed as they frantically looked for places to hide.

Stumbling back, Solan swore, grasping at Kamoore's cloak. "What have you done?"

"As I said, there will be no battlefield."

"Dragons!" Solan spat. "That's stupid even for you, Kamoore!"

Kamoore bristled. "Dragons have come to our land to remove the pestilence that is house Pallarus."

Nearby, a great red beast landed. Kamoore felt a twinge of annoyance that Galgothmeg landed of the roof of the audience chamber. If the red dragon carelessly damaged his throne room ... Galgothmeg tucked in his leathery wings, spearing a panicking Solan with ancient eyes that burned with an intense hunger for revenge.

"Welcome, Lord Galgothmeg!" Kamoore cried, making a sweeping bow. "As you can see, the coup of Pallaryn is almost complete."

Extending his muscled foreleg, his clawlike hand open, Galgothmeg spoke with the voice of a man. "Return to me the Dragon's Eye, *rokun*. I shall not be banished from Rama's shores again."

Kamoore felt a pang of fury as the dragon used a word that he knew wasn't complimentary. He pulled off his red ring and approached the dragon. He walked with caution.

Galgothmeg was first and foremost a beast. He needed to be careful around him. One day soon, he'd learn the secret to controlling the red reptile, and then Galgothmeg's army would be his to command. No one would ever defy Lord Kamoore again.

Placing the ring into Galgothmeg's palm, Kamoore bowed and hastily retreated. Galgothmeg slowly curled his claws around the ring, crushing it into his scaled hand. He cringed as the beast twisted the precious metal into a misshapen mess. "I would like to see Mandros take this from me."

"What was that ring?" Solan asked.

Galgothmeg lowered his head to stare down at Solan. "The key to Rama."

"*Key?*" The horror painted on Solan's face was almost too comical.

"With the key in Pallaryn, the seat of the Pallarus bloodline, the power holding my banishment faded. It also had the added benefit of shielding my *rokun* operative's thoughts from your king's little mind reader."

"Mind reader … Kamoore, why didn't you warn me the king had a mind reader?" Understanding dawned on Solan's face. "*Willyrd Hartcurt. That's why Thylyssa is after him.*"

"Having protection from Will Hartcurt's invasive gifting meant that he concentrated his efforts on discrediting you. And I was safe."

"Kamoore," Solan ground out, his lips barely moving. He thrust his thumb in the red dragon's direction. "He's Galgothmeg. You invited Vadroil's general into Rama, the dragon of Death and Despair."

Solan turned towards a few of his men who were brave enough to watch at a distance. "Seize him!" he cried in desperation.

There was a certain thrill of excitement watching Solan's face pale when none of his men moved at his command. He stomped towards the nearest man, grabbing the unsheathed sword from unresistant hands. As Solan turned the blade onto him, Kamoore rolled his eyes.

"Of course, once your men realised I had a dragon, they switched their alliance. Those who did not join me were slaughtered. You had no idea ... and you thought *I* was the fool."

Galgothmeg, who seemed to have very little interest in the squabbling humans, lowered his head to regard Lord Solan.

"You'll be your own ruin, Kamoore," Solan said. His eyes never left the dreadful sight of the red dragon's form.

"I only plan to be your ruin, Solan," Kamoore replied. He turned towards Galgothmeg. "Kill him."

It was useless. Kamoore knew Solan was aware of that fact. Still, he tried to flee. Galgothmeg chuckled, clearly amused by his prey's attempts to escape his fate. "You think to be king of Rama? Well, the symbol of kingship among the pitiful humans is a flaming crown."

The eruption of dragon flame stopped Solan's hasty retreat. A terrible inhuman scream tore from Solan's throat as he was encased in fire. Kamoore watched in fascination as Solan flailed in an effort to extinguish the flames. The arid smell of burning flesh quickly filled the afternoon air, and eerie shadows danced upon the walls of the palace.

Laughing, Kamoore grabbed a discarded spear from a guardsman too cowardly to face the dragon. He approached Solan and poked him with the end of the spear. Solan toppled from the wall, a trail of fire following him. His screams were abruptly cut off as he hit the ground below.

A few brave citizens peered out of hiding places to bear witness to Solan's still burning body.

High on the palace walls, Lord Kamoore smiled in victory. He had done it. His people abandoned Kieryn Pallarus, Solan was dead and Thylyssa was chasing Will Hartcurt. He alone was in Pallaryn. He alone would rule. He had the dragon. And for the first time, he had all the power.

Chapter Five

Orion

The Township of Silverdyne

"Lyntton Pressun, born of Farholm, King's Guardsman." Lyntton strode forward, saluting the Spearmaster as he drew cautiously closer.

Orion noticed that Spearmaster Natayn kept one eye on the dragons. He dismounted his prancing stallion, handing his reins to a subordinate, and approached on foot. "It's always a pleasure to host one of the king's men." As Natayn spoke, his eyes swept over Orion's uniform cloak and his horseman's lock. Orion squirmed under the scrutiny. "Words cannot say how pleased I am to see Orion Maysden. His father was well respected among the horsemen, and I'm fond of the boy. But from your serious bearing, I fear you have not brought him home to us."

Lyntton inclined his head. "Indeed, we've come on urgent business. His Majesty wished to grant Guardsman Maysden time to grieve as a son must before he is called back to royal service. I'd like a private word with you, Spearmaster."

Grabbing Theo's sleeve, Orion moved out of hearing range and turned his attention to the other horsemen. Their stance was relaxed but ready. Satisfied that they would not draw their weapons, he approached.

"Orion!" A young horseman dismounted his misbehaving mare and ran to greet him.

Tackled to the dirt road, Orion felt the wind knocked out of his lungs. He grunted as his friend landed on top of him.

"Tad!" Natayn's voice scolded. "How many times have I told you ..."

"Otherworlds, I've missed you." Orion laughed and thumped his friend's arm.

"I see Pallaryn has treated you well," Tad replied. He grinned sheepishly and helped Orion to stand. He studied the horseman's lock in awe as he brushed the dirt from Orion's cloak. "Since the king's first messenger, I've been hoping ... You look taller since I saw you last."

It seemed like another lifetime Tad had accompanied him to Pallaryn to seek a new beginning. His long-lost cousin had taken everything from him, and all he had was a letter of recommendation and promise he would have employment at the palace. He could still remember the forlorn look on Tad's face as he shot one last parting glance over his shoulder. The first night in the palace was the most difficult.

He had expected to be given a position as a palace guard, only for Lord Whitoak to lower his rank to a servant. It was a bitter blow to realise that he was to be Whitoak's spy and he was to serve an unwanted prince. Donatein saw his resentment the moment they met, and the old servant wisely sent him to the room they expected him to share with Valt without meeting Master Jodathyn. He lay in the dark for hours, cursing his existence.

"It gets easier with time," Valt said when he came into their chamber. "One day at a time. You'll not find the master difficult to serve."

Otherworlds, he missed Valt!

Tad retreated a few steps, shaking his head. His eyes returned to Orion's lock; he knew what question his friend was desperate to ask. Tad's lips parted. He sucked in a breath and instead turned to look at Theo. "He doesn't look like much of a guardsman," he remarked.

Theo glanced up at Tad, kicking the loose dirt off the road.

"Come meet him. I know you are curious." Orion grabbed Tad's upper arm and dragged him towards Theo. "Tad, this is Theo Torkelle, born of Korkalie. He's a good friend of mine. Theo, this is Tad Vyron, born of Silverdyne. He's Spearmaster Natayn's son. We grew up with each other."

Tad looked Theo up and down slowly and then shrugged. "Any friend of yours is a friend of mine."

"Aren't you going to ask?" Orion inquired, touching his fingers to his horseman's lock.

Tad bit his lip and rolled his eyes.

Orion chuckled as Tad sent a quizzical glance towards his father, who was still speaking in hushed tones with Lyntton.

"I don't understand," Theo said. "What's so funny?"

"Your horseman friend here knows very well that I cannot ask about the change to his horseman's lock."

"Why not?"

Tad glanced once more to his father, the Spearmaster. Almost as if he felt his son's eyes on him, Natayn looked up and made eye contact. He frowned and shook his head.

"Because I don't fancy the riding crop against my rear," Tad muttered. "He's watching."

"Traditionally, the Spearmaster is told first about the lock change," Orion said.

Theo blinked and snorted. "Sounds ridiculous. You should be able to tell whoever you want."

"It's a matter of respect and honour." Orion shrugged. "It's always been that way."

"Hierarchy is important in Silverdyne," Tad replied. "Come, Orion. I suspect you'll want to see … your parents."

"Where are they?" Orion asked. His chest felt tight.

"After *convincing* your cousin to relinquish your parents' bodies, Father took them to our land and honoured them there. Many in Silverdyne ensured they were properly looked after …"

Orion looked back at Tad. "I'm on the king's business …"

"I don't think His Majesty sent you home to stand around," Theo said. He turned back to where Lyntton was still talking with the Spearmaster. "I'll check with your ranking guardsman if you're dismissed, shall I?"

"Theo …" Before Orion could stop him, the thief scurried away and approached Lyntton with the confidence of one who did not care for rank. Orion could only watch with mounting trepidation as Theo interrupted the older men. Even the golden dragon, Zapyr, lifted his head to watch.

Nodding, Lyntton raised his hand and waved Orion off. On his way back, Theo grabbed the reins of their horses and tugged them along the road. Beside Orion, Tad snorted in mirth as Theo valiantly struggled with their mounts.

Orion nudged him with his elbow. "Don't be rude."

Tad was blessedly silent as he led Orion and Theo to his family gravesites. Confronted with the reality that his parents were actually dead, Orion paused. His friend squeezed his shoulder and pointed. "We laid them to their eternal rest between my Sionian grandparents."

Orion's knees buckled. For the first time in months, he felt the full force of his grief. His limbs felt like they were made of wood. His family was gone. He alone remained, the youngest child of Phill Maysden.

"Come," Tad whispered, "you don't have to mourn alone."

Theo touched his elbow on his opposite side, and Orion could see the compassion in his eyes. "You're never alone."

Between his friends, Orion allowed himself to be led to his parents' sides. Empty, he knelt by their graves and felt the soft grass under his fingertips.

"Wherever he is," Theo said, "your father would be proud of you."

"Hush, the gravesites are places to be quiet," Tad grumbled.

"Apologies, horse boy," Theo replied. "I hail from Korkalie, and there it's traditional to say something kind about the dead. As I don't know Orion's father ... well, I thought I should say something kind to Orion instead."

Craning his neck to look back at Theo, Orion could tell the thief was being perfectly serious. Before his parents' death, he had never left Silverdyne. He realised he had remained uneducated about other regions of Rama.

"Very well, fish boy," Tad conceded. He nodded to Theo curtly. "If that is your tradition and you wish to observe it ..."

Ignoring the common moniker of one born of the coastal towns, Theo dragged in a deep breath. "Your mother ... she would be pleased with her son."

Pressing his palm against the earth, Orion closed his eyes and tried to imagine his parents standing before him. He wished he could snatch back the time that had been stolen from him.

Rising to his feet, he wavered and swatted away Theo's steadying hand. He went back to the horses and retrieved his bow. Running his hand along the length of the weapon, he returned to the graves. Once more he knelt beside his parents and laid down the weapon.

"This is the last gift I can give to you," Orion whispered.

"That's a good bow," Theo said, stepping forward. "Use the sword you gave me …"

"He's relinquishing something of great value. The last gift should be something sacrificial," Tad said. He reached out his hand to stall Theo. "It's been this way for centuries."

Orion kept his gaze firmly on the graves. Theo meant well. "I'd like time …"

"Of course," Tad replied. He reached over and grabbed Theo's shirt and tugged.

Orion grunted and listened to their footsteps dying away.

"Hello, Father, Mother, I have so much to tell you …"

By the time Orion stepped over the threshold of Natayn's farmhouse, the Spearmaster's home was a hive of nervous energy. Natayn's wife, Yanna, met him at the door. He allowed her to fuss over him and exclaim how much he had grown since he last broke bread with them.

His mother had a very close friendship with Yanna Vyron, so much so that he had grown up alongside Tad. Many in the township had mistaken them as cousins.

"Your commanding officer told us briefly what happened on the road," Yanna said. She looked Orion over with a critical eye as if to ascertain for herself that he was well. "And to think, our Orion in the presence of the High King!"

"It's been a hard journey," Orion replied. A woman like Yanna would not be fooled. "I admit I wasn't prepared for …"

"You'd be lying to say you weren't shocked by your companion's death," Yanna said. "The first death is the hardest."

Orion nodded wearily.

"Quite a charming young lad, your friend Theo. I had the honour of showing him through the workshops in the Sionian quarter. That boy appreciates art."

"I'm sure he'll tell me all about it," Orion replied, pleased that Theo seemed to appreciate something from his hometown.

"Come, we've got quite an assortment of warriors in my kitchen. They've been waiting for you."

Orion let Yanna lead him into her kitchen. Due to Natayn's rank and her reputation as a hostess, their family kitchen was the largest in Silverdyne. He stepped into the room and let his gaze brush over the company of men and women at the table.

Lyntton was sitting with Natayn, surrounded by at least half a dozen of the most senior leaders of the town. Orion swallowed a lump. Not a year ago, his father would have been counted in their number. His absence seemed even more poignant now.

Among the confusion of warriors sat Theo and Tad. Theo looked distinctively nervous sitting between two burly horsemen who were arguing. On the other hand, Tad looked delighted with the proceedings.

"We're going to war!" Tad cried upon seeing Orion.

Yanna struck her son over the head with a wooden spoon. "Don't go inflating that ego of yours, son o' mine."

The room quietened as he entered. He was clapped on the back by many of the town's leaders as he was ushered to his own seat. Expectant eyes stared at him and then at Natayn. They were all eagerly awaiting the Spearmaster to ask the question that was on everyone's lips.

"Orion, might you regale us with the tale of your horseman's lock?"

Natayn's request was met with affirming nods.

"Oh, I can tell you a story," Theo said, leaning back in his chair, a sly grin on his lips. "Where's my lute?

> *Dare you to shoot me, horse boy?*
> *I know you never would.*
> *Orion o' Silverdyne ain't so coy,*
> *And let his arrow loose …*

"Theo!" Orion cried, "please stop. When did you have time to write this one?"

"They're not my words," Theo replied smugly. "Prince Carvelle wrote this song."

Orion's face fell, whether from astonishment or embarrassment, he did not know.

"Imagine, Orion Maysden, you have royalty singing your praises."

Orion longed to wipe the smirk off Theo's face.

"It is for Orion Maysden to tell his tale, Theo of Korkalie," Natayn said.

Orion nodded and looked down at his hands as he recounted his time in Pallaryn. He spoke briefly about Jodathyn, the kidnapping of Valt, Donatein's sacrifice, and how he stole from the king's stable. He kept the details of the burned bodies to a minimum before continuing on about the moment he shot the palace spy in the head.

There he paused for a moment, chancing a glance up at all the faces listening in rapt attention.

"Get used to telling the tale, lad," Lyntton said, his gaze lingering on Orion's face. "Most of your brothers-in-arms haven't heard your story. You'll be recounting it for years to come."

"And this is where your beloved Orion hatched a daring jail break with none other than Jodathyn Pallarus ..." Theo continued.

"Jodathyn didn't give me much of a choice," Orion replied. "I called him deranged ..."

"You called him *deranged* to his face?" Tad spluttered. "What was his response?"

"He turned around and kept walking, so I had no choice but to follow him." Orion sighed dramatically. "I'm sure he was grinning. Manipulative bastard."

Orion found himself staring off into thin air. After a pause, Theo took over mentioning the abandoned house, the discontent in Yanyima, meeting Voran and Aviah Valley. Listening to the gentle lilt of his friend's voice, he had to appreciate the way Theo could weave a story.

Orion finished the tale with the attack of Grey Shadows and how the king himself changed his lock. Stunned silence fell over the table once he finished his story.

"Well," Tad said after a pause. "I doubt there has been ever a horseman of Silverdyne that has had quite a splendid story."

Orion felt his skin warm under the praise. The woman beside him, who was still dressed in full leathers, clapped him heartily on the shoulder.

"What happened to my cousin?"

"Ran him off," said one of the horsemen proudly. "When he proved to be unwilling to leave, I set my dogs on him, I did."

Bewildered, Orion looked around at the horsemen as they erupted into a thunderous round of laughter. He turned towards to Natayn, who raised his eyebrows. The Spearmaster's lips were pursed to hold back his own chuckles.

"Orion has a letter written in the king's hand," Lyntton said. "Perhaps you could be so kind to help us in settling this matter before we have to go?"

"Yes," Theo said. "Let's see what's in the letter."

Tad slid a knife along the table, and Orion stopped it with his fingers. He had almost forgotten the letter he had tucked into his boots. His hands were shaking as he fished it out and used the blade to break the king's seal.

Orion felt a flutter of nerves as he unfolded the thick parchment. For a long moment, he stared down at the king's handwriting. It was a strongly worded letter addressed to the magistrate signed *Kieryn Pallarus, High King, Master of Rama and Lord of all her Regions.*

"What does it say?"

Orion let his eyes scan the entire letter.

The accusation that Orion Maysden born of Silverdyne is not Phill Maysden's child has been proven false. Palace experts agree that although Maree Maysden's older children were born of a Sionian man prior to her marriage, Orion Maysden is the natural born son and heir of Phill Maysden.

Spearmaster Natayn Vyron and Healer Maevyn Haelbard have verified these findings. Mistress Haelbard being the healer that attended Orion's birth.

While the property in question has a clause that no Sionian can lay claim to Ramian land, Orion is Ramian by the virtue of his father's bloodline.

Furthermore, records clearly state the service of both of Orion's parents and his grandparents (maternal and paternal) to the township of Silverdyne.

The Crown awards the property to Orion Maysden, son of Phill Maysden, and it is to be made ready for his return. Due to the stress of grief, his age, and the abhorrent way the dead were treated, the crown does not hold Orion accountable for the physical altercation between himself and Tavery Maysden. Any charges against Orion Maysden are forgiven and will be expunged from all town records.

It wasn't the whole letter. It seemed the king had a lot to say to the magistrate of Silverdyne. Orion could hardly believe it and looking around at the other horsemen, neither could they.

"They took the property by a lie," one horseman grunted. "Taken from one of our own."

"Did you know about this, Spearmaster?" Orion asked.

"Aye, on his deathbed, your poor pa was afraid something might happen. I thought at the time his words were the ramblings of a dying man. Then you were disinherited. When the king's messenger came to my door asking questions about the timing of your conception and birth … Aye, I knew what Tavery had done …"

"The king knows when I was born?" Orion asked, squirming on his chair. The last thing he needed was to be caught in a lie.

"Due to the nature of his inquiries, yes, your mother's pregnancy and birthing of you was thoroughly examined." Natayn raised his eyebrows in Orion's direction.

The horsewoman beside him barked with laughter. "Still remember the day Phill Maysden raced into town on his fastest stallion. Bad-tempered fiend, that horse was. Poor Maree, alone in the upper fields; the babe came hard and fast. The mares were her midwives and their foals witnesses of Orion's birth."

Theo strummed his fingers on the strings of his lute. "Goodness, Maysden, is every one of your life events made for a ballad?"

"Don't you dare." To avoid Lyntton's curious stare, Orion fumbled through the pages of the letter. The last page gave him pause.

"What is it?" Theo leaned forward in his chair to get a better look.

"The king has signed an arrest warrant for my cousin," Orion murmured.

"What charge?" Tad asked with a wicked smile.

"The disrespect of the dead and thievery through fraud."

The horseman to Orion's right stood, clapped him on the shoulder, and held out his hand. "Well, lad, let's wake the magistrate up to let him know this piece of news."

"He's probably at dinner," Orion replied, folding the letter.

The horsewoman on his other side grinned and proffered her hand. "Good, I hope I spoil it for him. I'll look after this nasty business for you."

Resolved not to think about his cousin or his fate, Orion handed over his letter. He flexed his fingers, remembering the feeling of his knuckles connecting with his cousin's jaw.

Orion returned his attention back to the table as the horsewoman left. She was joined by two others who were keen to disturb the magistrate. Lyntton's plate was being piled with more food by Yanna. Theo and Tad bent their heads together in a lively discussion. He was home and for the first time in months, he didn't feel weighed down by grief or guilt.

CHAPTER SIX

Jodathyn

Solan's Summer House, Aviah Valley

Much to Jodathyn's delight, Et-hir was alone in the kitchens when he entered. She moved around the benches, humming a tune that sounded suspiciously like "The Apple Tree Prince."

Unaware that she was being watched, she continued to work. Lingering by the doorway, Jodathyn observed her in silence. Instead of the food he had been hoping for, Et-hir was sorting weapons. Swords, daggers and axes were placed into neat piles along the benches. She picked up the dagger closest to her and ran her thumb along the blade. On her slender hands was a pair of guardsman's thick gloves. They were much too large for her.

"Our dragoness is sharpening her claws." Tornyth's desire flitted through Jodathyn's mind.

He knew that his drunken state had displeased her last night, and this was the first time they had been alone. Clearing his throat, he announced his presence. "Ettie?"

Et-hir whirled around, staring up at him with her large brown eyes. She reached up and ran her hand through her wet hair, her fingers snagging on a few knots.

"You scared me, Jodathyn." Et-hir's eyes scanned the doorway behind him. She gestured to a whetstone on the counter. "I thought I better make myself useful."

Jodathyn glanced at the rows of weapons. "It's a big job for one person."

"A young man once told me he was unafraid of work," Et-hir replied. She glanced up, her brown eyes filling with tears. She dropped the dagger she was holding back down on the bench with a clatter. "Curran was impressed with you. I'm sorry ..."

"You can talk about Curran," Jodathyn said. He took a few quick steps into the kitchen and then paused. He had thought to take her into his arms to comfort her, but he was unsure how she might react.

Et-hir threw her hands up in defeat. "Forgive me, I'm not sure if I should bow or curtsy or ..."

Jodathyn raised his eyebrows, tilting his head to the side to observe her shaking hands. A smile tugged on his lips. "I think we're past such formalities, Ettie. No one bows to me."

"It's just ..." Et-hir murmured. "Your brother, the king, is here."

"Yes, he's king. I don't see what that has to do with me," Jodathyn replied. A thought struck him. "Have you been hiding in the kitchens from Kieryn?"

Grimacing, Et-hir turned away, swearing softly in Sionian. "I was going to head to the village to get a dress that was less filthy, but he had already sent one of his elite soldiers."

"That doesn't sound so bad," Jodathyn said with a frown. He had noticed that she was wearing a well-made travel dress and sturdy leather boots.

He took a moment to admire how nicely the dress cinched in at the waist and draped into a full skirt. "The guardsman chose well for you."

"What must your brother think of my audacity?" Et-hir moaned. She slumped against the kitchen bench, her head in her hands.

"Why? What happened?"

"The king asked me what I wanted as a reward."

Jodathyn shifted. An uncomfortable feeling curled through his belly. "What did you ask for?"

Et-hir lifted her face from her hands. "You."

"*Me*?" Shocked, Jodathyn drew his eyebrows together. "I don't understand."

"I thought it was the only opportunity I'd get," Et-hir said. "I asked for the right to court you."

"*Court* me?" Jodathyn choked on his own tongue. He felt a momentary fear, wondering how Kieryn might have responded to such a request. Surely, Et-hir did not realise what she was asking of the king.

"Yes. But I have since gathered it was most improper of me."

"It's frankly ..." Jodathyn didn't know what to say. Even if he had been born as a beloved son of a king, any of the great lords would protest it was much too soon and oppose any courtship. "I might be considered ill-conceived, but I'm still a royalborn. What did Kieryn say?"

Et-hir shook her head. "He seemed amused. He said we may court but may not marry until ..."

"Until ..." Jodathyn stepped further into the kitchens, hardly believing his ears that it had been that simple. Kieryn had been *amused* about him getting married? It seemed impossible.

"He said he wanted you well recovered."

"The king granted us a chance ... We've only known each other a few days. Are you sure you want to *court* a royalborn?"

Et-hir nodded. She turned so that her back was pressed up against the bench. "I'm sorry if I overstepped."

"Et-hir, you've seen me on my very worst day and yet by some miracle, you still love me." He picked up her slim form and hoisted her onto the kitchen bench, which was mercifully free of weapons. She squeaked in surprise, but he silenced her with his lips against her own.

Within him, Tornyth rumbled in delight. *"My little vehyl."*

Leaning closer, he pressed his palms on either side of Et-hir's knees, a growl of pleasure escaping his lips. He nipped at her lip, and she gasped in surprise but the next moment, her fingers were in his curls, tugging him closer.

When Jodathyn pulled away to catch his breath, Et-hir ran her hand down his arm. Her head was bowed so that he couldn't see her expression. "What does your dragon think of me?"

Cocking his head to the side, Jodathyn regarded her. "I am the dragon. My human and dragon heart beats for you alone."

Et-hir threw her hands around Jodathyn's neck and drew him in for another deep kiss.

It was the sound of someone clearing their throat that caused Jodathyn and Et-hir separate as if burned. Raising his shaking fingers to his lips, Jodathyn imagined he could still feel the suppleness of Et-hir's soft lips on his own. And indeed, it had a pleasant burn.

"We're lucky. We've found our forever-mate." Deep inside, Tornyth was preening in triumph. *"She'll be mine, and I'll be hers ... and we'll make a nest together."*

"Lady Fydellah ... Nym," Et-hir stammered. "I was just sharpening some weapons."

"Sharpening Jodathyn's tongue, were we?" Nym smirked. She sauntered forward and plucked up a long dagger to inspect.

Arms crossed against her chest, Fydellah looked between them. She sat herself down at one of the tables. "Well, it is said by one of our wise men of old, 'the tongue is a double-edged sword'," she said.

The smirk on Nym's face was all-knowing. She swung her arm around Jodathyn's shoulder to pull him into a rough one-armed hug. "Seems like our palace brat is a natural," she cried. "I taught him to kiss like a gentleman, and here he is making poor Et-hir swoon with this bestial charm!"

Et-hir giggled. "He growled at me!"

"Did he?" Nym crowed, looking impressed. "He's growling, is he?"

Flushing, Jodathyn freed himself from Nym's clutches. "The dragon was attempting sensual purr, thank you very much."

"Oh, don't tease him so," Fydellah said. She turned her eyes onto Nym and smirked. "He's blushing."

Not entirely sure what to do while badly outnumbered by the women, Jodathyn straightened his shirt and eyed Nym and Fydellah. Nym seemed to be smiling. Her hazel eyes were alight with a cheerfulness he hadn't seen before. Fydellah's face was flushed, the sleeves of her shirt rolled up.

"Don't tell me you've kept yourself in the kitchens all morning," Nym said. She ignored Et-hir's glance at the door. "We've been out stretching our muscles with some of the King's Guardsmen."

"Nym is a good teacher," Fydellah explained. "I want to know how to use a sword in case …"

"You should join us after lunch," Nym offered. "Joddie might enjoy the show."

Et-hir shook her head. Seeing her anxiety returning, Jodathyn clasped her slim hands in his own.

He never gave Nym credit of how quick she was to read situations. "Oh, don't tell me you're afraid of your future brother-in-law. He's not that frightening."

Fydellah twisted some of her loose curls around her fingers. "I beg your pardon?"

The smirk never left Nym's face. "Et-hir asked the High King for Jodathyn's hand last night."

Fydellah's eyes widened in shock. "You asked for a *royalborn's* hand in marriage?"

"No, no, no," Et-hir replied, shaking her head, "that's not what happened. I asked to *court* Jodathyn."

Jodathyn silenced Nym's bark of laughter with a warning look. He wasn't as discreet as he would have liked. Et-hir saw the movement and looked around at them in confusion.

"Et-hir, in Rama, especially among the highborns, asking to court someone is the same as asking for their hand in marriage. Royalborns *never* break a courtship," Fydellah said, rescuing Jodathyn from having to explain.

"Oh no!" Et-hir cried, her voice draining of all colour. "What must he think of me now?"

Wrapping her arm around Et-hir, Nym pulled the smaller woman in close. "There now. Don't worry about it. It's not a big deal."

"I proposed marriage to a prince!" Et-hir cried. "After commenting on the king's age!"

"I'm not a ..."

"Prince," Fydellah and Nym echoed.

"The king had his men get you a more appropriate travel dress. One less tainted by your trials," Fydellah said. "It's a clear sign that he did so in respect of his future sister-in-law. The king is demonstrating that he has accepted you. He's the head of house Pallarus after all."

"Who has the king accepted?"

Surprised by the interruption, Jodathyn spun on his heel and came face to face with Voran. He felt a pang of sadness, wishing that it were his cousin, Valt. Guilt followed the sadness. The more changes he saw in Voran, the more he mourned. It felt like he had not only lost Valt, but also the man that Voran once was.

Sighing, Jodathyn turned away, running his hand through his hair. "I thought you would be long gone."

"My sword is needed here," Voran replied. He stomped into the kitchen and threw himself into a chair. He curled his lip in Et-hir's direction. "Get me something to drink, girl."

"Don't," Jodathyn snapped. He thrust out his hand to stop Et-hir from obeying him, but his eyes never left Voran's face. "Just don't."

"Typical to find you among the women," Voran sneered. "She's been working in the kitchen ... Don't care whose woman she is ... She can serve."

"He's threatening our Ettie."

Jodathyn froze, his mouth agape. His mind was telling him to do something, but he was too stunned to move. His eyes slid over to Nym. His silver-haired friend was snarling back at Voran. But it was Et-hir who acted. Her expression was perfectly demure as she picked up a pitcher of beer. Jodathyn rose his hand to stop her from serving Voran. However, Et-hir ignored him, walked over to Voran, and dumped it over his head.

"I don't care who you are," she said sweetly. She dropped the pitcher into Voran's lap. "I don't serve nasty."

Voran surged out of his seat, his jaw clenched. Jodathyn stepped in front of him, standing between his ex-guard and Et-hir. Placing his hand on Voran's shoulder, he applied enough pressure to let the guardsman know he was not going to allow him to pass. At the sight of Voran's beard dripping with beer and Nym's delighted face, Jodathyn burst into gales of laughter. He had never seen anyone put a misbehaving guard in their place with such finesse.

Voran's face flushed with anger, but it didn't have the desired effect. Jodathyn only shook his head. "Sit down, Voran, and control yourself."

"How dare you, boy."

"I think you fail to realise, Voran, I'm no longer a child. I'll not be intimidated," Jodathyn said, crossing his arms against his chest. "These women deserve respect. Fydellah helped me even though it put her in grave danger. I fought alongside Nym, suffered with her in ways you can't begin to imagine. And Et-hir has shown me strength in kindness and great courage in the face of death. They don't need to prove themselves to you or any other man."

The expression on Voran's face was thunderous. Snarling, the big man took a step forward to loom over Jodathyn. On his breath Jodathyn could smell alcohol.

Jodathyn tilted his head to meet Voran's angry eyes. "Go ahead. Hit me. I'm not going to stand down."

Voran stared at his clenched fists in horror. He stumbled backwards and landed heavily into a wooden chair, which groaned under his weight. He hung his head in his large hands and began to weep. Jodathyn looked to his companions, at a complete loss.

"What's happening in here?" Jael Aryk, along with two other guardsmen, entered the kitchen. The dark-skinned healer looked to Jodathyn, then to the weeping Voran, his lip curled in disgust.

"The healer is angry," Tornyth whispered. *"Calm him."*

"I'm sorry, Guardsman Jael," Jodathyn murmured. "He was in such a temper ... I may have said something wrong."

"Don't you dare apologise, Jod!" Et-hir cried, untying her apron and throwing it to the ground. "Even if he is some marvellous ex-guard that you loved at one time, doesn't negate what he's done."

Jodathyn turned towards Voran, who shrunk back. He could still feel his heart beating in his chest. For a moment, he had been sure that Voran would strike him.

"What. Have. You. Done?" Jael's normally gentle eyes were like chips of ice as he glared at Voran. The vein in his neck throbbed. Behind his back, his two companions shared an uneasy glance. It was never a good idea to make a healer angry.

"We handled it, guardsman," Jodathyn replied.

"He tried to hit Jodathyn!" Et-hir exclaimed.

"I'm confident he wouldn't have laid hands on me," Jodathyn said.

"Liar," Fydellah muttered.

Jodathyn sent her an exasperated look. He was trying to defuse the situation.

"His body language was clearly a threat," Nym said, leaning on a bench. She grabbed a long dagger and waved it in Voran's direction. "You make to go for Jod or Et-hir, I won't hesitate to stab you."

Jael pinched the bridge of his nose and turned to his companions. "Take your break outside. I'll deal with this."

The two other guardsmen hastened to obey. Jodathyn narrowed his eyes. He was sure the elder one of the pair outranked Jael, and yet he was still keen to leave the room without an argument.

Jael waited until his companions disappeared. "I'm only going to warn you once, Voran Axtin, so listen well. His Majesty told you to stay away from Jodathyn and Prince Carvelle. You've no business harassing Jodathyn or his friends."

"Only came in here to get away from you lot," Voran spat. "You all think you're better than me."

"Yes," Jael replied. Jodathyn winced at the calmness of the medic's statement. "I'm not the man who abandoned my post, so the boy I was supposed to protect was put in grave danger. I was the guardsman that found him, pale and lifeless. He wasn't breathing, Voran. You don't know what it is like to look into a child's agonised face, forcing air into his lungs. It hadn't been an easy death."

Jodathyn froze. *"Death?* I wasn't dead, was I?"

"He speaks true," Fydellah whispered.

"I'm not surprised that your memories of the weeks of healing are murky." Jael turned his gaze from Voran to look Jodathyn in the face. "When we didn't need you lucid for questioning, I kept you unconscious so you might not suffer. The poison kept trying to take you. Do you not remember losing weeks of your life?"

"No ... I thought it was unusual Voran had been replaced so quickly. The seasons ..."

"Donatein didn't want you to know how many times we nearly lost you."

Jodathyn's knees felt weak with shock. It seemed the poison he concocted for Solan worked a little too well. He had deserved the punishment. The suffering he had endured had been justice.

Sweat beaded on Jodathyn's brow. He felt Nym move beside him. Her hands were on his shoulders. He blinked past the confusion. Why would she try to comfort him? She knew his dirty secret. He couldn't hold his silence.

"I'm sorry, Jael," Jodathyn whispered. "I'm sorry you suffered on my account. It was my fault, not Voran's."

Jael frowned, his eyes sweeping over Jodathyn and then to Nym. What a sight he must look! "I apologise, Jodathyn. I should have held my tongue. Sit down; you're going into shock."

Jodathyn waved Nym's hand away. "I'm not a child to coddle. And I'm not confused. It *was* my fault."

"Sit."

Deciding it was better to appease the angry healer, Jodathyn sat with a sigh. Et-hir grabbed him a goblet of water and pushed it into his hands. He took it from her, with a strained smile.

"I wish it were wine," Tornyth grumbled.

Jael placed his hands on his hips and stared down at Jodathyn. "It's not as if you drank the poison yourself."

"Oh, but I orchestrated the whole thing," Jodathyn replied. He glanced up at Voran, who was eyeing him with something he could only describe as horror. "Don't you understand? I'm a murderer."

"Jod," Nym whispered in his ear. "That's not what happened."

"It was my poison," Jodathyn cried. His eyes darted up. Fydellah paled at hearing the truth in his voice. "My poison! That's why you never found the assassin."

"I know," Nym said. "You did what you felt you had to."

"Jodathyn." Jael crouched before him. "I need you to tell me what happened."

Jodathyn swallowed, feeling a terrible lump lodged in his throat. He swallowed a second time and finally took a swig of his water. It was more to delay the inevitable than to wet his throat.

"If you won't tell him," Nym said. "I will."

Jodathyn took another swig, swallowed loudly and glared in Nym's direction.

"Traitor," Tornyth snarled. *"She's supposed to be our friend."*

"She is," Jodathyn told his dragon. *"She's doing what she thinks is right for us."*

Jodathyn sucked in a deep breath, ignoring his sulking dragon. "The dragon stirred and showed me a plot to kill the queen and her unborn child. Kieryn was away, and I had no one to turn to. I stole Donatein's herbs and created a poison. Then I bribed the woman Voran was seeing to lure him away so I could poison the culprit. Voran's inattention was my fault."

Jael scoffed, folding his arms against his chest. "We of the King's Guard know your little secret. Voran left his post often and asked you, a child in his care, to lie about it. I daresay it happened frequently. You knew exactly how and when to lure him away."

"How long have you known?" Jodathyn looked up at Jael in horror.

"We knew from our investigations into the assassination attempt. Your brother, our king, was most thorough."

"Kieryn knows?" Jodathyn stiffened. He glanced in Voran's direction, feeling a spike of fear.

"I heard your pleas for Voran's life when I healed you. For your sake, I let him leave the citadel. When the king returned to Pallaryn, I weathered his displeasure and convinced him to let Voran live."

Jodathyn could barely believe what he was hearing. "You know the rest. I got caught, had my own poison shoved down my throat. It all worked out in the end. Me taking the poison saved the queen and unborn Carvelle. If I spoke out, they would have killed Kieryn ... so I held my tongue like they told me to."

"Master Jodathyn ..." Jael started, with a sad shake of his head. "We could have protected you if we had known."

"I couldn't take that risk," Jodathyn replied. "Carvelle may have survived, but the other babies didn't. I failed Kieryn in that respect."

"The *other* babies? What do you mean, brother?"

Jodathyn felt the blood drain from his face and experienced a moment of light-headedness. In the back of his mind, he had always known that the day might come when Kieryn would come to appreciate the depth of his own court's betrayal. He clambered to his feet, ignoring Jael's outstretched hand to keep him seated. He bowed at the waist stiffly. His limbs trembled beneath him.

"My king."

"Jodathyn? Surely you don't mean … my babies?" The king moved from the doorway; his firm footsteps sounded loud as he came to stand directly before Jodathyn.

Opening his mouth, Jodathyn tried to speak but found he could not. He knew he must answer his king. But with knowledge would come grief, and he did not wish to cause his brother pain. There was a certain amount of dread confessing the truth now that he was faced with Kieryn. Once the words were spoken, they could not be withdrawn.

"Look at me, Jodathyn," Kieryn commanded.

Jodathyn obeyed, willing his eyes to look the king full in the face. He was powerless to look away as the dawning horror swept over his brother. The king's expression crumbled.

"My daughters," Kieryn continued after a pause. "My children were murdered in the womb. Are those the words you cannot speak?"

Jodathyn looked up into his brother's stricken face. Grief was an ugly beast, he decided. He could see anger, guilt, fear and sadness warring for dominance over his brother's expression.

"Yes," Jodathyn gasped. "Forgive me, my king. I never saw their deaths … but I saw Carvelle's, and I had to do something so he might be born."

Kieryn's brows drew together as he put the puzzle pieces together. He spun on his heel, stalking over to the nearest bench, and slammed his fists down. Jodathyn jumped in fright even though he had seen his brother's temper many times before. He choked back a sob. "I'm sorry, Your Majesty. If I could take back the time and make it not so … I would. I would save them in a heartbeat."

Kieryn caught his movement in the corner of his eye. His shoulders slumped over, and Jodathyn could see him shaking with suppressed rage. Through his clenched teeth, Kieryn sucked in a deep breath. "Guilt does not lie with you, brother. You were only a young boy when my daughters were murdered. According to Mandros, your dragon was most likely trying to manifest around the time of Carvelle's birth. It was the dragon guiding your hand into poisoning the traitors."

"I'm sorry, Sire," Jodathyn muttered, staring down at his hands. "I didn't know what else to do. You weren't in the palace. My tutors only laughed at me, and no one was willing to let me see the queen."

"It was Solan, wasn't it?" Kieryn asked. His voice had a steel edge to it. "It was more than Aviah Valley that had you scared. It was Solan. It's always Solan."

Jodathyn nodded, feeling numb.

Kieryn leaned against the bench. His head bowed as he rocked from side to side. Jodathyn could see the king's knuckles growing white from the pressure of his grip. With a roar of frustration, the king grabbed a nearby plate and threw it into the wall. He grabbed a second and then a third plate. When he had successfully smashed any plate within reach, he stood, panting, staring down at the debris.

"Oh, my children." Kieryn turned upon his heel and stalked from the room.

"What have I done?" Jodathyn hung his head.

"A broken heart takes time, Jod," Fydellah said.

Et-hir reached over to take his hand in hers, while Nym looked dumbfounded in the empty space the king stood. "Should someone go after him?"

Jael placed a reassuring hand on Jodathyn's shoulder. "The king is grieving as a papa. He needs some privacy at this moment."

"I need a drink," Voran muttered.

"Leave," Jael said, lifting his finger and pointing towards the door.

Watching his ex-guard's back as he tramped from the room, Jodathyn could not help but feel wretched. Voran never looked back at him.

Without looking at Jael, Jodathyn stood, knocking his chair over, and swept out of the kitchen. By the time he made his way down to the garden path, Et-hir had caught up with him. She didn't say anything as she grasped his hand in hers. He turned his head and smiled.

When they reached the sweeping lawns, Jodathyn immediately noticed the lack of dragons. He tilted his head to the sky, wondering where they had gone to.

"Uncle, play with me." Carvelle jumped out from one of the bushes, a woven crown of leaves in his hair.

Jodathyn's misery was complete. He stared down at his nephew, his stomach cramping with the thought that they had nearly lost him before he had been given a chance to draw his first breath. The still forms of two guardsmen shadowing the prince's every move gave testament of how uneasy Kieryn truly was.

"I'm sorry, Carvelle," Jodathyn murmured.

Carvelle's face fell. "I'll go and find Papa if you are unwell."

Biting his bottom lip, Jodathyn contemplated his reply. There was no way that Kieryn would want Carvelle to see his grief over his deceased daughters. But his brother would never want his son barred from coming to him when he needed him.

Beside him, Et-hir crouched down to the prince's height and offered him her hand. "Today is such a lovely day. How about we go and enjoy the sunshine near the stream? Miss Fydellah is very willing to answer your questions about her island home."

Carvelle took Et-hir's hand without hesitating and tugged her towards the kitchens. "When can I call you Aunt?"

The two guards made to follow them, but Jodathyn held his hand to stall them. The guardsman who seemed to be of the higher rank paused and nodded for his companion to keep an eye on the prince.

"There's been a situation," Jodathyn said, realising too late that his words had put the guardsman on full alert. The man's impassive face clouded over, and he growled, his hand on the pommel of his sword. "No, not like that," Jodathyn frantically hissed between his teeth. He glanced around nervously. He was sure that Kieryn wouldn't want people to know of his reaction to the news. The king was a private man.

"His Majesty is in a ..." There was no other way to phrase it. "State. He wouldn't want Prince Carvelle to see him like this. Go find Jael. He'll know what to do."

"A state?"

"Find Jael and let the king know his son will want to see him when he is more ... himself."

The guardsman looked Jodathyn up and down. "Stay close to the house."

Jodathyn watched the guardsman leave with a mixture of amusement and annoyance. When the fiasco began, he was little more than a boy. But now he had seen so much, done so much, he knew that he was forever changed. What did the guardsman expect to happen to him if he was left to his own devices? He was a dragon. He could look after himself.

Inhaling, Jodathyn caught an unpleasant smell on the wind that tickled his nostrils. Inside of him, he felt Tornyth's hackles rising. He felt a strong urge to burn something and was curious what the dragons were up to.

Lifting his chin to the sky, Jodathyn saw a column of dark smoke. It was in the same direction as the skirmish last night. He realised the dragons were burning the bodies left behind.

"You're learning to listen to the Wind Song in our human body," Tornyth said.

"Anyone can smell," Jodathyn replied. *"They'll be doing it to prevent the spread of disease."*

"Who cares why they are doing it." His dragon stretched smugly. *"Let's go burn something."*

He manifested into Tornyth and leapt into the air. Although the place where they had the battle against the Grey Shadows was close to the house, he didn't want to walk the distance and risk one of Kieryn's guardsmen stopping him.

When Tornyth landed on the dust road where he had fought last night, Sidrah was gently nudging the dead mauve dragon with her snout. She lifted her gaze and stared at him with a knowing look. Mandros, along with many of his dragons in his command, stood watching over the burning of the Grey Shadows. Deovyn paced back and forth, his gait heavy and irritated.

Observing the smouldering remains of the Grey Shadows, Tornyth imagined he could still hear their last inhuman cries of pain and fear. He swung his head around to look at the slack face of the purple dragon that had been freed of her Grey Shadow prison. She looked to be merely asleep, and he fancied that she even looked at peace. Tornyth felt a pang of sadness. Who had she been in life? Who had loved her, grieved for her when she had become a Grey Shadow?

"Is there anything you can tell us, Sidrah?" Mandros asked.

Sidrah shook her head. "There's nothing."

"She was a Grey Shadow," Tornyth said.

"And now she's not. Most peculiar," Curarfur commented. He grinned at Tornyth and approached to bump him with his side. "What killed her, Sidrah, do you think?"

Again, Sidrah swayed her head side to side. "I cannot say."

"Dragons don't just die. There has to be a reason." Curarfur frowned. "I have never come across anything quite like this."

"My manservant Orion might tell you more," Tornyth said.

Mandros glanced at the purple dragon. "What powers does your servant hold?"

Tornyth was surprised. "I didn't know he had one. I was in the air when this happened. Perhaps he is a healer."

"Which means he either hid his power very well or didn't know how to use his power in the first place," Deovyn said. He fanned out his wings. "It might be the case the young *vehyl* doesn't know of the power he holds."

"Is this unusual?" Tornyth asked, gesturing to the dead dragon. "A Grey Shadow peeling off their disguise before dying?"

"This power is not something we have ever seen before," Roane, the olive dragon who was Mandros' general, said. "When this servant returns, should I look into him, *Pallu*?"

Mandros' lips curled into a grin. "No, my old friend. Zapyr has gone to the young man in question. I am confident it's as it should be."

"If he is what you suspect ..." The olive green shifted. "Surely my gifts are required, Mandros."

Mandros shook his head. "Your mission is to fly north to the place you will find a dragon-made tomb. There you will find *rokun* that need to be destroyed. I believe among the wreckage you will find someone who will quite frankly astound you."

"*Pallu?*"

"Go, please, before it's too late."

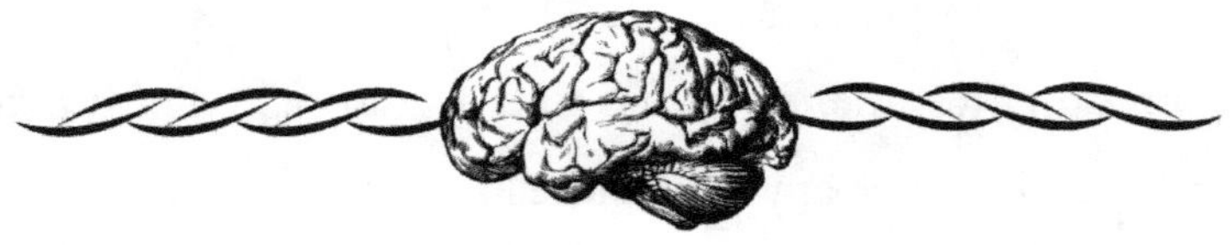

CHAPTER SEVEN
Will

The Village of Habron

Will had never seen anything like the molten, black dome that overlooked the village of Habron. There was a strong temptation to stretch out his hand and feel the smooth surface of the dragon monument. He decided against the action. It seemed disrespectful to touch the final resting place of a man who had suffered such a violent fate.

Beside him, the queen bowed her head to the tombstone. Through her thoughts, he caught strands of her regret. She slipped a small cream handkerchief from the sleeve of the shirt Will had purchased for her. She dapped her eyes, and he caught the clumsy stitching of the letters *OP*.

Such a small trinket she had taken from the palace, a little clue of the child she was missing. Will doubted that his own mother would choose to keep anything he had gifted her and keep it close to her person. His throat tightened.

The queen's now brown eyes shimmered with emotion. He would miss her kind blue eyes. The Sionian magic she had used to disguise them was permanent.

"Sometimes I feel trapped," the queen whispered. She folded her handkerchief neatly and tucked it into her shirt. "I love Kieryn dearly, I do, and I wouldn't give him up for anything, but I miss my old life when I was only a nobleman's daughter."

"I know," Will replied.

"I should have been able to save the old man," the queen continued. She attempted to smile, pushing back strands of short, dark hair behind her ear. "Never mind. It's late afternoon. We should head to the village and rest for the evening."

To give their tired mounts a break, they walked the rest of the way into the village. Dressed in humble leathers, no one paid any attention to the queen, for which Will was grateful. It must have been strange for her, he mused, for the most recognisable woman in the country to go about her business without the staring, the bowing, or the whispers.

As they walked into the middle of the town, Will could feel the queen's energy ebbing away. She would have liked to explore the village unhindered, but she was too exhausted to look around. With each step, she willed herself to keep moving, for the baby and the king.

There was a small fountain in the middle of the town. Grasping the queen's elbow, Will sat her at the edge. She looked up at him, her normally placid eyes flashing in annoyance. Will ignored her. This wasn't time for royal pride.

"Stay here, Della." Without glancing back to see if the queen would obey him, Will started to make inquiries of where they might find some rest and a good meal. There was a nervous energy in the village. The common folks' eyes often wandered to the outlining hills and to the dragon-built tomb. Most people didn't want to talk.

"The inn is full," a farmer barked after Will had grabbed his elbow to get his attention. "That dragon has attracted all the common folk from near and far."

"Is there anywhere we can go?" Will asked, trying to hide his irritation as the queen crept up behind him. "My companion isn't well ..."

The farmer looked the queen up and down. "You look like you could do with a good rest," he admitted, rubbing his hand down his greying beard. He pointed to a large stone building. "Old Ninah was once our healer. She'll be willing to help your friend, mark my words."

"Thank you," the queen murmured.

"Be patient with ol' Ninah." The farmer gestured wildly about, trying to find the right words. "She's old."

"Thank you," Will said, with an inclination of his head.

The farmer grunted and turned away. Will watched him leave before turning towards the queen. "We'll find this Ninah."

"I'm well," the queen protested.

Lifting his hand to his breast pocket, Will felt the bulge of Tryst's cloak pin. He could still hear the whisper of Tryst's thoughts as he handed the pin to him. The guardsman hadn't expected to survive the coming coup. Will's message had been his only hope of reaching his wife. He prayed for the young guardsman's sake he had misread the situation in Pallaryn and that when they returned, he would find Tryst alive and well.

"I have an errand here in Habron," Will said. "After we find a bed for tonight, I'll need to find someone."

The queen exhaled. "I'm pregnant, not diseased."

"I made a promise to your husband." Will shrugged. He started towards the building the farmer had shown them. "You'll have to forgive me on my ignorance on such matters, Della. Let's see Ninah."

Jogging up the steps, Will rapped his fists on the heavy wooden door. With a long-suffering sigh, the queen followed him. When there was no answer, Will knocked again.

"Hold on!" came a voice, which crackled with age. "It takes time to move my aching bones."

The door swung open, and Will looked down on an old woman. He was a little surprised by her sharp gaze and the strength of her thoughts. From the farmer's words, he had been expecting her to be less responsive. The old woman continued to stare at him. Her clawed hands clutched a cane made from a black hardwood.

"What business do you have disturbing Old Ninah, hey little west countryman?"

Will thought it ironic that she was calling him little. Hunched over with age, Ninah couldn't have been over five feet tall. On the other hand, he was nearly six feet.

"Stop staring," Ninah croaked and tapped his foot with her cane. "Speak up, boy."

Clearing his throat, Will gestured to the queen. "We've been travelling, and my friend could do with a rest."

"I'm no inn ..."

"She's with child," Will interrupted.

Ninah tilted her head, studying the queen with a gaze that reminded him of his father's hawks. Her eyes narrowed, and she tapped Will with the cane again. "Why didn't you say that, boy? You the father?"

"No!" Will said.

A calculating expression blossomed on the old woman's face.

"He works for my husband," the queen said.

"Got a name, boy?" Ninah rasped. She tapped Will's boot with her cane again impatiently. "I don't work with strangers."

"Wes Gunter, born of Pyth," Will said, using the first name that came to mind. "This is Della Maulay, born of Arah."

"Well, I don't normally allow weapons into my home ... but since there's a wee one." Ninah turned her back and tottered into the building. Bemused, Will followed her through the dark hallway. The old woman gestured to the table for them to sit.

"Far be it from me for someone to say Ninah of Habron doesn't know how to treat guests. You hungry?"

"Yes," the queen replied. "But I wouldn't want to take food from your table."

"Got plenty," Ninah replied. "At my age and experience, I'm a local treasure. The people keep me well stocked with food as long as I let their head 'healers' use my hospital. And since the king's visit, the people have been more than generous."

"Hospital? The king?"

"When I was young, my husband and I built my hospital. And further back is where we prepare the dead."

The queen shivered.

"Don't let it bother you, dearie," Ninah cackled. She rummaged through her cupboards and selected a loaf of bread, cheeses, and dried fruits. "The dead don't mean you no harm. Someone has to look after them."

"You look after the living *and* the dead?" Will eyed the fruit. His stomach cramped.

"At my age, death isn't so frightening," Ninah said. "The dead still need care and attention. The lawmen found a young man recently, beaten and left to die in the wilderness. Tragic. I looked after him as if I were his doting mamma. Eat up."

Thankful that he wouldn't have to spend more coin on a decent meal, Will plucked up a piece of fruit. He glanced at the queen and thought a change of topic was in order. "I was hoping someone might help me."

"What do you think I'm doing?"

Will snorted back a laugh. "You remind me of my grandmother before she passed."

Ninah blinked at him. "I hear that a lot in my old age."

"I'm looking for someone. Hallea, a wife of a King's Guardsman. His name was Tryst. I have a message for her."

Ninah plonked herself into a chair opposite the queen and gawked. Then she turned to Will. "You've had a rough journey, my dear. Long and hard. I can tell by the wrinkles in your youthful brow that your message troubles you. Hallea sent a missive two days ago to Tryst in Pallaryn. She birthed a healthy boy."

Distressed by the thought of a new mother separated from her husband, the queen looked at her hands in her lap. "We should have brought him with us."

"He wouldn't come, Della," Will said. "He wouldn't leave his post."

Ninah cleared her throat. "Bad news then? I can tell by the way you sit and ogle your weapons."

"I would like to speak to her on Tryst's behalf," Will said.

"Eat. Then I'll take you to see her and the baby. She laboured hard, and she is still staying with me."

While they ate their simple meal, Will kept one eye on the queen. She was silent, and her thoughts were ones of home. In one respect, she was relieved she had been able to leave the citadel. On the other hand, she despaired for those left behind. There was also a heavy guilt that weighed on her mind.

That she might live while others perished. He leaned over and took her slim hand in his, knowing she would forgive his impertinence.

"There was nothing we could have done."

"I should have fought for them," the queen whispered. She withdrew her hand from Will's grasp. "I know how to use a sword."

"There still may be reason to use it."

Will knew he cut a striking figure, so it did not surprise him when all conversation ceased as he stepped into Ninah's hospital. The room was a large rectangular space lined with rows of cots. His footsteps echoed as he walked between the beds, and the queen followed closely behind. Before she came to Pallaryn and married the king, she had grown up in a rural lakeside mansion. He doubted she would have ever had the opportunity to visit a sick house before.

Will kept his eyes forward. He recognised Hallea, Tryst's wife, the moment he stepped into the room. Watching her nursing a small child, a lump formed in his throat. Whenever he was off duty and they crossed paths, Tryst always acknowledged him and asked after his health. One summer festival, he had invited Will to his home so that he wouldn't be alone. A smile tugged on Will's lips, remembering Hallea's shock at seeing a lord on her doorstep. It had caused quite a scandal at court, that he should visit a guardsman's humble home. The rude whispers did not upset him. He was the young lordling that lived with his brother in a brothel to escape his father. Rumours only had power when you allowed them to. Besides, it was worth enduring poisonous gossip to have time away from the bitterness that lurked within courtiers' shallow minds.

A girl who was hugging a cloth doll to her chest clambered up on the end of Hallea's bed. She tugged on Hallea's nightshirt and lifted a little finger in Will's direction.

"Lord Will!" Hallea cried, lifting her head. She smiled up at him, and Will felt his stomach knot. "What are you doing in Habron?"

"You know this woman?" the queen whispered.

Will sighed and gestured for the queen to stay a few steps back. He didn't turn his head to see how his silent command was taken. He stepped forward. "Hallea, we've just come from Pallaryn."

"Is my Tryst doing well?" Hallea asked, tucking her mousy brown hair behind her ear.

Will's eyes flicked down at the small bundle. The babe seemed at peace with the world. He hated to be the one to shatter that sense of security.

"Tryst asked me to come to you," Will replied. He swallowed, feeling the weight of the clasp in his pocket. Drawing it out, he stepped forward and placed it on Hallea's lap.

"This is my husband's ..." Hallea said. "Something has happened. Why have you come to me instead of Tryst?"

Will could feel his hands shaking. He averted his gaze. "Perhaps you should have the child visit another patient."

The small girl looked up at him inquisitively. Clutching her doll close to her chest, she slipped from the bed. "The king called me Larelle, Lake Maiden," the child informed them. "He says he's coming back to protect me from the bad men."

The queen made a small, choked noise in the back of her throat. Will turned sharply to her and shook his head. "This is my friend, Della. She would very much like to play with you. She has a little boy your age."

Larelle leaned forward and pointed. "She has a baby in her belly too! But it's only a small bump. Hallea was much larger before Addryn was born."

The queen recovered quickly and held out her hand to the child. "My baby has many seasons of growing. Come, tell me about the king's visit."

Larelle considered her seriously, twining her long, dark hair around her fingers. "I like your sword. Ninah told me I can play out in the back garden as long as I don't go too far."

"Can you show me your favourite place to play?"

Larelle nodded, and Will watched as the young girl dragged the queen into the garden.

"The pregnant woman?" Hallea's eyes shone with suspicion. "Is she … Will, what have you done?"

"Don't speak of her to anyone."

Hallea nodded her head, cuddling her small babe close to her chest.

Will inhaled and braced himself for the message he had promised he would deliver. "Pallaryn has fallen."

"Fallen?" Hallea gasped. "My Tryst?"

"He asked me to seek you out and tell you he did his duty and to give his child his cloak pin."

"Tryst? What about Tryst?"

"I'm sorry, Hallea, I don't know," Will replied, shifting from side to side. "He remained at his post."

Shoulders shaking, Hallea started to weep until great gasping sobs racked her body. Uncomfortable with the display of grief, Will stepped forward and gently took the baby in his arms to allow Hallea time to grieve.

The sound of Hallea's cries disturbed the other patients, and soon Will could hear Ninah's shuffling footsteps. The cantankerous healer stared down at Will with the baby and then the inconsolable Hallea.

Will was ushered out of the way as other women gathered around Hallea. He hoped one of them might take the babe. But they ignored him in favour of the crying woman. Stepping away, he wandered to the far side of the room. He sat perched on the edge of an empty bed and looked down at the wriggling bundle in his arms. Small children were usually a delight to be around. Their thoughts weren't corrupted by the worries and the pain of the world. The baby's dreams were ones of well-fed contentment.

"I would have saved them if I could," Will whispered down at the baby. He hung his head, resisting the urge to cry at the unfairness of it all. The young babe would grow without the guidance of his father and although he didn't always see eye to eye with Illeanah, she didn't deserve her fate. He could only imagine the destinies of those they had left behind.

A door opened and slammed shut and sensing danger, Will shot his head up. Clutching Larelle's hand tight in her own, the queen hurried between the hospital cots. She stopped in front of him. Her body was trembling.

"Ma'am, are you in some sort of trouble?" Three burly lawmen entered the hospital room behind the queen.

With one hand cradling the baby, Will reached out to grasp the queen's sleeve. He stood and stepped in front of her, not sure what he could do.

"Gentlemen, what is the meaning of this?" Ninah's stern tone startled the baby in Will's arms, and he woke with a little squeal, scrunching up his face as he did so. The queen looked at the babe with some surprise.

"We've got some unwelcome visitors in Habron, Ninah. This woman has a small army of men searching for her, and they're not friendly," the oldest looking guardsman said, ignoring Ninah's pointed stare.

"They went to the inn first, said you had stayed a night at Arimac, and their barkeep told them she got you a midwife and helped disguise you," one of his companions continued. "We're here to help. What can you tell us?"

"Will, give the child to his mother." The queen lifted her chin and unsheathed the sword at her hip. "We're going to fight our way out."

Will shuffled over to Hallea and handed her the baby. "We may be able to leave unnoticed."

"I would not advise it. These intruders seem intent on catching you. Mark my words, they'd have men on the roads watching," a lawman said.

"Larelle, darling, find somewhere small and dark to hide and stay there." The queen knelt beside the little girl and pointed to a dark corner. Larelle nodded her head and scampered away to hide herself under the bed. The queen watched her disappear.

"Ma'am?"

Rising from the floor in one fluid motion, the queen turned her attention to the impatient lawmen. "My name is Odelle Pallarus, born of Arah, wife to the High King of Rama. Pallaryn has fallen, and I have escaped the citadel. And I fully intend to fight my way out of Habron if necessary."

"Otherworlds," one of the women who was comforting Hallea swore. "First the High King, then his queen in our little village."

One of the lawmen swore. "My queen, we don't have much time."

"Your Majesty ..." Will tried to reach out and touch the queen's elbow. "This is not right."

"No," the queen said, "I'm a queen of Rama, and I'm ready to take up my sword for my husband, my children, and my country."

"Don't stand there like ninnies," Ninah said, gesturing to the patients. "Arm yourselves with whatever you can find."

The patients that were able grabbed whatever they could to defend themselves. Chair legs, a poker from the fireplace, and a wicked-looking knife were all wielded as weapons.

"Ma'am, this isn't your fight," one of the lawmen said. His gaze lingered on her belly. "Rumour says you're with child."

The queen lifted her imperious gaze onto the lawman. "These men are here to butcher me, pregnant or not. I prefer to die with a sword in my hand."

"Fair enough," another lawman replied.

They waited in silence. Will could feel the sweat dripping down his brow. It was only a matter of time before they were found.

When the violent knocking at the door came, he startled. His heart leaped out of his chest.

"Open up!" a voice yelled from the other side of the door.

"Sir, if you must know, I am a lawman of this town. We're armed and prepared to detain you." The lead lawman glanced back at Will and the queen, mouthing the words *get ready*.

There was a scoff, then a thunderous bang. Patients who lined the wall pressed themselves against the stone. A frail-looking farmer, with dark circles under his eyes and a hacking cough, stood in front of Ninah.

The queen grimaced at the door. She curled her fingers around the grip of her sword, her eyes hard. Widening her stance, she nodded in Will's direction. "Ready, Will?"

"No." Will could hear some brave villagers on the other side of the door trying to persaude the armed men into leaving their village.

"Keep it steady, lads," the more experienced lawman said, glancing at his companions.

The door splinted and shattered under the assault. Immediately, two bearded men rushed into the room, their swords raised above their heads. The lawmen met them with a clash of steel.

Patients shrieked, and Will gritted his teeth against the disruption of several panicked thoughts. Three more assailants pushed their way into the room, and Will lunged to the right to intercept a particularly large man. Their swords met, and he felt the tingle of his foe's thoughts. The brute believed he was an expert swordsman and Will a clumsy amateur. Violence and swordplay may not be one of Will's giftings, but his mind reading skills gave him an advantage he intended to use.

A wet gurgling sound to Will's side alerted him that one of the lawmen was in trouble. He turned to see the man's eyes widen in shock as he studied the sword impaled in his belly. Leering down at his victim, the assailant wrenched his weapon back. The lawman fell to his knees, his lips quivering on the first few syllables of a prayer.

Busy with his opponent, Will tore his thoughts away from the dead man. He darted forward to stop more attackers from reaching the queen. He intercepted one, but the other stepped around him.

Much to her credit, the queen raised her sword and moved forward to meet him. She snarled as her blade connected with his. Not expecting the queen to be on the offensive, the burly attacker swore and stepped back. He regarded the queen with ferocious eyes before jeering at her.

The queen didn't wait. She stepped forward again and attacked. Where the man was relying on sheer brute force, the queen was light on her feet. As he took time to intimidate her, she lunged forward, pushing her sword through his throat.

The queen's attacker thought she was incapable, too delicate to put up much of a fight. He had let down his guard to try to frighten her, and Queen Odelle had used it as an opening. Her movements had been smooth and swift, without a hint of hesitation. She had attacked to kill. Will winced as the queen yanked her sword back. She was not playing.

"Like stabbing my husband with a needle," the queen said. Looking into her blood-spattered face, Will could see determination gleaming in her eyes.

Three attackers came at them from nowhere. She spun on her heel and lifted her sword to parry the first man's blow. The second man nearly barrelled into Will while the third punched the queen. She stumbled, kept her footing, and tried to step out of reach.

It was no use. Will darted to the side and attempted to stab his opponent. Their attackers would soon overwhelm them. Not hearing the lawmen's thoughts, Will cast his eyes about. All of them had been killed in the struggle. Leaving Will, the queen, and the patients.

An earthen vase flew over Will's head and smashed against the wall.

"Leave 'em, you wretch!"

"Ninah! No!"

Will couldn't bear the thought of the old woman being hurt by the brutes. The fight was lost. He had one last gamble to make.

"Gents," Will gasped. "I'm Willyrd Hartcurt. I know Lord Thylyssa wants me alive. Leave the queen, tell them she's dead, and let no harm come to the people of Habron. I'll come with you without a fight."

"Too late." Will was knocked off his feet, and his head struck the hard flooring. He was aware of his arms being grabbed. The sensation of being hurled to his feet and bundled outside left him feeling disorientated.

From the murkiness of their attackers' thoughts, Will knew they were planning on making an example out of them. Queen Odelle would die here, while his fate would rest on the mercy of Thylyssa. Knowing that any protests would be ignored, he felt his stomach lurch. These men had been paid too well to take a bribe.

"Take your hands off me!" Queen Odelle continued to fight as she was dragged between two monstrous men.

Old Ninah's cane soared through the air, hitting one of them in the back of the head. While he stumbled and cursed, his companion turned to snarl at Ninah.

"Cowards!" Ninah taunted. "I'm that woman's midwife. Let her go, you steaming pile of dragon dung."

Will cried out in dismay as the man she had hit with her cane stalked after her. Ninah remained unmoving on the steps of her hospital, her head held high. He bit back a curse. The stubborn old woman was ready to meet the deadly armed man head on. He wondered if the healer had a plan.

The armed man only took a dozen steps before the village erupted into terrified screams.

Craning his neck, Will spotted a looming shadow that was circling the village. He couldn't quite make out the shape against the glare of the sun. But whatever it was, it gave him a sense of foreboding.

Chapter Eight
Jodathyn

Solan's Summer House, Aviah Valley

The only known dragon-made tomb was the one Tornyth had built on the grassy hills overlooking Habron. It was the last resting place of Donatein. While he had mourned the loss of his servant in his vision, he met Mandros for the first time. Watching until Roane's large frame disappeared on the horizon, he turned his head to glance quizzically at Mandros. "You're sending Roane to Habron? What's happening in the north?"

"That's something for Roane to discover for himself. He'll return in a few days."

Mandros stalked past him, nudging him playfully with his shoulder. "Whether *vehyl* or dragon, when a mistake is made, you can choose to learn from it or blame others. You're not responsible for choices of others, *mynrell*."

"You know what happened at the house?" Tornyth shifted back into his human form, and Jodathyn looked up into Mandros' face. The green dragon's expression gave away very little, but he sensed that Mandros was alluding to Voran. He wished he knew how much his *aluel* knew.

Mandros drew in a deep breath and lowered his body closer to the ground so that he could better pierce Jodathyn with his amber gaze. "Yes, the Sight gave me a glimpse."

"And yet you have no questions for me, *Aluel*, about what you saw?"

"Jodathyn, I am well aware you overheard my private conversation with your brother," Mandros said.

Jodathyn hung his head and kicked at the grass.

"I know that something drastic happened before Carvelle's birth. He's the promised Dragon King, and you're the Herald to his coming and the vanguard of the return of dragons to Rama."

"My mother's predictions foretold of Carvelle's coming. He's the foretold Dragon King, not me?" Jodathyn raked his hands through his hair. How much pain and suffering could have been avoided if his mother hadn't made such dire 'prophecies' about him?

"Your mother saw many things. But from everything you have told me, her interpretation was abysmal." Mandros snorted, flashing his fangs. "She saw her son bring redemption to Rama, not destruction."

"I hate this place," Jodathyn murmured. His change of subject was a deflection. Thinking of his uncertain future was frightening. He was on the precipice of greatness or doom. He dared not think about what would happen if he failed. Could he be personally responsible for hundreds or possibly thousands of deaths?

"I know, *mynrell*, I know. I felt your suffering at the time of your first manifestation. Your inner child revealed himself to me as the Apple Tree Prince. He told me of his pain." Jodathyn was relieved that Mandros respected his desire to change the subject.

"You already knew it all, then?" Jodathyn whispered. Tornyth raised his head in agitation. "Why send me here? You knew this was a place of suffering for me, and yet you still ..."

Mandros huffed, and warm air blew over Jodathyn's face. "That may have been a mistake. I knew your nephew was here. Your dragon would have tugged you back no matter what I did. So I gave you a little nudge. I hoped that you might have found some peace here. I've underestimated the depth of your pain."

Jodathyn remained silent.

"Please forgive an old dragon," Mandros said. "I've been centuries without my human heart. I've forgotten how painful healing can be. I wanted to do right by you as *aluel*."

"I was desperate to see Carvelle," Jodathyn replied. "I would have come despite the pain."

"Why don't you fly with Deovyn, pump some warm blood through those wings of yours?" Mandros said. "Wing Song is an invigorating remedy."

Jodathyn turned in time to see a crestfallen expression cross Deovyn's face.

"We won't be long." Mandros raised his head, observing the impatient movements of the other dragons in his command.

"What are you planning?" Jodathyn felt a spike of suspicion.

"*Aluel* plans for two groups of dragons to fly to human settlements to collect men and supplies for the coming battles. Of course it doesn't involve me," Deovyn snarled.

Sidrah, who was nearby, lifted her head in her brother's direction. "You are a small dragon, Deovyn. You cannot take such a load without fatiguing."

"I could at least do one trip," Deovyn snapped. "I'm capable."

"You'll be slower," Mandros replied. "We need you rested and fast for the battle to come."

Deovyn didn't seem comforted. "This has to do with the battle of Haven Bay."

Mandros speared him with a stern amber eye. "Careful, hatchling ... You will do as your king commands."

Deovyn frowned at the other dragons, who were all unfurling their wings and preparing themselves into two groups. A few of them sent him worried glances, which only made the russet dragon bristle.

Mandros lowered his voice. "I trust you to remain as my representative here and to be with Tornyth."

Sidrah moved to close the gap between herself and Deovyn. She nudged him with her wing. "Tornyth could do with instruction on manoeuvres small dragons can execute in battle. It could very well save his life. There's no one better to teach him, *sudunyn*."

Deovyn brightened at the suggestion. "Come, *sudunyn*, to the skies!"

Jodathyn groaned.

"My son, Deovyn the Small and Mighty, is an excellent teacher," Mandros replied. Exasperated, he shook his head. "He also needs to be in the thick of the action. Pairing him with you will give him purpose and direction ... and hopefully fly off some of his nervous energy."

Curarfur unfurled his wings and laughed. "I seriously doubt that, *Pallu*."

Deovyn was relentless. They spent the afternoon flying over Solan's summer house, which held the interest of the humans below. They spotted half a dozen men who had come out onto the lawn to openly gawk at them.

"Watch this!" Deovyn said, with a grin, winking one large tawny eye. He spun in a tight circle and dove at the guardsmen. The men scattered in every direction as Deovyn gave no sign of stopping.

"Quit staring and get to work!" Deovyn roared. At the last moment, he twisted and shot up into the air again. Laughing, he returned to Tornyth's side.

"Oh, Zapyr ..."

In the afternoon sun, Zapyr's golden scales were easy to spot. Upon his back, Tornyth spied Orion and Theo, while a King's Guardsman was riding on the back of a silver female dragon. The horses were grasped firmly but gently in their talons. Tornyth studied his friends closely and was relieved to see they were unharmed.

"Don't mind Zapyr. Like most beast-talkers, he prefers his animals. He didn't remarry after ... Well, it was duty, horses, and dogs," Deovyn murmured. He suddenly brightened. "Once, when we were much younger, he had a horde of rabbits."

"To eat?"

"Ancient One's Talons, no! Once Zapyr has spoken to another beast, there's no way he eats them ... They were his *companion bunnies*."

"What does Zapyr eat then? He's a big dragon."

"Fish, mostly. You might convince him to teach you to fish when he's in a good mood. He and *Aluel* love the sea."

"Tornyth!" Zapyr bellowed. "You should have been aware of approaching dragons much earlier than you were. Keep your wits about you, or you'll end up at the wrong end of a Grey Shadow's claws."

"Can't you ever say well done?" Deovyn grumbled.

"No," Zapyr snapped. "I want him to survive. So *teach* him, Deovyn."

Mischief glinted in Deovyn's eyes. He glanced over to Orion, who had his chin lifted, eyes closed, clearly enjoying the wind tugging his long hair. Theo, Tornyth noticed, was less than enthusiastic at being on Zapyr's back. He looked positively ill.

"I see you have your talons full," Deovyn said, gesturing with a lazy claw to the whinnying horses. His grin grew as he returned his gaze on Orion.

"Deo ... don't you dare!" Zapyr growled, flashing his fangs.

"Why?" Deovyn shrugged. "Are you fond of this one, *sudunyn*?"

"Deo ..."

"*Vehyl*! Jump!"

Orion's eyes widened. For a glimmer of a moment, Tornyth thought he saw movement in his manservant's eyes. He held his breath as Orion stood in one swift motion and leaped into mid-air. A cry of alarm stuck in Tornyth's throat. He squeezed his eyes shut, imagining Orion's splattered body underneath him.

Rumbling in annoyance, Zapyr was too slow to catch Orion. Deovyn was ready. The smaller dragon held himself steady so that Orion landed neatly on his back.

Tornyth shuddered at the befuddled expression on Orion's face. His manservant looked dazed and confused by his own actions. He flicked his eyes in Theo's direction. The thief was clutching on to Zapyr's back, shaking his head furiously.

"Deo!"

"Come, brother, don't you remember doing this when I was younger than this *vehyl?*" Deovyn rumbled with laughter at his brother's reprimand.

"That's different," Zapyr snapped. His scaled lips twitched.

"How so, brother?"

"We knew what we were doing!"

Deovyn was unconcerned by Zapyr's growing temper. "You know I wouldn't have called the *vehyl* if I was uncertain if I could catch him."

Tornyth dipped to move out of Zapyr's line of sight. If Deovyn wanted to annoy the golden dragon, he could shoulder his anger alone.

"Enough play," the King's Guardsman called out. "We need to report back."

"Took the words right from my mouth," Zapyr grumbled. He turned back to Tornyth. "You are tiring, white scales. It's time to land and rest. Follow us down."

"Hold on, *vehyl*." Still grinning wildly, Deovyn tucked his wings and spun into an abrupt dive. On the wind, Tornyth caught the delighted laugh of Orion.

With a long-suffering sigh, Zapyr followed Deovyn to the ground, taking it slower for the clearly terrified Theo.

"I'm Gylleah." Tornyth glanced towards the silver female dragon and the King's Guardsman upon her back. She smirked and swayed her head back and forth. "Don't be alarmed by Deovyn and Zapyr bickering."

"I'm more concerned about Deovyn being in harm's way," Tornyth replied. He nodded his head and allowed Gylleah to start her descent first.

By the time Tornyth's claws touched the earth, Orion had jumped off Deovyn's back while his brothers continued to argue. Without glancing at either of the dragons, he did an about-face, grabbed their horses' reins, and marched along the green lawns towards the house.

Rolling his shoulders, Tornyth returned into his human skin. Zapyr's head shot up, startled by his change and Orion's abrupt departure. The golden dragon rumbled, and Jodathyn raised his eyebrows. Blue eyes flickered towards him, and Zapyr huffed. The golden dragon did not lift his stare from Orion's retreating back.

The older King's Guardsman stepped past Gylleah and paused by Deovyn and Zapyr. His brow furrowed as he considered the dragons. "My thanks for your help." He lowered his voice. "It seems our young companion is eager to report and rest. We of the King's Guard will look out for him when it comes to battle."

Without breaking his gaze from Orion's back, Zapyr rumbled. "What makes you think I am concerned?"

Stumbling forward on shaking legs, Theo shook his head. "I think you've made your intentions clear, Lord Zapyr."

Jodathyn opened his mouth to ask Theo exactly what he meant. But Theo shook his head and jogged to catch up with Orion.

"You should rest, Zapyr," Deovyn said. "*Aluel* is out ferrying weapons, supplies and men. No doubt you'll be expected to join him ... unlike us." Deovyn shifted his weight, frowning. Jodathyn knew he was recalling the sting of being left behind.

Zapyr's eyes flashed, and the silver dragon quickly took her leave.

For a long moment, neither of the dragons spoke. Then Zapyr drew in a deep breath. "I pray that you'll never feel the pain and fear *Aluel* has known, brother. I don't wish that upon you."

"The battle of Haven Bay was one thousand, two hundred and thirty-six summers ago," Deovyn muttered. "I'm not the same dragon I was then."

"Indeed, that is true." Zapyr glanced towards Jodathyn, then back at Deovyn. Jodathyn had a sense that Zapyr feared he might have revealed too much. "Yet there is no recovery for *Aluel*, no matter how many summers have passed."

"What happened at Haven Bay?" Jodathyn asked. He bit his tongue and cursed his curiosity. "Is that where *Aluel* killed Vadroil? Historians have assumed that was the place. But they got so much wrong ..."

Deovyn grimaced, as if something unpleasant had been wafted under his nose.

"It was a long and bloody battle, *sudunyn*," Zapyr said with a sharp nod of his head. "Killing Vadroil and running off his generals cost us dearly. For some, the price was high."

Blowing smoke, Deovyn spread his wings and leapt into the air. Jodathyn watched him disappear with a frown.

"We all paid a price," Zapyr murmured.

CHAPTER NINE

Jodathyn

Solan's Summer House, Aviah Valley

It was a silly superstition. Yet even after all these years, Jodathyn refused to enter Solan's summer house through the front door. The servants of Aviah Valley believed that ill luck befell anyone of lowly birth who entered through the master's entrance. He hated that the servants' superstitions were so well ingrained in him, that he still could not force himself to look at the front door. That was for the master.

Hoping to find someone to distract him, he walked along the path towards the gardens behind the back of the house. He was not ready for the sight of several men building a makeshift pavilion.

Kieryn stood to the side with Orion, who was clearly reporting back. To the casual observer, it seemed like the king wasn't listening. His stare was firmly fixed on the pavilion. The telltale frown on the king's face told Jodathyn he was carefully taking in every detail of what Orion was saying.

Captain Tiernan stood by the king's shoulder, alternatively watching his men and Carvelle, who was attempting to help with the build.

On a makeshift table, Nym was arguing with Carew over what seemed to be a map. He watched as Nym jabbed at the paper and Carew shook his head. Guardsman Jael joined them, clapping Nym on the back. Standing to her full height, Nym stared back at the healer. Even at a distance, Jodathyn could see the wary distrust in her hazel eyes.

Returning his gaze back towards Kieryn, Jodathyn decided it was best to not interrupt Orion's report and strode towards Nym and the mysterious map.

"I don't think using ruins is a good idea," Nym said.

"Which ruins would that be?" Jodathyn asked.

Running his hands through his hair, Carew's eyes slid back towards the map. "Torryn has a great deal to offer in the way come battle. Miss Nym is concerned."

"Nym has moved around Rama. Her insights could be valuable," Jodathyn replied.

Crossing her arms against her chest, Nym glared up at Jodathyn. "I can speak for myself, you mulish, lumpy-stew brain ..."

"Maggot, codpiece or hound ...?" Jodathyn grinned at Nym's sour expression.

Nym swatted him. "Palace brat."

Jodathyn executed a bow with a flourish, ignoring the raised eyebrows of the guardsmen. "Your brother has returned safely with Orion. He looked ill from the flight."

"Something we can agree on then," Nym said. "Flying is a wretched affair." She stalked past Jodathyn, shaking her head and mumbling threats on how she planned to wring Theo's neck. Jodathyn watched her go and noted with some amusement Carew's unwavering gaze on her back.

"You sure know how to pick your allies," Carew muttered. "She's ..."

"Cantankerous, argumentative, obstinate ..." Jodathyn said.

Carew drew in a deep breath, exhaled, and then let his shoulders slump. "I was thinking more ... wonderful."

"You hurt her, and you'll have to deal with me," Jodathyn replied, his grin betraying him.

Carew stared him up and down. "You'll do what exactly?"

"I could rip your manhood off and punch you in the face. Alternatively, I could kick your kneecaps ... or I could hand Nym a knife." Jodathyn smirked.

"You grabbed someone's manhood in a fight?" Jael raised his eyebrows.

"You should have heard him howl. In my defence, he had a knife to my throat, and I could hear Carvelle's cries for help."

Carew stared off into the distance where Nym had disappeared. "Did she teach you that?"

"Keep your mind on your duty, Guardsman Carew. We're at war," said Jael, with a bark of laughter.

Jodathyn smiled. "No, a young King's Guardsman gave me some pointers one afternoon behind a certain captain's back."

Carew's brow furrowed, and then his expression cleared in understanding. "You were paying attention."

"Your advice saved my life in a few fights," Jodathyn said. Embarrassed by the way Carew and Jael were now looking at him, he turned his attention back to the map. His eyes bore into the parchment, and he tapped his finger on the words *Ruins of Torryn*. "There're mountains here. They could be used for a military advantage. It's been done before."

"We may have no choice but to engage in battle in the citadel," Jael said.

"Can't let those slimy lords hide themselves behind the stone walls. Luckily, we have dragons." Carew smiled mischievously up at Jodathyn. "Any chance of riding you into battle?" At Jodathyn's incredulous stare,

Carew burst into laughter, making those around him pause their tasks. "That sounded like a terrible thing to say out loud."

"I would be honoured if Mandros allows it," Jodathyn said.

Jael smiled thinly, nodded towards Carew and moved away to where Captain Tiernan was gesturing for him. Both Carew and Jodathyn watched as the troop medic approached the king. Carvelle had now joined them and was swinging off Orion's arms.

"It's harder than it looks," Carew said, nodding in Orion's direction. Jodathyn swore he could almost see beads of sweat dripping down Orion's forehead. "The dragons have certainly taken a liking to our newest guardsman."

Jodathyn hummed in response, not knowing what to make of Zapyr's interest in Orion. He returned his gaze onto the map; not able to resist, he grabbed a nearby quill and ink pot to fill in the missing details.

Carew watched in silence as he added his own neatly curled handwriting to the parchment. Jodathyn didn't know why he felt the insane need to add labels that weren't needed. He marked Sant Burgundy, Thrangul, Kudah, and even the abandoned house they had spent that one drunken night. He was so engrossed with his task that everything faded into the background.

Lost in the world of parchment and ink, he only came back to awareness when he heard the sound of a blade being drawn. He lifted his head, dazed as Carew's hand closed around his bicep. Before him stood Voran Axtin, his expression crumbling.

"You're not to approach," Carew spat in Voran's direction. He stepped around Jodathyn to stand in front of him.

Voran surveyed the naked blade and lifted his hands in surrender. He raised his chin, refusing to look in Jodathyn's direction. "You're as tenacious as your father, boy."

"I am Carew Candyde, born of Arelle, King's Guardsman," Carew replied. Jodathyn saw his fingers flexing. "And I take that as a compliment."

Voran snorted. "Tell Jodathyn I apologise for earlier ... for everything."

"Speak to me," Jodathyn said, thumping his chest in frustration. He went to step forward, but Carew flung his free arm out to hinder him.

Voran's hazel gaze narrowed but didn't leave Carew's face. "I'm not to speak to Jodathyn."

Jodathyn could have roared his outrage. "Is this Jael's doing, Carew?"

"His Majesty's," Carew replied. "Go, Jodathyn heard your apology."

When Voran turned his back to trudge back to the house, Carew sheathed his sword, and Jodathyn stepped past him. He darted forward to catch Voran's elbow in his fingers. The big man stopped, staring down at Jodathyn's hand. He made to jerk his arm away, but Jodathyn held on tight.

"Please don't ignore me," Jodathyn begged. "I couldn't bear it."

"I've always loved you, as if you were my very own," Voran grunted. "Do you know what it did to me, to know that I failed to protect you? I'm condemned to live with my failure."

"Voran ..."

"There's no denying it ... Let me go. His Majesty doesn't want you near me. It's a reasonable enough request."

Jodathyn's fingers betrayed him and released Voran's shirt. Voran looked down at him, his face twisting into a pained scowl. His chin lifted, and he glared at someone over Jodathyn's shoulder.

"Voran ..." Tiernan had joined Carew.

"There's something else you should know," Voran said after clearing his throat. Jodathyn noticed that his ex-guard was refusing to look him in the face. "Lord Kamoore has been paying Solan's men to betray him. He's been doing it for some time. My company died for their refusal."

Jodathyn could only stare in confusion. "Why didn't you say something earlier?"

"Don't look so betrayed. Sometimes holding information close is the only thing that keeps you alive. Best you learn it," Voran answered, his eyes hardened. "If you want to have your guardsmen arrest me … fine … arrest me."

"Jodathyn!" Kieryn's voice cracking like a whip was enough to break the silence that followed. He watched in despair as Voran turned upon his heel and stormed towards the house.

Glancing up, he caught sight of his brother staring at him, and he knew the king had seen the exchange. The deep lines on Kieryn's face creased as he beckoned Jodathyn near.

Jodathyn's traitorous eyes swivelled to watch Voran's retreating form.

"Jodathyn!" Kieryn's voice wasn't angry, but there was no mistaking the command in his tone.

"Voran's diatribe was all about him," Carew said, stepping closer. He whispered so that his words did not carry to the guardsmen working around them. Jodathyn hated that his tone held only contempt for Voran. "Let him go. He's only concerned about himself."

"*Jodathyn!*"

Jodathyn suppressed a sigh and without looking behind at Carew and Tiernan, he trudged over to his brother. He heard the captain's footsteps following closely behind.

Kieryn watched his approach with a steady gaze. Remembering their last conversation, Jodathyn bit his lip and felt the familiar feeling of anxiety bubbling in his stomach.

"Jodathyn, I want you to stay away from him," Kieryn said sternly. His gaze lingered on the house. "A man like that will only bring you calamity."

"My king." Jodathyn couldn't stop the frown tugging at his lips. He lowered his head in reverence and then blurted the first thing that came to mind that wasn't anything to do with Voran. "I'm so sorry ... I would have saved them if I could."

"The blame for my daughters' ..." Kieryn paused, remembering Carvelle, who was pressing himself against his leg. The king ran his hand down Carvelle's hair, a soft smile on his face. Jodathyn saw him blink frantically. He had little doubt his brother had spent much of his afternoon weeping for his lost children. "You're not responsible for what happened, Jodathyn. I am truly very sorry that you felt you could not break your silence."

"I'll make Solan pay, I swear it, Majesty," Jodathyn said, feeling Tornyth's anger spilling over. His head twinged at an abrupt pain splitting through his skull. The others about him must have felt the force of his fury. Orion eyed him cautiously while Carvelle hid his face into his father's leg.

"Revenge does not suit you, Jodathyn," Kieryn murmured. He stepped forward, grasping Jodathyn's hands in his own. "Solan will answer for his crimes. But we'll act within the boundaries of what is fair and just."

"Forget justice. I'm going to make him burn," Jodathyn whispered. He stared down at his trembling hands. "Do you think I'm not capable?"

"Perhaps Solan will burn. Maybe rightly so," Kieryn replied. He released Jodathyn's hands and gripped his shoulder firmly. "Promise me this, brother. Stay the man who loves justice; don't repay his evil with evil."

Jodathyn blinked. The spell of anger dissipated. His shoulders slumped as he beheld the small prince still hiding against Kieryn's leg. He felt a wave of shame wash over him. "I promise, my king, if I have the opportunity to take Solan, I'll drop him at your feet to do whatever you see fit. There is no justice in this world. Not for what he's done."

Kieryn pulled Jodathyn close to him. Carvelle tripped over his own feet to join them. "Let your justice be that he's not broken you. Live a full life as a free man ... a free dragon, who is untwisted by hatred and bitterness."

Jodathyn nodded his head against his brother's shoulder.

"Your Majesty!"

Lifting his head, Jodathyn stepped away from his brother's embrace and started at the voice shouting at them. He spotted Theo running across the lawns, his silver earring glinting in the sunlight. The cheeks of his pale face were crimson from exertion.

When he was a few feet away from Kieryn, he fell to his knees, puffing and panting. "Riders!" Theo gasped.

"Guardsman Orion has already told us about the men from the village. My men have gone out to meet them."

Theo shook his head. "No. Gylleah saw the glint of armour and weapons in the distance. Lord Mandros is not here, and the dragons await your command."

Jodathyn felt a jolt of surprise. "I'll fly out and see for myself."

"No," Kieryn replied. "Not alone. Find your dragon brothers and ask their counsel."

Zapyr and Deovyn appeared on the green lawn only moments after Jodathyn called for them. Kieryn went to speak with both dragons in a hushed tone and when he finished, Zapyr nodded. He stalked past the king and grasped a stunned Orion around his middle and placed him on his back.

"No jumping from back to back," Zapyr rumbled. "Be a good *vehyl* and stay put. Tornyth, stay close to us."

Zapyr ignored Deovyn's sniggering and leaped into the sky. It seemed that Deovyn was content to allow their brother to take the lead without a fight. He bowed his head at Kieryn and blew hot air over Jodathyn. "Manifest, and off we go."

Bowing deeply to Kieryn, Jodathyn turned and joined his brothers in the sky. He flew alongside Deovyn, keeping half an eye on Zapyr and Orion. Zapyr intimidated him more than Mandros ever had. The fact that they had gotten off on the wrong foot didn't help matters. Tornyth got the distinct impression that he was a nuisance that required him to be put up with.

He inhaled a deep breath and realised Deovyn was watching him. The russet dragon's eyes slid to Zapyr and then back to Tornyth and then returned to Zapyr again. He opened his mouth to say something but then clicked his jaw shut.

"Keep vigilant!" Zapyr barked. "There are potentially Grey Shadows about."

Tornyth flinched.

"He's right," Deovyn whispered from the corner of his mouth. "It's never wise to rely on other dragon's diligence. Being taken by surprise can have nasty consequences for everyone."

"Has that happened before?"

"More times than I would like to admit." Zapyr's gaze was firmly ahead. It didn't take Zapyr long to find what Gylleah had spotted.

"Do you suppose they are for us or against us?" Orion bellowed. The wind buffeted his long hair so that his horseman's lock hit him in the face. Tornyth saw him press his body closer to Zapyr.

"One way to find out." Deovyn laughed.

"This situation requires delicacy," Zapyr replied.

"So raining dragon fire on *vehyl* is out of the question, *sudunyn*?" Deovyn's cheeky grin only grew.

"I could approach them in my human form," Tornyth said.

"No," Zapyr growled. "I'll not leave you vulnerable to potential threats."

"*Aluel* will have our hides." Deovyn flew in a lazy loop, and Zapyr rolled his eyes at his antics.

"That leaves us to call out to them," Orion murmured.

"Keep your distance, *sudunyn*. Humans can be skittish little creatures." Zapyr dipped his wing and started a slow, graceful descent. Obediently, Deovyn and Tornyth followed his example. From the ground, the soldiers cried out, and a fair number of them broke ranks. From the sky, Tornyth thought they looked like retreating ants.

"The moment they get aggressive, you fly higher, *sudunyn*," Deovyn said from his side. All traces of his earlier humour were gone. This was Deovyn the battle dragon. Tornyth shivered and not for the first time, he wondered what had happened to Deovyn in the past.

When Tornyth caught sight of the banner men among the human ranks, he gave a shout of glee. He recognised the family crests. He sped up to catch up with Zapyr.

His golden brother spared him a sidelong glance as Tornyth flew level with him.

"Most of the soldiers are from Androssah ... and Pyth."

"Pyth?" Orion asked. "Who's the lord there?"

"Whitoak, the king's favourite, is from Androssah, and Frayn for Pyth," Tornyth answered. "He's the one I saw ... lose his head in the vision."

"Now their men are mobilised." Zapyr nodded. "Keep your distance until we know it is safe. Deo, if you would do the honours…"

Deovyn didn't say anything as he zipped past to then fly towards the human army. He kept his height just far enough that spears and arrows would not reach him. His speed hovered over them.

"We wish to parlay with your commander," Deovyn said.

Tornyth strained to hear what the human reply was. "My lord dragon, forgive us for being wary of your presence. But we'll not send a man out to you."

"Why did you send Deo in?" Tornyth whispered.

"An excellent question, white scales. He's smaller and more able to ma-noeuvre out of danger if need be," Zapyr replied. "Hush. Let Deo work."

"Understandable," Deovyn called out. "I'll hover here and talk with your commander in peace."

"Very well, dragon, you have our attention."

"We want to know your purpose."

The men exchanged weary glances between each other. A man dressed in the blue and silver of the house Frayn pushed his way forward a little way. He was older than most of his company, his face hard. He was a man of rank. "My lord sent us a letter requesting arms and men for the king. Long live King Kieryn!"

There was a roar of approval from the men about him. They brandished their swords and banged them against their shields.

Deovyn smirked as he looked back at Zapyr and Tornyth.

"Stay on your guard," Zapyr said, his voice a low growl.

"I believe you would like to meet the humans in our little band," Deovyn said. "Would you be comfortable if we landed so we can talk face to face? We can land at a distance."

Tornyth watched as the humans shuffled uneasily, conversing among themselves. They finally came to the conclusion they would allow the dragons to land. Feeling the strain of his afternoon exercise, Tornyth was quite glad to have his claws on the ground.

"May I present Orion Maysden, born of Silverdyne, King's Guardsman," Deovyn said with a flourish. Zapyr landed, and Orion clambered down and approached on foot. "He has come from His Majesty King Kieryn's side in order to find out your purpose."

The decorated soldier from Pyth looked Orion up and down. "Well met."

"May I please see Lord Frayn's letter?" Tornyth manifested into Jodathyn, which elicited startled gasps from the men. Although he was only a small boy when he lived in Androssah with Lord Whitoak, it was likely that some of the older generation recognised him.

The man from Pyth stepped forward, walking the distance that separated them, and offered Jodathyn a folded parchment. Jodathyn took it, running his thumb over the wax seal. He had always admired Frayn's love of blue wax and the symbol of his house, a ship at sea. It was said in Pallaryn that Frayn adored the ocean. After opening up the letter, Jodathyn quickly scanned the contents.

"It's as they have said," Jodathyn declared. "Lord Frayn has asked his men to mobilise and find the king if necessary. It's dated some time ago ..."

Jodathyn cast his mind back. From his clumsy estimate, this letter had been penned a few days after Donatein's death. What had happened in Pallaryn to cause Lord Frayn to do something so risky? Why hadn't he seen

Kieryn about his concerns? He could only assume last night's visions had been real. Was this letter the reason he saw Lord Frayn's head on a pike?

"My Lord Frayn sent a messenger first to Pyth, and then we have travelled to Androssah with another letter asking for Lord Whitoak's men ... If the king needs us, we are ready to answer the call."

Folding the parchment, Jodathyn nodded his head. He swallowed thickly. Frayn had always been his rival, a constant reminder that he was unloved and unwanted. Now he was dead. Looking at the situation, Jodathyn realised Frayn wasn't much older than he was, only twenty-four summers. He had done something to upset Lord Solan, and he had been killed for it.

"There are rumours."

"These are your people, white scales. Time to practice your diplomacy skills." Zapyr's voice, low and commanding, echoed in Jodathyn's mind.

Jodathyn handed the parchment back to the soldier. "If the rumours speak of war, then they are correct. The king needs every able-bodied and loyal man that we can muster."

"Here we are."

"I'm afraid I have some bad news," Jodathyn continued. "From our sources, Pallaryn has fallen and Lord Frayn, your master, is dead."

"The enemies of house Frayn will find no mercy with us," the soldier replied. "Tell us where to march."

Jodathyn opened his mouth to speak. But Zapyr cleared his throat. "Send the best of one hundred and fifty of your finest fighters to Aviah Valley to await the orders of your king. We have approximately thirty battle dragons ready to fly to the liberation of Pallaryn."

"But ..."

"There are too many of them for us to carry all the way to Torryn," Zapyr replied. A small smile tugged on his scaly lips as he looked down at

Jodathyn. "We need to have them moving of their own accord. We'll send our strongest dragons to start ferrying them to Torryn."

"The dragon is wise. Preparing for battle can take days. We'll move with all haste and gather more men and supplies as we go."

The man before them bowed and shouted some orders. Jodathyn watched as they began to choose among their number who would go to Aviah Valley and who would march onto Torryn.

"Here's to hoping you do not become accustomed to the ways of war, little brother," Zapyr said, cocking his head to the side. "A dragon who catches fish in his claws is a happier dragon than one who smites foes." Spreading his wings, Zapyr gathered Orion back up with his claws and took off. "Come, you two!"

Tornyth blinked in confusion and turned to Deovyn. The russet dragon rolled his eyes. "It's his way of saying he hopes for you to live a happy life free of suffering. Our brother is obsessed with fishing."

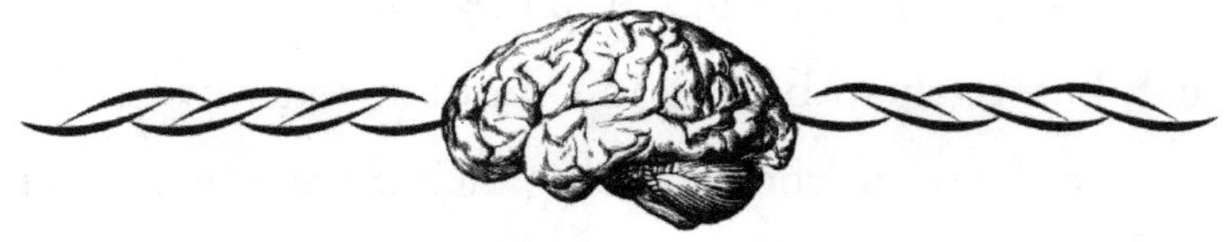

Chapter Ten
Will

The Village of Habron

Will blinked past people's confused thoughts and struggled against his captor. He drove his elbow to the man's stomach, and he heard a soft grunt at the impact. The man's grip on him tightened, forcing him to keep moving. Craning his neck, Will tried to get a better look at the looming shadow.

Behind him, the queen was thrown to the ground. She thrust her wrists in front of her to cushion her fall, and Will heard her soft cry of pain. The man who had been jostling her turned tail and fled.

Sprawled on her hands and knees, the queen tilted her chin to stare up at the man holding Will captive. "Let him go."

The man holding Will ground his teeth together. "What are you going to do about it, darling?"

The queen pushed herself to her feet and dashed forward with a shout of rage. She lowered her head and rammed into the man's side, punching him with her fists. Air whooshed out of his lungs, and he released Will.

The man intended to subdue the unruly queen and then return to Will. Before he could lay a hand upon the queen, Will took his chance and punched the back of his head. All the years he had spent under the violent thumb of his brother had paid off. As a boy, he had watched Tomas' fights, sifted through his thoughts and taught himself how to brawl.

As the man crashed to his knees, Will bent and grabbed a piece of discarded wood. He lifted it above his head and clubbed his attacker.

It was not his or the queen's destiny to die in the village of Habron. He would not be dragged back to Lord Thylyssa. He thumped the man again. The wood connected to the man's skull with a dull thud. There was no room for mercy. Will knew he had to win this fight, and that meant this man had to die.

Dropping to her knees, the queen grasped a dagger from the unconscious man. Will stumbled to his feet. Thylyssa had sent several soldiers to take him. He groaned, wiping the sweat off his forehead.

Surging forward with a scream, the queen held her dagger aloft, stabbing the man who had mistaken her for an easy target. With a hoarse cry, she wrenched the blade back and pivoted on the balls of her feet, daring for another to attack her.

"Dragon!"

The effect of the word had everybody scrambling for cover as the shadow drifted over the village. If they didn't get peeled alive by the dragon, they could use the chaos to escape, taking as many villagers as possible.

"Where's Ninah?"

Frantically, Will swept the area with his gaze. There was no sign of the old healer. He grabbed the queen and pulled her towards a hut in the opposite direction to where he had seen Thylyssa's men flee. "We can't help her if we're dead. We need to hide!"

Bloody dagger clutched in her delicate hands, the queen followed him. He could sense her rapid heartbeat as she attempted to calm her own mind.

Will slammed into a door at speed. His trembling hands tried the latch, only to find it locked. Banging his palm against the wooden door, he screamed to be let in. There was no answer.

"*Rshon mahthyt!*" Will caught sight of an overturned cart. Without looking back at the queen, he tugged on her arm and bolted for the shelter. As he dove into their hiding spot, he heard a solid thump in the middle of the market square.

"A dragon," the queen whispered.

Lying face down, Will could feel the ground trembling beneath him as the dragon rumbled. He swallowed his fear and held his breath.

The dragon spoke in a voice that rumbled like thunder. "My *pallu*, my king, has sent me here to punish *rokun*. I sense your thoughts. Stay behind the cart while I dispatch of your enemies."

Will felt the queen's hand on his shoulder. He briefly wondered if it was his laboured breathing or his erratic heartbeat that had given away their hiding spot. He shuffled closer towards the queen, determined that he would at least shield her body with his own if required.

Terrified bloodcurdling screams punctured the hush of Habron village. Squeezing his eyes shut, Will recalled the sound of his brother's body breaking under the power of Illeanah Whitoak. He could hear his brother's last cries mingling with those of Thylyssa's men ... and he swallowed a mouthful of bile.

The dragon made short work of the humans he decided to hunt. The noises faded until all he could hear was the soft symphony of crickets. Licking his lips, Will huddled with the queen behind the cart. Had the dragon simply flown away?

Then the ground quaked with the footsteps of the dragon.

"He's coming this way," the queen whispered.

Will swallowed. He kept his eyes firmly shut against his own rising fear. He never imagined that he would die by a dragon. "I'll distract him. You run."

"Come out, *vehyl*," the dragon rumbled. "I very much want to meet you."

Will's eyes snapped open, and the first things he saw were two wide nostrils flaring at his scent. In awe, he looked along the olive-green snout and into two large bronze eyes. The dragon was so close that Will could feel his warm breath on his skin and see the almost invisible spiderwebbed scars that were littered among the scales of his face and sinewy neck. The dragon's lips twitched with what Will could only assume was a smile. He reached for his power to see if he might examine the beast with his mental powers. But all he could sense was a fortress.

"I'm an ancient one, Willyrd Hartcurt," the dragon said. "You'll read nothing from my mind. I'm practised in defending my thoughts and mind."

"What do you want, dragon?" Will asked, still crouched behind the cart. He felt ridiculous. The dragon could easily topple the cart or set it on fire. In retrospect, it wasn't the best hiding place from a dragon.

"I have been sent north to find one who was in trouble," the dragon said. He sat down on his haunches, looking less terrifying. "My name is Roane, Sky Strategist."

The queen ignored Will's hand as he tried to stop her from moving. She crept further away from their hiding space and closed the gap between herself and the dragon.

"Pleasure, Lord Roane," Queen Odelle replied, dipping into a curtsey. Her movements were fluid even though Will could still sense the lingering terror in her mind.

The dragon dropped into what Will could only assume was a bow. "Your husband will be much relieved to hear you're safe. The last of what I read from his mind, he was troubled."

Clasping her hands, Will felt the queen's mind light up with hope. Her expression was hungry as she stared up at Roane, desperate for news. "Please, great dragon, what news do you have of my husband?"

The dragon dipped his head, and Will winced, looking up at the long, bronze horns on his head. He noticed that one horn had been damaged; the break was jagged, and it was considerably shorter than the others. He shuddered; he could only imagine what might have caused such an injury.

"The loss of a horn is such a minor thing," Roane said. "Especially in comparison to a friend's life."

Ashamed, Will looked away from the injury.

"Please, sir dragon, what news?" The queen took a few more tiny steps forward.

"King Kieryn has reunited with your son, the prince. We hold grave concerns for Pallaryn. Now we are readying for war." The olive dragon cocked his head to the side.

"My son," the queen gasped, bringing her hands to her mouth. "He's alive!"

The dragon's grin widened. "Yes, many of our kind have had the pleasure of meeting his royal highness, Prince Carvelle."

"My brother by marriage, Jodathyn?"

"Safe."

The queen promptly burst into tears.

"What's happening here?"

Will could have laughed at the ridiculous sight of Ninah with her walking stick raised above her head, charging up to the dragon with the shuffling steps. Roane peered down at the old woman and rumbled with laughter. "Queen Odelle is overcome with joy."

"She's with child, and you've made her cry," Ninah shouted. The healer toddled past the dragon and beckoned the queen into her arms. The dragon watched bemusedly as the healer brought the queen to her chest and crooned to her. Meanwhile, Ninah glanced over the queen's shoulder and spotted Will still crouched behind the cart. "Right useless you are, boy."

Cheeks burning, Will straightened and took a few steps away from the cart. He let his hands fall to his sides as he watched Ninah hush the queen.

Will could not help but admire Roane's impressive wingspan as he stretched out one wing and then the other. A scaly smile lit the dragon's face as he turned to him. "Yes. I am quite magnificent. You and I have a lot in common, *vehyl*. I see why *elt pallu* chose me for this errand."

"I don't understand."

"We share the same power, two-legger," Roane said. "I sensed it screaming in my mind the moment I landed. It seems you're untrained."

Sniffling, the queen pulled away from Ninah's embrace. She wiped her eyes and smiled apologetically. "There's no one else like Will in Rama."

"Now the *vehyl* named Will has an ancient dragon to teach him better control. Tell me, tiny *vehyl*, can you shield your thoughts and quieten the thoughts of others?"

"No, I cannot," Will admitted, toeing the ground. "Can you help me?"

The dragon chuckled. "I was an old dragon even in the days of Arturyn ... These will be my last battles. Age will soon make me a liability on the battlefields. It's time I cool my battle fire."

"I'm very sorry to hear that," Ninah said.

"Bah," Roane said, his ancient eyes peering down at Will. "Age will not clip my wings. I'll soon have a new role among my kind."

Ninah wrapped her arms around the queen's shoulders. "Are you hurt?"

The queen shook her head.

"She's exhausted and in shock," Roane rumbled. "Evening approaches. Take her inside and ensure she has a good night's rest. I'll take her to her husband and child in the morning. Willyrd and I have some work to do."

Will sat cross-legged between Roane's forelegs. The cool of the evening swept over him, drying the beads of sweat that were forming on his forehead. He listened carefully to the dragon's instructions and encouragements, but he felt he was missing something vital.

A feeling of anger washed over him. He clenched his fists against his knees and tried to concentrate on his own thoughts. Roane had told him the key was to be master of his own mind first.

"It's time to stop," Roane rumbled.

Scrunching his eyes, Will shook his head. "One more try."

"Willyrd," Roane said. "Stop."

Will sighed and opened his eyes. He blinked and looked around in surprise. The sky was dark, and the stars shone down upon them. They had been at this for hours. Will felt another spike of annoyance. He hadn't improved in all the time he had spent with Roane.

Roane laid his head down on the cobblestone streets. "You will improve. It is inevitable. I have never met a mind that casts such a wide net."

"I'm cursed," Will groaned.

"The kind magistrate has left you some food." Roane indicated with his snout to a tray.

Will scrambled to his feet. His stomach groaned, letting him know he was ravenously hungry. His mouth watered at the sight of a couple of buns, dried meats, and cheeses. Snatching up a bun, Will was delighted to see that it was still fresh. It had been cut for him, still warm and lathered in golden butter.

"He also said to come knock on his door when we've finished here," Roane continued. "He has offered you a bed for the night."

"That's kind of him," Will said, biting into the buttery warmth of the bun. He snatched up a slather of dried meat. Looking at it, he assumed it was prime venison. "If we are going to war, what is the king doing about his forces?"

"Mandros, the dragon of Flame and Fury, has our kind collecting humans and positioning them in Torryn. I'll speak with the magistrate and the lawmen in the morning."

Will's hand dropped from his mouth. "They lost three lawmen today."

Roane sighed. "It may be all the help we can expect from Habron is riders to go out searching for men. It's late. Go seek the magistrate and get some rest."

Will woke late the next morning and tumbled out of bed.

Last night he had been nervous knocking on a stranger's door at such a late hour. Before he could raise his fist to knock, the door swung open, revealing the magistrate and his wife both dressed in their nightrobes. They greeted him warmly and ushered him upstairs to a modest room. He sunk down into the very comfortable mattress and drifted immediately to sleep.

Will didn't want to overstay his welcome, so he crept cautiously downstairs. The magistrate's wife greeted him, pressing a simple breakfast into his hands.

"Hurry, Master Will, the dragon is impatient to leave."

Will nodded his head in thanks and glanced down at the food she had offered him. Dried sugar apples and a bun filled with nuts and fruit. He looked up at the magistrate's wife, dumbfounded. This wasn't the usual breakfast fare for a Ramian.

"Every now and then, we all deserve a sweet treat." She winked at him as she pushed him out the door.

Will thanked her again as she shooed him from the doorstep. He bit into the bun, savouring the subtle sweet spices and the tang of the dried fruits. Deciding it was best to save the dried sugar apples, he tucked them inside his jerkin for later.

Roane stood right in the centre of the village, overlooking the eager humans. The ancient dragon looked no less magnificent in daylight. The smirk on the beast's face at Will's entrance was enough for him to know that Roane heard his thoughts. It was disconcerting. For the first time in his life, it was his thoughts that were being read. He wasn't sure he liked the idea.

Queen Odelle stood proudly beside the dragon. The young child, Larelle, was holding on to her pant leg. In her arms, she held a small babe swaddled in blankets. The mother, Hallea, nervously looked up at the dragon.

Ninah tottered forward and whispered something to the queen. She turned and spotted Will.

"Wherever I am," the queen said, gesturing to Larelle with a nod of her head, "there's safety."

Will stepped forward.

Roane lowered himself so that Will might mount him first. He bent down and motioned for Larelle to come. When he was sure the little girl was ready, he climbed upon the dragon's back. He settled the child in front of him and reached down to help the queen, who was nuzzling the baby before handing him back to his mother.

"Stay strong," Odelle said, grasping Hallea's shoulder. "We'll make sure that both you and Addryn are looked after."

Hallea's eyes filled with unshed tears, but she straightened her shoulders and nodded.

Roane assisted the queen onto his back, and her hands came to rest lightly around Will's waist.

"What about you, Ninah?" Will asked.

"Don't be foolish, boy," Ninah replied, brandishing her cane up at him. "I'm off to Torryn. If there's battle to be had, healers are needed."

"You're a brave woman," Will said.

"Naw," Ninah said. "These old hands still have healing to do. I'll be healing to my dying day. Bravery ain't got nothing to do with it."

"Rama thanks you for your service," the queen whispered. "How can I ever repay your goodness to me?"

Stepping up to the dragon, Ninah patted his foreleg and looked up at the queen. "If I survive this nasty business ... let me be your midwife."

A gentle smile lit the queen's face. "I would like that very much."

Roane stretched his wings out wide. Will felt the rumble run along the spine of the beast, and Queen Odelle's grip on him tightened.

Soon they were looking down at the Paldera River. Between his thighs, Will could feel the power of the dragon as they flew among the clouds.

It seemed impossible that Solan or even Thylyssa could do anything in response to a dragon army.

The war would be over swiftly. Of that Will had no doubt.

Chapter Eleven

Kamoore

The Citadel of Pallaryn

Galgothmeg had taken residence on the tallest spire of the palace, which happened to be directly over the throne room. Every time he dug in his claws, the structure crumbled. Shards of rock rained down in the audience chamber, doing irreparable damage. From his lofty vantage point, the red monstrosity observed the pillaging of Pallaryn, uncaring of the chaos.

The screaming and wailing of the common folk continued day and night. Gritting his teeth, Kamoore told himself he would show restraint as he stomped up the steps of the palace's outer walls.

He had brought dragons into the citadel to subdue the stubborn Ramian people, not to ransack the bustling city. But what did one really expect from an unthinking, loathsome beast?

Galgothmeg had been a necessary evil to consolidate his power in Pallaryn. Very soon he would be the High King of Rama, with no one left to stand in his way.

As a child, he had been schooled in a manner befitting a highborn lord. The remnants of the great heroes of old still lived through him. He was born of dragon slayers, fighting beside the great Unifier. Without them, Arturyn would have been slaughtered, his corpse left to be picked apart by scavengers.

Throughout his lifetime, he had watched the dwindling power of the Pallarus dynasty through three kings. First, Ayran, who relied on the powers he gave to the great lords during his long reign, then his son Hadryn, whose decade of kingship further chipped away his family's power, and finally, Kieryn.

By the time the now deposed king came to the throne, he had been too long left to his own devices by his father. Uneducated on the true difficulties of kingship, Kieryn had inherited a country that was slowly being torn apart by the great lords. He was destined to fail from the very beginning, and Kamoore had been waiting in the wings for his opportunity.

Before the proud people of Rama could submit to him fully, he needed to bring Galgothmeg to heel. It seemed the beast had no understanding of power and how to wield it against humans.

Kamoore paused his trek up the palace walls to stop halfway and peer out over his city. He had been on the walls when the people rioted two days after Galgothmeg's arrival. They swarmed the gates of the palace, killing his sentries. He heard shouted accusations of the Grey Shadows consuming the poorer folk and of homes and livelihoods destroyed. They cried out for justice and for their leaders to do something about the loathsome beasts. The Grey Shadows, attracted to the sound of their whining, flew in from behind them and attacked. Many had died clambering for safety.

Since then, the streets had been abandoned. The people had ceased their trading, and they cowered in their homes.

If he was truly honest with himself, this was what Kamoore was angry about most. If the people were too afraid to go about and live their pathetic lives, then they weren't making coin to pay their taxes.

Galgothmeg had done absolutely nothing to stop his damnable Grey Shadows from terrorising the citadel. And discontent was brewing among the citizens.

While fear was a good thing to have among the common folk, discontent was dangerous. Galgothmeg needed to learn that people needed to fear in order to show proper respect ... but pushing the people into discontent was dancing on the edge of a revolution. His reign was young, and Kamoore couldn't risk a coup.

Intent on having a serious discussion with the red dragon, Kamoore stalked along the palace walls. He tilted his head to glance up at the heads of the guardsmen who had died for their king.

"Soon, your king will join you," Kamoore said.

Eyes frozen in death, looking into the Otherworld, the guardsmen stared down at Kamoore. Was it his imagination, or did their eyes gleam in the waning afternoon light? He hurried past them. He wasn't a superstitious man, but he would have to ask his soldiers to remove them. Just in case.

Drawing close to Galgothmeg, Kamoore noticed his men were on edge. This pleased him, as guards needed to keep their wits about them. He knew his necessary steps of removing Kieryn Pallarus from the throne would result in assassination attempts. The guards would stop any foolishness before it caused him any inconvenience.

"Dragon!" Kamoore bellowed.

Galgothmeg raised his crowned head, curling his scaly lips into a sneer, and then turned his gaze away from Kamoore.

"We need to have a talk about proper behaviour."

"Very well. Your first lesson. You should bow to me, *rokun*," Galgothmeg replied. "I'm Artrothian, your natural master."

"I am the High King of Rama!" Kamoore spat.

Galgothmeg yawned wide. As he did so, Kamoore saw rows upon rows of deadly fangs. "I have no interest in your complaints."

"The people are not going about their daily lives."

"Not my concern," Galgothmeg said. His tail flicked as he ran his tongue along his sharp fangs. The red dragon's grip tightened upon the spire as he leaned forward to glare at Kamoore. "I care not for humans."

"Your Grey Shadows are harassing the people. There are reports of them consuming humans."

Galgothmeg chuckled. "Grey Shadows need to eat. It's the natural order of things."

Feeling his anger rising, Kamoore stomped his foot. He would not be made a fool of. "Tell your dragons to leave the people be. I demand ..."

Galgothmeg blinked slowly, staring at Lord Kamoore in contempt. "I'm the dragon called Death and Despair. Tell me, *rokun*, what did you think would follow in my wake?"

"You must stop!"

Galgothmeg snorted.

"I am the High King of Rama!"

Galgothmeg lifted his head and laughed. "You're a pawn, Kamoore. Nothing more. Once I'm done, there won't be a Rama, just a food source for Artroth to gorge on."

Kamoore felt the flush of rage prickling his skin. "That wasn't our arrangement."

"Guards, take him to his rooms. Lock him in. I have some use for him before I eat him."

To Kamoore's utter dismay, his own men laid their hands on him and dragged him from the palace walls. Horror blossomed in his chest as he realised he no longer had control of his own men. They belonged to Galgothmeg. They knew as long as Galgothmeg had a use for them, they would live. Those who became bothersome were dragon food.

No one wanted to be dragon food.

The untrustworthy lizard had betrayed him. *Him.* He who had orchestrated the coup and held the red jewel that had been the gateway for Galgothmeg's return. He had delivered Solan to the wrath of Galgothmeg, and this was how he was repaid for his services. It was a disgrace.

He was dragged throughout the halls of his newly gained palace, kicking and screaming. The doors to the king's personal chambers loomed before him. What once was a prize was to become his prison.

He was propelled through the doors, and he landed on the floor with a thud. Cursing, he turned towards the guards to let them have a piece of his mind. But the door clanged shut.

Kamoore's red-haired serving boy strode in from the adjoining room. The freckled little cretin stared at him, his lip curling. "I take it things did not go as you planned with your overlord?"

"Insolent slug, help your king off the floor before I remove your head from your proud shoulders."

"*Proud?*" The boy stepped closer, a strange fierceness shining in his green eyes. He paused, his frown tugging into a smile. "They've locked in you the king's rooms with me."

"Obviously, you insufferable wretch! And I am the High King of Rama, whelp."

The boy shrugged. "You're the same as me now."

"What are you on about?"

"We're both prisoners. The only difference now is that you wear a stolen crown."

Growling, Kamoore rose to his feet and took a few steps forward.

The young servant darted back a few steps and brandished a knife in front of him. "I am Filyx Ostyn, born of Garrowmyth, the son of Lord Royn Ostyn, and I'm not afraid of you."

"Pathetic." Kamoore scoffed.

"I've the only object in this room that's sharp. I took it before they locked us in," Filyx said. "Perhaps you should show me more courtesy. Lord Thylyssa gave me an escape. The only thing I have to do is put this dagger in your black heart."

"What are you waiting for?" Kamoore spread his arms wide.

"The anticipation makes this all the more fun, don't you think?" Filyx had the audacity to laugh. "You'll never know when to expect my dagger."

Tilting his head, Kamoore studied his servant more closely than he had for months. When he had taken him from his father's land as payment for a debt owed, the boy had fought him. Kamoore had spent the last few years chipping away at the lad's confidence. With the help of the treacherous Thylyssa, it seemed the boy had found his courage. Either that or he had descended into madness.

"Sit down." Filyx waggled the knife in Kamoore's direction. "Let's enjoy each other's company, you and I."

"I could have you executed for this."

"I know," the boy replied. "We both know I am a dead man walking. But at least this way I get a little revenge. Now. Sit."

Kamoore hated the way his feet moved in the direction of a chair. He did not like being forced into obedience. He'd have to search to find his weak point and then exploit that. "What now, my clever little boot licker?"

A cruel smile spread across Filyx's face. The boy licked his lips in nervous excitement. "When I heard your traitorous men making plans a few days ago, I knew I wanted to see your face one last time before my soul was sent to the Otherworld. I wished to see your expression when you realised Galgothmeg is the new king. Not you. It was *never* you. Why do you think Thylyssa left so quickly?"

Kamoore blanched. "You knew … you knew their plans all along and said *nothing*!"

The boy shrugged. "You never gave me a reason to look after your interests, my lord. When you took me from my father's house, I told you I would survive and find my way home. You laughed."

Kamoore growled, banging his fist uselessly against the hardwood table. All the while, his servant continued to observe him with his eerie, crooked smile.

When he got his hands upon Filyx, he would tear him limb from limb and string him up on the walls of the palace for all the cowardly lowborns to see.

He was the High King, and he wouldn't take disrespect from anyone.

CHAPTER TWELVE

Jodathyn

Solan's Summer House, Aviah Valley

Safely hidden high in the branches of the old apple tree, Jodathyn watched as Jael stopped by the trunk. The healer placed his palm against the tree and looked up. "This is a quiet place."

"The healer found us." Tornyth was displeased that they had been caught hiding. Jodathyn stifled a long-suffering sigh.

"Have you been looking for me for long?" Jodathyn asked. "Most people don't look up."

"I'm not most people." Jael shook his head, his lips quirking into a smile. "When Ruevyn told me you could be found near the apple tree, he failed to mention you were *in* the tree."

"Traitor," Jodathyn replied, with a snort of humour. "You mean to say he spotted me when he walked past an hour ago?"

"Your friend is wise to know that sometimes it is good to have some quiet time to reflect in peace. But sometimes it's good to have company."

Much to Jodathyn's surprise, Jael took a hold of a low branch, braced his boots against the trunk and began to climb. He waited until the troop medic was alongside him before he spoke. "You want me to speak with you, I gather."

Tilting his head to the side, Jael looked into Jodathyn's eyes. "If you wish to speak, speak. I'm listening."

"Not today," Jodathyn whispered, his eyes downcast.

"Maybe one day." Tornyth wasn't going to make a promise that he was unable to keep.

"I've been puzzling over something for years. Perhaps you can help me?" Jael asked, plucking a stray leaf out of his hair.

"What is it?"

"The poison," Jael said. "What was it? In all my years, I have never come across anything like it."

"Oh." Jodathyn shrugged his shoulders sheepishly. "I created it myself. Donatein taught me some herb lore, so I made something that I was reasonably sure was lethal."

"Reasonably sure was lethal," Jael parroted. "That explains a great deal. I gather you didn't know what it would do to its unfortunate who ingested it?"

Jodathyn looked down at his hands. "I had no idea."

"Always said you were too smart for your own good. A grim, well deserving death if it had only found its victim." Jael chuckled. The sound of his laugh was oddly dark. The healer reached out to grasp an apple, but Jodathyn stopped him with a shake of his head.

"The tree has been neglected ... The fruit is terrible. Ruevyn found out the hard way."

Jael withdrew his hand and wiped it across his brow. "I can see why you enjoy climbing. It's physically demanding."

"Don't give the captain any ideas." Jodathyn laughed. "I'd lose my only advantage over the King's Guard."

"I can think of a big advantage you have no one else has," Jael teased. "I've seen you in action."

Jodathyn smiled weakly. "I don't think any of you realise how terrible dragons in battle are to behold."

Jael said nothing. His face remained politely attentive.

Jodathyn drew in a deep breath and when he started talking about the dragon battle in the Paru Mountains, he couldn't stop. It seemed that having a captive audience listening caused the words to bubble out of his mouth.

"Dragons in battle sounds …"

"Horrific," Jodathyn said. "It is, and the noise …"

I like the chaos of the flight. But I hate the blood and death, Tornyth added.

"I can only imagine," Jael replied. "It must have been frightening."

"Not in the moment." Jodathyn shrugged. "But watching the large orange dragon, Averyn, die and doing nothing …"

Jael hummed.

"Can I ask you something, Jael?" Jodathyn inquired. "If you don't want to answer, I understand."

Jael's head shot up. "Do you want to know about my scars, master? The one in my shoulder was from an arrow—"

"No, it's a little more personal," Jodathyn said, interrupting Jael's story. "What is it?"

Jodathyn swallowed. "I wanted to know about your power and … Are you a dragon too? Have you met other dragons before?"

"Ah." Jael rearranged himself in the tree. "I see. I was born in Farholm, in the west country. My father had the same healing ability as I possess.

Now, in certain places in Rama, before your mother's rise and downfall, while not socially acceptable, powers were kept quiet and ignored. I lived a comfortable life until my grandfather took me from my father's home. I was nine summers when the old man started drugging me with the tonics to stop the powers. It seems I was old enough that the herbs couldn't dampen my power or my grandfather wasn't able to purchase enough. The damage was done; my dragon stopped growing. In order for my abilities to keep flourishing, he let go ..."

"When you say ..."

"My dragon perished before he could manifest, but my powers remained."

Jodathyn gasped. "That's terrible. I'm sorry."

Jael shook his head, smiling up at Jodathyn. "Don't. I'm at peace with it. I had faith that my powers could change the world. My dragon left behind a legacy. Every time I use my power, I feel the spark of him ... just a spark return."

Jodathyn blinked rapidly. "I wish I could have met him, your dragon."

Reaching out, Jael grasped Jodathyn's arm. "I left my grandfather's house and the west when I was fifteen. I am proud of the life I have been able to lead. I've no regrets."

"How do you do it, Jael? Live free of anger?"

"Forgiveness is a long, hard journey. I released my fury and grief to step into the future waiting for me."

"*Forgiveness...*" Jodathyn sniffed. "Do you think I'm wallowing in grief?"

"Patience, my young friend," Jael admonished. "The body, heart and soul need time to appropriately grieve and heal. But please don't make the mistake in thinking forgiveness means that one is free of being held accountable and safe from consequences."

"You're fond of your consequences."

"Yes," Jael said. "It's the natural order of things. The men who have harmed you will be held accountable. Your forgiveness does not save them from consequences."

"Do you think—"

A great rushing wind above them turned Jodathyn's attention away from the troop medic. He caught sight of Roane's battle-scarred underbelly as the olive dragon cruised overhead. On the dragon's back were human passengers. With his curiosity needing to be satisfied, Jodathyn climbed down from his perch.

"Where are you going?" Jael asked.

Jodathyn's feet landed on the ground, and he glanced back up at the puzzlement on the healer's face. "Don't tell me you are stuck, guardsman?"

Shifting, Jael followed him to the ground, brushing off his trousers. "I'm not as young as I used to be," he grumbled.

"The battle dragon who flew overhead, Roane, was sent north on a mission. I want to see what he has come back with."

Jodathyn didn't wait for the healer. Without looking behind him, he jogged around the gardens to the green lawns the dragons were using close to the house. There was already a large gathering of guardsmen greeting the dragon. He caught sight of Et-hir and Nym offering a hand to the human passengers.

Much to Jodathyn's surprise, Will Hartcurt was the first to descend. He nodded curtly to Nym and turned back towards the dragon. A small girl, not much older than Carvelle, slipped from the dragon's back and into his arms.

Seeing the guardsmen were still nervous of Roane, Jodathyn strode forward to help. Jael followed closely on his heels.

Jael knelt on the ground and offered his gloved hand to the child, who Will set on the ground. "Are you hungry, little one?"

"I remember you. You're one of the king's men." The child took Jael's offered hand and tugged him towards Roane's snout. "I think I should say thank you to the dragon first. He let us ride him."

The dark-haired woman who still sat astride the dragon spoke. "I want to see my husband and my baby."

"Tell us who he is, and I'll go find him," Nym offered. "I'm sure our sweet palace dragon-fodder will be tripping over himself to help."

Deep brown eyes swept over Jodathyn as the woman pursed her lips in amusement. The voice ... that face ... but how? He stood rooted to the spot, transfixed on the dark eyes. A gasp escaped his lips as he forced himself to step up to Roane's side to offer his assistance.

As he came level with the young lord, Will's eyes met his own. There was a genuine smile on his face as he beckoned to the woman. The woman slid from Roane's back and into Jodathyn's arms, wrapping him into a tight embrace. "Odelle ..." Jodathyn sighed. "You're here."

"Ma'am, I need to inform you Jodathyn Pallarus has an intended," Nym said, coughing and looking away.

"Does he?" Odelle asked, stepping back and cupping Jodathyn's cheeks. "When did this happen?"

"It all began when the palace brat decided to strip nude and go bathe in the river."

"Nym!" Jodathyn cried, his cheeks flushing as the guardsmen nearby chuckled at his expense. The King's Guardsmen, all who knew the queen on sight, had all fallen to a kneel, but Nym and Et-hir, unaware of who the queen was, seemed intent on embarrassing him.

"It wasn't his nakedness that—"

"Et-hir!" Jodathyn cried.

"Don't mind Jod. He flusters easily," Et-hir said, chuckling and shaking her head at Jodathyn and then turned a quizzical eye to the guardsmen.

She seemed confused, watching Carew stepping forward and tugging Nym into a kneel. "Jod ..."

"Odelle, might I, uh, present Et-hir of Sion, my intended. Et-hir, this is my sister-by-marriage ..."

"Your Majesty!" Et-hir squeaked, her knees buckling.

Odelle reached out a delicate hand to stop her. "Don't ... It's not necessary, my dear. We must find some time to get to know one another. I admit, I would dearly love to know what my little brother has been up to ... Spare no details."

"Oh, I have details." Nym covered up her laugh with a cough, looking away at Carew's stern glare.

"The king!" someone called out.

That was all Odelle needed to hear, and she was sprinting past Jodathyn. All that Jodathyn could do was watch as she made her way to her husband, crying his name.

Kieryn paused, watching her running towards him. Jodathyn knew the moment his brother realised that the woman was his wife. The king knelt beside his son, speaking rapidly. A gentle palm on his son's back, and the king propelled him forward.

"Mama!" Carvelle cried.

Sobbing, Odelle fell to her knees as Carvelle ran into her arms. Little hands ran down her hair and then rested on her tummy. Even at the distance, Jodathyn could hear Carvelle's high voice parroting away.

Kieryn followed at a sedate pace, his arms crossed against his chest and a wide smile on his face.

"He's letting the queen have her moment with her son," Will said at Jodathyn's elbow.

Jodathyn glanced at Will, his eyebrows raised. "How could you possibly know that?"

Will flashed a wide smile at him, stepped forward, and clapped him on his back. He glanced at Et-hir before his gaze settled onto Jodathyn. "Congratulations, you two."

Nym chortled, and Will observed her, his eyes glinting, a pleased smirk on his face as he turned to look at Carew.

The mirth soon melted from Will's lips. He sighed heavily, closed his eyes, and reached out to grasp Jodathyn's shoulder. "I need to speak with you." He glanced at the guardsmen. "Alone."

Jodathyn's eyes swept over his family. Kieryn, Odelle and Carvelle were all wrapped up in a tight embrace. He smiled. It was as it should be. "You protected the queen?"

Will nodded. "Yes."

"Were you ... in Pallaryn?" Jodathyn swallowed past the lump. "Were you there when the citadel fell?"

Surprise lit up Will's handsome features. "You know about that?"

"I saw it," Jodathyn confirmed.

"We got out before," Will admitted. His voice lowered. "I need to tell you about Illeanah."

Bile filled Jodathyn's throat for the second time that afternoon. He cocked his head to the sky in an attempt to stop the tears from coming. Et-hir was behind him, her hand on his back. He could feel her rest her forehead on his shoulder blade.

"She's dead, Will." Jodathyn's voice shook. "I saw that too. They ..."

"Who's Illeanah?" Et-hir whispered. "I've been hearing that name whispered."

"A cherished childhood friend," Will murmured with a dip of his head. "She regarded Jodathyn as her brother."

Standing in the warm autumn sun, it seemed impossible that Illeanah was gone. His mind rebelled against the thought. He would never see her again. He would never share wine with her, walk in the palace gardens or share a text with her. He glanced back at Roane, half expecting Illeanah to be upon his back ... The olive dragon stared back. Jodathyn felt as if his heart were on display.

"You saw your friend die?" Et-hir asked. Her words were whispered in Sionian. Jodathyn wondered if she would be angry with him. "She was the one you saw ... executed."

"Yes," Jodathyn replied in kind. "I can't believe ..."

"She regretted the fight with you," Will said. "She grieved for you."

"You don't know that," Jodathyn replied.

Will's fingers on his shoulder tightened. "I do, Jodathyn. I know."

Jodathyn shook his head. "It's not possible. You can't have known what was happening inside her head."

"Jodathyn," Will whispered, "I can read minds."

Jodathyn stared up at Will. A mind reader. He should have guessed there was something more to Will.

"I *know* what her feelings were. She loved you as a brother, her dearest friend."

Jodathyn sniffed. "I wish we didn't fight."

"I'm sorry. I really am." Will smiled sadly. "I want you to know that she saved the queen's life. She saved my life."

Jodathyn's eyes flicked down so that he might not look into Will's earnest expression. He nodded glumly. "I saw her in the Otherworld ..."

Will spoke the words that Jodathyn could not. "She gave you a yellow flower and wished for you to know love." Will's eyes travelled over to the sombre Et-hir. "She would have loved you, Miss Et-hir. If you love Jodathyn half as much as what I can read, she would stand by your match."

Jodathyn nodded. "The note you gave me at the Autumn Festival?" he asked, more to change the subject than really wanting an answer.

"I wanted to warn you," Will said. "I sensed that there was plotting against you ... I had no idea how far it went."

"I found your safe house. Thank you."

"I know," Will said. "I got there too late. You had already left."

"Fydellah got away safely."

Will blinked. "She did?"

Jodathyn nodded. "She's up at the house."

"She is?"

"There will be a war council later tonight," Roane rumbled, shifting his great weight. "I suggest you *vehyl* go and rest. I suspect it will go well into the night."

Jodathyn looked up again to see Kieryn leading his queen and son into the house. He smiled at the sight of his brother's protective hand around Odelle's waist. Carvelle trotted alongside them, a grin on his small face as he regarded his parents.

"War is coming," Tornyth said. *"I feel it in the wind."*

CHAPTER THIRTEEN

Jodathyn

Solan's Summer House, Aviah Valley

When Jodathyn stepped into the king's war tent, he couldn't help but think it resembled the illustrated scenes from one of his myths and legends books. The light of dozens of lit torches reflected in the luminous eyes of the dragons present. Zapyr's scales seemed to blaze in the torchlight, and Sidrah's silver specks winked every time she shifted.

Jodathyn's elder dragon siblings sat to Mandros' right-hand side, while Curarfur and Roane were on his left. The sides of the tent were left fully open so that Mandros and his advisers could be involved in the proceedings.

Jodathyn turned his gaze away from the dragons to note the humans present. Kieryn had brought to his council Captain Tiernan and a few of his senior guardsmen. Orion, as the youngest of the King's Guard, was given the task of serving the council.

In times of war, the honour of serving the king and his council was never given to a servant but a trusted guardsman. King's Guardsmen were sworn to loyalty to their king and hence were harder to corrupt. Odelle and Will had also been invited. Up at the house, Will had confided to him he was the king's spy. Which explained his presence.

Jodathyn felt like an interloper. What did he have to offer?

To keep his mind away from negative thoughts, he strode over to the map that Nym and Carew had been arguing over earlier. He ran his finger along the Stonethaw Ranges and the ruins of Torryn nestled at their base. That was where Mandros and his mighty dragons had been ferrying humans and weapons. It would be here that they planned to draw out the enemy.

"If we only knew what to expect from the opposing forces," Kieryn said.

"I could infiltrate their ranks, Your Majesty," Will replied.

"Absolutely not," Roane answered. He lifted his head with a low growl. "Your life will be lost for nothing."

"I could relay messages, Lord Roane."

"The answer is no, *vehyl*," Roane replied, his hackles rising.

Visibly surprised by the dragon's reaction to his suggestion, Will stepped back, holding his hands up in surrender.

"Has your Sight revealed nothing, brother?" Kieryn stroked his beard.

Surprised at being addressed, Jodathyn looked up from the map. "I'm afraid not, Sire."

"The Sight, as you humans call it, cannot be controlled," Mandros said. "The demands on Jodathyn's physical body may contribute to a lack of visions. It is not unknown for mind powers to lie dormant in times of high stress."

"And what of you, Lord Mandros? Have you seen anything?"

Mandros lifted his head, piercing Kieryn with a large amber eye. "Only your people and pain. The walls of Pallaryn, your city, must fall."

"If I may be so bold, Your Majesty," Orion murmured. "Toppling a wall ... Might long range weapons or something explosive be the best strategy to take?"

Zapyr blinked his azure eyes and grinned, revealing his fangs.

"Why do I get the feeling, Lord Mandros, you knew what Orion's suggestion was going to be?" Kieryn lifted his goblet and drank.

Mandros laughed. "Sometimes dragons like to leave a little surprise. It keeps the *vehyl* on their toes."

"Go ahead, Orion one-who-whispers," Zapyr continued.

"The use of foot soldiers against the Grey Shadows is not a wise use of our resources," Orion said. "Archers from dragon back or humans upon the walls is a better strategy. Do dragons have the muscle power to ..."

"Oh, I assure you, we have the power to topple walls," Curarfur said. "We need to be safe from Grey Shadows first."

Jodathyn turned back to the map. "It needs to be done quickly if what—"

"Kill him ... Kill the king. Together we can rule."

The first time Jodathyn heard the voice that was not his own, he had been terribly drunk. At the time, it had seemed like a nightmare. The next time his mind had been invaded, he hurt Deovyn. His lips parted with a soft cry as his head began to turn without his permission.

"Who are you?" Tornyth twisted and writhed within his mind. There was a certain amount of horror that came when one realised they were no longer in control of their own body. He wanted to scream a warning that all was not well, but all that escaped his lips was as strangled cry.

"Jodathyn, dear," Odelle asked. "Are you well?"

Beside him, Will stiffened and grabbed his wrist, and Jodathyn felt pin prickles of heat shoot up his arm.

"Tiernan!" Jodathyn cried, even as his feet moved forward. "Help me! I can't stop!"

Everything seemed to happen all at once. Tiernan was striding forward, confusion wrinkling his brow. Roane and Mandros rose, both rumbling, their teeth bared. Orion dashed forward, spilling the contents of a goblet into the king's lap.

"We will rule ... Mandros will die. He'll never harm one of his own hatchlings. Never. You are safe from him. He would rather die at your claws than hurt you."

"You don't own me!"

"I own all, boy!"

"I'm not yours!" Jodathyn shouted aloud. Tiernan stood in his way, blocking Kieryn from his view. There was a flame nearby; without stopping to think of the consequences, Jodathyn thrust his hand into the fire. Gritting his teeth, he ignored his body's desperate cry to remove his hand.

"Rshon mahthyt!" Tiernan swore, grabbing Jodathyn's wrist to remove his hand from the flames. Jodathyn struggled in the guardsman's firm grip.

"I'm not giving you control. You cannot get through my pain." Tiernan pulled Jodathyn's hand from the flames as he sobbed out the words. Crossing his arms against his chest, the captain pulled him close in a vicelike grip and forced him to the ground. Exhausted, Jodathyn didn't fight or try to free himself from Tiernan's suffocating embrace.

Orion reached his side and reached out a hand to touch his temple.

"Let him be!" Orion's voice cried in his head. *"I command you to leave."*

"Don't let me go," Jodathyn whispered, leaning his head back against Tiernan's shoulder. "I'm too dangerous. He's here ..."

"I won't ..." Tiernan's voice was gruff. "I promise, I won't leave your side."

"Lord Mandros, what's happening?" Kieryn wrapped his robes protectively about himself.

Mandros nudged both Tiernan and Orion out of the way and snaked his clawed hand around Jodathyn to draw him close.

"Is this normal, dragon?" Kieryn's tone bordered on demanding.

"Kieryn," Mandros rumbled. "Remove your unnecessary guardsmen."

Jodathyn shivered with dread. Upon his throne, Kieryn stared at Mandros and then slowly Jodathyn. Reaching over, Odelle grasped Kieryn's hand in her own. "Very well. Guardsmen Maysden, Captain Candyde, stay. The rest of you are dismissed for this evening. Go."

The King's Guardsmen were too disciplined to let their curiosity or discomfort show. They all bowed as one and left the king's pavilion in silence. Jodathyn swallowed, watching the last man's retreating back.

"Some dragons hold terrible power, King Kieryn. We haven't known a power like this in centuries," Sidrah said.

"Someone more powerful than Galgothmeg is behind this," Zapyr continued. "There's a dragon attacking Jodathyn's mind, trying to control him from within. He's fighting back."

"Who, lord dragon?" Kieryn demanded.

"I don't know," Mandros replied. "It seems Pallaryn and Galgothmeg may be a distraction. I have considered ... the Grey Doom. My brother has the flare for dramatics."

"There are very few with that power," Roane muttered.

"Even fewer that are able to command them back," Zapyr continued, his deep azure gaze upon Orion. "Well done, *vehyl*. Whoever it was seems to be gone."

Jodathyn lay panting on the ground, Mandros' claw still around his belly, anchoring him to reality. His head felt like it was stuffed with straw.

"You have a brother?"

"Moroth isn't important. What can you tell us about this voice, *myn-rell*?"

"The first time I was … drunk. I thought it was my imagination," Jodathyn admitted, closing his eyes in shame. "Then when I was sparring with Deovyn … I pushed the voice back, and the vision took me."

"What did it want, *sudunyn*?" Zapyr asked.

"To kill Kieryn … or rather, let the Grey Shadows have him. So I flew out and killed the Grey Shadows."

"The one time your penchant of doing the exact opposite to what you're told worked to your advantage." Sidrah snorted with laughter. "That would have annoyed whoever it was."

"When you were wrestling Deovyn?" Mandros' voice was a low rumble.

"It wanted me to kill him … and tonight it asked me to kill Kieryn. It was controlling me."

"To be fair," Orion said, his voice seeming to come from far away, "you gained control back before I got to you."

Sidrah leaned her long, elegant neck over and breathed over the burn on Jodathyn's hand. He reached out and patted her snout.

"I'm no longer safe to be around," Jodathyn murmured. "It's true after all."

"Nonsense," Roane said. "The power relies on a few factors. It's usually insidious in nature. Most would dismiss its presence, making total manipulation possible. Now you know for certain you are under attack, it becomes a battle of the wills."

"And whoever is attacking you is relying on the fact that you remain unprotected. We just have to find something to ward your mind," Curarfur said. "Putting one's hand in the fire was effective but foolish. Do you have any magic rings in your possession?"

"A magic ring?" Jodathyn asked. To Jodathyn the notion seemed ridiculous.

"Yes, the only treasures we Ramian dragons hoard are *mynrell* and magic jewels for protection," Curarfur replied, as if the whole situation was self-explanatory.

Kieryn stood from his chair and lifted his jewelled hands underneath the teal dragon's snout. "These are the rings that symbolise the kingship of Rama. Will any of these protect Jodathyn?"

Looking deeply amused, Curarfur drew his snout back, cocking his head to the side. "What we need, *vehyl* king, is a magic ring that once belonged to Vadroil or something Artrothian."

"I don't have anything of Vadroil's," Jodathyn muttered. "Or Artrothian."

"But at one time, you did!" Will cried. "That night at the alehouse. You went to free a slave ... What did you give her?"

"A ring from my maternal grandfather ..."

"Who was ...?"

"A descendant of Vadroil."

"We find this slave then," Mandros decreed.

Roane smiled toothily. "She's here. It seems fate gave her the ring for safekeeping."

"I gave her the ring of my own free will," Jodathyn protested.

"Orion," Mandros said, lifting his head to pin Jodathyn's servant with an unwavering gaze. "Bring her here."

Orion had been still as a statue, looking mortified at the wine stain on Kieryn's robes. In one hand he held out a cloth to the king and in the other he had a refilled goblet.

Kieryn turned upon his heel, plucking the goblet from Orion's loose fingers, and lifted it into a salute. "Most refreshing, Guardsman Maysden. The woman they are talking about is Fydellah."

Even with his head bowed, Jodathyn could see the red tinge on Orion's cheeks. "My king."

"Come now, not to worry," Kieryn said. "This has to be the first time a guardsman has dumped wine in my lap. Go do Lord Mandros' bidding and get some rest."

Orion bowed and swiftly left the tent.

Fydellah didn't come to the king's tent alone. Nym and Et-hir followed on her heels and behind them, Carvelle tugged the little girl from Habron. The three women knelt at Kieryn's feet, who gestured impatiently to Mandros and Jodathyn. Jodathyn still sat between Mandros' great claws.

Pink-cheeked, Carvelle dashed into the tent. He ran past the women and straight into Jodathyn's lap.

"I heard Orion saying something happened to you, Uncle. Are you well?"

"It's late, and you should be in bed," Jodathyn replied.

Carvelle ignored him and wriggled closer so that Jodathyn had no choice but to wrap his arms around both of the children. Small hands tapped his cheeks. "Did you faint? Have you eaten? Does your tummy hurt?"

"Your uncle is fine, prince of Rama," Kieryn said. "He's right; you should be tucked up in bed."

Carvelle turned his head towards his father and smiled winsomely. "Larelle couldn't sleep, so I told her the story of Zazzir and the Snapdragons."

"That may very well be," Kieryn replied. "This is a war council, my son."

"A prince ought to learn," Carvelle said.

Jodathyn choked back a laugh. He had heard Kieryn use this phrase when arguing with Carvelle about listening to his tutors. His brother had said similar to him when he was young.

"Carvelle," Odelle admonished. "A good son listens to his father."

Sighing dramatically, Carvelle released himself from Jodathyn's embrace. He toed the ground. "I'm sorry, Papa. Uncle doesn't look well. He needs a good nap."

A smile tugged on Kieryn's lips; he could never stay stern with his son for very long. "I will personally ensure that your uncle is delivered to Guardsman Jael shortly for a nap. Goodnight, Carvelle."

"Goodnight, Papa."

"Goodnight, Larelle Lake Maiden."

The little girl, who had stayed frozen and stiff in Jodathyn's lap, eyed the adults and the dragons of the war council. She bit her lip as she locked gazes with Jodathyn.

"This is Uncle Jod," Carvelle said. "Uncle, this is Larelle. Papa says she'll stay with us in Pallaryn."

Curious about the strange turn of events, Jodathyn glanced up at his brother, who shook his head. "I'll tell you that tale another time, brother."

Carvelle took Larelle's hand. He looked pleadingly up at his mother for permission to stay, but Odelle shook her head and pointed towards the house.

"Your Majesty," Et-hir said, brushing her hair from her face. "If Jodathyn is well, I can escort the prince and the girl back to bed."

"A story, Miss Ettie?" Carvelle asked, his eyes lighting up with hope.

Et-hir looked toward the king for guidance and at his frown, she said, "One Sionian trading song."

"Deal," Carvelle announced, holding out his hand.

Jodathyn watched them go with a soft smile on his face. He blinked rapidly when he caught Kieryn's and Tiernan's twin looks of amusement. He could see curiosity gleaming in Odelle's newly changed eyes as she tilted her head to observe Et-hir with her son.

Zapyr cleared his throat, the sound sending vibrations through the ground. "Now we have sufficiently watched Jodathyn's *vehyl* woman leave ... back to the matter at hand."

"Can you imagine, baby dragons, at last!" Curarfur cried. "I want to teach them to fly. Oh, I can't wait. Uncle Curarfur!"

Jodathyn felt his cheeks heat at Nym's chuckles.

"There'll be another dragon before Jodathyn's brood," Sidrah replied. "There's plenty of time to talk the circle of life later. Now it's war."

"You must forgive us, *vehyl* king," Mandros rumbled. "Dragons get excited talking about our young. But Sidrah is right. Our objective tonight is war."

"Fydellah, do you have the ring my brother gave you?" Kieryn asked. "Please show our dragon friends."

Nodding her head, Fydellah pulled out the ring in question. It lay flat on her palm, and she lifted her hand so that Mandros could inspect the ring.

"It's Vadroil's ring," Mandros declared. "It has some residual power that will protect Jodathyn."

Jodathyn stared at it. It seemed like another life that he had given Fydellah the ring. Not for the first time he wondered what would have happened if he had stayed ensconced, hidden in the palace. What would have happened to Fydellah? He flicked his eyes to Will, and the lord stared back at him.

Will would have saved her alone. He wouldn't have upset the great lords, they wouldn't have plotted against him, Carvelle wouldn't have been kidnapped ... Galgothmeg ...

"Jodathyn," Will whispered. "The great lords were already plotting. They would have tried to remove you sooner or later, and Galgothmeg ... I suspect he already had a foothold in Rama."

"Furthermore," Roane added with a lazy yawn, "would you have had this ring in your safekeeping now if you hadn't given it to Fydellah?"

"No," Jodathyn muttered. "I took it with me on a whim. In case ... in case I needed to get myself out of trouble. I hated it. I hated that I am Vadroil's bloodline."

"Vadroil's bloodline is still prevalent through Rama," Mandros replied. "He was a powerful dragon. A fierce ruler with many sons and daughters. I didn't kill all of his many children."

"The ring is indeed one that belonged to Vadroil himself," Roane said. "Fydellah, we have use for it."

"You are saying this piece of jewellery will protect me from further attack?" Jodathyn asked.

"It's a weapon, *sudunyn*," Zapyr replied. He gestured to the ring with his claws. "Put it on."

Without lifting her gaze from the black dragon, Fydellah knelt beside Jodathyn and offered the ring. He wondered what questions she had asked of his sister and what answers she had received.

"He speaks truth, Jod," Fydellah said as Jodathyn curled his fingers around the ring. "A wise man uses the weapons handed to him."

"I didn't think I counted among the wise," Jodathyn said with a slow smile.

"I think you're smarter than you look, hatchling," Nym muttered.

Jodathyn barked out a laugh and slipped the ring onto his finger. "This will keep Kieryn safe from me?"

"I don't think the king was truly in any danger," Will replied. "I felt your struggle. You were winning even before you placed your hand in the fire."

"Will speaks truth," Fydellah said. She looked up at Will, and her expression softened. "He always speaks truth."

"The greatest weapon fighting a mental attack is firstly recognising you are under attack. Whoever it is will not be happy that you not only realised you were in trouble, but you could fight back," Curarfur said.

"True," Sidrah rumbled. "The ring is added security to ensure your visions and your mind are free from further attack."

"Soon we'll fly out to Pallaryn. We cannot delay." Mandros stirred and nudged Jodathyn to his feet. "It's late, and our mortal friends need to rest. Goodnight, *elt mynrell*. May the stars bless and guide you."

Jodathyn murmured his goodnights. He paused to watch the dragons take off into the night, to feel the air stir with the beating of their wings. He blinked, realising he was left alone with Kieryn and Odelle; the others had already departed the king's tent.

Kieryn stared, brooding in the firelight, Odelle's hand clasping his forearm.

"My king," Jodathyn murmured.

"Sleep well, brother." Kieryn's gaze did not move from the fire. Jodathyn wondered what he was thinking.

He exhaled and turned to leave. Odelle stood and stalled him to give him a quick embrace, kissing his cheeks. "Goodnight, brother. Thank you for defending my son."

"My queen." Jodathyn bowed deeply and stepped from the tent.

Will Hartcurt was waiting for him in the shadows and fell into step with him as he made his way to the house. Up ahead, Fydellah and Nym strode, heads bent together and talking adamantly.

"They seem unlikely friends, don't they?" Will asked.

"Indeed," Jodathyn agreed. He sent a sidelong glance in Will's direction. The lord was not there to discuss the women. "Nym's not as tough as she would like us to believe."

Throwing his head back, Will laughed, causing Nym and Fydellah to stare back at them. Jodathyn couldn't see their expressions clearly in the dark, but he knew they were suspicious that they were being spoken about.

Will cleared his throat and held his hand up in apology. "Your friendship with Nym seems even more unlikely."

Jodathyn tilted his head in acknowledgement.

They walked on in silence.

"She kissed me," Jodathyn said. "We were drunk, and she kissed me."

Will grinned up at him, flashing his perfect teeth.

"Oh, right, mind reader," Jodathyn murmured. "You already knew that."

"Pray, go on," Will said. "Don't let the fact I can read your mind stop the conversation."

"You know what I'm going to say," Jodathyn replied.

"Yes, you have the most endearing thoughts."

Jodathyn's face fell.

"Lord Roane has agreed to work with me to show me better control," Will admitted.

"Wait," Jodathyn gasped. "He can read minds too?"

Will nodded. "Seems like a handy skill to have for the upcoming battle."

Jodathyn's stomach churned at the thought of the coming bloodshed. He knew now that he had it within him to kill with his own human hands.

Tornyth could certainly make short work of human enemies ... The vision of the orange dragon crashing came unbidden to his mind. Beside him, Will flinched.

"Sorry," Jodathyn murmured. "Do you see what I see in my head too?"

"Sometimes, when the person's imagination is strong," Will replied. "You've always been that way inclined. It's like watching a troop of actors."

Silhouetted by the light of the house, Jodathyn made out the form of Guardsman Jael. The troop medic was waiting for him to return. He wondered, perhaps uncharitably so, if Orion had told him of the attack as well.

"Jael is a trustworthy mind healer," Will said. "He doesn't just see to the guards. He saw me when I first came into His Majesty's service."

Jodathyn raised an eyebrow.

"It was to Jael I brought any slaves I freed that needed help. At first, I trusted him as a fellow west countryman, then as a healer, and then as a friend. He's heard some pretty horrific stories," Will continued. "He won't judge or betray you. He'll do everything in his power to help, whatever that might look like."

"I'm not entirely sure you know what you are talking about," Jodathyn said. He felt his cheeks redden, and he went to step away.

Will gripped his elbow. "You're not alone. Not anymore."

There was a hint of a promise in Will's voice.

CHAPTER FOURTEEN

Orion

The Citadel of Pallaryn

If someone had told Orion a season ago that he would be flying into battle astride a gigantic golden dragon, he would never have believed them. Yet here he was. Standing among his new brothers-in-arms, a black King's Guard cloak around his shoulders and weapon in his hand.

The king strode among the ranks, shaking hands and speaking to the men as Captain Tiernan organised them into flight groups. Each dragon could take a dozen men or so on their backs. Lord Zapyr had made a bid to take him into battle early, which had Orion baffled. He was the greenest recruit, and the golden dragon requested him personally.

"Explain to me the plan again."

It seemed that Theo's way of coping with his fear was rehashing the plan over and over. Orion stifled his sigh. If going over the plan provided his friend with reassurance, then he would oblige him.

"We're flying in three groups. The first group led by Mandros and His Majesty is the initial onslaught. The second group, us, will engage once the front lines have collided. There'll be Grey Shadows, and the dragons will concentrate on killing and maiming as many of them as possible. Armed humans can provide cover for dragons and if necessary, engage in combat with any human resistance."

"And the third wave. Tell me about the third wave."

"Led by Deovyn. The smallest of our groups. They will be breaking down the outer walls or gates of the city to allow any civilians to flee the capital."

"And that's why we are doing it," Theo muttered to himself. "Our people. Think about the people." Theo nudged him with his elbow, nervously peering through the milling crowd of men. Orion followed his line of sight and saw Voran's red hair. It seemed Jodathyn's guard was skulking around the outskirts of the ranks, trying to avoid Captain Tiernan. "What do you think Voran's up to?"

"Don't waste time worrying about what others are doing," Orion replied. "Concentrate. No matter what, stay calm. Even if I fall ... keep fighting."

"I promise I won't throw my sword at the enemy this time," Theo said, hefting his weapon.

Despite having little to no training, the thief was determined to follow him into battle. Orion could respect that. And because Theo would not be parted from him, Nym demanded to accompany them. Then Carew had insisted that he join, and on it went until Zapyr's flight crew had been filled with fighting men and women.

"Et-hir's feeling some pain. She wants to fight," Theo said. Orion turned around and sure enough, there was his master in his white dragon form, snuffling Et-hir and trying to extract himself from Prince Carvelle. Et-hir's face was pinched, and she was blinking rapidly.

"Sionian women are strong," Orion said. "It's still a place of honour that she will form Prince Carvelle's last stand if today goes poorly."

"Live Valiantly, Master Maysden, Master Torkelle."

Orion jolted in shock. Before he could react, the king first gripped his forearm and then Theo's.

"Die Honourably," Orion echoed.

"Don't do anything stupid, Orion," the king said. "I'd like to see you at the other end of this battle. You too, Theo."

"Your Majesty." Orion inclined his head.

"Mandros is waiting for me. Come, the dragons are impatient." The king's gaze lifted towards the house and back to the queen, who was now holding Prince Carvelle back. He waved his gloved hand. Orion could tell the smile for his son was forced.

The whole sky thrummed with the sound of dragon wings. From his very first flight, Orion adored the feeling of the wind against his face. Theo clung to his waist, his grip so tight his fingers were trembling A shame, really, that his friend didn't feel the same way.

"Nearly there, Theo silver-ear." Orion marvelled at Zapyr's ability to feel Theo's unease.

"If I keep my eyes tightly shut, I think I should be able to avoid vomiting," Theo said.

Lifting his hand from one of Zapyr's spines, Orion reached behind to grip Theo's arm. "Whatever you do, keep your head, stay close." Orion could feel Theo's fingers digging into his ribs. "Try and relax."

"I'll be close by, Theo," Zapyr rumbled.

"Fancy that. A dragon bodyguard," Nym grumbled under her breath.

"You are both important to Orion, so you're important to me."

"Just keep your eye on that white dragon," Nym replied. "He can be painfully unpredictable."

"We're all looking out for him. Unpredictability comes with shield-fire," Zapyr answered levelly.

Looking out over the battalion of dragons, Orion caught sight of Mandros flanked by Roane. Behind them were Sidrah, Deovyn and Tornyth. He would have loved to ask what Zapyr meant by shield-fire, but now wasn't the time.

Closing his eyes, Orion meditated, just as his father had taught him. Before battle, it was beneficial to be calm and focused. His eyes flickered open, and he could now see the great walls of the palace. He shifted, staring wide-eyed in horror at the number of lifeless eyes staring back at him. He heard Theo's sharp intake of breath as he too saw the forest of impaled heads.

Born of a Silverdyne horseman, Orion had not been spared the hard facts of life. He had seen heads removed and traitors' bodies displayed. This was different. Many of the slain were now his brothers-in-arms. If they lost the battle, Orion could expect the same treatment.

Behind him, Theo's grip tightened. "Keep your head."

The thief repeating his own words back to him left a sour taste in Orion's mouth.

"They died with honour," Orion replied. His tongue felt strangely dry and stuck to the roof of his mouth.

"Tell that to the families," Nym gritted out. Orion could picture her severe face twisting into a scowl and her long, nimble fingers flexing on the handle of her sword. He swallowed. Even with his training, he wouldn't want to meet a vexed Nym with a blade in her hand.

Orion knew the moment the enemy spotted them. Sluggish and content from their plunder, the Grey Shadows were slow in taking to the sky. To Orion, facing his first battle, he likened them to a grey swarm of flies on a hot summer's day. Their otherworldly shrieks set his teeth on edge.

"I can possibly subdue—"

"No!" Zapyr barked. "You may not attempt to free Grey Shadows ... Battle is chaos enough without adding an untested power."

Orion inhaled a deep breath to steady his racing heart. He knew a direct order when he heard one. Arguing would get him nowhere. He nodded, even though the golden dragon could not see him, and notched an arrow.

Mandros and his contingent surged forward, charging the Grey Shadows. Zapyr hung back; they were to be the second wave of attack. Orion could only describe the booming sound of dragon on dragon like thunder, and he was in the very centre of the storm.

The Grey Shadows, empty of thought, concentrated solely on the first wave of dragons. Zapyr and his contingent dipped and flew under the melee.

"*Araae helphelwyn*," Orion muttered. He loosed an arrow into the bulbous eye of the unsuspecting Grey Shadow. The poor creature's shriek was cut off as its wings stopped beating. It spasmed and fell.

"*Terini gorthorawyn*," Zapyr echoed. "War is a cruel mistress. Harden your heart to your foe whilst the fighting is thick."

"'Tis the only way not to go mad," Carew added. Orion barely heard his voice.

"Pretty sure I'm already mad," Theo complained. Orion felt him shift to notch his own arrow. He held his breath as Theo fired. The thief missed the target. By a long way.

"*Rshon mahthyt*," Theo swore.

"Dragon dung indeed," Orion said. "Take your time to aim. It's more difficult on the back of a dragon."

"Cursed, cowardly swine!" Nym cried. "Look!"

Orion lifted his head, his eyes darting around, looking for what she had spotted. He felt the tremours of Zapyr's soft growl through his thighs. There was little sound that accompanied the gold dragon's anger, but a shock of alarm snaked its way up Orion's spine.

There was no doubt in Orion's mind that Zapyr's growl was a threat. The golden dragon was promising violence would follow in his wake.

Lines of bound King's Guardsmen were being lined up on the infamous northern wall of the palace. Some were tied to stakes like dogs, some lay battered and bruised, while others were forced to their knees to be executed. Orion could hardly believe his eyes. While the dragons battled in the sky above, the murder of those loyal to house Pallarus continued.

"Take us down, oh great golden one!" Carew cried.

"With pleasure."

Nym's strong battle cry rent through the air as they descended.

"If you wish to engage the humans in battle, you will need to dismount quickly. I'll do as much as I can," Zapyr said. "Theo silver-ear, stay by Orion."

Zapyr dipped lower. The wind swept about Orion's face, loosening his hair. He felt the whisper of vengeance as the air warmed around them. Lifting his hand to his face, he glanced back. Three other dragons followed Zapyr's flight path. He did a quick calculation. Each dragon was carrying at least a dozen men. With four dragons, that was approximately fifty men they had at their disposal to create havoc among those who would betray the people of Rama.

Orion curled his fingers around an arrow, notched, and took aim at the burly executioner who loomed over a common palace guard. She looked to be at least sixty summers. Holding his breath, he waited for the perfect moment to let his arrow loose. As soon as they were in range and he was confident of his aim, Orion fired. The arrow whizzed through the sky and hit the executioner between his eyes.

Orion's victim's knees buckled; the axe tumbled from his fingers. Shocked by the sudden reprieve, the old guard's fingers searched for the fallen axe, and she stumbled to her feet.

Orion whipped his head around, looking for the next person who required his help. He spotted a King's Guardsman bent over in pain. Two vicious men dressed in Kamoore's colours held him down. Blood poured from his side; his golden skin was flushed with agony.

Orion loosed two arrows in quick succession, hitting both of his targets. The King's Guardsman grasped his side, fell to his knees, and grabbed his fallen enemy's blades. From his ribs, Orion caught the glint of a dagger. Deep red blood coated the man's fingers, but he continued to collect the weapons. He glanced up and spotted Orion astride the giant dragon. Nodding his head in thanks, he stumbled to his feet and joined the fight. Orion knew he would not survive. He was going to bleed out.

"Get ready to move, Orion!" Theo called.

To show that he heard, Orion nodded.

Zapyr landed, and the north wall quaked under his might. With Theo, he slipped from the golden dragon's back. He fired an arrow the moment his feet hit the ground.

Carew and Nym rushed past him, their swords flashing.

Confronted with an armed threat willing to kill them, Kamoore's men didn't stand a chance. Those who had landed upon the north wall in order to take it back fought with fire and passion.

"Form ranks, you maggots!" The bark of this foe's voice reached the men around him, and they shuffled closer together to organise a counterattack.

Orion let another arrow fly; he didn't think about it. All he knew was a man who could organise fellow soldiers was a threat. Threats needed to be eliminated.

The arrow pierced the man's throat, and Orion watched in detached horror as the life left his eyes. While he had feelings of revulsion at his victim's gruesome fate, another part of him, a darker part, was pleased … no, amused.

"Great shot!" Carew called over his shoulder.

"Eyes on the enemy, Carew!" Captain Tiernan was on the north wall too. Orion looked around frantically and spotted the High King at his side, hacking away with his sword at the enemy.

The first kings and queens of Rama had all been warriors. It was not shocking that King Kieryn was on the battlefield, right in the centre with his men. A king who would not bleed for his country was no king at all.

Carew shrugged good-naturedly at his father's chastisement, smirking as he grabbed Nym's shoulder and swung her out of danger. Nym's eyes widened as a blade narrowly missed her chest.

Gritting his teeth, Orion shot another three arrows in quick succession, downing three enemies who thought to converge upon the king. As each man fell, he felt the warmth of pleasure washing over him and flowing through his veins.

Orion viciously buried his thoughts. He could not afford to be distracted by horror or pleasure. There would be time after the battle to sort out his raging thoughts.

In the end, it wasn't either horror or pleasure that distracted Orion. It was the terrified bellow of a purple dragon that had accompanied them to Silverdyne. Salvea, Orion recalled. She was a quiet dragon, preferring to listen and watch. Now she made a terrified sound as two Grey Shadows pinned her down and drove her closer into the wall.

He parted his lips, his eyes wide.

It was Theo who voiced the words to his garbled thoughts. "They'll die!"

The three dragons hit the wall with a shuddering bang. Humans, friend and foe alike, were crushed under their bodies. Orion rushed forward with a cry. Feeling faint, he wished to find a place to sit and rest … Yet his body moved forward, his sword biting any wayward enemy who hindered him. Bile rose in this throat. Battle was different to what he had imagined. It was unyielding and relentless. Around him was senseless death that seemed to have no rhyme or reason.

In his frantic charge to reach Salvea, Orion lost awareness of his surroundings. A large hand grasped him and pulled him off balance. Orion screamed in frustration, only to feel the air being sliced by a cruel blade seconds later.

"Keep your head, Maysden!" the king barked.

Orion had been so engrossed with what was happening before him that he didn't take note that Theo was shadowing his footsteps. "The Grey Shadow!" the thief cried.

The fall hadn't killed one of the Grey Shadows. It lifted its head, looking around dumbly. The creature's grey wings were twisted in three different directions. The fallen Grey Shadow would never fly again. But there was death in those soulless eyes. The injury would not stop it.

"Captain!" Orion screamed, knowing he needed to act. "I need to get to that Grey Shadow … before it goes on a murderous rampage."

"I'm with you," Theo murmured, gripping his elbow.

The King's Guardsmen about him, many who knew of Orion's strange hold over the Grey Shadows, moved forward to create enough of a distraction so that Orion could get close to the mangled creature.

"Stay!" Orion yelled at the Grey Shadow, never mind that he felt foolish screaming an order to a mindless beast. One foot in front of the other, Orion surged forward. "Surrender ... Don't kill."

The Grey Shadow's lifeless eyes turned to stare at Orion. For a flickering of a heartbeat, he was within the creature's mind. It shocked him to learn the terrible foe before him had once been a young soldier, not quite a man when he had been captured. His human part was slain, and his dragon subdued. He was a leftover relic from the days of Vadroil.

Orion couldn't imagine being trapped in a body for over a thousand years. Behind the curtain of blackness, he could feel the torment and grief. Against the cloak of oppression, the Grey Shadow's former self was still struggling.

"Please!" Orion screamed. He pressed his hands against the Grey Shadow's flank. The skin on his hands burnt and fire built within his belly, but Orion did not let go. He felt wave after wave of power crashing over him. His body convulsed as he joined the Grey Shadow in its torment. "It doesn't have to be this way. I can help you!"

"Orion. No! You're burning from the inside!" Theo grabbed his arm. The thief was so closely pressed up against his side that Orion could feel him quivering in fear. Removing his hand from the Grey Shadow, Orion grasped Theo and hurled him to stand beside him rather than behind. The last thing he needed was for his friend to take a fatal blow while he was busy.

Theo yelped, jumping back. "Orion. *Please* ... this is dangerous!"

Squeezing his eyes shut, Orion grunted with the effort of pouring his power within the now wailing beast.

"Orion ... danger ...!"

Orion could now make very little sense of Theo's words. He felt an anger that wasn't fully his. Beneath his hands, the Grey Shadow shuddered. Pain flared behind Orion's eyes, and his insides melted and churned like molten liquid. A searing pain in his shoulder blades had him falling to his knees.

Screaming, he pushed further into the Grey Shadow's mind. Even though it wasn't the first time he had done so, it still shocked him at how such a powerful being could be brought so low and controlled. The malevolent power was strong. The dragon was a hostage, a body for something far more sinister.

"Leave!" Orion screamed. "Leave!"

He felt his body melting, being consumed by the flames of fury. The power inside the grey dragon was fighting back this time. Hysterical screaming filled his ears.

"Captain, something is terribly wrong!" Theo's fingers dug into Orion's arms. "Orion, stay with me!"

The Grey Shadow roared as its scales fell. He was bronze underneath, his belly adorned with flecks of black. His deadened eyes blinked, and dark blue orbs stared down at Orion. He collapsed with a thud, his broken wings fluttering in a panic.

"Where's Lord Zapyr?" A hand reached out and grasped Orion's cloak and pulled him backwards.

"He can't land!" Theo's voice was muffled, like the thief was underwater. Orion could feel the blood pumping in his ears. "There's too many Grey Shadows."

"Zapyr?" rumbled the newly freed bronze dragon. His speech was slurred. "Where am I?"

Black spots danced in Orion's voice. The sound of the voices surrounding him melded together in a symphony of confusion. His head lolled to the side.

"Get the king out! Galgothmeg's Grey Shadows are coming for us!"

"The king! The king!"

"They're after Orion!"

"Otherworlds, they are looking at him like he's lunch!"

Orion rallied himself enough to lift his head at a tremendous thud. It took everything within him to pull his mind back to a state of consciousness. Five Grey Shadows had scattered what living humans were still on the wall. They were advancing, their teeth bared. They trained their fathomless black eyes on Orion. As one, they thundered, *"Kairn! Kairn!"*

The bronze dragon heaved himself up from where he lay, his head lowered and panting. He swung his tail at the Grey Shadows. His flank trembled with the effort. "He's not the mongrel," he gasped. "Off with you!" Exhausted blue eyes blinked down at Orion. "I'm not well," the bronze dragon said. "Leave me ... They want him ... Vadroil must not have him."

"What's happening?" Orion managed to ask. His head felt like it would explode.

"Congratulations, you've got the Grey Shadow's attention," Theo muttered. "Run!"

Orion was propelled along. His feet didn't seem to be hitting the ground. He reached for the power that was within him. This time, however, instead of the warm, pleasant tingle, all he could find was confusion, chaos and pain. He closed his eyes to the inevitability of his fate.

"Leave me," Orion gasped. He blinked and for a moment he could see Theo clearly, Captain Tiernan too, who was hurling them both along the north wall.

Theo shook his head, sweat dripped hair slapping his flushed face. "I'm here. No matter what."

The wall groaned under the weight of another dragon landing. Teal scales glimmered in the midday sun. Powerful dragon fingers curled around Orion's and Theo's middles. Orion was brought close to large, angry amber eyes, and he cried out in fear.

"Curarfur ... please ..." Orion licked his lips, his voice slurred. He wasn't quite sure what he was asking of the dragon. Only that he wanted the torment to end.

"Your dragon is trapped," Curarfur rumbled.

Body racked with pain, Orion slumped in the dragon's claw. His muscles felt like melted wax. He slowly blinked his eyes shut, his body convulsing as a terrible cry was ripped from his throat.

"Rhox!" A bellow, full of agony, from a voice that Orion knew very well, pierced the pain in his mind. The anguished blue eyes of Zapyr were above him.

"I'll go to Rhox! But this *vehyl* cannot last!" Curarfur cried. Orion was laid upon the ground almost reverently. "You must act!"

Zapyr's massive scaly claws pinned him down, and he cried out in alarm.

"What are you doing?" Theo screamed.

"It's the safest way for a dragon of my size to hold him."

Zapyr lay his snout close to Orion, who was now writhing and keening. His body stilled, taut and rigid, as the golden dragon emitted a low, pleasant sound.

"Hush, fledgling," Zapyr rumbled. "Battle wasn't the time for you to listen to the Wind Song. Peace now. Your manifestation will be difficult. Dragons who manifest through violence suffer; your two halves are warring with one another."

"Help him!" Theo's voice was full of horror.

"His dragon is afraid and is attacking the only threat it can ... his human side. Without help he could lose his mind ..." Zapyr rumbled. "Quiet, human. I will join Orion in his chaos and help him to manifest whole."

Under the weight of Zapyr, Orion quailed and screamed. Zapyr's breath washed over his face as the golden dragon lay down his head and rumbled low sounds. Through the haze of the confusion, he watched pain wash over Zapyr's face as he focused on something before him. Not once did the golden dragon blink or move his gaze.

Orion's world was on fire. He surrendered.

Chapter Fifteen

Tornyth

The Citadel of Pallaryn

Nothing prepared Tornyth for the grim reality of returning to his home overrun with enemies. He thought he might feel fury and grief. Instead, the first sensation he felt was a strange emptiness. And cold.

From the air, he heard faint screams and wails. His eyes scanned the citadel, searching for any sign for normalcy. The destruction of the market streets gave him little hope of finding *vehyl* alive. Chunks of rock scattered the buildings of trade. The cobblestone streets were charred and in some places, spattered with blood.

"No." The single syllable slipped from his tongue. His wings faulted. "No. This cannot be."

Gylleah, who was Deovyn's second, drew alongside him. "It's a shock, white scales. Breathe."

Tornyth dragged in a deep breath, and a surge of fury heated his blood. He snarled at the Grey Shadows, who were still too far away to hear his anger.

When Mandros had commanded him to stay away from the initial onslaught, he felt a flash of annoyance. He wanted to stretch his wings to prove himself in a way his human heart could not. Looking down on his people, he saw honour in his role. In his wisdom, Mandros had given him an important task. Many vulnerable men, women and children were waiting for him to swoop down and decimate the city walls penning them in.

Scaly lips peeled back into a vicious snarl, promising retribution to any who dared to get in his way. A shiver of anticipation trickled down his spine as Deovyn looped around.

"You're burning with shield-fire, brother," Deovyn said. "Feel it. Use it."

Tornyth returned his gaze to the walls. The gates were the weakest part. Any human looking for an escape would be hiding near the natural exit points of the city. The plan was simple: half of their team would dismantle the gates, while the remaining dragons were sentries.

"I sense noncombatant *vehyl* below," Edisyn said. The dark red dragon was the largest male in their group, and Tornyth thought his impressive bulk would have been more useful battling Grey Shadows. When Edisyn was given the command to join Deovyn, he grinned and bowed regally. "There's a group of them huddled near the gate."

"Edisyn is one of our trackers," Deovyn said before Tornyth could open his mouth to ask how he knew the hiding place of the humans.

"I sense their body heat." Edisyn looked quite proud of himself.

Beside Tornyth, Gylleah turned her graceful neck to blow smoke into Edisyn's face. "Don't do anything stupid, *ketur*."

Edisyn raised his head with a bark of laughter. "Beloved, I'm sure the humans along your back will keep you out of trouble."

Tornyth's gaze swept over the armed men and women along the larger dragon's back. His eyes locked onto Voran. He wasn't sure how his ex-guard managed to wrangle his way onto his team, but he knew from the stone-set expression on Voran's face that it was no accident.

His heart swelled with hope. If the king found out Voran had joined his team, intentional or not, his ex-guard would face severe consequences. Despite that, Voran had chosen to be near him. All was not lost.

"Tor!" Deovyn shouted. "Stay with me. Gylleah, take your team down for the first gate. *Aluel* and Zapyr have engaged the enemy."

Tornyth swallowed and to keep himself busy, he counted the number of men that the dragons were carrying in their team. Thirty-seven humans in total, carrying either swords or spears.

Perhaps once this was over, he might seek out Voran and have a frank conversation. The King's Guard was watching them both and intervened anytime he got close to cornering Voran. He had tried arguing with Kieryn, but the king had been insufferably stubborn about the matter. Mandros had told him gruffly to 'mind his *pallu*'.

Below them, Gylleah's team made swift work of the gate. It fell with a thundering crash, and the two dragons moved on to crumbling the rock around the door frame to create a larger escape hole. The dragons grabbed the rubble in the way and cleared the path. The process had taken a matter of seconds.

There was no opposition. Protecting the city gates wasn't a priority for Grey Shadows.

As soon as Gylleah and her companion lifted their reptilian bodies in the air, the humans nearby made themselves known. Craning his neck, Tornyth observed the *vehyl* tripping over each other in order to reach the escape. He felt a thrill of pride that he had been a part of something that preserved human life. Edisyn caught his eye and winked.

"Tornyth, Edisyn, the next one is ours," Deovyn said. He swiped playfully at Tornyth's tail as he flew past into a dive. "Go get 'em, *sudunyn*."

Keen to be of assistance, Tornyth landed beside Edisyn. "This is the Eastern Gate. The poorer live here."

"Let's take it out!" Edisyn said. "Push with me."

Tornyth braced his front legs against the giant doors. His claws dug into the wood, and he turned toward Deovyn, who was on the ground nearby, guarding their backs. He knew his brother was only doing it because he was on team. "You're being awfully stringent with lookouts."

"A simple mission can turn into chaos in a matter of seconds," Deovyn grunted, coming alongside Tornyth to help with the gate.

The hinges creaked and groaned under the pressure. Tornyth could feel the moment the door failed and fell with a heavy thud. A plume of dust burst forward, and he choked back a grin.

"Let's get this rock ..."

"*Vehyl!*" Gylleah cried from above.

Tornyth turned his head at her cry. Instead of the expected horde of angry soldiers, he counted half a dozen small boys and girls hurtling towards him, screaming. They were dirty, trembling, terrified little creatures. Their fear sent shivers up his spine. His wings flapped in agitation.

"Grey Shadows!" Edisyn growled. "Tor ... up ... now ..."

Tornyth lifted his eyes and saw indeed the children were being pursued by two eager Grey Shadows. An uncomfortable burn seared his throat, and he knew he would never take to the skies; not with children fleeing for their lives.

"Under me!" Tornyth yelled at the children. "Under my belly!"

"Soldiers down!" Edisyn shouted to the humans on his back who were already preparing to fight. "Protect the white dragon!"

Gylleah dove, almost shaking the humans from her back. Voran Axtin led the charge towards Tornyth.

The men joined Tornyth's cry for the children to hide under his belly. Little hands brushed his scales as they reached him to clamber under him. He felt their fear as if it were his own, but he would not take flight. When the last, a small boy with a head wound, ducked under his belly, he hunched over and roared a warning to the sky.

Deovyn, Gylleah and Edisyn had launched themselves into the air to intercept and battle Grey Shadows. Belly burning with cold fury, Tornyth glanced up. With the promise of an easy, living dinner, four more Grey Shadows had joined the fray. He crouched lower over the cowering children. That made six enemy dragons.

"What are you doing, master?" Voran cried, reaching his side. A giant, trembling hand brushed down his scales.

"What I must," Tornyth replied.

The grimace that twisted on Voran's face seemed sheepish. He took his position along Tornyth's left flank and widened his stance.

"Watch ..."

Tornyth's heart fluttered in his chest as a Grey Shadow broke free. It spun into a tight dive, its claws outstretched. Bracing himself for the impact, he squeezed his eyes shut, expecting sharp talons to rake down his exposed back. Underneath him, the children screamed. He did not move a muscle.

At his side, one of the soldiers cried out. Tornyth felt the disturbance of the air around him as the man threw the spear over his back. The spear struck true. Even with his eyes tightly shut, he could hear the wet impact of a spear hitting flesh.

Another one of their men grabbed his scales. Tornyth froze, grunting in discomfort as the human's boots dug into his side. The soldier was climbing him.

"Throw me my spear."

Tornyth's eyes snapped open. It was Voran's voice. His ex-guard had clambered onto his back.

"Stay steady, dragon."

"What are you doing?"

"Guarding your back," Voran replied. "The injured one has limped off, but it won't be long ..."

Tornyth knew the truth of Voran's words. Deovyn and the air team had kept most of the Grey Shadows at bay. But one moment of hesitation, and an enemy dragon broke free into a dive.

"Voran!"

"Steady! I say!"

Voran's stance widened on his back, and Tornyth tensed his muscles. As the creature came closer, Voran threw his spear. Spiralling in the opposite direction, the Grey Shadow narrowly evaded the spear. It shrieked, and enraged, lunged again.

There wasn't time to shout a warning. Even as he turned his neck to snap at the enemy dragon, the Grey Shadow plucked a struggling Voran from his back.

"Stay! Jod, stay!" Voran yelled. His frightened eyes looked down at him in horror. A strangled cry left Tornyth's throat as he witnessed a flash of defiance, then acceptance in Voran's expression.

Voran's lips parted, desperate to utter a last word as the beast took his arms in his claws.

Tornyth blurted the only words that would come to his numb mind. "Not like this ..."

One moment Tornyth was looking at his ex-guard, the next the Grey Shadow tore him from limb to limb. Tornyth screamed in rage as what was left of Voran's torso was dropped unceremoniously to the ground. Voran had made mistakes, Voran had changed, but he was still fond of him. He had wanted Voran to know how much he had taught him, how much he still meant to him. Now those words would forevermore remain unspoken between them.

The human guards who stood between Tornyth and the Grey Shadows fearfully looked up.

"Take the children and go," Edisyn shouted. "We'll guard your back."

"Come, children," Tornyth muttered. There would be a proper time to mourn Voran later. He reached under his belly and grasped as many of them as he could. They screamed and wriggled in his grip; there wasn't a choice. He was able to take hold of four in one fist. The other two, two larger, defiant boys with tear tracks down their cheeks, fought. He stepped away, placing the four smaller ones on his back before taking the elder ones. "Enough of that."

"Tornyth! To the wooded area!" Deovyn cried. "We can't hold them off forever."

Tornyth nodded, unfurled his wings, and took off. He kept his dragon ears deaf to the cries and whimpers of the *vehyl* children.

"If you want to tear us to pieces to eat, monster, you'll have to kill me first!" one of the boys screamed.

"I have no desire to do such a thing," Tornyth replied. He eyed the little one out of the corner of his eye. Under a mass of brown curls, large blue eyes glared back at him. His clothes were a little better than the other children. But his face was just as dirty and tear streaked.

"I swear I'll stab you if you don't put us down this instant!"

Tornyth rumbled in annoyance as the boy fished out a little dagger, one many of the great lords used at feasts, and dug it into the tender flesh of his hand.

"Did that sting, lizard?"

"You know it did," Tornyth grumbled. "Let me get you to safety ... It'd be a shame to drop you."

The lad glanced at the ground below, and the pale skin of his face drained of blood so that Tornyth could see the freckles along his nose. His spindly limbs trembled, and Tornyth could feel the fluttering of his heart.

"Safety?" the other boy asked. There was hope in that one's voice.

"There's a wooded area you can hide in until this little skirmish is over."

"This is not a *little skirmish*!" the boy with the curls cried out.

Tornyth let the child have his tantrum. He ducked under two charging Grey Shadows. He cursed as the children on his back cried out. Since he was flying away from the battle and not towards the fighting, most of the Grey Shadows didn't pursue him. The children weren't the target.

Landing among the King's Orchards, Tornyth released the boys from his claws and helped the small ones from his back.

"Stay down," Tornyth growled. "Wait for the sounds of battle to quieten, then get away from the citadel."

"You're not going to help us?" the angry boy demanded.

"War is coming," Tornyth replied. "Arelle Forest is close. You'll be able to scavenge food and stay out of sight."

"We're survivors," the other boy said. He turned to watch as the younger children wandered away to hide among the fruit trees. "Don't eat the king's fruit ... That's stealing."

"Eat your fill," Tornyth said. "The king would have you fed."

"You don't know that." Blue eyes glared up at him.

Tornyth's lips quirked into a smile. "I know my brother well. It's safe to eat the fruit."

"Brother, ha!" The boy brandished his dagger in Tornyth's direction. "The rumours are true; you are a huge man-eating beast."

"I have issue with the man-eating description," Tornyth replied. He turned his back to rejoin the battle.

"Don't you want to know about Kamoore?"

Tornyth turned, glaring into the blue eyes of the boy. Looking closely, he could see a small palace insignia on his vest. A servant. "Galgothmeg had him dressed for battle in the king's clothes ... He'll be paraded on the red dragon's back."

Grin widening, Tornyth couldn't help but smile. "He's mine."

With a few quick wing beats, Tornyth was back in the air.

"Are you going to eat him?"

"I'm not that kind of dragon!" Tornyth roared back.

The sky above Pallaryn was full of smoke when Tornyth returned to the battle. He caught sight of the heads of the men and women who had been executed. The fighting was thickest there. Squinting through the smoke, he saw Orion and Theo beside a fallen Grey Shadow. Even from the air he could feel the pulsating power pouring from Orion as unearthly screams ripped from his throat.

He watched the miracle of the scales falling from the writhing Grey Shadow. He was a bronze creature underneath. Confused dark blue eyes stared up at him. His jaw was slack, and the muscles along his serpentine back convulsed in exhaustion.

Tornyth sighed in relief as Captain Tiernan joined Theo and Orion. The captain wrapped his strong fingers around Orion's bicep and tugged.

"Captain!" Tornyth cried. Five Grey Shadows landed, their horrible sightless eyes on Orion, who was slumped in Theo's arms.

"*Kairn! Kairn!*" the Grey Shadows chanted.

It was with a great effort that the now freed bronze dragon dragged himself to his feet. He swung his tail at the Grey Shadows, panting with the effort to move.

Tornyth dived as Tiernan and Theo fled with Orion, who seemed to be barely conscious. His claws hit the ground. He snarled and lunged for the first Grey Shadow. He fanned out his wings to look larger and more threatening. He reasoned that if the Grey Shadows were nought but dumb beasts, they might be intimidated.

"Damn shield! Fly, you fool!" the bronze dragon cried. "A downed dragon is a dead dragon!"

"You sound like Deovyn," Tornyth replied. He snarled again and snapped, "Get yourself into the sky!"

The bronze dragon flapped his ruined wings. His voice came out in a sardonic drawl. "In case it has escaped your notice, I'm not exactly whole!"

"In case you haven't noticed, the effort to free you from the Grey Shadow hasn't *killed* you! Move."

A strong wind buffeted three Grey Shadows back. Digging in his claws into the rock, Tornyth turned his snout to the sky. Above, Deovyn cried out in victory. Beside him, the bronze sighed and slumped. His eyes were closed, his breathing becoming shallow.

"Rhox!"

The world was chaos. To the side, he saw Zapyr had landed, his noble face twisted in agony as he beheld the bronze dragon.

Curarfur was nearby, magnificent in his fury. The teal dragon lowered his head and came to Tornyth's aid.

Attention on the movements of the other dragons, Tornyth left his right side vulnerable to attack. A sharp sting in his shoulder brought him back to the fray. Roaring in shock, he turned his head, coming eye to eye with a Grey Shadow.

"Tornyth, concentrate!" Zapyr's voice screamed into his mind. *"Free yourself quickly!"*

Snarling, Tornyth lurched forward, his teeth only able to graze the Grey Shadow's neck. He pulled back. The bronze dragon who he was trying to protect lunged over his back to puncture the enemy dragon's skull with his teeth. The condemned creature still refused to let go.

Anger pooled in Tornyth's belly. He felt his blood pounding first hot and then the odd cooling sensation. Counting to three, Tornyth snapped at the Grey Shadow, and his teeth anchored into his enemy's scales.

The cold of his bite was enough to make the poor creature shriek, and it released Tornyth from its grasp. But Tornyth held on as ice formed on the Grey Shadow's wings and horns. The creature spasmed and collapsed at his feet.

In the next heartbeat, Deovyn was at his side, snapping down on the Grey Shadow, finishing him off.

More Grey Shadows were pressing in. Curarfur had killed three of them. Blood ran over his scales and claws. Whoever the bronze dragon was to the enemy, they were coming to kill him.

Above, Tornyth saw the red shadow of Galgothmeg. Upon his back, in all the finery of the High King of Rama, sat Kamoore. If he leaped into the air now, he could snatch the pompous nitwit from Galgothmeg's back and revenge would be his …

The bronze dragon groaned; his eyes looked dull from exhaustion and pain.

Tornyth pressed his scaled hide closer to him.

"Mandros, Aluel!" he screamed. *"We need help! We need Sidrah!"*

"Stand firm! We're coming!"

Tornyth nudged the side of the bronze dragon. A blue eye opened slowly. "Mandros is coming."

"Mandros?" the bronze dragon slurred. His voice was weak, but at the sound of the green dragon's name, he seemed to perk up.

"I need you to ignore the pain and move!" Tornyth nudged the bronze's side.

Panting, the bronze dragon forced himself to his feet. "I can't fly," he gasped, "but I can …"

The air around Tornyth and the bronze dragon shimmered. In confusion, Tornyth blinked. It looked like he was peering through water. He saw himself slumped on the wall. The bronze dragon was lying in a bloody mess beside him. Tornyth hissed in surprise at seeing his own corpse, but Rhox hushed him.

Deovyn, Curarfur and the others that had joined the fight slowly backed off. The Grey Shadows looked to the lifeless forms and retreated.

Mandros' claws hit the wall as the bronze dragon curled himself up. Sidrah was right beside him. The bronze dragon, Rhox, stared at them, visibly upset, and the illusion faded. His eyes welled with tears as his tail flicked from side to side.

"Where am I?" Rhox asked miserably. He sniffed at the air. "I sense battle, and my *vehyl* … I can't feel my *vehyl*."

Mandros shook his great head, looking incredibly sad and old. "You have my eternal thanks for being with Rhox, *mynrell*."

"He's yours?" Rhox whispered. "How can this be?"

"It's been a long time," Deovyn muttered.

"You've aged, Deo," Rhox said. "How long?"

The older dragons shifted uneasily.

"How long?"

"One thousand, two hundred and thirty-six summers," Mandros rumbled.

"Oh." Rhox's brows knit together. "My *vehyl* ..."

"Your *vehyl* passed at the Battle of Haven Bay, aged nineteen."

Rhox's eyes shut as if in great pain. "I remember *Lullah* ... they ... she ... fell ..."

"You went after her," Mandros continued. "Your human was killed and your dragon ..."

"I was a Grey Shadow for over a thousand years?"

"Yes."

"*Aluel*?" Rhox asked. Two pearly teardrops fell down the scales of his face. "I thought I heard his voice."

"You did," Deovyn assured him. "He's near."

"Where?"

"A dragon tried to manifest in battle," Sidrah said.

"I know. Tenacious little *vehyl*. Stubborn too. Vadroil's power didn't want to let me go." A smile finally lit Rhox's face. "Is he well?"

"Your *aluel* is with him," Sidrah said gently. "We have a second newly manifested dragon. And you have a *sudunyn*."

"Orion is a dragon?" Tornyth muttered. "How could I not know?"

Deovyn shrugged. He crept closer to Rhox, belly close to the ground, and lay down next to him. "The power was virtually rolling off him. I don't know how you didn't sense it."

"Such a sense comes with age." Mandros looked amused. "Sidrah, if you please."

While Sidrah stepped close to Rhox, Tornyth manifested back into Jodathyn. The dark blue orbs of the bronze dragon looked at him longingly, and he reached out to touch his snout. He couldn't imagine the shock of finding himself over a thousand years in the future with a dead *vehyl*. He shuddered. Poor Rhox had a lot to take in, and Zapyr was not around to help him.

"Nineteen," Rhox murmured. His gaze never left Jodathyn. "I thought myself a man. And now the *vehyl* look ... young."

He noticed Edisyn and Gylleah observing nearby and made his way over to them. The dark red dragon marked his approach with gleaming amber eyes.

"It seems miracles do happen."

"He's someone important, isn't he?" Jodathyn asked, glancing over his shoulder.

"Indeed, Rhox the Illusionist, the only son and heir of Zapyr," Gylleah replied.

"Guess that makes him your nephew," Edisyn said.

"I guess so ... I thought I better give them some space."

"The path to the guardhouse is safe," Edisyn said. "It's where they are taking injured *vehyl*."

Jodathyn's footsteps faltered as he approached the guardhouse. Being the Son of the Crown, he had never dared to venture in. He knew once he heard news of the human cost of the battle, he couldn't unhear it. He wondered if he was ready to know.

Nym and Carew were lounging by the entrance. Hearing his footsteps, they looked up at him, surprise on their faces.

"Are you well, Jod?"

Jodathyn shrugged in answer to Nym's question. The feeling of light-headedness lingered. "This doesn't feel like home. The heads …"

Grimacing, Carew sauntered forward, grabbed Jodathyn's elbow and escorted him into the guardhouse. Jodathyn blinked in the dim light. There were at least two dozen men and women crowded at the tables. A few lay on the ground. They were a strange mix of King's Guardsmen, palace guards, lawmen, and common folk. Rank no longer mattered among them; they had all fought under one banner.

"Found a stray, Jael."

Without looking up from his task, Jael pointed to a spare chair. The healer was busy healing a nasty slice along a man's belly. "The stray can wait there for me."

Grinning at him, Carew pushed Jodathyn into the chair.

"How badly are you hurt?" Nym asked, coming over to stand over him.

"Who says I am hurt?" Jodathyn replied.

Nym raised her eyebrows.

Jodathyn glanced at his shoulder. "I was bitten. The dragons are busy …"

The dark-skinned healer looked up and frowned. "Jodathyn? Carew, get a look at it for me while I finish up here."

"It's just a graze." To Jodathyn's observation, Jael looked exhausted.

"Disrobe. I don't want to be dealing with a nasty infection."

Jodathyn slumped, too tired to make a fuss over Carew unlacing his shirt. "Is Theo …"

"He's with Lord Zapyr. He was there when that hay-brained stable boy exploded."

Jodathyn blinked. "That's for dragons only."

"Don't think the dragon had much of a choice," one of the guards grunted.

"Get the feeling it wasn't supposed to happen like that," a woman with burns down her legs said. "Otherworlds, the screaming ..."

"Manifesting is painless," Jodathyn said.

"What happened to Orion wasn't painless," Jael replied. The healer's voice was laden with irony. "I would like to check him over, but Lord Zapyr wasn't keen on my approach."

"Sidrah has seen him," Jodathyn said. He glanced away from Carew, who tugged at his shirt to pull it over his head. His knees jiggled with nerves. He couldn't help but think over what he had seen during the battle.

"Voran's dead," Jodathyn whispered.

"Can't say I liked the man," Nym replied. "Oh, Otherworlds, Jodathyn! That's not a graze; that's pulverised meat."

Carew winced and poked the wound on his shoulder.

"I can feel the pain now," Jodathyn muttered.

Jael shook his head, but he kept his tone steady. "Cleanse the wound, Carew, if you would."

"He died trying to save me. He intercepted a Grey Shadow ... It tore him to pieces."

"Who?" Nym asked.

"Voran. He knew he was going to die ... I could see it in his eyes," Jodathyn said.

Carew's gloved hand landed on his uninjured shoulder, and he began the process of cleaning the abrasion left by dragon teeth. "Soldiers face death every day. I, for one, can only hope that he found that piece of himself he lost."

"Even those of us who aren't soldiers made the choice to fight today and face our deaths. To think only a season ago I was a blacksmith," the burned woman said. She rubbed the palms of her hands together, her eyes looking glassy. "How can I go back to my forge, my home after losing so much?"

A few of the guards murmured soft words of encouragement to her.

"What happens now, do you think?" Jodathyn asked.

"This isn't the end," one of the gruff older men muttered. "That red beast was able to flee with the puppet king."

Nym rubbed her hands together. "War is brewing. This was just a taste."

"Think I've had my fill of war," Jodathyn replied. "Does that make me a coward?"

"A realist, I would say," Jael said. He finished with his current patient and came to stand before Jodathyn. His long, elegant fingers pressed into his flesh.

"It's a nasty bite," Carew said.

Jodathyn blinked, grinning sheepishly up at the healer. "Good thing I know a decent healer or two."

Grunting, Jael pressed his fingers to the gash. His power was pleasantly warm as his skin began to knit together. Jodathyn turned his head to watch.

"There's a question I've been too afraid to ask."

"Ask."

Jodathyn licked his lips and closed his eyes. "Donatein ... Why did Kieryn sign his death warrant ... He would never ... I'm angry, Jael. I'm so angry ... Kieryn is king and ..."

"Jodathyn," Jael said, "you have the right to feel angry. The king didn't sign the death warrant. He was right riled when he found out what happened under his nose."

"It was one of the reasons Solan used to dispose the king. That and he didn't allow anyone to go after the manservant who stole a horse," another guard added. "I was here when the coup happened. Rumour says the king sent a letter to Sion trying to find you sanctuary."

Jodathyn looked around at the guardhouse, feeling foolish. "Solan was responsible? I'm going to kill him."

"Too late," a guardsman replied. "Galgothmeg lit him up for all Pallaryn to see. He fell burning and screaming."

"Well," Jodathyn said. "Every year, I'm going to build an effigy in Solan's likeness and burn him on the walls."

"Sounds fun." Nym snorted back a laugh.

"The King's Guard will join you," Carew declared.

Jael rolled his eyes. "Do you have anything else you wish to ask, Jodathyn?"

"You'll think I'm foolish."

"Ask me."

"My dogs." Jodathyn sighed. "They're gone, aren't they?"

Jael nodded his head. "I stayed with your older dog so he wasn't alone. The other was already gone when the king found him. I'm sorry, Jodathyn, I truly am."

Jodathyn slumped. "Now I can stop wondering."

Chapter Sixteen

Orion

The Citadel of Rama

Orion's world was on fire. The scent of smoke and blood was heavy in the air. Memories of the battle and ferocious pain surfaced. The last he remembered was the Grey Shadows converging on him. He was still alive; he could only assume he lost consciousness and someone had pulled him to a place of safety.

Cautiously, Orion opened one eye, groaning as he rolled his shoulders. Large, dangerous claws were the first thing he saw. He raised his head, staring down at the wide nostrils that followed his line of sight.

"Peace, Ayrdonyth."

"Oh, he's awake!"

Orion blinked down at Theo, who was much smaller than he remembered. The thief lifted one hand and patted his scaled foreleg. He watched. The sensation was different, but not unpleasant.

"I kept your *vehyl* friend safe."

A powerful scaled body rippled at his side, and Orion stumbled to his feet. It was only then he realised that his hind quarters were resting on Zapyr's back legs.

A shooting pain laced its way up Orion's spine. He fell to his nose, his leg muscles spasming. He was faintly aware of the protrusion on his back, unfurling and fluttering in the wind.

"No flying for you just yet," Zapyr said. He nudged him gently. "Here is protected well enough. You must rest."

"What happened? I hurt."

"You happened," Theo said. "You wouldn't listen."

"Your dragon manifested in the middle of the battle," Zapyr replied. "It's a dangerous feat, Ayrdonyth Shadow-Eater. A dragon who manifests out of fear is in danger of losing himself."

"I don't understand," Orion muttered.

"Your dragon was stressed and was attacking its human heart. We nearly lost you."

"I don't want to be a dragon."

"I don't think it's a matter of wanting or not wanting to be a dragon, my friend," Theo replied. "It's a matter of what is. Look, you now have four legs, wings and a *Rshon Aluel*."

Orion could only blink.

"Lord Zapyr has been kind enough to spend the last few hours talking to me about dragon culture. Most fascinating."

"Curl up and rest, Ayrdonyth." Zapyr stood, his golden scales glittering in the sun. Ayrdonyth watched him closely. The older dragon looked magnificent. He briefly wondered what the other dragons would think of him releasing the Grey Shadow and doing whatever he did in the midst of the battle. "Theo will keep you company here until my return."

Ayrdonyth looked down at himself. "I'm bigger than Tornyth."

Zapyr, who was standing right at the edge, his wings spread wide, turned to look at him. "Yes, *mynrell*, we suspect that the sheer amount of herbs Tornyth was given from infancy resulted in his diminutive stature. While Sidrah has ascertained you have taken such herbs, you have consumed less. Also, you are younger, with more time to grow into full-sized adulthood."

Shifting his weight, Zapyr didn't look back as he took off. For a long moment, Ayrdonyth watched him go. The feeling that the golden dragon couldn't wait to leave gnawed at him.

Theo came and sat between his front forelegs.

"Where do you think he came up with the name?" Ayrdonyth asked.

Startled, Theo glanced over his shoulder and then lay down to rest his head further up on his leg. "Ayrdonyth has always been your name. It's something that your dragon was born with. Remember Jodathyn knew his dragon's name before the dragon manifested."

"How come I didn't know?"

Theo smirked up at him. "I guess Tornyth was stubborn and made himself known."

"You're probably right. Are you hurt?"

"Surprisingly, no." Theo chuckled.

"He couldn't wait to leave ..." Ayrdonyth couldn't keep the despondency from his tone. Everyone left him eventually.

Theo's hand ran down his side. "He's very protective of you. He growled something shocking at the King's Guardsman that came to check on you. He only let Sidrah near out of necessity."

"He left ..."

"Ayr, if I may call you such, the other dragon ... I think he's someone important. Lord Zapyr has been torn between staying at your side and going to the other. He'll be back as soon as he can."

"Did I kill the other dragon?"

"No," Theo replied. "He must have been stronger than the first one you freed. He was alive. From what I could see, weakened. There was quite a battle over him ... It was terrible to watch."

"No more terrifying than watching a dragon struggling to manifest from a screaming boy."

Ayrdonyth's head lifted at the new voice. He recognised the tone. Guardsman Lyntton stood a few paces a way. A few other King's Guardsmen, many unknown to Orion, stood behind him. Orion shuffled over so that he might peer at the older guardsman.

"Might we approach?"

"Papa lizard said nothing about visitors now that he's awake," Theo said. "Dragons really don't like anyone or anything near their sleeping hatchlings."

"*Hatchling?*" Ayrdonyth screwed up his nose.

"Oh yes, to Zapyr you're *his* hatchling."

A few of the King's Guardsmen chuckled at the indignant look on Ayrdonyth's face.

"Think of it this way, my friend," Theo continued. "In human form, you have a whole bunch of older men watching your every move. As a dragon, you have an ancient one who'll rip out anyone's throat if they mess with you."

Ayrdonyth groaned.

At Theo's hand gesture, Lyntton approached until he was level with him. For a long moment, he stood at the new dragon's side, silently contemplating.

"Were our losses heavy, sir?"

Lyntton looked up at him, perhaps with the ridiculous notion that a dragon might still refer to him as sir. He glanced back at his comrades, who had all taken cautionary steps forward to get a good look at their newest recruit's dragon.

"Heavier than we would have liked."

Ayrdonyth nodded. This wasn't unexpected news. "Jodathyn?"

"You're right friendly with him, aren't you?"

"Running for your life brings people together."

Lyntton turned to his companions. "Orion was Jodathyn's manservant, the one that stole the horse ..."

"He's curled up in the guardhouse with Jael," another guardsman answered. "Best place for him, I reckon."

Ayrdonyth let his chin drop to the ground and huffed.

"You in much pain, recruit?" yet another guard asked.

"Everything hurts," Ayrdonyth muttered.

"Here," the guardsman said, striding up boldly. He used Ayrdonyth's curled forearm to climb onto his back. Ayrdonyth was about to open his mouth to demand what exactly the guardsman thought he might be doing when firm hands kneaded his shoulders. He lay his head back down and huffed again so that his breath unsettled the dust.

"When you're ready, report to the guardhouse. We can work out the exact nature of your appointment as we go." Lyntton gestured to the other guardsmen, and they turned to leave.

"Is that him?"

Orion blinked and opened his eyes. The first thing he noticed was that he was back in his human form. Relieved, he brought his legs underneath him and sat. At his side, Theo helped him to remain upright. He raised his hand to his hair; his horseman's lock was matted and wet with sweat. He was covered in dirt.

"Welcome back, Orion."

Zapyr loomed over him. At his side was a familiar bronze dragon with a black underbelly. From the twisted look of his wings, it seemed that flying would prove to be painful.

"Orion, this is Rhox, your *sudunyn*, your brother. Rhox, this is your brother's *vehyl*, Orion. His dragon is Ayrdonyth."

The bronze dragon, Rhox, eyed him curiously. "I owe you a great debt, *sudunyn*."

"I felt your torment," Orion said. He flicked his eyes over to Theo. "I could have killed you."

"Your power makes no sense. How is it a beast-talker can free Grey Shadows?"

"It seems that the new dragons' powers may be amplified. Roane surmises that their dragons have had to fight at a very young unmanifested stage to stay alive. It isn't the first time your *sudunyn* has freed a Grey Shadow."

"I could have *killed* him," Orion pointed out.

"Death would have been a preferable fate than to stay trapped in my own mind and body." Rhox pulled a face and lumbered over to a spare space. He slumped down and watched Orion with two eyes full of misery.

"The Grey Shadow wasn't you, *elt mynrell*," Zapyr rumbled.

"You have no idea of what I may have done, *Aluel*," Rhox said.

Zapyr nudged his bronze scaled son with his snout, budging him over so he might curl down beside him. Grudgingly, Rhox moved over to allow Zapyr to lay at his side.

Orion felt uneasy watching such a moment between father and son. He glanced towards Theo, who also averted his gaze.

"Have either of you seen Tornyth?" Zapyr asked. "I should thank him."

"The white dragon?" Rhox asked. "He was quite tiny."

"The words we are using are petite or modest," Zapyr replied. "Yes, he's my new *sudunyn*."

"He has shield-fire ..."

"Yes, he'll drive *elt aluel* mad."

"He was holed up in the guardhouse," Theo said. "Guardsman Jael is with him."

"The healer?"

"He was bitten, *Aluel*," Rhox said. "No one was paying much mind to him ... He slipped away."

Zapyr lowered his head and gazed down at Orion. "Thank you, *elt vehyl*, but please learn to listen to your dragon instincts. If your body is on fire ... Ancient One's Talons, stop pouring out your powers. Now, go, feed your *vehyl* body. Rest. I'll teach you to fly later."

Orion looked over to Rhox, who had grimaced at the word 'fly'. His new brother flapped his useless wings. His frown deepened.

"I can't say I'm sorry for what happened, Zapyr," Orion muttered. "A little pain and ... Rhox is back with you."

Zapyr nudged him. "*Rshon Aluel*. I am your dragon father, *vehyl*."

CHAPTER SEVENTEEN
Jodathyn

The Citadel of Pallaryn

As much as Jodathyn enjoyed watching Jael work, he was impatient to return to his rooms. While Carew and Nym were at home conversing with the guardsmen, Jodathyn felt out of place. He sat in silence and studied Jael tending to the wounded. The healer's power held a tender quality to it, and yet it was no less powerful than some of the gifting he had felt. Healing suited Jael.

The moment word spread that the palace was safe, Jodathyn stood, thanked Jael and left. It had taken several hours to complete the purge of Kamoore's men.

When Jodathyn rounded the first bend, he heard footsteps and spun on his heel.

"Well, his reflexes are good," Nym said.

"We thought you could do with some company." Carew ran his hands through his hair. "A lot has happened in the time you've been gone. There's no knowing the state of your rooms."

"Thank you," Jodathyn replied.

"Won't this be fun. I've never been in the Son of the Crown's private rooms before, and I'm sure Nym is curious about the lifestyle of a palace brat. Now let me tell you the story of when we found him covered in beer, collapsed in the corridors …"

Wedged between the pair, Jodathyn half listened to Carew's tales of palace life. Their footsteps echoed in the corridors, giving the palace an eerie feeling. He did his best not to let his eye wander and take in the devastation around him. A quick, hesitant glance at Nym's face told him she was overwhelmed by his childhood home. She opened her mouth but seeing Jodathyn watching her, she clenched her jaw shut. He would have preferred she spew whatever barb she had thought of and not worry about his feelings. Her silence was not natural.

When they reached his personal chambers, Carew stepped past him and swung the door open, gesturing for Jodathyn to enter ahead of him. Crossing the threshold, he had to choke back a gasp of dismay as his knees hit the floor.

His rooms had been ransacked. Jodathyn ignored the ripped curtains, the slashed bedsheets, and even his destroyed books. A cry of outrage left his lips as he took in Donatein's precious herbs and ointments spilled across the length of his rooms. The candles the old man had experimented with for hours for Jodathyn's personal use had been smashed. He spied one of Valt's uniforms torn and tattered in his fireplace.

Jodathyn reached out to scoop up the herbs at his feet.

Arnica, for bruising, his mind supplied. The aromatic scent filled his nostrils. He breathed in deeply, and in his imagination, he could see Donatein waiting for him to come home.

Carew stepped around him and disappeared into the servant's quarters, leaving Nym standing in the middle of his rooms, shifting her weight. She ran her fingers along the hardwood of his desk.

"Such artistry. Your rooms are beautiful, palace brat," she said. She picked up papers and tried to straighten his desk. Jodathyn glanced up at her, but she ignored him. "What did I expect? You're royalborn."

Carew returned and knelt by Jodathyn, resting his hand on his shoulder. "I found something of Valt's in his rooms."

Hopeful, Jodathyn looked up. In Carew's hands were a pair of leather gloves and a small ornamental knife. Reaching out, Jodathyn took the knife. "Where did you find these?"

"Sometimes servants hide things in the walls."

Fingering the knife, Jodathyn smiled sadly. "This was his first weapon. It was given to him by his pa. He showed it to me once."

"It was special to him," Carew said. "It wouldn't have been hidden in the wall otherwise. The gloves are frankly an odd find."

Jodathyn laughed, taking the gloves and holding them to his chest. "He was fond of nice supple leather gloves. He had his favourites."

"You knew your men well," Carew said.

"They were family," Jodathyn replied. "Even though it's forbidden."

"Human emotions can't always be denied." Carew patted his knee. "Forgive me for saying this. When the day comes for you to cross to the Otherworld, I hope it's your servants that greet you and not your father."

"I always wanted to become worthy of my name to please my father, make him proud ..."

"Can I tell you something, lowly guardsman to a son of a king?"

Jodathyn snorted and gestured helplessly.

"You were always worthy to your men. Donatein spent his last breath defending you. And Valt, Pa told me how much your guard cared for you. You were more than an honour bound duty to him."

Jodathyn's eyes welled with tears. "I miss them so much it aches."

"Jodathyn," Nym whispered. She traced a delicate quill that had been bent in half with her fingers. It was one of Jodathyn's favourites. "Mourning takes time."

Glumly, Jodathyn nodded. "And I have nothing."

"I found something on your desk." Nym picked up a piece of parchment and offered it to him. "I don't know what it's doing here but ... this is obviously something from your childhood."

Jodathyn took it from Nym's hand.

It was a simple child's drawing. And it made his heart ache. He thought Donatein would have destroyed any evidence of how much their relationship had evolved.

At the top of the page, he had written, *I love you Donatein. I wish you were Papa. Your Jodathyn.* The picture was of a small Jodathyn holding the hand of a bearded servant. Above the figures was a clumsily reptilian head with wings. On the other side, he had written, *I dreamed I was a dragon.*

"I don't remember doing this," Jodathyn said. He touched the drawn figure of the dragon. "Do you think young me knew of Tornyth?"

"There's a part of you that knew," Nym said.

"I'm surprised that Donatein would have kept such a piece," Carew commented.

"Ah, the simple, pure love of a child."

Jodathyn jumped. He turned upon his heel and spotted Captain Tiernan in his doorway. The captain looked about at the destruction, a frown upon his face.

"Why don't you three see about cleaning up? His Majesty wishes to see Jodathyn in the audience chamber."

Jodathyn was about to open his mouth in protest when Tiernan threw a bundle of clothes at Carew.

"How did he know where we were?" Nym asked as Tiernan left without speaking another word.

"Captain of the King's Guard," Carew replied with a shrug. "He knows just about everything."

When they arrived at the king's audience chamber, the door was open wide. Jodathyn dithered on the threshold. In the past, a servant would be by the doors, admitting people permitted by the High King. Now there was no servant. It was another reminder that his home was forever changed.

"Go on." Carew's hand in the middle of his back pushed Jodathyn forward. In order to keep his façade of confidence, he stepped fully into the audience chamber. He heard Nym's appreciative intake of breath, but his stomach dropped.

While the great columns still stood tall and proud, the great lords' chairs were crumbled nubs of stone and Kieryn's throne a twisted mass of gold. His eyes trailed along the domed roof, which was damaged. Through the crack, he could see Mandros' face as the green dragon pressed his snout to the hole. More shocking was the sight of Deovyn, whose scaled body was wrapped around the stairs leading to the throne.

"What's Deovyn doing?"

"Intimidation." Dressed in full uniform, Tiernan approached. He bowed, which turned Jodathyn's attention away from his dragon brother to the Captain of the King's Guard. "Lord Mandros does not fit through the hole in the roof. He sent Deovyn to wriggle through in his place. Come, His Majesty awaits."

Jodathyn's footsteps echoed throughout the chamber as he followed in Captain Tiernan's wake. The room was filled with the surviving King's Guardsmen, ordinary guardsmen and what seemed to be common folk. It was an unprecedented sight. Traditionally, the decorated members of the King's Guard would be arranged in perfectly lined ranks while the great lords presided over the matters of state. Kieryn would be on his golden throne. Common folk standing before their king in this room was unheard of.

With a fine black and silver cloak draped over his armour, Kieryn stood waiting for him. The crown of Rama was noticeably missing from his brow. At the king's side, Queen Odelle looked elegant in her high collared black gown trimmed with silver threads. The train was artfully folded so that the embroidery of the royal emblem of a flaming crown was clearly visible.

The small girl who Odelle had rescued was clutching the king's hand. She had her whole body pressed against Kieryn's side as she watched, wide-eyed, the adults before her. Carvelle stood close to his mother's side and beamed down at Jodathyn. He wondered how long he had spent in the guardhouse.

"Et-hir of Sion, might you do the honours for me?"

If he harboured any doubts of his brother's acceptance of her, he could now lay them to rest. She was dressed in an admittedly simple gown of black and silver. Her Sionian scarf was tied loosely around her waist like a belt. Around her neck was a silver sword pendant strung with black pearls and diamonds. In her hands was a man's cloak.

"Mate …" Tornyth purred.

Jodathyn hid the smile at his dragon's enthusiasm. Silently shushing his dragon, he knelt. "My king."

He couldn't help himself; his eyes wandered back to Et-hir. She strode forward, the sound of her footsteps muffled by the soft slippers she now wore on her feet. She stopped directly in front of Jodathyn, and there was a teasing glint in her eye.

"Jodathyn." She draped the cloak around his shoulders.

"Kiss her," Tornyth whispered as he looked up into her eyes. *"Her heart beats for us, and I pine for her!"*

Jodathyn bit his lip, his eyes darting up to Mandros and then Kieryn.

"What is it?" Et-hir whispered.

"Tornyth is being vocal about his yearning for you."

Pursing her lips, Et-hir's cheeks took on a rosy hue as she turned her gaze upon the king as if gauging what the correct response might be. High upon his throne, Kieryn couldn't hear what they said to one another, but Jodathyn noticed the king's interest.

"Aren't you one with Tornyth?"

"Yes," Jodathyn replied, lowering his tone to a teasing rumble.

"Rise, brother," Kieryn commanded. "And approach boldly the throne of Rama."

The wording of Kieryn's command was odd, but Jodathyn did as he was told. Et-hir couldn't help herself. She reached out and smoothed the material of his cloak. The pressure of her fingertips was almost enough to put his unease to rest. He wondered how many times she had done this when she worked with the silk traders.

Jodathyn let his eyes linger over the simple lines of her gown and smiled at the strip of red fabric around her waist. His eyes travelled to her lips and then noticed she had a very few carefully placed black pearls in her hair.

"I am so pleased you are well." Et-hir's hand grasped his upper arm tightly. She dipped her head towards him so they might not be overheard. "I've spent the last few hours imagining the most horrible—"

"I am well," Jodathyn said to reassure her.

He scanned the room. Ruevyn and Will stood together, and Fydellah was only a few widths away from them. Carew and Nym had entered behind him and located Theo, who had found himself a lute.

"Jodathyn, come," Kieryn repeated. His lips twitched upward into a smile. Jodathyn hastened to obey and when he made it to the bottom stairs, Kieryn continued to speak. "Today you are my council. It is you, the men and women who fought for Pallaryn, that I petition on the behalf of my brother. Among us we have farmers, ex-slaves, guardsmen of all ranks, a lord and ex-thieves. We have those with great powers and those with none."

Tilting his chin up, Jodathyn knew that the cloak around his shoulders and the black gown of Et-hir was not a coincidence. He decided he would keep his mouth shut and wait for the king to reveal what he was up to.

"When you were born, oh brother of mine, you were given the title Son of the Crown. While you're a legitimate son of a king and his wife, this title has been used to cause you pain. I'm petitioning that the title be removed from your name. Henceforth I would ask the council to agree with me that you'll be known as Jodathyn Pallarus, Prince of the Realm. I would also like to seek approval to provide you with a birthright that has been denied to you. You will have your own inheritance, your own title and your own lands for your family. To each of your natural born children will be granted land and titles. Is there anyone in my council who disagrees?"

"You jest," Nym called out from the crowd. "Anyone who disagrees, I'll pull out their wretched tongues."

Kieryn's smile widened. "As Prince of the Realm, you have an oath to make. You're of age to understand the importance of any oath made before the High King and his council. I trust you know the words."

Jodathyn knew the words of the prince's oath. There had been a time as a child he had dreamed of a moment like this, a moment where he would be accepted for who he was born to be. He had fantasised that one day, his father might return and claim him as his own. He had diligently learned the words in secret, sometimes whispering them at night to himself.

This was better than his dream. The majority of the great lords were missing. They did not matter, Jodathyn realised. Not when there were people in this room whose opinions of him far outweighed Kamoore or Solan. In this room were people who believed in him, supported him when he was nothing. It meant the world that they were here.

He locked eyes with Et-hir, then Odelle and his brother, and knelt.

"There is no need to use our father's name," Kieryn said. "Use Mandros' titles. He has done so much good for you, brother, and he deserves the recognition."

Jodathyn nodded and drew in a deep breath, briefly glancing towards Mandros. "I, Jodathyn Pallarus, the son of Mandros, the dragon of Flame and Fury, Arturyn's Heir and Prince of the Realm of Rama, solemnly swear to serve the people of Rama. To put their interests above my own. To be a man of honour and uphold the values of Rama. I will serve faithfully with valour. My right hand shall shield the weak, and my left hand shall love mercy. This I solemnly swear for the rest of my days."

Kieryn bent and gestured for Larelle to go to the queen. Odelle reached out for her, and the girl stepped away uncertainly. She nestled close to Odelle and clutched at the queen's skirts. Smiling indulgently at the children, the king turned his attention back to Jodathyn and strode forward, speaking as he descended the stairs. "I present Jodathyn Pallarus, Prince of the Realm."

Jodathyn was still kneeling, dumbfounded, as Kieryn helped him to his feet and wrapped him into a tight embrace. "I am so proud of you," the king murmured in his ear as he kissed both of his cheeks. "So proud. Come, both of you."

Arm in arm, Kieryn led Jodathyn up the steps, something as a mere Son of the Crown he was never permitted to do. This was what had perplexed him about Et-hir's presence with the royal family. Bouncing excitedly, Carvelle met them halfway and practically dragged Jodathyn to the top. "We're not finished yet."

Kieryn chuckled and ran a gloved hand down Carvelle's hair. "Patience, my son."

At the top of the dais, Kieryn paused and gestured for Et-hir to come to him. Et-hir stepped forward, looking a little anxious but at the same time eager. To Jodathyn's surprise, Kieryn took Et-hir's hand in his own. His brother smiled as he took Jodathyn's hand to join with Et-hir.

"I made another promise," Kieryn said. He kept his hand over their intertwined fingers. Et-hir blinked and smiled shyly up at Jodathyn. "To Et-hir of Sion, I promised her Jodathyn. Let it be known that Jodathyn and Et-hir have expressed their intentions to be a courting couple, and I have gladly given my blessing."

Kieryn stepped towards Et-hir and dropped a kiss upon her brow. He had to bend significantly to do so. "Welcome, Et-hir, to my family."

Jodathyn felt Et-hir's fingers squeeze his hand.

"Kiss!" cried Carvelle. "It's tradition!"

Under his brother's watchful eye, Jodathyn stepped forward. He would have thought he'd be shy taking Et-hir into his arms with so many witnesses. But just letting his hands fall to her waist and pressing his lips to hers, his world melted away. His eyes fluttered shut, and he deepened the kiss.

"Alright, you two." Kieryn chuckled. "This isn't a wedding. We have some serious business to attend to."

Pulling away, Jodathyn blushed, his eyes still upon Et-hir, who seemed to be glowing with happiness.

"Tonight, brother o' mine, judgement is yours and yours alone." Kieryn released Jodathyn's shoulders and sat himself back on his throne.

"I don't understand, Your Majesty."

"You will." Deovyn's rumbling laughter had the ground trembling.

"Yours is a non-speaking role, *mynrell*," Mandros said from his vantage point.

"Bring them in ... Let the games begin," Deovyn replied, flicking his tail.

"Deovyn ..."

Kieryn interrupted Mandros' warning growl. "Let us have this moment of levity, Lord Mandros."

"What these prisoners did has my dragon skin crawling," Mandros said.

Jodathyn's eyes narrowed in suspicion, but then the doorway was shrouded by palace guards and three very miserable prisoners. Swallowing his gasp of horror, he immediately recognised their faces. They were forced to march between those who had gathered in the audience chamber.

These were the men who had sold him into slavery. They haunted some of his worst nightmares. When he had been handed over to the captain of the *Tribulation*, he had never thought to see them again. Even so, their likenesses were forever branded into his brain. Burning anger swelled in his chest.

Jodathyn didn't realise he had brought his hands to his chest and that his breathing was laboured until Et-hir took his hand in hers and squeezed his fingers.

"He's angry," Jodathyn choked. "Tornyth is angry."

"Of course the dragon is angry, love," Et-hir whispered back. She looked at him with her lovely brown eyes. "I'm angry too."

The unfortunate men were harried forward with the butts of the guardsmen's spears and were forced to their knees.

Rumbling low in his throat, Deovyn curled back his lips to reveal his fangs. If he wasn't so angry, Jodathyn would have rolled his eyes at his brother's theatrics. He was beginning to realise how dramatic dragons could be. He had to admit that his brother's scare tactics were working. Deovyn lifted his head off the ground so that his shadow loomed above the quaking men.

"I believe one of them has pissed themselves," Deovyn said with a disgusted sniff.

Jodathyn tried to dredge up some sympathy for the cowering men and found he could not.

"They sold us," Tornyth whispered. *"For gold."*

"Do you know why you are here, *rokun*?"

Deovyn is doing a spectacular job of ignoring his non-speaking role, Jodathyn thought. He glanced towards Mandros, whose snout was pressed even closer to the hole in the dome. The green dragon was growling. It was a very soft noise. But the sound sent shivers of dread up Jodathyn's spine.

"We've committed no crime."

Jodathyn wanted to spit in the leader's bearded face. Atek Rytter was still trying to seem unfazed by his situation.

Deovyn made a show of yawning wide and running his tongue along his fangs. "Didn't my brother tell you that you are the enemy of house Pallarus and you would be forced to kneel?"

"We've harmed no dragon."

"Ah, foolish *rokun*," Mandros said from above. "Do you not recognise the one you marked? Do you not recognise the Son of Flame and Fury, his royal highness Prince Jodathyn?"

Jodathyn thought his heart might thud its way out of his chest as the men looked up at the dais and their eyes met.

"Impossible ..."

"My brother suffers because of your heinous actions and as a result, house Pallarus suffers with him." Kieryn's voice boomed through the audience chamber. "When he hurts, I hurt. He is my flesh, my blood, my brother and prince of this realm."

"He is no prince."

"Silence, fool!" Kieryn barked. "I have learned many great, valuable things during my reign. I could sit in judgement today, but I would have my dear brother granted peace. He's your judge."

Kieryn's motives should have been obvious. Everything had been for show, from the cloak about his shoulders to the dragon on the floor flashing his fangs. It had never occurred to him that one day he'd shoulder the duty of sitting in judgement. Today the king was relinquishing his sovereignty and handing it to him. It was a rarity that his own feelings were considered when decisions were made ... and today, he was the one in control.

Et-hir's long, slender fingers intertwined with his and anchored him to reality. He parted his lips and reminded himself to breathe.

Tilting her head back to look at him, Odelle caught his eyes and smiled at him encouragingly. Her strangely dark eyes still held the same warmth as when they were blue. But Jodathyn wasn't sure he would ever get used to them. "You don't need to rush, brother."

Above his head, he heard Mandros' low rumble of agreement.

He stepped forward. "No."

"No, brother?" Kieryn asked.

"I don't need time to deliberate." Jodathyn's eyes hardened. There was a savage joy he felt as the men who caused him so much pain flinched back. "There is only one outcome. It is only a question of method. Do you mean it, brother, my king? The choice is mine?"

"Fully yours."

Beneath his skin, Tornyth rippled, and Jodathyn felt unease. He thought of all the ways he might accomplish justice—but there was also danger.

"Death," Jodathyn said, turning his eyes towards his brother. "That is the only option in this case. Even if I was so inclined to show mercy, I cannot foresee that either you or Mandros would suffer them to live."

Deovyn made a scoffing noise.

Jodathyn's eyes swivelled towards the prisoners. "Do you know how many ways I could have you executed? I could have you flogged or flayed. Burned or torn from limb to limb. Impaled or have your intestines drawn from your body as you watch."

He watched as the men did their utmost to seem unaffected, unafraid of their fate. They were frightened, and they should be. The one they mocked and tormented was now the one in control. They were helpless mice before a dragon who longed to ripple free and show them what true fear was.

"We're not a beast," Tornyth whispered. *"We're more. We are the prince of scales ... Herald of the Dragon King."*

Descending the stairs in silence, Jodathyn watched as the echo of his boots caused the prisoners to draw back in alarm. He crossed the stone floor until he stood before the leader, Atek. In a fluid motion, he knelt and grabbed the man's chin. When he tried to jerk his head free, Jodathyn dug in his nails and forced the man to look him in the face.

"You drugged me, marked my body and sold me into slavery that would have been centuries worth of torment. You sought to destroy me. But here

I am, unbroken and stronger. You thought to harm a boy, and he has returned to you a dragon. A lesser man than I would ask for torment ... for fire."

Jodathyn glanced towards Kieryn. He released Atek's chin and stood to his full height. He watched with a detached sense of power. "Let it be done swiftly, I care not how. No more time will I give them residence in my mind."

"Are you sure, brother?"

"I am sure." Jodathyn swallowed past the lump in his throat. "Their torture will benefit me nothing. I want them to know that after everything I have been through, the beatings, the humiliation and flogging, the burning alive, that I am victorious. Pain and fear have no place ruling me."

Kieryn seemed to consider Jodathyn's words, but Jodathyn knew the pause was only for dramatic effect. Spreading his arms wide, the king gestured toward the guards. "Let it be known, my brother, Jodathyn Pallarus, Prince of the Realm, is a gracious man full of conviction and honour. Guardsman Lyntton, I trust you'll see to the matter to its completion, and then please join us in celebration."

Jodathyn recognised the guardsman who took hold of the prisoners as the same man who had accompanied Orion to Silverdyne. His face remained calmly professional as he dragged Atek kicking and cursing from the audience chamber. The burned woman from the guardhouse came forward to assist with the prisoners. She was followed by a palace guard and a man who looked like he might have been a servant.

Jodathyn stared after them until his brother grasped his shoulder.

"A great leader must always be sure when he passes judgement," Kieryn said. "You did well, brother."

"Would you have let me decide anything?"

Kieryn cleared his throat, an uncomfortable expression crossing his face as he looked back to his queen. "If you asked to have their entrails removed, Jael would be having a lengthy discussion with you to ensure that you were at peace with your decision."

"I am at peace," Jodathyn said. He turned back to the open doorway. "It's just …"

"It's a heavy burden, handing down a death sentence," Odelle said.

"I'm a bit disappointed," Deovyn muttered.

Jodathyn eyes flicked back towards Mandros. "Hush, Deo. Well done, *mynrell*. I am pleased," Mandros said.

"I'll let you eat the next lot, Deovyn," Jodathyn replied.

Kieryn clapped Jodathyn on the back, turning so that they were facing the forgotten crowd. "Tonight, friends, we celebrate not only a victory, but a wise new prince of the realm and a royal courting. Let the wine flow, just for tonight."

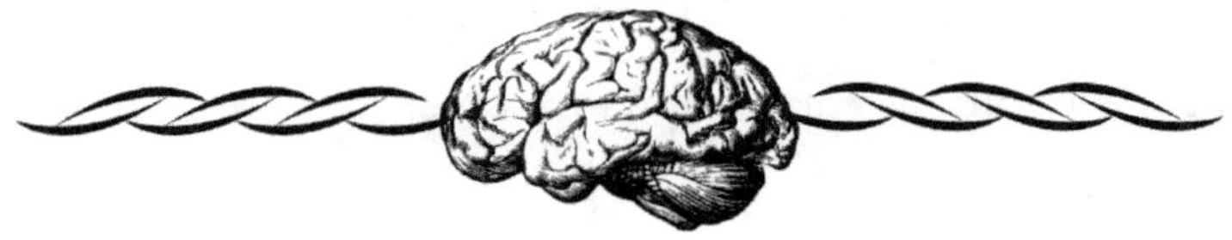

Chapter Eighteen
Will

The Citadel of Pallaryn

Centring his power, as Roane had attempted to teach him, Will felt the gentle presence of Tornyth under Jodathyn's thoughts. How he had never sensed this before was beyond him. He sidled a few steps closer, his eyes trained upon Jodathyn's beaming smile. Underneath that smile were feelings of hope and anxiety mixed with his dragon's warm glow of contentment.

Jodathyn had certainly grown. Will wondered if the newly proclaimed Prince of the Realm knew how much he had changed.

"He's always wanted this," a blond farmer on his right-hand side said. The man turned to him with a pained smile. "Ruevyn Kelvie. We've not met formally."

"Yes," Will replied. He kept a straight face as he felt a strong wave of jealousy and grief washing over Ruevyn. The image of a young woman with flour in her dark hair appeared in his mind eye. He saw the moment of her death, the anguish and crushing guilt that was on this man's shoulders. "A childhood friend of Jodathyn. I know who you are."

"I feel a royal wedding coming on!" Guardsman Carew cried, joining them, pushing a goblet into Will's hand. The young guardsman seemed to be already deep into his cups. Captain Tiernan was eyeing his son with a frown on his face.

"Don't you think you should slow down, Carew?" Will asked. "The night is young."

"And you're all beautiful." Carew saluted and sloshed his cup.

To the side, Ruevyn shifted.

"Ruevyn, this is Carew."

"We've met!" Carew cried. "He don't like me much after I arrested him in Habron."

Ruevyn curled his lip at Carew, turning his shoulders away. Getting the message that his presence was unwanted, Carew took a swig of his drink and ambled away. "Lady Fy! A dance!"

Ruevyn growled under his breath.

"He's not that bad once you get to know him," Will said.

Ruevyn rolled his eyes and searched for Jodathyn in the crowd. "I should be happy for him."

"You are," Will said, passing his unwanted wine to a passerby. His head still thrummed with the thoughts of the dying. Alcohol would not help his headache tonight. "Your grief is stopping you from expressing it."

Looking angry with himself, Ruevyn glared at him.

Will shrugged. "I can read minds."

Ruevyn swore.

"You should tell Jodathyn about Elyssa."

"A truth." Will had been so caught up reading Ruevyn's emotions that he didn't notice Fydellah's presence.

"I wish you'd stop doing that." Ruevyn did not look impressed. "She's dead. There's nothing to be done about it. I don't want, nor do I need, Jodathyn's pity."

The farmer gave them both one last parting stare and stormed off. His footsteps were hurried, his head down as he tried to plough through the milling people. Unfortunately, this meant he didn't see Jodathyn until he ran into him.

"Oh no," Fydellah moaned.

Face lighting up to see his friend, Jodathyn gestured for Ruevyn to join him. The crestfallen look of hurt that crossed Jodathyn's face as his overtures were rejected was hard to watch. No doubt he was trying to figure out what he did wrong as he watched Ruevyn retreat. His hand went to the gold ring around his finger and fidgeted.

Glancing at the gold ring on Jodathyn's finger, Fydellah scowled. It would be easy to interpret her expression for one of displeasure, but there was another stronger emotion she was feeling.

Concern. She was worried about the attack that Jodathyn had endured during the war council. She was unbelieving that a little piece of gold might be sufficient protection. She swore to herself to keep an eye on him.

Will straightened his shoulders and strode towards Jodathyn. When he was close enough, he touched his sleeve. He watched the new prince's face split into a grin at seeing him.

"Will! Good. I'm glad to see you well."

"Your Highness, congratulations."

Jodathyn blinked at him, looking bewildered.

"Don't tell me I'm the first one to use your title? For shame, ladies and gents!" Will raised his voice, laughing as those nearby yelled a chorus of cheers. Leaning his head closer to Jodathyn, Will continued, "It'll take time to get used to the new title."

Will took a step closer, and Jodathyn inclined his head to listen. "He needs some time. He's hurting."

"Of course," Jodathyn whispered. "He had a girl in Androssah he had to leave behind ... We could find her."

"Jod, you won't find her," Will said.

"What do you—"

"Dead."

"*Dead*?"

"Murdered," Will said. "I saw it in his mind."

Jodathyn's face paled. "What do I do?"

"Let him grieve," Will replied. His heart felt heavy. "I'll let Jael know ... He's already been speaking with him. Rue isn't alone."

"Thank you, Will."

Jodathyn's attention was soon swept up by the other onlookers. Soon he was manoeuvred away in a sea of well-wishers. Will watched for a little while, knowing that Jodathyn ached for his friend. Then as the press of human bodies and thoughts became too much, he turned and left the audience chamber.

Without conscious thought, Will's feet took him from the palace and into the citadel. In the dark it was eerily quiet, and he felt like an intruder as he walked the streets he knew so well.

When he first arrived in the citadel, Will hated the bustle, the press of human bodies and the smells. Living with his elder brother Tomas and being used to cheat the wealthy in the gambling houses, he grew to hate the city more.

It changed the morning he was saved by Kieryn Pallarus. He had been willing to give up. The king had other ideas.

His role as spy may have started out as a convenience for the monarch, but over time he had earned the king's respect. His skills were unparalleled.

The king was not a stupid man. He had known that Will had his own side projects. But he never made a move to stop him. The king had trusted him to have his own secrets. And for that Will was grateful.

Pallaryn was his playground. Once Will had been sure of his protection in the king's shadow, he began to defy his brother. If he was honest with himself, he started freeing slaves and helping the destitute to cause his brother difficulties.

The people, the lowborns and the downtrodden, stole Will's heart. He began to work for them even if it did not negatively impact his brother. His purpose had morphed from revenge into something more. Tomas was no longer in control of his thoughts and of his mind.

Pallaryn was his.

Before long, Will found himself in front of one of the many fountains in the middle of a meeting square. As a child he had fantasised about dancing in a fountain. Now, the city was abandoned. He was alone. No one would be here to see him. He wandered up to the steps and pulled his shirt over his head.

He tugged at his boots, pulling them from his feet, and threw them to the side. In only his trousers, he swung his legs over the side and slid into the water.

Gooseflesh rose to his skin. He cupped the water in his hands and splashed it over his shoulder.

He bent to drink the water and washed his face, running his hands through his short, tight curls. He had the wild thought that he needed soap and a sudden desire to feel clean.

Plunging his hands into the water, Will attempted to scrub under his nails. His movements started gentle but turned frantic. Despite his gifting, he hadn't been prepared to drive his sword through the bellies of his fellow countrymen and hear their desperate last thoughts.

In truth, their dying thoughts echoed the same themes as the men he fought beside. It was the same for them all. They thought of families, of their children and of unfulfilled dreams.

He was alone now, but their thoughts remained. The weight of the dead and dying's most intimate thoughts pulled him into depression's dark embrace.

Will pressed his fingernails into the soft skin of his palm. He grinned, relishing the feeling of pain. Pain was his friend, his escape of the accusations of dying men.

"Calm down, *vehyl*. Human skin is delicate."

Startled, Will jolted back to reality and looked for the speaker. Normally he heard people's thoughts before they reached him. It was unusual that he would be found unaware of someone's presence. He decided he didn't like being taken off guard.

"Pain is not your friend."

Brushing the water out of his eyes, Will peered up into the glowing amber eyes of Roane. He felt a blush sweep over him. How crazed must he have been that the giant beast was able to approach him without him hearing.

"That's it, calm down," Roane murmured.

"I can go, Lord Roane, if you wish."

"You're not disturbing me, Willyrd," Roane replied.

Will grimaced. Roane had insisted on calling him by his full name. It was a dragon thing, he decided. A dragon always used the proper names for people and animals. To them it was a matter of respect.

"Mandros told me where I might find you tonight."

"The green dragon was watching me in his visions?"

Roane shrugged. "We like to keep an eye on *vehyl* that interest us."

"And I interest you?"

"We are alone, just as Mandros said. It will make this easier." Will noticed that Roane hadn't answered the question. That was something else dragons were fond of. Avoiding questions.

"What easier?"

"You need to relax, Willyrd. I'm not here to hurt you."

Will eyed the olive-green dragon speculatively. "I know you can read my mind."

"Tell me, what has you so defensive?"

"You're testing me."

"Perhaps."

"I am Will, not Willyrd."

"Perhaps you are wiser than I, *vehyl*." Roane tilted his head, flashing his fangs as he grinned. He was looking at Will as if he had done some great feat. "Your true name is not a label someone has given you, but the label you give yourself."

Will took an uncertain step back. "You're trying to teach me something."

"Your human *aluel* and *lullah* disgraced themselves. Your *sudunyn* too. You're not what they say. Only you, Will Hartcurt, get to decide what type of man and dragon you are."

Will frowned. "Lord Roane," he said, "I think I would know if I was a dragon."

Roane stretched out his neck and breathed into the water, which bubbled. The temperature rose to a pleasant warmness. Will longed to sink down and let the world melt away into nothingness.

"There, warm water. Sit, relax. Let us celebrate together."

Will let his knees bend and let the water lap around him. It seemed ridiculous that he would bathe in warm water while the city lay silent and desolate.

"It won't remain desolate for long."

The warm water was absolutely wonderful. Will sunk further in so that his shoulders were covered. He decided he could stay there all night. All he needed was a bar of soap. He closed his eyes and let his mind drift away.

"Why do I feel that you have an ulterior motive for doing this, dragon?" Will asked. He must have laid there for over an hour, soaking in the stillness. He cracked his eye open; the dragon hadn't moved.

"Because I do have an ulterior motive."

Will's eyes sprung open.

"Oh, relax. If I was tenderising you for a meal, I would have eaten you by now. I brought you a cloth to dry yourself."

Roane held up a large rectangular piece of material. Peering at it in the dim light, Will realised it was a bedsheet.

"I'm out of practice with human habits," Roane said. "I am almost over three thousand summers."

Reluctantly, Will stood and left the warm water of the fountain. He took the sheet from Roane's claw, rubbing his skin dry. Instead of getting dressed, he wrapped himself in the sheet and looked up at the dragon. The gouged scars along his face looked stark in the night.

"I'm guessing you wanted to talk to me, Lord Roane. Why not talk?"

"You are ready," Roane rumbled. "Tell me, are you sleepy, little *vehyl*?"

Will found that yes, he was exhausted. He would like nothing more than to lie down somewhere comfortable and sleep. The conspiracy unfolding in Pallaryn had been enough to drive him to madness. He hadn't slept well in days.

"Come, my side is warm. I'll guard your thoughts tonight."

"You didn't answer my question," Will said, stepping up to Roane's side. "Am I to assume you have come just to put me to sleep?"

"Well, yes, I guess I'm putting you to bed, *mynrell*. Aren't you tired? Didn't the warm water trick work?"

Will blinked and decided to succumb to the dragon's invitation. He knew Roane; the old dragon could be trusted. And if it meant he could sleep away from human thoughts, then so be it.

Will was warm and safe. He blinked his eyes open, realising that his mind was still, devoid of others' intruding thoughts. It seemed foreign to be alone in his own head. He stretched and yawned, remembering the strange interaction he had with Roane last night.

He was tucked up close to the softer underbelly of the ancient dragon. Roane seemed to be asleep. The deep, rhythmic breathing beside him was comforting. How had the dragon's snoring not woken him earlier?

Lazily he stretched out, startled to find his arms were replaced by long, dark blue appendages. Long claws shone like silver daggers at the end of his fingers. The act of stretching unfurled large, leathery wings, which bumped Roane.

"Welcome, Rigyl."

"This is impossible!" dragon Will cried. He struggled to his clawed feet and stared Roane full in the face. "What have you done to me?"

"Come now, you saw Jodathyn's dragon, and you must be aware of the one they call Orion and his dragon."

"No, no, no, no, no ..."

"Rigyl, you were ready. And no one wants another unfortunate manifestation in a battle. This way was gentle."

"I'm not a dragon."

Roane shook his head. "Why should your dragon remain imprisoned?"

"How long has it been in me?"

"Since your birth, *mynrell*. You were born to become Rigyl. Calm down. You're the last to awaken this morning, sleepy scales. Time to take flight."

"Fly?" dragon Will cried. "You want me to *fly*?"

CHAPTER NINETEEN
Fydellah
The Citadel of Pallaryn

Fydellah found that she was well equipped to mingle with both high-borns and lowborns. Born into one of the most ancient and noble houses of Myryn, she had started training in her infancy. For centuries, her mother's family had studied the ancient texts hidden in the great libraries of the island. As her mother's daughter, it had been expected her life would be devoted to preserving the history of Rama. It had been birthright and duty.

She hadn't been the most diligent of daughters. She left that to her beautiful, perfect sister. Unhappy with her lot in life, she made friends with the lowborns on the island. At night she would sneak away to gamble and drink. She preferred the lively alehouses to the drudgery of her mother's halls.

She briefly contemplated telling the king who she was and how her sister's jealousy had found her betrayed, bound and sold into slavery. When she had been caged, beaten and starved, she had dreamed of revenge on her sister. But as angry and hurt as she was, she could no longer imagine what life would be like without the friends she had made since escaping.

Fierce Nym spoke her own mind. The silver-haired woman was loyal, tenacious and unapologetic. When he wasn't brooding, Ruevyn was sweet. Honesty ran through the words of whatever Will spoke. It was rare to find a nobleman with such sincerity. And then there was Jodathyn. He had been understanding of her dislike of highborns. His reputation of kindness was well deserved.

Strands of music filtered into her hearing, and she saw the objects of her thoughts. She knew in that moment she had a home in Pallaryn with her friends. Her desire to return to Myryn was gone.

She had the opportunity for a new life, and she wasn't going to let go.

Her feet started taking her towards Jodathyn's group. Et-hir was at his shoulder, listening to Theo strumming his lute. Nym sat beside her brother, watching Carew as he happily chatted and drank.

She would congratulate the happy couple and retire for the night.

It was Carew who spotted her coming over to them first. Rosy-cheeked from his drinking, he thrust a goblet into her hands. "It's all we could find," he said in apology.

Fydellah winced at the volume in which he spoke.

Jodathyn handed his goblet to Et-hir, snatched Carew's cup and sculled the guardsman's drink. Returning the now empty cup to Carew, he clapped him on the back. "I thank you, Carew. The ale is much better than the wine."

The men around him cheered and lifted their own cups in salute.

Fydellah laughed as Carew gawked at Jodathyn, hiccupped and stared into his empty cup.

"It isn't funny, Lady Fy. Now I need to refill it." He ambled away, shaking his cup, unaware that Nym's keen eyes tracked his every movement. Catching Et-hir's eyes, Fydellah hid her smile behind her hand.

Et-hir sampled the wine. She swallowed it, scrunching up her nose. "That's awful. I wonder where they got it from?"

"Not my brother's personal stores," Jodathyn said.

"Maybe one day I'll find my way into your brother's wine," Theo said, strumming his fingers along the strings of his lute. "I have a new chorus ..."

Galgothmeg, Galgothmeg,
You're going to die.
Let me tell you why.

Galgothmeg, Galgothmeg,
You're going to fall.
Don't you hear our call?

"Nothing quite like blasted positivity to bolster your spirits," Nym said, finally looking up at them and releasing Carew from her gaze.

Theo's fingers halted and rested upon the strings of his lute. He glanced at Nym, smirking. "You don't have to sit here and listen to me."

Nym snorted.

"Play a dancing tune," Jodathyn suggested. "I can go and convince a certain guardsman to drag Nym onto the dance floor."

Nym's hard eyes pinned Jodathyn where he stood. "Don't you dare, palace brat."

Jodathyn grinned. "He's quite merry. It wouldn't be difficult to convince him to sweep you off your feet."

"Jodathyn ..." Nym growled.

"Then when the music stops, you kiss him *gentle, soft and sweet*." Jodathyn nodded in Et-hir's direction and winked. "It worked for me."

Et-hir bent and grabbed Nym's hand and despite her small stature was able to pull the reluctant Nym to her feet. "Do you know any Sionian reels, Theo? That'll get us some attention."

Chuckling at the disgruntled expression on Nym's face, Jodathyn watched as Et-hir effortlessly spun Nym about. Theo saluted and attempted to play something that may have sounded Sionian. Et-hir tilted her head back and laughed at Theo's efforts to mimic the fast beats of a Sionian reel while Nym desperately tried to keep up.

A few of the guardsmen stopped what they were doing to clap a rhythm. As Jodathyn had predicted, Carew bounded forward, grasped Nym about the waist and twirled her about. The expression on Nym's face was a cross between furious and delighted.

Fydellah touched Jodathyn's elbow lightly. "I just wanted to say congratulations and good night."

"Goodnight, Lady Fydellah," Jodathyn replied. His grey eyes searched hers. "If you ever feel the need to return home, all you need to do—"

"Jodathyn," Fydellah whispered. "Myryn has no place for me. That old part of me is dead."

Jodathyn's fingers brushed her hand. "Then I pray that you'll find a place worthy of you."

"I already have," Fydellah answered. "Goodnight, Jod."

"Goodnight," Theo echoed. His deft fingers danced across the strings of his lute, the raucous sound of laughter drowning out the sound of the music. The thief didn't mind.

Feeling that her work here was done, Fydellah turned and left the audience chamber before she too was coerced into dancing.

The night air was cool. She walked along the inner courtyards and climbed the great winding stairs upwards, towards the highest points of the palace walls. She had heard the dragons talking about communing with the Wind Song.

When she reached the highest point of the palace walls, she buried the instinct to open her arms up to the cool breath of wind. She was just a human woman. The wind could not whisper sweet nothings to her.

Unclenching her fists, she closed her eyes and breathed in deeply.

"Tell me, *vehyl*, do you hear the promises the wind sighs tonight?"

"I hear nothing, Great Lady."

Sidrah, the large black female dragon who had taken a special liking to Jodathyn, was crouched on the wall. Her obsidian scales camouflaged her in the night.

"Nothing?" Sidrah repeated. "A lie."

"Promises are nothing but spoken disappointments." Fydellah felt the twinge of annoyance being trapped in a lie. She knew of her untruth even as she spoke it. She felt the sharp prickles of deceit the moment she parted her lips to reply. She didn't need a nosy dragon to tell her.

"Ah, you're afraid of disappointment."

"It's merely experience."

"Yes, I can see you have had *years* of experience."

"Don't mock me, dragon," Fydellah gritted. "I'm not in the mood for mind games."

Sidrah lowered her head. "Who says I'm playing?"

"Everyone is playing a role."

"A rather cynical way to look at it." Sidrah raised her head again, and Fydellah couldn't help to admire her crown of horns.

"Jodathyn seems happy tonight."

Sidrah cocked her head to the side. So even though the dragon didn't answer, Fydellah knew she was listening.

"You're fond of him."

"He is family," Sidrah replied. "He reminds me of Rhox and one of my own sons."

"Time has not changed the Pallarus boys?"

Sidrah snorted. "Indeed not. I think seeing Jodathyn in the flesh was like a fang in Zapyr's side. It hurt him to remember what he lost. Would you fly with me, *vehyl*?"

"You want me to climb onto your back?" Fydellah asked. "I didn't think a dragon would invite a human up unless it was necessary."

Sidrah swayed her head side to side. "Shows you exactly how much you know about dragons."

"I studied at the Great Libraries on Myryn," Fydellah said. "I have read plenty about dragons."

"Yet you know very little," Sidrah replied, unconcerned. "Let me show you through experience, not a dusty scroll."

Fydellah considered the offer. How often did one get an invitation from a dragon? She stepped forward, and Sidrah grasped her about the middle and placed her on her back. Sidrah lurched forward, and Fydellah held on awkwardly, holding her breath as the black dragon launched herself into the sky.

When they had flown into Pallaryn to liberate the city, Fydellah had been too engrossed with the sounds and smells of battle. She hadn't dared looked down at the citadel she thought she loathed.

When Will had rescued her from the guild, she had sworn she would never willingly return to Pallaryn. In her mind, it was a cruel and twisted place. But since then, she had returned twice of her own volition. Once to try and tell the king where Jodathyn was and again on the back of the dragon.

Now she looked at the citadel as if for the first time. Evil and pain did exist in Pallaryn's streets, but there had also been goodness. People made their homes and lives here. There was trade and life. Good people made communities. She witnessed the comradery of the King's Guard. She experienced the kindness of other highborns such as Will, Jodathyn and even their king.

Pallaryn was now smoking and dark. The time would come to rebuild her, starting from the foundations, removing the chokehold of the guild and many of the great houses. Ramians would rise from the ashes, stronger than ever.

She looked down closely. Under them, she caught sight of a man in a fountain. The olive-green dragon was with him. She couldn't be sure, but she thought it might be Will.

"Leave them to their own time," Sidrah rumbled before Fydellah could speak. "It's your time now."

"What do you mean, my time?" Fydellah asked.

"You're ready."

"Do you dragons always speak in riddles?"

"Yes," Sidrah answered. "It infuriates the *vehyl*."

"Where are you taking me?"

"You're not yet comfortable in the citadel. It's best done somewhere you're at peace."

"Again, that tells me very little."

Sidrah harrumphed. "Tornyth hid some *vehyl* young. I'm going to find them in the morning. It'll be good practice."

"Good practice for what?"

"Patience."

Fydellah was a little shocked when Sidrah landed among the trees of the King's Orchard. The black dragon lay upon the grass and let her dismount. When her feet hit the ground, Fydellah turned around.

Growing up on the Isle of Myryn, she had played in the forests at night. Her mother hadn't been particularly attentive, and she had been at home among the trees. There were no predators on the island, just hundreds of birds. She had spent many countless hours exploring her homeland. In the orchard, she could pretend she was back home.

"Are we camping under the stars tonight?"

"The stars make good company." Sidrah watched her with glowing amber eyes as she looked for somewhere comfortable to lie down. She found a place where grass was spongy, soft and flat.

"No," Sidrah said. The black dragon lifted her head, and her nostrils flared. "That's not a place for you."

"Why not?"

"I can sense malevolence there. Come, lie down at my side."

"Malevolence?" Fydellah scoffed. "You're doing it again, dragon."

"Come here, Fydellah. Trust me when I say the ground swallowed up a *rokun* here. His last breath was crushed out of him. A terrible but necessary death," Sidrah said sternly. "Are you going to be a troublesome hatchling? I don't wish to quarrel."

Exhaling, Fydellah settled herself down next to Sidrah. She felt her breathing relax as she slipped into sleep.

"Is that another dragon?"

Fydellah felt a small finger poke the sensitive skin of her nostrils. Annoyed that someone had disturbed her slumber, she snuffled and attempted to roll over.

"This is my hatchling, Vydris."

"She's really pretty."

"She doesn't look like a baby dragon. Did you lay an egg?"

"No, Ramian dragons are not hatched from eggs. Vydris is a fully grown dragon."

"Then why call her a hatchling?"

"If she didn't come from an egg, where did she come from?"

Fydellah sneezed as another finger found its way into her nose. She lifted her head only to find herself surrounded by half a dozen children. She wriggled back in alarm.

"Vydris hatched from her human soul."

Cocking her head to the side, Fydellah looked towards Sidrah, who smirked at her. "Good morning, Vydris Truth-Seeker."

"I'm a ..."

"Dragon." A little girl with large brown eyes finished for her. "Your mama said you were originally born on an island and that's how you got your scales the colour of sand."

Fydellah looked down at herself. She had a long, slender reptilian body covered in scales of pale yellow. In wonder, she looked to her claws, which were sharp and the colour of stone.

Sidrah looked smugly on. "Your first task, Vydris, is to fly the *vehyl* children safely back to Pallaryn without dropping one."

"You want me to fly?"

"The mother dragon gave you wings, did she not?"

"You want me to *fly*? With wriggling little children?"

Sidrah turned her head towards the children. Who all looked to Fydellah with wide, hopeful eyes. All except a little lad with mousy brown hair and angry blue eyes.

"Up you go."

The children didn't need to be told twice. At Sidrah's invitation, they rushed forward, pushing and shoving to get closer to the dragon who was once Fydellah. Sidrah shushed them and one by one placed the children carefully along the newly awakened Vydris' spine. Terrified that one of the children might fall off, Vydris tensed her muscles and stayed perfectly still. Soon the last child was left, the defiant little boy.

"I want to kill Kamoore," the boy said, stomping his feet. "If he's not dead, I want to do it."

"Feisty little thing," Sidrah murmured. "It's time to behave yourself. What would your mama think?"

"She's gone. The ghost dragons took her to the Otherworld."

Sidrah seemed to consider the boy's words. "Well, little one, let's get you back to the citadel and find you somewhere safe to stay."

"Ma's sister is a laundry maid in the lower town," the boy said. "I was trying to find her."

Feeling sorry for the feisty little fella, it was Vydris who replied, "When the danger has passed, someone will help you find your aunt."

Sidrah seemed pleased by the direction of the conversation. "When you are ready, Vydris, copy, follow, learn."

Vydris had never been so terrified in her life.

Flying with passengers wasn't as scary as Vydris had feared. She watched Sidrah from the ground for what seemed like ages. Then her legs bent of their own will, and she joined the black dragon in the air. The children upon her back squealed. It took a few seconds for her to realise they were crying out in delight and not in fear.

She flew cautiously and carefully. And was relieved to see the walls of Pallaryn looming ahead of her. Keeping her eye on the target, she never wavered.

A mile out from the palace walls, the children cried out again. A familiar white dragon flew towards them.

"It's the white one who saved us from the ghost dragons!"

"His name is Tornyth, Winter's Dragon. He's my brother," Sidrah told the children.

"He's so pretty." A little girl sighed.

"Don't tell a male dragon he's pretty," Sidrah warned. "Males can be so vain."

"You can tell me I'm pretty," Vydris said.

The little girl patted her scales. "You are. Your scales are like warm butter on bread."

"Lealah!"

"What? I really like buttery, warm bread."

"Sidrah!" Tornyth cried. His silver orbs glanced over Vydris in curiosity. "I've been looking everywhere for you. I can't find *Aluel*."

"*Aluel* had his own mission last night. Tell me, do you recognise my new *mynrell*?"

Tornyth's wings fluttered in excitement. "*Fy*? Is that you? I would know those big brown eyes anywhere."

"Can we get our claws on the ground?" Vydris gritted out. "What if I drop one?"

Sidrah laughed and had mercy. They landed on the palace walls.

The children tumbled from Vydris' back, eager to greet Tornyth, who happily snuffed each of the children. Little hands patted his scales and rubbed his belly, and Tornyth closed his eyes, basking in their attention.

"Is Kamoore dead?" the defiant boy demanded. He stood apart from the others.

"I think you'll find that a man like Kamoore's fate is far from pleasant," Tornyth rumbled.

"Is he gone?"

"He's gone," Sidrah replied.

"Well, what are we going to do now? Mama is gone." One of the little girls scrubbed at her eyes.

"Hush now." Tornyth manifested back to Jodathyn and drew her close to his side. "We'll find you somewhere safe to stay in the palace."

"You can do that?" Fydellah asked.

Jodathyn lifted his chin. "I'm a prince now. There's no better use of my power."

A dragon crowing with delight ruined their moment of peace. From the ground below, Deovyn, the dragon Vydris had labelled as rough and outgoing, barrelled upwards. Close on his tail was a blue-grey dragon.

Vydris lowered her belly to the ground as the two males sped past.

"Zapyr, your son is a beast!" Deovyn cried into the wind. "He flies like a maniac."

The blue-grey dragon laughed and lunged, catching Deovyn's tail with his teeth. Deovyn cried in shock and delight.

The heavy thump of the stern gold dragon turned Vydris' attention from the pair.

"Again, congratulations, *sudunyn*. It's a boy."

The gold dragon smirked at Sidrah. "Likewise, *sudunah*. I see you have a female fledgling."

"How did Roane go last night?"

"He has a brand new, very handsome, midnight-blue son who is snoozing the day away."

"You planned this," Vydris said, raising her head to glare at the older dragons. "You ambushed us last night and planned the whole scenario out."

Zapyr looked at her and blinked, as if he was astounded by her anger. "You did not wake screaming with rage and power, Vydris. Ayrdonyth nearly died under my claws."

"He's looking good this morning," Sidrah murmured, watching him.

"He's flying well," Jodathyn said. "He's keeping up with Deovyn."

Zapyr watched the two dragons a moment longer before rounding onto Sidrah. "I need you to speak with Rhox."

"He's been through a lot, Zapyr," Sidrah replied. "He needs some time to adjust."

"He can't fly, Sidrah," Zapyr growled. "It's enough to drive a grown dragon mad."

"He can't fly *without pain*," Sidrah continued. "It's different. He needs to fight for his wings. Sitting in a lonely courtyard, defeated with his tail between his legs, won't help the healing process."

"I would give him all my strength."

"Because you're a good father, despite what you've been telling yourself these last thousand years," Jodathyn said, interjecting himself into the conversation.

Zapyr harrumphed.

Sidrah sighed heavily. "Very well, Aunt Sidrah will have a word with Rhox. Don't be surprised if he gets his scales bent out of shape. He was almost grown and as tenacious as his regal father."

"Or I could try. I haven't formally met Rhox, and I would like to help."

Vydris thought that Jodathyn's offer would be rejected. But Zapyr stared down at Jodathyn, his gaze contemplative. "Thank you, *sudunyn*," he rumbled, taking one last assessing gaze over Vydris before turning his back to fly away.

Sidrah nodded her head gravely. "Come, Vydris. I'm not finished with you quite yet."

Chapter Twenty

Jodathyn

The Citadel of Pallaryn

Jodathyn left the palace walls, a trail of children following him. He was determined to find a place for each of them to stay.

In one of the inner courtyards, he happened upon Kieryn and Carvelle. Noticing the king's bemused expression, he swept into a deep bow. The children crowded behind him. Little hands touched his back as they tried to use him to shield themselves from the sight of their High King.

Carvelle stepped away from his father's side to openly stare at the other children. "What do you mean to do with them, Uncle?"

Jodathyn licked his lips, his eyes trained upon Kieryn's face. "I was hoping, with Your Majesty's permission, to harbour the children in the palace until other arrangements could be made."

"It does not look like you were asking for permission, brother."

"I guess I wasn't," Jodathyn replied, standing. "The palace is the securest building in Pallaryn."

"Indeed."

"They could stay in my rooms. They're large and I've toys and books, and we know my rooms are safe." Carvelle nodded sagely, lifting his hand to beckon to a little girl. "Come, I have another little girl who is my companion."

"That's very generous of you, my son, but—"

Carvelle waggled his fingers again in invitation. He grinned up at his father. "Papa is not as scary as he would like to think. Come, come."

Kieryn sighed dramatically. "Very well."

One by one the children left Jodathyn's side to follow Carvelle, who skipped ahead of them, looking quite pleased with himself. The last to leave him was the boy with the brown curls and the surly attitude.

"I won't rest until Kamoore is brought to justice," he said as he stepped from Jodathyn's side.

"Boy," Jodathyn called after him. "Don't focus so much on Kamoore that you forget to live the life you want."

The boy turned on his heel. "My name is Myrus."

Jodathyn fought the urge to smile at him. Pride shone in Myrus' eyes. "Someone very wise once told me not to allow my anger to rule me, Myrus. Can I trust you to look after the others while I'm not in Pallaryn?"

Drawing himself to his full height, Myrus nodded, looking solemn and determined. Just as he turned to run after Carvelle and the other children, his stomach rumbled loudly. His hand flew to his stomach, his cheeks reddening.

"Ask that son of mine to have food brought to you," Kieryn said. "Go now."

"Your Majesty." Myrus fumbled into a bow and scampered away.

Kieryn watched his son and the children disappear from view. He chuckled and shook his head. "It seems I have two dragons in my palace that don't worry about what I think," Kieryn said. He crossed the distance that separated them and lay his hand on Jodathyn's shoulder. "Carvelle admires you. He told me this morning that he wants to be your attendant on your wedding day."

"Sire?" It was by no means unheard of for a royalborn to be the attendant of honour in a royal wedding. But Carvelle outranked Jodathyn. That along with his age might raise some eyebrows.

"I told him you'll marry when you're ready and he's not to pester you," Kieryn said. "He's quite impatient to call Et-hir his aunt and for you to give him a cousin."

Jodathyn blanched, and Kieryn patted his shoulder.

"There's no rush, brother. I must go. There are many pressing matters I need to see to." Kieryn swept his gaze over the walls of the palace, nodded curtly and strode away.

"And I need to find Rhox."

Jodathyn found Rhox curled up in an abandoned palace courtyard. The bronze dragon's snout was raised to the sky as he watched Ayrdonyth and Deovyn flying in the sky above him.

The bronze dragon sighed heavily, hunching his shoulders. He was the very picture of dejection. Slowly the bronze dragon unfurled his damaged wings to catch a gentle breeze.

Deciding it was best to approach Rhox in dragon form, Jodathyn manifested and slipped into the courtyard. Moving stealthily in his reptilian body was not an easy task. When his tail whacked an archway, he gave up hopes of subterfuge.

Rhox didn't move at the sound of his blunder.

"Hello," he called. "I'm Tornyth."

Rhox slowly opened one eye. "I know who you are. I'm Rhox the Illusionist."

Tornyth sidled closer. "Your gifting was quite impressive."

Rhox huffed. "I can't fly. I can't stand the way *Aluel* looks at me as if I'm some pathetic, helpless little ... A downed dragon is a dead dragon. They sent you to talk to me."

"No ... well, yes," Tornyth replied. He shifted from side to side as Rhox speared him with a furious glare and rumbled. "Zapyr is worried ... and Sidrah says you can fly."

"I fly as well as a limp lizard. You should have left me to die. I'm now a worthless battle dragon." Rhox rounded onto Tornyth, snapping his jaws.

"I know it hurts," Tornyth whispered, refusing to move a muscle in the wake of Rhox's anger.

"You know nothing of suffering. I was born with battle-fire, and now my wings are clipped," Rhox snarled. "Go away!"

Tornyth took a few steps forward and lay on his belly so that he was now snout to snout with Rhox. "We don't have to talk. I can keep you company."

"I don't feel like company." Rhox lifted his snout up to watch Deovyn and Ayrdonyth, growling.

"Well, I know suffering, and there's one thing that has got me through it all ... and it's the people who believed in me and fought at my side even when I wanted to give up."

"I thought you said we didn't have to talk. Your empty words don't help me. *Aluel* is being insufferable."

"He doesn't want to see you hurt," Tornyth replied. "He's scared too."

"Nothing scares my *aluel*."

"He's scared," Tornyth said. "So there's one thing for it."

"And that is?"

"Fight for it. Wings are muscles." One way or another, Tornyth was determined to get Rhox into the sky again. "Humans can learn to get along with hurt limbs. I'm sure we can learn to get you into the sky."

"I'll never fly well."

"Rhox," Tornyth replied. "A day ago, you had spent over a thousand years under the power of the Grey Shadow. A day ago, it would have been said to be impossible to help you. Yet here you are."

"What would you have me do?"

"Stretch out your wings and strengthen them, to start," Tornyth said.

"I'll look like a fool." Rhox's eyes slid back to the sky, his eyes lingering on Ayrdonyth. "That used to be me. The world has changed."

"I'll work alongside you."

Sardonic eyes turned to looked Tornyth up and down, and for the first time Tornyth heard Rhox's laugh. "Do you really think you can keep up with a battle dragon?"

If dragons could sweat, Tornyth was sure he would be covered in a river of it. Once Rhox had started to exercise his wings, he became fiercely focused on continuing. The bronze dragon had stamina and a will of steel.

Unable to keep up with him, Tornyth stopped and manifested back into his human self. He lay on the gritty stones and watched the grim determination on Rhox's face. Each repetition of movement was painful. Jodathyn could see it in the bronze dragon's expression.

"I think that's enough for today," Jodathyn muttered.

"No. Not yet."

Jodathyn grunted and closed his eyes, ignoring the pull and the burn in his muscles. Dragons were stubborn, he decided. Rhox would not stop until he was near collapse. Now that he had started, he wasn't going to admit defeat. There wouldn't be telling him otherwise. The frenzy of activity was better than Rhox lying in a sad lump. Now the bronze dragon was ready to fight for what he wanted.

Whether it was the strain of the last few weeks or he had become accustomed to sleeping in awful places, Jodathyn fell asleep on the stones of the courtyard. He was awoken by Carvelle, who decided to sit on his stomach and jump up and down. Groaning, Jodathyn clasped Carvelle around the waist and pulled him off so that he could sit up.

Rhox was still pumping his wings up and down.

Carvelle stared at him. "Time to stop, bronze boy."

Rhox's wings faltered, and he stared down at the child who addressed him. He flared his nostrils and glared.

"A smart warrior knows when to rest," Jodathyn said. "Stop before you injure yourself."

"You might be the same age as uncle," Carvelle said. "And you might be sad and lonely, but I know you've been very rude to him."

Rhox blinked, staring down at the prince. Jodathyn's hand snuck around Carvelle's waist, preparing to get in between them if he needed to. Huffing, Rhox tucked his tired wings close to his body.

"Carvelle ..." The last thing Jodathyn wanted was Carvelle defending him from another dragon.

"He's right, I have been awful since coming back to myself," Rhox admitted. "And I am sorry I have been incredibly rude."

Carvelle nodded and flounced away. "That wasn't so hard now, was it?"

In the days following the battle, the palace became a sanctuary for anyone in need. During the dragon battle, some of the citizens had stayed holed up in their homes. After the fighting had finished, Kieryn sent out his men to coax terrified people from their hiding places. Guardsman Lyntton took charge of completing a census to calculate the remaining people. He was also responsible for locating the dead and ensuring they were treated well.

Many citizens who had been able to escape returned. Hope of finding their missing loved ones had the people returning in droves. It broke Jodathyn's heart, hearing stories of mothers looking for their children.

Et-hir threw herself into sorting out rationing issues. Food was scarce. Kieryn had commanded that the wealthy share their food with the vulnerable, keeping only what they needed for themselves.

While the population of Pallaryn had drastically fallen, the outer courtyards were a constant hive of activity as Et-hir dealt with the distribution of goods and disgruntled city folk.

Jodathyn spent his mornings with Rhox and Ayrdonyth. The bronze dragon was regaining strength and mobility with his wings. When Zapyr wasn't in Pallaryn, Rhox would take to the skies.

After lunch, he took to teaching Myrus how to read and write. The boy had come to him the day after the battle, formally requesting to become Jodathyn's manservant.

"You have no attendants," Myrus had said, straightening his jerkin. "I'd like to take that position."

Jodathyn had been unsure of what to make of such a request. "Why serve me? Isn't there something more you want?"

Myrus licked his lips and shifted nervously. "By the time I'm grown, I've the chance to be your chief servant, like Master Manideep. The pay is excellent, I could afford to have a family one day, and I know you won't mistreat me."

So Jodathyn told him once the realm was safe and it was time for him to appoint servants, he would consider him. He had then taken to teaching him and had learned the boy was now an orphan. His aunt was still missing.

Jodathyn considered the issue that was Myrus as he strode through the corridors. He didn't let his footsteps linger and let the haunted minor nobles, servants and common people part before him. Murmurs of 'Your Highness' followed him, but he kept his chin up high and didn't let his discomfort show. In the past, it was rare for him to be shown respect.

Passing a woman who may have been a kitchen hand, he plucked an apple from her basket. She paused to watch him toss it in the air and catch it in his hand.

"Your Highness." She curtsied before him, her eyes curiously taking him in as if his dragon might burst forth and devour her. "Is there anything I can do for you?"

"I like the respect," Tornyth whispered, *"but not the fear."*

"Do you suppose I have changed?" Jodathyn asked.

The woman rose slowly.

"She thinks us a predator to be wary of."

"I think you are very much changed, Your Highness."

Jodathyn considered her words. "Yes, my adventure has taught me a great deal of things," he agreed. "Flying builds one's appetite. I tell you, woman, I have missed home and the fruit bowl dear Donatein kept by my desk."

Making a show of biting into the firm flesh of the apple, Jodathyn hummed in appreciation for the sweet juice. It wasn't enough to satisfy his dragon. His appetite was growing, but it seemed to be unfair for him to complain about hunger when everyone else was suffering.

"Your Highness!" Myrus ran towards him, waving a parchment above his head. The woman smiled, watching him as he came to a skidding halt just before reaching Jodathyn. Jodathyn took the opportunity to grab an extra apple from underneath the woman's nose. He winked at Myrus and tucked his extra prize into his jerkin.

"I have a message."

"I can see that. Open it and read it to me, please." Knowing that Jodathyn was teaching the boy to read, Kieryn had begun to pen him simple messages so Myrus might practice his reading.

Myrus' nose wrinkled, but he did as he was told. He shook out the parchment and looked pointedly to the woman with the apples.

"Please excuse us," Jodathyn said. With a dip of the head, he stepped past her and sauntered down the corridors. Myrus jogged to catch up. "What words or letters can you recognise?"

"The king's handwriting is awfully neat," Myrus said. "I see 'to' and 'go'. The first word starts with P for Pallarus, and there's a place that starts with K and ends in 'ah'."

Jodathyn held out his hand for the missive. It was a one-line sentence. "You are correct. It says, 'Prepare to go to Kudah'. Well done."

Myrus beamed at him. "Why would you be going to Kudah?"

"We have some great lords missing," Jodathyn replied, folding the parchment. "There may be answers from the southern magistrates to give clue what their traitorous lords were up to."

"Is Kamoore still missing?" Myrus frowned, his expression darkened.

"Yes," Jodathyn answered. "But his time is limited. He can't hide forever."

"Galgothmeg is protecting him," Myrus grumbled.

Jodathyn lay a comforting hand on the boy's shoulder and squeezed. "Kamoore has made a poor choice of ally. Galgothmeg is not trustworthy. One day that bumbling, great oaf will reap the fires of retribution on his head ... He will pay. For everything. That I promise you."

CHAPTER TWENTY-ONE

Kamoore

The Citadel of Pallaryn

No one wanted to be dragon food. So when Galgothmeg command-ed him to come to the palace walls during the battle of Pallaryn, dressed in the king's finery, Kamoore obeyed. Filyx, the little red-haired cretin, had rammed the crown of Rama on his head and escorted him to the red dragon by the point of his dagger. When he attempted to escape, the boy had slashed his face, twirling his blade in his nimble fingers.

"Do it again," Filyx said, licking his lips. "Please try to escape."

As soon as it was safe to do so, he would convince the red dragon to eat his servant. There was madness brewing in that boy's mind.

Galgothmeg was waiting for them, serenely watching the pillaging of the great citadel. Filyx urged him to climb upon the red dragon's back with his dagger, laughing manically.

"Why is he coming with us?" Kamoore demanded. The scales along Galgothmeg's back were hideously warm and dry.

"He is a gift for my lord and master," Galgothmeg replied.

When gigantic red wings unfurled and the beast's claws left the ground, Kamoore knew he needed to study the state of the citadel if he was to have any hope of gaining control. Pallaryn had been burning; great clouds of smoke curled in the air. Kamoore sucked in a gasp of surprise. Dozens of dragons had fought with Galgothmeg's Grey Shadows.

Galgothmeg dipped and flew low over the battlefield. Kamoore could smell the arid smoke of the burning city. Opening his maw, Galgothmeg rumbled and spewed forth a jet of fire down upon the people below. Kamoore cried out in outrage, but the red dragon didn't care who was caught in his flames. Friend and foe burned alike.

Behind him, he felt Filyx's grip about his waist tighten; the servant laughed in unadulterated glee at the scourge of Pallaryn.

"This is what you have brought me to Rama for, *rokun*," Galgothmeg said. "Death is my balm and war my masterpiece."

Behind him, Filyx continued to chuckle.

"Human homes are but walls of stones," Galgothmeg continued. He rumbled and exhaled. A jet of fire spewed from his open maw and sprayed the battlefield below once more. "Buildings are but pens for our sheep."

Kamoore practically howled in rage. "You monster."

Amused, Galgothmeg laughed, and Kamoore flattened himself along his spine in order to hold on. "We're both monsters. The only difference is I am the apex predator, and you're prey … a little piggy in a fancy robe."

Gritting his teeth, Kamoore seethed. "I demand …"

Filyx made soft pig noises in his ear. If they weren't flying miles above the ground, he would have beaten the boy for his audacity.

"Be quiet," Galgothmeg said. "Sit there. Let the humans see you, and then we will begin the next phase of the invasion."

"Next phase?" Kamoore asked. "Invasion?"

"You're not very bright," Filyx said. He spoke as if he thought Kamoore was nothing but dust on the bottom of his shoe. "Did you think you knew all the plans of Lord Galgothmeg? Did you think that you could control an Artrothian dragon, one of pure, unpolluted blood?"

"Quiet, humans," Galgothmeg snapped. "I have no issue eating you earlier than I planned."

For a few days, Galgothmeg flew in dizzying circles around Rama. Nights when Galgothmeg landed to rest, the red beast remained stoically awake. Under the black stare of the evil one, Kamoore had trouble sleeping. Filyx, he noticed, was not bothered. The boy was definitely mad.

On the fourth day, Galgothmeg flew east. When they landed, Kamoore dropped to his knees. His trembling fingers reached out to caress the solid land. Filyx dismounted beside him, dusting off his trousers, and brushed his windswept hair back. A wide grin split his freckled face.

Pushing himself up to stand to his full intimidating height, Kamoore looked around. While they were flying, he had estimated that the red dragon had flown them into the great mountains of the Rhson Spine. High in the air, he had caught sight of the remote Lake of Tears. It was clear as the stories led him to believe. He wondered how many living men had seen the lake with their own eyes.

Galgothmeg had landed somewhere in the mountains, and Kamoore was exceedingly glad for his long, warm cloak. He wrapped it around his body, sneering at a shivering Filyx.

"Never mind, milord, I won't be cold for long," the boy said.

Lifting his chin, Kamoore turned away from his wretched servant and studied the sight before him in awe.

Cut into the side of the mountain was a palace. Gigantic pillars carved with dragons, horses and all sorts of beasts were crumbling. They were a testament that this was an ancient place. In all of his studies, he had never heard of this palace. This was a place that was evidence of the greatness and superiority of the human hand.

Galgothmeg's lips peeled back, and the great dragon had the audacity to laugh at him.

"Are you in awe, human?" the red dragon asked.

"Indeed, look what my ancestors—"

"This was not built by human hands," Galgothmeg said. "This was built by an Artrothian *lyron finyr* ... a great dragon lord."

Kamoore frowned at this revelation, barely understanding what Galgothmeg told him.

"This is called the Stronghold," Galgothmeg said. "One time it was used by the *rshon* who hid themselves upon this land. Now my kind has returned to use its lairs. Enter, human."

Growling, Filyx stomped forward and grabbed his upper arm. The boy tightened his grip and pushed him forward. "You heard Lord Galgothmeg."

There was very little that Kamoore could do but listen to the red dragon. His footsteps were hesitant as he moved up the stairs. The dragon lumbered in behind him.

"We'll wait here for the arrival of my lord," Galgothmeg said. "Prepare yourselves."

Kamoore was relieved to find that Galgothmeg was a poor host. He disappeared into the shadows without glancing back at them, leaving him alone with his useless servant. He could hear the sounds of dripping water and went to investigate. He needed something to drink.

It had been a few days, and still Kamoore had not seen any sign of Galgoth-meg. Filyx had also relaxed his guard, which Kamoore took advantage of. He found a source of water, dripping down the stone walls, and he started plotting.

He stumbled around in the dark, knowing that he had the intelligence to work out a way out of the mountain. He walked until he had blisters upon blisters on his feet and his stomach cramped with hunger.

Sighing, he let his knees give way. Determination was a hallmark of a Kamoore. In his youth, he had been quite spindly, and physical pursuits held no interest. His quick tongue and physique had made him a natural target in the tiltyards. While the boys born of inferior stock toiled for their daily bread, he had been free to come and go as he pleased. They resented his freedom. When his father was absent from the family estate, the uneducated, lice-ridden brutes made his life a living nightmare.

An educated man would always win, which was why he never educated his servants. To demonstrate how much power he had, he began to feed his father's swordmaster the names of those who had *not* wronged him. Kamoore knew that when he started reporting younger, smaller boys, his father's man didn't believe him. Not wanting to upset his master, the swordmaster punished the innocent boys. Within a few short seasons, the bullying stopped.

War and bloodshed was not for him. He was more suited to the shadows and pulling of puppet strings. The mere thought of bloody deaths, with all the sweat and grime associated with it, made him feel ill.

Galgothmeg was about to learn that he was a force to reckon with. The red dragon was going to die, and he was going to take control of the Grey Shadows. Mindless dragons to do his bidding would be helpful in tracking down Thylyssa and removing him from the field of play.

Kamoore pushed himself off the wall and kept trudging forwards. It was sometime later that his ears caught a sound. Pausing, he listened, his heart thumping in his ribcage. Running water. Lots of it.

He laughed. Surely if there was a waterfall nearby, the water had to go somewhere. He had done it. He had found the exit.

Rushing forward, he blindly stumbled in the dark. He did not stop until he came to a cavern. A luminous torrent of water rushed from the ceiling, falling into a deep blue pool. He bent down and cupping his hand, drank from the pool. There was something magical about the rushing water. It lit the cavern, and as Kamoore rocked back on his heels, the water renewed his strength.

Laughing in relief, he sat on the wet ground. He was exhausted and weak with hunger. He removed the crown of Rama and studied it in the light of the cavern. Disgusted by the sight of it, he threw it into the deep pool. Let the history of the Pallarus family be lost forever. When he was king, he would have a proper crown made.

Cold and wet, he dug his hands into his pockets and touched a piece of parchment he had forgotten about. Kept prisoner in Kieryn Pallarus' rooms, he had rifled through the king's desk and come upon a journal. He loved the feel of the aged leather and flicked through the pages.

Many of the pages had been illustrated with people and places that were familiar. There was one particular picture that had given him such glee to look upon that he tore it from the journal and stuffed it inside his robes. Hands shaking, he pulled it out from his hiding place and unfolded it so that once more he might look upon the picture of King Hadryn lying face down in a puddle of blood. Remembering how he had been a part of Hadryn's assassination sent a thrill of satisfaction up his spine. All these years, and he had never been discovered. To this day, the country believed that King Hadryn, Otherworlds bless his soul, was killed in a hunting accident. Not even the King's Guard suspected foul play.

He let his eyes wander from the red ink and to the handwriting at the top. *Rokun will kill a king of Pallarus blood.*

Contrary to popular belief, he wasn't an idiot. It hadn't taken him long to deduce that the journal belonged to the woman who had started the downfall of the great and powerful Pallarus dynasty. He chuckled to himself. He had Jodathyn's mother, Consort Ammerie's, journal in his hands.

Tilting his head back, he laughed.

"What you laughing at?"

Four little words, and Kamoore's mood plummeted. He had thought himself free of his manservant, and here he was standing only two lengths away. Licking his lips, Filyx strode forward and snatched the parchment from Kamoore's numb fingers.

"Interesting," the brat said.

Growling, Kamoore surged forward to push the boy into the churning water. Without looking at him, however, Filyx sidestepped him.

"It's time. The Lord Galgothmeg calls for you," Filyx said.

Tilting up his chin, Kamoore stared defiantly back. "I am the lord and master of Pallaryn. I am king."

Filyx scoffed. "You're the king of damnation."

That was when he heard it. Another low rumbling.

Two large, fiery red eyes gleamed behind the curtain of water. The new dragon stepped through the pounding of the water and into the pool. Water lapped around his gigantic reptilian body as he ploughed through the depths with ease. Galgothmeg was terrifying but this dragon, Kamoore could sense something more sinister and dangerous in him.

To his side, Filyx dropped into a kneel of supplication.

"Welcome to Syrif's Pool. Three thousand years ago, a dragon mother killed her newborn babe, believing him to be dragonless. His song can still be heard on the wind for those who have the wits to hear it."

"I beg your pardon." Kamoore lifted his chin. He would not cower. He would not be afraid.

"A warning not to underestimate the power of Artroth, *rokun*."

A heavy thump signalled the arrival of Galgothmeg. The red dragon lowered his head and peered into the darkness of the cave, his nostrils flaring.

"Ah, what is this you bring me, my general of death?" The sound from the new dragon was a low purr, but Kamoore could hear the danger in every syllable the creature spoke. The stale air about them shifted as the dragon stood from the water. Fear coursed through Kamoore, and he was rooted to the spot.

At first, in the gloom, Kamoore had thought he was looking at a black dragon, but as his eyes adjusted to the light, he realised this dragon was closer to a midnight blue.

Kamoore turned his head slightly to see Galgothmeg's slow, terrible smile as he bowed his head. His brain felt numb with fear. Who was this that the great Galgothmeg would bow?

"An amusement, *Pallu*," Galgothmeg said. "It has been many years since we have played with foolish *rokun*."

Kamoore half expected an evil chuckle from the dragon. The red eyes narrowed. "Is he of Pallarus?"

"No," Galgothmeg admitted, "he's the one who thought to take Pallarus' place."

"Foolhardy." There was something savage in the beast's eyes as he stared down at the cringing Kamoore.

"The boy of flame hair is a gift from Lord Thylyssa. Our emissary," Galgothmeg said.

"He'll do. He has enough power to sustain the dragon within him?"

"A small, weak one, my lord."

"Very good."

"I have further tidings, milord," Galgothmeg said. "We lost the illusionist."

The dark blue dragon lifted his head and roared in fury. "I told you to leave that one in Artroth ... Why bring him on a suicide mission?"

"Forgive me, milord."

"I am not in the habit of granting forgiveness."

Swallowing his fear, Kamoore stepped back.

The dark dragon sniffed. "And the white dragon?"

"Alive," Galgothmeg confirmed with a nod of his head. "He has shield-fire, not much use for anything."

The dark dragon grunted, his terrible eyes looking over Filyx, who in Kamoore's opinion was too calm. "Shields have a nasty habit of getting in the way."

"Mandros cares for him deeply," Galgothmeg said. "He's young and inexperienced. And we know what young, inexperienced Pallarus men are like on the open battlefield."

"The white dragon must die," the dark dragon said. "All predictions about Winter's Dragon, the one with the impossible white scales, tell stories of doom if we cannot lure him to Artrothian ways."

"He's next to useless to Mandros on the battlefield, *Pallu*. There is nothing special about Tornyth."

"Tornyth," the dragon scoffed. "*Return to glory* indeed. Mandros is about to find himself disappointed in his white scales. He will pay for underestimating me and taking the white dragon for himself."

Galgothmeg shifted. "Of course, *Pallu*. There's more."

"You bring too much news of failure, Galgothmeg."

"Indeed, what I have to say is troubling; I heard it among the Grey Shadows' screeching minds that there is one that can free them."

"*Free them?*"

"Indeed, that is what I heard, milord. It is how we lost the illusionist."

The dark dragon snarled and snapped his teeth. Kamoore retreated, imagining himself broken and mangled in the dragon's maw. His movement caught the dark dragon's eye. He flashed his long, sharp fangs. And took a lazy step forward and returned his eyes to Filyx. "Rise, my ember. We shall release your dragon and when the time is right, you will fly as you 'escape' the clutches of the evil one. You will relay a message to Mandros, the dragon of Flame and Fury, and tell him of our numbers."

"But my lord ...?"

"That's not your real message, lizard," the dark dragon said. "I'll be merciful and give white scales one more chance. Now, show me how you take a life."

Turning towards Kamoore, Filyx's face was hidden in shadow. There seemed to be an unnatural glow in his eyes as he regarded Kamoore and lifted his knife.

Panicked that he was cornered, Kamoore lifted his hands to ward off Filyx, even as the boy lunged with a feral yell. The knife bit down into his chest, and he tried to open his mouth to scream, but there was no sound.

Filyx yanked his knife back and stabbed down once more. Kamoore's fingers reached out for the blade, eyes bulging as his quivering lips attempted to beg for mercy. He tried to suck in a breath to hold on to precious life.

Blood bubbled down his lips. The last thing he saw before he tumbled into a terrible, empty darkness was Filyx's grinning face.

Chapter Twenty-Two

Jodathyn

The Citadel of Pallaryn

Jodathyn's stomach lurched as he stepped through the archways into the outer courtyards. The metallic scent of blood was thick in this part of the palace. He glanced up at the walls. Immediately following their victory, the heads of the great lords' victims had been removed. But he could still see them. He had wanted to find Illeanah, to ensure she was treated with respect. Captain Tiernan heard of his plans and adamantly refused to let him go up onto the walls. Jodathyn had to be content with Tiernan's assurances that the guardsmen would ensure her remains would be blessed with water as was her people's custom.

The early morning mist shrouded the ground, and he shivered. Soon low autumn would give way to winter. Once high winter took Rama in her cold embrace, supplying food to the citizens of Pallaryn would become more difficult. He was aware that Kieryn had sent messengers to outlining villages asking for help.

There had been no rest for any able-bodied adult who elected to stay. They all did their part, whether it was removing rubble, hunting or preserving food. Zapyr had done trips along the coastline bringing back fish to preserve for the long winter nights.

Mandros had told him not to worry about his *vehyl* kin. Lifting his head to observe the dragons who stationed themselves along the walls, Jodathyn knew their scaled allies would hunt for the humans.

Zapyr must have felt his scrutiny. He leaped lightly from the wall and landed in the courtyard. His muscles rippled as he strode forward, unconcerned of the humans nearby. His shoulders were set. The frown lines on his face made him look quite severe.

"Winter's Dragon," Zapyr rumbled, lowering his crowded head to peer at Jodathyn with his deep blue eyes. "I wanted to thank you for staying at Rhox's side during the battle."

"Galgothmeg got away with Lord Kamoore the usurper. He was in my sights ..."

Zapyr lowered his head yet further. "Sometimes it takes greater courage to stay your hand. A strength I'll never know."

Jodathyn reached out and touched Zapyr's side. "Something is bothering you, *sudunyn*. You're speaking nonsense. You're the most uptight, disciplined dragon I know."

Zapyr snorted. "Careful, hatchling, you might find yourself at the end of a nip if you keep up the cheek."

"That was not cheek," Jodathyn replied, his hands on his hips. "I was being serious. But if you want cheek ..."

"I lost everything at the Battle of Haven Bay. I never thought my dragon heart would beat again ... and now Rhox ... Ayrdonyth. They deserve something more than me ..." Pain washed over Zapyr's face. "I do not have the strength to be the *aluel* they need."

"You're strong, Zapyr," Jodathyn replied. "You'll find your way. Besides, you wanted Orion the first time you sensed his dragon. I know you did."

Zapyr chuckled darkly, looking up to the wall where Ayrdonyth and Rhox were roughhousing. "I never wanted a young dragon to manifest more than I did in that moment. I thought I was protecting him by waiting until he was ready. I was a fool. He manifested in battle, and I almost lost him."

"I don't think I could ever get used to living through battles." Jodathyn gestured wildly about. "I can still smell blood."

"Good, your dragon senses are strengthening," Zapyr rumbled. "The atrocities of war shouldn't be something you're comfortable with."

"Are you?"

"Battle-fire burns in my blood. The only comfort to be found is in knowing that innocent lives are avenged."

"And I have shield-fire?"

"It's no small thing," Zapyr replied. "Battle-fire is often wrongly placed upon a pedestal. Dragons like myself are predisposed to battle, the hunt, protection and soldiering. Shield-fires like you, Curarfur and Sidrah are more inclined to protect the young and vulnerable. Shields are natural teachers, nurturers, healers and builders. Both fires are noble and needed for dragonkind to flourish."

"Sidrah has shield-fire?"

"Aye, she's the great general of Rama, but her natural gifting is in the healing arts. She was a fantastic mother to her children and to the realm when she was queen. Me … not so much."

"I know you're a good father."

"When I lost my mate, my *ketur*, and our unborn child to Vadroil, I lost a piece of myself. My son … reckless, tenacious Rhox was taken before my eyes." Zapyr choked back his words, his blue eyes blinking, lost in the horror of a memory. "My boy killed avenging his mother … Otherworlds, holding his broken body broke me. I promised myself I would never be vulnerable again, never take an heir. Never open myself up to …"

"What changed your mind?" Jodathyn whispered.

"Orion. An old dragon like me … I sensed the hum of his power, and it mingled with a deep grief. Behind his mask, he was alone and hurt. I wanted to protect him."

"You're proving my point that you're a good father."

"Using my own words against me? When did you become so wise?"

"It happens on occasion," Jodathyn replied. "Shocking, I know."

Noticing something nearby, Zapyr lifted his head. His scaly lips lifted into a sly smile as he looked back down at Jodathyn. "Looks like wise Uncle Jodathyn is required."

Jodathyn turned around to see what his dragon brother had spotted and suppressed a sigh. The royal family had entered the courtyard, and Kieryn looked distinctly unhappy. Holding on to his mother's hand, Carvelle was sulking, while Larelle's eyes darted around.

Seeing Jodathyn watching him, Carvelle released Odelle's hands, launching himself across the courtyard and into Jodathyn's arms. "Papa is sending me away! Tell him he's wrong!"

Frowning, Jodathyn scooped up his nephew and waited for Kieryn to join him. He was hoping something in his brother's expression might give him a clue on how to handle the matter. The king's dark eyes stared down at him. He could see the shadow of doubt, but also determination.

"Come, Carvelle," Jodathyn replied. "Whatever your father has asked of you is done for good reason. You know that."

"Not you too, Uncle!" Carvelle wriggled, demanding to be put down. Jodathyn obliged, and the young prince stamped his foot. "You're supposed to be on my side."

"I am on your side," Jodathyn replied. He brushed Carvelle's hair away from his flushed face. Two tears of anger ran down his cheeks.

"While we go to Kudah, Lord Mandros wants my heirs to fly with the majority of his dragons to Torryn in preparation. He feels it would be safest in the mountains," Kieryn murmured.

"I see."

"Papa isn't coming with me," Carvelle pouted. "I want to stay near Papa."

"Your uncle and I have business elsewhere. We'll go to Torryn after, Carvelle," Kieryn said, pinching the bridge of his nose.

Jodathyn shifted and glanced up at Odelle, who glanced away. She looked teary and confused by Carvelle's reaction. Larelle shrunk back to hide behind the queen's skirts.

"He's anxious, my king," Jodathyn said. He remembered how he felt when he had been taken from Aviah Valley and into Whitoak's home as a child. He hadn't liked it when Lord Whitoak left the estate. In his childish mind, Whitoak was safe. "Might I have one of your rings?"

Kieryn's brow creased, but he complied with Jodathyn's request. Taking the ring, Jodathyn pressed it into Carvelle's palm. "It's okay to be scared, Carvelle. Your papa doesn't really want to send you away with your mama and the baby, but we must keep you safe. We have a job in Kudah, and then we'll fly back to you. I promise. Hold on to Papa's ring; he'll come back for it. He's vain about those types of things, you know."

Carvelle sniffled. "What if Papa doesn't come back?"

"I will look after him," Jodathyn replied. "I swear it."

Kieryn knelt and swept Carvelle into a hug. He kissed his boy's cheeks with his bearded face and whispered something in his ear. When he released his child, the king looked up into the impassive golden dragon. "Lord Zapyr, pray watch over them."

"I will. I know what it is like to lose a son," Zapyr replied. He glanced up at Mandros; a momentary flicker of discomfort crossed his face.

"Guardsmen Jael and Lyntton are who I trust in my absence. Lyntton is good with green recruits and an excellent strategist."

"I know of the men you speak of, King Kieryn. I will consult with them while you're away." Zapyr dipped his head in acknowledgement, and his blue eyes swept over Jodathyn. "*Aluel* and Sidrah can teach you much about leading *vehyl* with integrity. You're ready to learn from them."

Jodathyn nodded.

"I foresee that battle is not where you will find the greatest achievement in life, *sudunyn*."

"You're a seer now, Zapyr?"

Zapyr flashed his fangs. He extended an open palm for the queen and the children to climb onto. He placed them gently on his back, and Jodathyn watched as his sister by marriage settled down, with the children sitting in front of her. "No. But you are young and destined for greatness. Such a shame that you will learn battle before ways of the hunt or fishing."

Lifting his crowned head, Zapyr roared and spread his wings. He leaped into the air, rumbling at his sons as he passed them. From the wall, Ayrdonyth looked back at Jodathyn almost apologetically and followed suit. Soon the sky was full of the colourful scales of the departing dragons.

"Looks like you're flying with me, my king," Jodathyn said, craning his neck to watch as the golden speck of Zapyr winked on the horizon.

The delegation to Kudah was quite small. Mandros, Sidrah and Roane formed an escort along with Tornyth, Rigyl and Vydris. Tornyth had been much put out that both Vydris and Rigyl were larger dragons than him.

Vydris, who once was Fydellah, was the largest of the new dragons. Sidrah had patiently explained that Fydellah had taken very little of the suppression herbs in her formative years. Tornyth remained disappointed.

"You fly confidently," Rigyl, the midnight-blue form of Will, said. He came up on Tornyth's left-hand side and turned his snout to look back at Vydris. Tornyth followed his gaze and could see that Vydris' face was screwed up in concentration.

"Vydris' confidence will grow in time," Tornyth replied.

"Disadvantages can always be turned into an advantage," Rigyl said.

"Deo uses his smaller frame to execute manoeuvres that the larger dragons can't," Nym cried out from the back of Sidrah. "I've seen you do the same thing."

Rigyl bumped him playfully with his wingtip. "See, nothing to be jealous about."

"I'm not jealous!"

Rigyl gave him a knowing look.

"Listen, hatchlings," Mandros boomed. "Take your cues from me. I want you to observe and feel the use of your gifting while you are in dragon form. When the time is ripe, you'll have the opportunity to inform me what your powers have revealed to you."

Vydris snorted, and a plume of smoke left her nostrils. "Isn't that what Lord Roane is for?"

"This is a time to learn," Sidrah said, her voice taking on a hint of sternness.

After his botched execution, Tornyth had been too sick with pain and shock to study Kudah from the sky. From the air, he could easily spot Magistrate Swyft's house, the community hall and the dirt road that would have led to Curran's tucked away tavern.

Mandros landed first. In the abandoned market square, the green dragon was greeted by a lone hunched over woman.

"Kya," Tornyth rumbled, pleased to see the old woman who had shown him such kindness.

Tornyth swept down to land beside Mandros and lowered his snout so that Kieryn might dismount with some dignity.

The king paused his foot in mid-air, hesitant to step along his face. "Are you sure, brother?"

"Quite sure."

Kieryn stepped out onto his snout, and Tornyth kept still.

"Come, Et-hir. Come, Tiernan."

Kieryn offered his hand to Et-hir, and as she drew level to him, she grasped the king's hand and stepped from the edge of Tornyth's snout. As Captain Tiernan followed Et-hir to the ground, Tornyth eyed the captain's socked feet. "It seemed wrong to step on Your Highness' face with my common man's boots.'"

Tornyth didn't comment as Tiernan used his side to balance so he could pull his boots over his feet.

With her arms spread wide in welcome, Kya tottered forward. "I have been expecting you, lord dragon."

Mandros stretched out both of his wings. "Have you now, old one?"

"Yes, your black scaled friend promised there was one that was greater who had the duty of exacting revenge." Kya tapped her ear with a wrinkled hand. "I've good hearing, sir dragon."

"That is correct. I am Mandros, the dragon of Flame and Fury, father of this land and the deliverer."

"I very much desire to speak with your magistrate," Kieryn said, stepping out of the shadow of the dragon.

Kya's old, wizened eyes took in the number of dragons landing in the marketplace and the High King before her. She recovered quickly and puffed out her chest. "I'm the magistrate of Kudah."

"*You?*" Tornyth couldn't help but choke.

"I'm dying, not dead, lizard," Kya snapped. "I'm more than capable of keeping the lawmen in check."

"If you would be so kind to bring to me those who were responsible for the governance of Kudah, I would be most appreciative."

"Forgive my old, tired hips ..."

"Tiernan will help you."

Tornyth had been watching Tiernan's face closely. He wasn't sure if the captain was amused or taken aback by Kya. He was a dutiful man and stepped forward and let the old woman escort him. Kya seemed delighted by her gallant escort, beaming she took the crook of his elbow. Tornyth bit his lip as Tiernan had to adjust his powerful strides to something more sedate.

"I had a boy like you once. He was tall as a tree and ate like a bull. Are you hungry?"

Rigyl made a chuffing noise that sounded like a choked laugh. He sidled close to Roane, who looked at him with an amused glint in his eye. Tornyth wondered what they both sensed.

Sidrah prowled along the market square. Her hackles rose, a growl in her throat. He sniffed.

Dragon blood. He could still smell the scent of his blood in the village. He knew that his dragon senses were keen, but he never appreciated how superior they were until now. He turned his head in Mandros' direction. The green dragon stood, stiff-backed and still. Roane, likewise, had lifted his crowned head and was sniffing the air. With his cracked horns and scarred face, he would have been a terrible sight to behold if Tornyth didn't know any better.

Both Rigyl and Vydris seemed nervous of the reactions of the older dragons. Vydris shuffled closer to Rigyl's side, her large eyes never leaving the form of Sidrah, who continued to pace.

It was almost half an hour later when Tiernan strode back into the market square. In his grip, he held a wriggling, dissatisfied Magistrate Swyft. Not only the captain had the magistrate but all the lawmen of Kudah. Behind the lawmen, Kya hobbled.

"Get yourselves into line, you mangy, good-for-nothing ..." Kya grumbled, shaking her fists at the lawmen. They looked at her uneasily and shuffled into a neater line.

"My king, might I present Magistrate Swyft?" Tiernan thrust the magistrate forward so that he fell to his knees. Swyft looked up; his blond hair was matted about his sweating skin.

Tornyth's nostrils flared, sensing the magistrate's fear.

"Who do you work for?" Kieryn barked.

"You, my king, and only you," the magistrate stammered.

Mandros turned his head. "Vydris, what do you sense?"

Vydris' brown eyes were cold. Deep in her chest she began to growl, and Magistrate Swyft trembled under her scrutiny. "He speaks lies."

"Rigyl?"

Wings outstretched, Rigyl seemed to be enjoying the cool wind. Every muscle in his body was taut as he stared into an empty space before him. His tail twitched, and he shuddered before he answered. "He takes bribes. Gold. Under the bidding of another, he has oppressed the citizens of Kudah."

The magistrate's head was turning in every direction. His face was slack with confusion until he locked gazes with Sidrah.

"You!" Magistrate Swyft snarled. Desperation sometimes made people stupid. Without a weapon in his hands, he lunged at Sidrah. Tiernan's fingers curled around the magistrate's shoulder, yanking him back onto his knees.

"Tell me, from whom you take the bribe?" Kieryn asked. He glanced to Rigyl's calm form. The dark blue dragon's eyes were still closed in concentration. And Tornyth knew then that his brother had used Will's powers in interrogation before.

The magistrate trembled but should have taken seriously the king's darkening expression. "I am loyal, my king."

"A lie."

Rigyl huffed in agreement with Vydris' statement.

Nodding at Tiernan, Kieryn seemed to watch impassively as the magistrate was hurled to his feet.

"You beat my brother bloody."

"I swear I did not."

"A lie," Vydris growled.

"He took great pleasure in mocking one born of house Pallarus and one he knew had a dragon. Greed was a motivator." Rigyl's flanks shivered with whatever he sensed from the magistrate's mind. Beside him, Roane turned his horned head to look sympathetically in Tornyth's direction.

Tornyth remembered Will saying that sometimes he could see what people imagined in their thoughts.

Kieryn took a slow step forward. "Consider your next words carefully, sir. I am High King, and to speak lies to me is a serious crime."

"I swear—"

"Think carefully," Rigyl interrupted. His tone was clipped, earning himself a pleased look from Roane.

"Who is controlling you?"

"Kamoore! It's all Lord Kamoore ... he threatened me."

"Yes, it's Kamoore," Vydris said. "But he wasn't threatened."

"If it pleases you, Your Majesty," Tornyth said. "I have a question."

"Go ahead, brother."

"The people ... the prisoners they said they were going to the mines to work off their debts," Tornyth said. "Is this true?"

"Yes ... yes ..."

"He has his suspicions it's untrue. Rigyl, what do you read?" Whatever Vydris sensed from him, she seemed uneasy.

Rigyl shifted, the scales on his brow furrowing. "The number of prisoners requested was high. They're hiding them in the mountains, but mining hasn't happened for seasons."

Tornyth felt Et-hir stir beside him. "My brother, Tyr the Sionian ..."

"Dead."

"True," whispered Vydris.

"How?" Et-hir demanded. Her eyes stared resolutely ahead.

"He escaped and fell."

"True."

Taking in a deep, shaking breath, Et-hir touched Tornyth's scales. She seemed unsteady on her feet. "I can take you somewhere quiet," Tornyth whispered.

"No," Et-hir said, her voice sounding small and far away. "Let's see justice done."

Kieryn made his way over to Et-hir's side and lifted a gloved hand to squeeze her shoulder. "We'll rest the night here, and tomorrow we will go up into the mountains. If there is anything I can do to assist you honour your brother please ... tell me."

The expression on Kieryn's face hardened as he turned to survey the lawmen before him. "Each of you stood aside in the name of 'just doing your jobs' and allowed injustice to infect Kudah. Good people suffered, one of them my brother. War is upon us. Each of you may decide for yourselves if you are fighting, but once the war is over, every one of you will be removed from your post. You're not worthy of your position in your communities. You'll need to find other employment."

Murmurs ran through the ranks of lawmen. Tiernan watched them with his challenging blue gaze.

"Tiernan, Lord Mandros said my brother predicted the magistrate would be stripped naked and shamed. So please strip him, flog him and then remove his head from his shoulders."

Tornyth started at the king's judgement.

Kieryn merely dropped his hand from Et-hir's shoulder. "It seems I'm not as even-tempered as you, brother."

Chapter Twenty-Three
Jodathyn

The Village of Kudah

To watch the proceedings, Jodathyn manifested back into his human skin. His jaw tightened as he clenched his teeth. He wanted Magistrate Swyft to see his humanity before he was executed. He wanted the townsfolk to see he was unharmed and unafraid after his ordeal. He exchanged an anxious glance with Kieryn, who nodded in approval.

"Please!" Magistrate Swyft cried, trying valiantly to lunge out of Captain Tiernan's grasp and into Jodathyn's direction. "Mercy!"

Tiernan wasn't in a forgiving mood. He clamped his hand on the unfortunate man's shoulder, wrenching him backwards.

Jodathyn schooled his features into what he hoped was polite indifference. He lifted his head to observe how the villagers crept out of their hiding places. Most of them hung back, watching from afar.

"Humans are just like dragons. Curious creatures at heart," Tornyth declared.

Kya hobbled past Sidrah and over to give him a warm embrace. She made him bend down to brush her fingers through his Pallarus curls and kiss his cheeks.

"My poor, poor husband, he isn't long for this world," Kya said, taking his hand and patting it. "Oh, it's such a blessing he'll pass to the Otherworld as a free man."

Before this adventure, he would never have thought a lowborn would approach him while his brother was in close proximity to him. He sent a sideways glance in Kieryn's direction. The king observed the old woman fawning over him, clearly amused at being ignored.

"Fie for shame, gents! One of you fetch a chair for your magistrate." Kieryn lifted his gloved hand in the lawmen's direction.

The lawmen shuffled, and one of them broke away at a run to do as the High King bid. The chair was brought forward, and Kieryn made a grand gesture of taking Kya's hand and seating her as if she were a visiting dignitary in his court.

"Well!" Kya barked, waving her hand imperiously in Tiernan's direction. "We haven't got all day. Get on with it."

Tiernan's lips quirked, and his eyebrows rose. "As milady commands."

Et-hir's small hand clasped Jodathyn's while Tiernan tore the magistrate's clothing from his quivering frame. The memory of his own humiliation brought a cold sweat to his skin. Et-hir murmured something to him in Sionian, but he was unable to take in what she said. He nodded woodenly, his eyes never leaving Magistrate Swyft.

Faced with the grim reality of his actions, the magistrate's proud mask fell. Tiernan wrenched his arms up to chain him onto the same whipping pole Jodathyn had been flogged on. Jodathyn stiffened and glanced over to Mandros.

The green dragon didn't speak directly into his mind, but he felt a soft pressure and assurance that he could leave anytime he wished. Jodathyn shook his head. He would remain strong as was expected of someone of his lineage.

The first blow hit the magistrate's skin, and the man's scream was enough to have Tornyth writhing in horror. He swallowed his gasp at the stark memory of his own skin ripping. The second blow had him visibly flinching. Et-hir's hand tightened on his own.

He stared straight ahead, determined to show no emotion or weakness. It was best that he turned his thoughts away from the present and dwell on anything that would deafen him to the crack of the whip and the magistrate's screams.

"I want to leave," Tornyth whispered. *"Or burn something. Let's burn his house."*

He thought his dragon would have been happy to see their tormentor suffering. Somehow the retribution left a bitter taste in his mouth. He felt alone, lost among his memories of pain and suffering.

"Hush," Jodathyn whispered, his quiet word earning him a strange look from Et-hir. "It'll be over soon."

Nym moved over then. She stood by Jodathyn's other side and lifted her hand to squeeze his shoulder. She didn't say anything; she didn't have to.

Jodathyn wished he could stop what was happening, but he knew he could not. The magistrate's crimes were many. It wasn't just the violence he had inflicted upon him that he was reaping. Et-hir's own brother had lost his life. He squeezed her hand back, and she looked up at him, her deep brown eyes welling with tears.

Jodathyn bowed his head as the magistrate was untied from the pole and left sobbing on the cobblestones.

Unsheathing his sword, Kieryn turned towards Et-hir and offered her the handle. "Sister, in honour of Sionian justice?"

Et-hir looked at the sword uncertainly and then back to the king. In Sion, if a member of the king's household was murdered or killed, the next of kin was the executioner.

"Tyr was but a merchant, Your Majesty."

"You're Jodathyn's intended. You'll be a princess and a member of my household. Your brother would be Jodathyn's brother by marriage."

Et-hir reached out a shaking hand to grasp the handle. She looked to the magistrate and then back to Kieryn. "He has such a thick neck, and I am such a little woman."

Jodathyn lifted his head towards Mandros and Sidrah, who both seemed unbothered by the magistrate's fate. Magistrate Swyft was nothing but a snivelling lump of flesh. He took Et-hir's elbow and drew her closer to his chest. "Captain Tiernan can assist with technique better than I."

"Don't be surprised if it takes a few goes," Nym said. She crossed her arms against her chest and leered at the magistrate.

"My king." Et-hir nodded and took the sword from Kieryn's grasp with both hands. She looked back at Jodathyn and Nym as if seeking reassurance. Then her back stiffened, and she strode towards Captain Tiernan, her chin held high.

Nym sidled closer to Jodathyn. "Are you well?" she whispered.

Jodathyn smiled weakly. "The sound drew me into past memories. I'm much recovered now."

Kieryn patted Jodathyn on the shoulder.

Et-hir reached Captain Tiernan and said in a loud, clear voice, "Captain, might I have some instruction?"

Jodathyn suppressed an inappropriate snort of amusement at the way the magistrate's head tilted to look at Et-hir in horror. "A woman!"

"You think an angry lass can't take your complaining head off?" Kya called out. "When I was a spritely twig of a girl, I used to train with the lawmen."

Jodathyn exchanged a bemused glance with Nym, who wasn't doing anything to conceal her smirk.

Magistrate Swyft attempted to crawl away from his fate. Growling, Tiernan grabbed his hair and pulled him backwards. "On your knees."

Whimpering, the magistrate was given no choice. Tiernan beckoned Et-hir to draw closer. He positioned her and patiently adjusted her grip on the sword. Her stoic, proud bearing slipped for a moment as she looked to the blond captain. Tiernan nodded gravely and gestured for her to take her time.

Et-hir widened her stance, drew in a breath, held it and swung with all her might. Her first swing was impressive for her size. The magistrate's body tumbled forward, his head mostly attached. Et-hir stepped forward, peering down at the corpse. She lifted her foot to pin the body down and swung again to finish the job.

Silence reigned in the wake of the magistrate's death. Et-hir stared down at him as if she couldn't quite believe it was over.

Tiernan took the sword from Et-hir's slack fingers. "It takes mastery of skill to decapitate a man in one go. Well done, my lady."

"Yes, well done, well done," Kya said, hobbling out from the crowd with a basin of water and a washcloth. "Looked like a real warrior princess, you did."

Kya offered the washcloth to Et-hir and with her head bowed, she cleaned her nails and then offered it to Tiernan.

"Don't you worry your great big giant fingers over cleaning the sword," Kya said, confidently taking the king's blade from Tiernan. "I'm sure I can find some worthless lawman to do that job for you."

Beside Jodathyn, Kieryn chuckled at the audacity of the old woman snatching his sword right out of Tiernan's hands and walking away with it. Surprised, Tiernan looked toward the king, who shook his head.

Jodathyn reached out to Et-hir and drew her close to his chest. He could feel her heart racing as she pressed her face into his shirt. Both his arms wrapped around her and tightened. "You wielded King's Talon well."

Bewildered, Et-hir looked up into Jodathyn's face.

"It's the name of the sword wielded by the High Kings of Rama," Jodathyn explained.

"And an old woman just wandered off with a priceless royal treasure ..." Tiernan was still staring after Kya.

"As entertaining as this afternoon has been," Mandros rumbled, "I will get back to ferrying our men and weapons. Sidrah and Roane will remain behind to help with the search in the mountains."

"Thank you, Lord Mandros," Kieryn replied. "I'll see you in Torryn."

Mandros turned towards a scraggly little boy who had been watching the proceedings. "You. Go get every willing fighting man. We're flying to war."

The boy nodded and ran off to spread the news. Jodathyn knew it wouldn't be long until the willing men assembled. He wondered how many men would unwillingly go.

"Are we flying to the mountains tonight?" Et-hir asked. She still looked a little stunned with her ability to decapitate another human being.

"Best wait till morning," Fydellah replied where she was standing with Will. They had been shoulder to shoulder through the afternoon, whispering. Jodathyn thought perhaps they were comparing notes on their powers. As far as the mental arts went, they seemed to function in a similar way. A mind reader and a truth discerner in his brother's court could be a powerful combination, especially since they seemed to work well together.

Will must have picked up his thoughts because the dark-skinned lord locked eyes with him and grinned.

"We can find some rest at Curran's tavern," Et-hir said. "We should eat."

Jodathyn couldn't agree more. The flight and the excitement of the afternoon left him strangely ravenous.

Staying in Curran Norrys' tavern without him felt wrong. The moment Kieryn entered the tavern, Jodathyn had expected to see the ex-guardsman come out and greet them. He could tell from the expression on her face that Et-hir felt the same way.

Roane and Sidrah stationed themselves outside, so that anyone wanting to approach them would truly have to be bold.

Dinner was an informal affair. From the kitchens, Jodathyn could hear Tiernan's lower murmur as he spoke to Et-hir while they searched for something to eat and drink.

Jodathyn collapsed at the nearest table, and Kieryn dragged another chair over to join him. At another table, Fydellah, Nym and Will engaged in a lively debate. He watched a small, playful smile on the king's lips as he unobtrusively observed them.

"I think Nym has found more palace brats to be friends with," Jodathyn said.

"She's certainly an interesting character, brother," Kieryn replied. "Strong, fierce and loyal."

"I didn't think you would approve of her."

Kieryn paused. "How could I not? She fought beside you as bravely as any of my guardsmen. And then there's Et-hir ..." Jodathyn's head flew up in anticipation of what his brother might say about her. "She's strong, fierce and loyal in her own way."

"You approve, Sire?"

Kieryn gave him a sideways glance. "Have I indicated otherwise?"

"No," Jodathyn replied. He watched as Tiernan and Et-hir left the kitchens. It seemed that they had found some choice flagons of ale. Tiernan placed a jug in front of the king.

Reaching out, Kieryn touched Jodathyn's sleeve and whispered urgently, "She may have need of your support tonight, brother."

"It's simple fare tonight, Your Majesty," Tiernan said, pouring the king, Jodathyn and himself a drink.

"No roast with gravy like our last tavern?" Kieryn quipped.

Jodathyn raised an eyebrow. When had his brother had time to visit a tavern before?

"Afraid not. We've got hard bread, some leftover fruit and vegetables and some cheese," Et-hir said. "Can't blame the villagers for pilfering off the meat."

"Where did the ale come from then?" Jodathyn asked.

"Curran was a wise man," Et-hir replied. She shook her head with a laugh. "He hid the best ales."

"I'll drink to that!" Will jumped up from his chair to help with the food, and soon everybody had something to eat.

Et-hir sat next to Jodathyn, grasping his hand under the table and giving it a squeeze. While everyone seemed to have an appetite, she seemed to have very little. Her brow was creased in distress as she looked down upon her plate.

Jodathyn watched her with mounting worry. Kieryn finished his meal quickly, sending him a significant look, which Jodathyn interpreted to mean as 'comfort her'. The king stood clapped Jodathyn's shoulder and left. Tiernan followed him shortly after.

Et-hir's goblet of ale remained untouched. Scooting closer, she leaned her head against his shoulder, and Jodathyn ran his fingers through her hair. She stayed close to him in silence for a long while before Jodathyn spoke. "Is there anything I can do?"

"No," Et-hir said. "I knew for so very long he wasn't coming back. It shouldn't be a shock."

"Suspecting something and knowing the truth are two different things," Jodathyn replied.

"I've no hope of seeing Tyr's face again," Et-hir whispered. Her small voice sounded choked. "He'll never ride the caravan horses bareback or play tricks on the trade masters or even meet you."

"He sounds like a good brother."

"He is," Et-hir replied. "He was."

When Nym, Will and Fydellah also decided to go and find somewhere to sleep, they stayed in the dark. Silent tears fell down Et-hir's cheeks. Jodathyn leaned over and gently brushed them away with his thumb.

"I love you."

Et-hir blinked up at him in the dark. "I love you more," she said.

"Not possible," Jodathyn replied.

Laying her head on his shoulder, Et-hir breathed out a tired sigh and closed her eyes. Jodathyn pressed his lips against her forehead. "I'd take your pain away if I could."

"In Sion we believe that great pain after a loved one has passed is a great honour to the dead."

"Ettie ... I don't know what ..."

"Hold me, Jod. Don't let me go." Et-hir released another shuddering sigh, pressing herself closer into Jodathyn's side. He could feel warm tears seeping through his shirt as Et-hir began to weep in earnest. His fingers brushed through her hair.

"I'm here," Jodathyn whispered in her ear. "I'm here."

High in the mountains, Jodathyn stood by the grave of Curran Norrys. The wind buffeted his cloak. It whispered of others in the mountains. It tugged on his hair and begged him to come. Humans had brought death and misery to her bountiful mines.

He edged away from the grave and stared up into the cloudless blue sky. And then let the Wind Song whisper to him in the voices of death and oppression. Cocking his head to the side, he realised that it wasn't in fact just the wind speaking with him—it was human voices.

"It goes deeper, boy," a voice weathered by pain and betrayal grated in the dark. "It goes deeper than kidnapping and Galgothmeg. This is an ancient war."

Jodathyn shivered.

"Why are you here?"

"We're tribute for Artroth," the voice continued. "Food and men for the dragons of Artroth."

Artroth, an ancient enemy many leagues from Rama. Jodathyn recalled hearing Mandros telling his brother that dragonkind had originated in Artroth, and they felt they had a claim over Rama.

When he was younger, his main interest had been in the heroes. He had seen little reason to study long absent enemies. Artroth hadn't made a bid for Rama in centuries. Why would they choose now?

But that had been foolish. To know one's enemy was to know oneself. He could never understand the beauty and depth of Ramian history and culture without understanding the villains in her story.

The air about him rushed, and he was flying. The colours danced before his eyes in swirling patterns. Below he thought he saw craggy rocks and the ocean ... Perhaps a village and the silver scales of fish.

"The white dragon has risen," the voice said. "They will lay claim and waste to our land."

Jodathyn was no fool. He knew he was the white dragon. But what did he have to do with the invasion?

"Rama must never have the hope of the white dragon. They've come to destroy him."

Swallowing painfully, Jodathyn blinked, and the dizziness fled. Gone were the rushing wind and confusing pictures. He had to find his way back to Pallaryn. The invasion was coming. Galgothmeg was the vanguard.

The bright sun greeted him with her warmth. Behind jutted the crumbling rock of proud ruins ... below a grassy field that ran thick with blood. He could see the king's standard among the press of human bodies.

The sky erupted with fire, which tore through wings. He shouted, looking about. The sky was a mass confusion of dragon against dragon. Not only were there Grey Shadows but other larger dragons that were commanding them.

He heard Mandros' cry of pain as Galgothmeg and another mightier dragon slammed into him. Mandros screamed a warning ...

He saw Kieryn's bearded face; he heard his brother's yell as his great sword came crashing down. Jodathyn's jaw and belly seared with pain.

There was a glint of a dagger, and Jodathyn lay in a puddle of blood. Around him were falling leaves of a peculiar shape falling from the sky. He reached out a hand to touch one and brought it close to his face. Rather than the fragile texture he was expecting, it was hard. It was green in colouring. The sight of it filled him with horror, and he crawled to his knees to pick up another. This one was white ... He saw a multitude of leaves on the ground—blues, red, whites, purples—and the breath was stolen from his lungs. From his past visions, he had thought them leaves ... he was mistaken.

Dragon scales were falling from the sky.

Stifling a scream, Jodathyn jolted awake. He was still slumped over in his chair, Et-hir wrapped in his arms. The vision of Galgothmeg's powerful jaws around Mandros left him shaken. He glanced around the room. It was still and grey. There were still a few hours until sunrise.

Groaning, he delicately extracted Et-hir from his arms and lay her head down on the table. It seemed like a lifetime ago that he stood out on the dusty road. Curran had come out to him to stand beside him in the dark.

"Aluel?" He reached out hesitantly with his mind. *"Are you well?"*

"I am well, mynrell. What bothers you?" Mandros' voice came steady and sure in his mind.

"Where are you?"

"We are ferrying men and equipment to Torryn. We are preparing for battle, remember? Tell me what ails you."

"I had a vision. You were right about an invasion, and there was another dragon mightier than Galgothmeg, and you were hurt ..."

"I am aware of all of this, mynrell," Mandros replied. *"Were you not listening when we discussed this?"*

"I was hoping you were wrong."

Mandros' rumbling laughter filled Jodathyn's mind. *"I'm an ancient dragon, white scales. I am very rarely mistaken."*

"You're not very humble."

"Hatchling, when you are my age, you don't need to be humble." There was a pause and a great huffing sigh. *"Is there anything else you need to let me know?"*

"The prisoners were taken for Artroth ..."

"I was afraid of this ... and?"

"You were hurt."

There was a pause. *"The future is not yet written. Injury is likely,* mynrell. *"*

"Promise me you'll stay away from Galgothmeg."

*"*Mynrell, *you know I can't promise that."*

Jodathyn sighed and rested his forehead against the wooden table.

"Galgothmeg and I have a long history. He's never been able to defeat me in battle. Go back to sleep. Sidrah will take you up into the mountains soon ..."

Jodathyn had a brief flash, feeling the weight of dozens of soldiers along his back. Mandros was carrying as many as possible. It was hard work, but he was like the other battle dragons. He would not ask his dragons to do something he himself would not do.

Jodathyn closed his eyes again and decided that he wasn't going to be able to return to sleep. He left the grey stillness of the dining hall and crept out of the tavern. He wandered out to the dirt road and stared out into the darkness.

Just like that night where Curran had comforted him, Jodathyn stood looking in the direction of home until his toes began to feel numb.

"Hello?"

Jodathyn startled at being spoken to.

From the gloom, Jodathyn could see a hunched figure. He sensed the drawn blade and instantly rippled into Tornyth. The figure paused, thinking better than to challenge a dragon.

"Sidrah!"

He felt his sister's momentary annoyance at being woken.

"Who goes there?" Tornyth growled. His human eyesight morphed into a sharper focus.

"Lawman Floyde. I want to speak with you, dragon."

"Then speak, *rokun*." Tornyth hunched down, his tail lashing. He remembered the part that Lawman Floyde had in his capture and botched execution. His dragon half was less forgiving than his human heart.

"I don't mean you any harm," Lawman Floyde replied. To his credit, he kept approaching slowly.

"Experience tells me otherwise," Tornyth muttered.

Lawman Floyde kept his gait steady until he was directly before Tornyth. He threw another man, still dressed in his lawman's coat, at his clawed feet. Quivering in fear, Floyde's prisoner lifted his gaze. Sweat dripped from his balding head. His jaw opened and shut but instead of words, he made whimpering sounds. "I bring His Majesty's sword cleaned and polished by my own hand and a gift."

"A gift, you say?" Tornyth could feel his lip curling. "What can you offer my king?"

"He's here to offer more information." Sidrah appeared out of the darkness. She moved gracefully; the silver specks glistened in the waning moonlight. "Stand down, Tornyth."

"He won't eat you." Roane's voice cut in from the darkness. On his knees, the prisoner tucked his scrawny limbs into his body. "I know that's what you fear ... Our Winter's Dragon is simply bothered by your presence."

"I could eat him if I wanted to," Tornyth said.

Sidrah rolled her eyes. "*Males. Manifest back into your human and go wake your brother.*"

Jodathyn didn't bother to take in the stunned expression of the lawman as he manifested back into his human form. He turned upon his heel and marched back into the tavern, running straight into Will.

"What's happening?"

"Lawman reckons he's got more information," Jodathyn grunted.

Will nodded. "Get the king. I'll get Fy."

"Jodathyn ..." Et-hir looked up at him, confusion written all over her face.

Jodathyn took the flight of stairs almost two at a time, his anger not allowing him to respond to either Will or Et-hir.

"Gosh, you scale-brained, inconsiderate harpy!" Nym poked her head out of a room. Her silver hair curled in multiple directions. "What's all the noise about?"

"Lawman on the road claiming to have more information."

"Well, be quiet!" Nym hissed, slamming her door.

Jodathyn shrugged and was then faced with the dilemma of figuring out where his brother might have retired for the night. His problem was solved by Tiernan opening a door.

"The king is required," Jodathyn said before Tiernan could open his mouth. "A lawman is out on the road claiming to have information."

Tiernan looked at him as if he had never seen him before. "Your Highness?"

"I'm angry, Tiernan," Jodathyn burst out. "I asked this man for help in my hour of need … I begged for my life like a dog, and he didn't have the decency to bother even looking at me when he told me I was going to die."

"Jodathyn …"

"I told him how to get rid of the magistrate of Kudah," Jodathyn said. "He refused to even consider telling Kieryn what was happening in his own village … to his own people. He didn't care."

"What is it you need from me?"

"He's not to ride me." Even Jodathyn was surprised by the outburst. "My dragon doesn't want him anywhere near us."

"I'll keep him away."

Jodathyn sniffed, his anger spent now that he wasn't so close to the lawman. His dragon perceived the man as a threat, and therefore he had reacted strongly. It was why Sidrah, wise to the ways of dragons, had asked him to leave. "I could bite him in half if he truly became a bother, Captain."

Tiernan's expression shifted from perplexed to amused within seconds. "Let's try and avoid unnecessary chomping, shall we?"

Jodathyn harrumphed as Kieryn opened a door and stared back at them, clearly overhearing the last moments of their conversation.

"Messenger outside, Your Majesty."

Kieryn studied Jodathyn's face, then nodded regally once. He stepped past, and Jodathyn watched him go. "Tiernan is right. Let's keep eating of messengers to a minimum, brother."

Jodathyn kept his gaze averted from Tiernan. "I'm well. Let's go and see what this lawman wants."

By the time Jodathyn and Tiernan made their way downstairs, most of their party had assembled. Lawman Floyde was on his knees in front of the king, holding out the king's blade. Kieryn's face was inscrutable as he looked down upon Floyde.

"You are a brave man, lawman," Kieryn said.

"How so, Your Majesty?"

Kieryn's lips twitched. "You were instrumental in the harm of my close kin. You've approached dragons, and you've no way of telling what mood I'm in. I can tell you that Jodathyn doesn't look upon you with favour."

Floyde's eyes momentarily left the dirt road and sought out where Jodathyn was standing. He immediately looked away. "I don't blame him."

"Tell me what you have to say quickly," Kieryn said folding his arms across his chest. The king looked over his shoulder as if to ascertain the whereabouts of Will and Fydellah.

"I had been suspicious of this lawman for some time," Floyde said indicating to the slobbering mess of a man that until now everyone had been ignoring. "He was highly favoured by Magistrate Swyft. He can tell you more about what is happening in the mountains."

"I saw the mountains last night," Jodathyn said.

"If I may?" Floyde asked, careful to keep his eyes on the king's face in order to avoid Jodathyn.

The king nodded.

Floyde stood and went over to the prisoner. He grabbed him up by his collar. "Tell them what you told me."

The hapless man opened and closed his mouth like a fish that had been dragged out of the water.

"Tell them!"

"The prisoners have been taken from the caves. The magistrate became agitated when the black dragon came and rescued Jodathyn." The scrawny lawman nodded to Sidrah. "He sent word to those in the mountain to move the slaves."

Lawman Floyde grimaced at his colleague's wording.

"Move them where?" Roane's voice was a low growl.

"They'll be out in the open soon. The village of Paruhulise is on the coast. It's remote. The lords have complete control there."

Sidrah purred, her tail lashing out behind her. "Not for much longer."

CHAPTER TWENTY-FOUR
Orion

The Ruins of Torryn

Soaring over the skies of Rama, Ayrdonyth wished that his human father could see him now. He was a free dragon, no longer bound inside his human flesh. Another smaller part felt guilt that he was the monster that his father had feared.

He lifted his snout and glanced over to his *Rshon Aluel,* and he knew he was fortunate. Military trained and wise, Zapyr the Splendid could teach him everything he wanted to know.

Zapyr blinked back at him with his large blue eyes and turned his head. Ayrdonyth followed his movements and suppressed a sigh. Looking exhausted but determined, Rhox lagged behind.

"I'll fly with him," Ayrdonyth said. "Theo and I can keep him company."

"No," Zapyr replied. "Deovyn is war trained. You are not."

Hearing his name, Deovyn nodded his head and wheeled back, forsaking his usual banter.

Ayrdonyth watched as Deovyn approached the bronze dragon to nudge him higher. Rhox looked miserable.

"Eyes forward, Ayr," Zapyr commanded. His voice took on a sharp tone. "You don't want to embarrass your *sudunyn* more than he is."

Ayrdonyth felt the reassuring weight of Theo shift above him. For most of the journey, the thief had been silent. He had been careful to fly smoothly as possible, knowing the heights bothered his friend.

"Are we nearly at Torryn, Lord Zapyr?" Prince Carvelle clung to Zapyr's spikes, his little face screwed up at the wind lashing around them. His mother, the queen, sat behind him, her arms wrapping him up in a cloak.

"We'll land soon, little prince," Zapyr replied.

"Good," Carvelle said. "The baby is making Mama feel bad. Mama is stressed. Larelle is asleep. And Theo is going to throw up."

Zapyr rumbled, and Ayrdonyth looked over to the queen. He was no expert on women and babies, but she did look like she was on the verge of collapse. The little girl had curled herself up into a little ball and fallen asleep.

"The prince is right, *Rshon Aluel*," Ayrdonyth said.

"Queen Odelle, my dragon eyesight can see the ruins. We will be landing shortly."

The queen nodded, her short brown hair whipping around her face.

"Praise be to the Otherworld," Theo said.

"Should have brought another *vehyl* woman with us," Zapyr muttered.

"There should be one in the camp for me," Queen Odelle said, patting Zapyr's scales. "Don't worry about me, lord dragon, I'll make do."

"A woman deserves to have a *vehyl* that they are comfortable with," Zapyr muttered. "What would a dragon remember about *vehyl* babies ..."

"I could go back to Pallaryn."

Zapyr's blue eyes rounded onto Ayrdonyth. "You will do no such thing. Until I say so, you will not fly anywhere unaccompanied, do I make myself clear?"

Ayrdonyth was taken aback by the vehemence in Zapyr's tone. "I understand."

Zapyr huffed, smoke curling from his flared nostrils. "You're a young dragon with unusual powers; you'll be easy prey to Galgothmeg and his Grey Shadows."

"I said I understood," Ayrdonyth muttered.

Zapyr growled and lashed out to nip Ayrdonyth's nose. Ayrdonyth startled at the sharp pain of his *Rshon Aluel's* fangs in his snout. Theo cried out in alarm.

"Behave," Zapyr rumbled.

Feeling irritated over his *Rshon Aluel's* overprotectiveness, Ayrdonyth turned away to look below. The ruins of Torryn, the ancient capital of Rama, were exactly how he imagined them. There were jumbled stone blocks and regal pillars that stretched for miles. He could see the ant-sized shapes of humans bustling about their business, making camp. But Zapyr flew over the ruins.

Confused, Ayrdonyth watched as most of their company settled themselves around the outskirts of Torryn, but Zapyr flew on.

"*Rshon Aluel ...*"

"We're taking the queen and the prince to a safe place," Zapyr said. "We will not keep vulnerable *vehyl* in the camp proper."

"The mountains!" Carvelle cried. "You're hiding us in the mountains."

"Yes," Zapyr said. "Here is where we hide our human treasures."

Ayrdonyth wisely decided to keep his mouth shut as Zapyr led them into the mountains. They didn't fly too far into the range when Zapyr landed before a cave. He lowered himself so Carvelle could dismount.

Ayrdonyth shuffled closer to help the queen down and set her feet on the ground. Then, very carefully, he plucked up the sleepy girl. The child blinked up at him and yawned. She looked about in confusion but otherwise didn't seem bothered being handled by a dragon. He placed her feet on the ground, and Prince Carvelle took her hand, dragging her towards a cave. "Come, Mama, you could do with a lie down."

Theo jumped down and took off his cloak. For a moment, Ayrdonyth wondered what the thief was doing, but it soon became clear as he bundled his cloak up. He approached the queen, where she had almost collapsed in relief. "Here, Your Majesty, for your head."

"Oh, how kind," the queen said.

Carvelle took the bundle and lay it down on the ground. He bid the queen to lie down and patted the hair away from her forehead. "I'm sorry, Mama, for the trouble I caused this morning. I didn't mean to hurt you. I just didn't want Papa to leave me again."

The queen's reply was cut off by Deovyn and Rhox landing. Zapyr turned away from the *vehyl* and eyed Rhox wearily. "Are you well?"

"I am well, *Aluel*," Rhox said. "Only exhausted."

"Good, I could use your power to hide the cave where we are keeping the vulnerable *vehyl*."

Rhox's face fell further. "Of course, *Aluel*."

"You are the only illusionist we have, Rhox," Zapyr said. "What else would you have me do?"

"I'll do my duty, *Aluel*."

Zapyr seemed discouraged by Rhox's stiff response. He turned toward Ayrdonyth. "Stay here with your brother for a little while. Deovyn will run through some drills with you when he feels you have sufficiently rested."

"Yes, sir."

For some reason Zapyr still seemed displeased. "I'll be in the camp."

"You know why we've been exiled to the mountains, right?" Rhox asked as they crowded around the campfire that night. Orion stretched out his human legs, enjoying the warmth. He looked beyond the crackling of the fire to his bronze brother, who had been quiet since Zapyr had left.

Orion felt a twinge of fatigue from the flight from Pallaryn to Torryn. Deovyn had assured him his stamina would improve with each flight. He had suggested Orion spend time in his human body while his dragon form was not necessary. While his human lived, this was his natural form, and it was less taxing on him physically.

Deovyn snorted. "We're the three dragons that aren't used to ferry *vehyl* into camp. Ayrdonyth and I because we're too small, and you ..."

"Because I'm broken and twisted."

Prince Carvelle jumped up from where he was sitting in Theo's lap and grabbed a twig to shove into the fire. "I hate being told I'm too little to do something."

"Rhox, my dear," the queen said, "not long ago you lamented you would never fly ... Perhaps with more time the injury wouldn't cause you so much bother."

"It did seem to be a fatigue problem," Deovyn murmured. "You'll never have the speed you once had ... but I'm believing for a full recovery."

Rhox snorted. "Time has changed you, Uncle. You who were younger than me sound so much older now."

Theo choked. "He's younger?"

Deovyn grinned. "Three years separated us ... I was the unexpected child of my father's old age."

"Explains a lot," Theo replied.

Deovyn nudged him with his snout. "Careful, Theo silver-ear ... I could snap you up in one gobble."

Theo tilted his head back and laughed.

Rhox huffed and drew his back legs closer. He blinked his large blue eyes. "I should be honoured to be free of the Grey Shadow curse and that my powers can be used against the evil ones. I should be honoured that my gifting could be used to secret away the bloodline of Pallarus from Vadroil."

"Vadroil is dead," Carvelle said.

Lifting his head, Rhox looked confused. He turned to look at Deovyn. "It's true. *Aluel* killed him during the battle. Suffocated him. Held him down until there was no life in him."

A frown crossed Rhox's face. "It seems I have missed so much."

"Don't worry," Deovyn soothed. "I'll tell you everything that has happened in the last one thousand, two hundred and thirty-six years."

"Does *Aluel* still fish?"

"Your *aluel* is obsessed with fishing," Deovyn said. "Rare is the day he returns to his den without sea salt on his scales."

"I miss swimming in the ocean."

"I don't," Deovyn replied. "I hate getting seawater up my nostrils."

"You can swim in your dragon form?" Orion asked. "Can you teach me?"

Rhox chuckled. "You're now the son of Zapyr the Splendid. You won't be able to avoid the ocean."

"I've not seen much beyond Silverdyne, Pallaryn and the few villages to be honest," Orion admitted.

"You've never seen the ocean?"

"No."

Rhox and Deovyn exchanged looks. "A crime!" they bellowed together.

"While it does my old dragon heart good to see the young ones getting along, I can hear you clearly from the camp. Be quiet."

Orion jumped out of his skin, his heartbeat racing, which set Deovyn and Rhox into peals of dragon laughter. Zapyr peered at them from the other side of the fire.

Hand to his chest, Orion tried to still his racing heart. "*Rshon Aluel*, how do you do that? Can you teach me?"

Zapyr's nostrils flared as he prowled forward. He sent both Rhox and Deovyn a dark look.

"Looks like you have a keen student, *sudunyn*," Deovyn said.

"Shame, Deo. You know better than to caterwaul like a strangled cat," Zapyr growled.

Rhox snickered, which earned him a disapproving glare.

"As for you, *mynrell*, I have taught you better. We are at war."

"Sorry, *Aluel*."

Laying his body down, Zapyr closed his eyes. "It's time to settle down and rest. We all have a busy day tomorrow."

Orion listened as one by one, the members of their camp started to drift off to sleep. Deovyn was the first, followed by the soft hum of the two children, then the queen and then Theo. He lay completely still, looking up at the stars through his lashes, sleep eluding him.

"*Aluel* ..." Rhox asked in the dark. "Is Vadroil really dead?"

Zapyr exhaled. "Yes. *Elt aluel* and Sidrah chased him down and shed his blood on the battlefield that day."

For a long moment, there was silence, and Orion held his breath.

"I wish ..." Rhox began. "I wish I were there to see the victory."

"So do I."

"*Aluel* ... When Orion first broke the chains, I couldn't feel my *vehyl*. I still can't. But now, he's at peace where all *vehyl* souls go."

Orion could hear Zapyr swallowing. "I know. He's at peace with my own soul. I only wish that ..."

"*Aluel* ..."

"What now, Rhox?"

"Ayrdonyth; Galgothmeg cannot find out about him. They'll do worse than kill him."

"I know."

"Do you think they already know?"

Orion sucked in a breath, hardly daring to believe what he was hearing. "From what *elt aluel* has seen ... they know about you being free but think you're weak."

"I am weak."

"Rubbish. There's no indication that they understand what Ayrdonyth is ... but that doesn't mean they suspect something."

"The white dragon ..."

"Rhox, honestly ..."

"We haven't spoken for so long."

"I'm sorry, I'm tired, *mynrell*. What about Tornyth?"

"He's not what I expected. How can a tiny dragon fight Galgothmeg and win?"

"I've taught you better than that." Zapyr chuckled. "Not all strength is brute force."

"Not everyone believes he is the white dragon."

Zapyr scoffed. "I think the colour of his scales speaks for itself, and many, many dragons doubted the power of Mandros. Many denied his ability to stand up for our kind."

"Do you like him? Jodathyn?"

"My new little brother?" Zapyr paused. "Very much so. He reminds me of you."

Rhox scoffed.

"Truly. Same age, dark curls and a penchant of trying to prove yourselves, never realising that you don't need to."

The two dragons' conversation faded away, and Orion lay on his back, staring up at the stars, wondering what he had overheard. Was there something wrong with him? What did Zapyr and Rhox not want Galgothmeg to know about him? He had a feeling that the dragons held Tornyth the white dragon in some high regard. But did that mean his newfound royal friend was in some type of danger?

His father had always taught him not to eavesdrop. These sorts of conversations led to trouble. But what he had heard left him much to think about.

Wriggling, he tried to find a comfortable spot.

"Go to sleep, mynrell." Zapyr's voice clearly cut through his mind. Orion's eyes sprung open at being caught eavesdropping. He resisted the urge to slap his face. *"We'll talk later."*

CHAPTER TWENTY-FIVE

Jodathyn

The Hills of Paruhulise

Tiernan was as good as his word. The moment they were prepared to leave, he strode forward, grabbed Lawman Floyde by the back of the neck and thrust him in Sidrah's direction.

"If you know what's good for you, stay away from the white dragon," Tiernan said.

Sidrah leered at the confused lawman, who stared back at Jodathyn. At the sight of the lawman, he could feel Tornyth's hackles rising. His lips curled back into a snarl.

"Your actions taught the young dragon that you are his enemy," Sidrah said. "You won't be able to change his mind."

"Might I apologise?" Floyde asked.

Grabbing Jodathyn's elbow, Will hurriedly dragged him to the other side of the road. "Might be a little too fresh for that, I'm afraid."

Roane lowered his face, his wide nostrils flaring as he sniffed at the lawman. "While I know you're not a *rokun*, you'll fly with me. Sidrah, our general, will keep to her *sudunyn's* side."

Jodathyn could feel his teeth clenching but didn't say anything about the arrangement. If he had his way, the lawman would have been left behind. He manifested into his dragon form, snapping his teeth at Floyde. He snorted in amusement as the man paled.

"Enough," Et-hir murmured at his side. She lifted her hand and brushed her fingers down his cheek.

Tornyth lowered himself to the ground and let Et-hir mount him. He watched from his position as Floyde clambered onto Roane's back. Tiernan grasped Floyde's sobbing prisoner and thrust him in the direction of the village as he too mounted Roane.

"With me, King Kieryn," Sidrah said. "Nym, your choice."

Kieryn bowed in Sidrah's direction and approached Tornyth's side. Tornyth turned to look at him as his brother patted his scales. "It's perfectly natural to be angry," Kieryn said. "But let's not stay in the state of fury."

Shaking his head, Tornyth blew hot air. "I won't."

"I'm truly sorry for what you have suffered," Lawman Floyde said.

"He speaks true," Fydellah murmured. She looked to Sidrah and manifested into her dragon, Vydris. She bumped Tornyth playfully with her wings.

"Me speaking truth does not change the pain I have caused," Floyde acknowledged.

Will was standing beside Tornyth still. He too manifested into his form. He didn't need to say anything. Tornyth knew the moment the lawman had any treacherous thoughts, Rigyl and Roane would act. He was safe, even if he was uncomfortable.

Nym still stood upon the road and looked up at Vydris with a thoughtful look on her face. "Lady Sidrah," Nym said, "might I fly with Vydris? She is still nervous taking passengers; should she not practice with someone she knows?"

"Indeed, Nym blade-tongue. That is a kind offer," Sidrah replied.

"Nym," Vydris interrupted, "you're afraid of heights."

Straightening herself to her full height, Nym looked Vydris in the eyes. Her jaw was clenched, as if she was determined not to show how worried she was. "That makes two of us that don't like flying. We might as well help each other out, you flying furnace."

They flew west with the wind. Tornyth allowed his mind to hear the whispers of Wind Song as Et-hir's fingers clutched onto his scales. He glanced in Vydris' direction. Her movements to his dragon sight seemed stilted and unsure. She held herself stiff, unpliable to the wind currents, and Nym ... his silver-haired dragon-friend was holding on for dear life. There was a green tinge to her cheeks. Astride a dragon whose whole body was tense and battling against the Wind Song was not an easy ride.

Tornyth couldn't understand how a dragon, born to fly free and rule the skies, could be so afraid of flying.

At his side, Rigyl chuckled. He looked over to the midnight-blue dragon and smirked, knowing his thoughts had not been private. Tornyth's side trembled in his attempt to hide his dragon giggles.

"What are you two cackling about?" Et-hir asked.

Tornyth guiltily looked towards Vydris, grinned and shook his head. "Dragon business, my dear."

Roane flew past with a burst of speed and bumped Rigyl with his wings, tipping him off balance. "Behave, you two."

Tornyth bit his lip and burst into peals of laughter, which had Sidrah and Kieryn staring at him in befuddlement.

"Just like a hatchling, drunk off Wind Song," Tornyth heard Sidrah mutter.

"Males ..." Vydris echoed.

"Aren't they hatchlings still?" Et-hir asked.

"Any dragon whose human is alive is considered a hatchling," Roane replied. He looked heavenward at Rigyl's answering grin. "We're approaching the hills of Paruhulise. Now, Rigyl, is the time to turn your attention listening for human thoughts that are somewhere down below. Everyone, quiet, and let us do our jobs."

Tornyth clamped his mouth shut and edged away from Roane and Rigyl, partly to give them some distance from his own mind and partly to get away from Lawman Floyde. They seemed to circle about the hills for some time, following Roane's direction. Every now and then, Roane and Rigyl would look at one another and change directions.

Sidrah seemed well at ease with their tracking, and so Tornyth decided to trust their process. After what seemed like an excruciating hour, he spotted movement in the hills. Humans!

"Sidrah!"

"Good spotting, *sudunyn*," Sidrah rumbled.

"We'll stalk them first," Roane continued. "We can decide their numbers and what threat they pose before we dive on top of them. Rigyl ... follow and concentrate."

Nodding, Rigyl followed in Roane's wake. His eyes were lidded as he attempted to do whatever Roane was trying to show him. Tornyth watched in fascination.

Roane wheeled about and glanced towards Rigyl. He waited until the younger dragon looked back at him and blinked.

"What do you sense?"

"Perhaps twenty prisoners ... three guards?"

"Close," Roane rumbled. "Sidrah, we have thirty prisoners and five guards."

Rigyl huffed in defeat.

"It takes time, practice and skill to get it right, *elt mynrell*," Roane rumbled. "Especially when we are at a distance. I was doing this long before Arturyn was even born. I am asking a lot from you."

"What are we going to do with thirty humans?" Vydris asked. "We can't carry that many, surely."

"No," Sidrah agreed, "we cannot. That is a conundrum."

"Humans have legs," Nym said. "Surely our black she-lizard can heal the injured and send them on their way."

"Good," Vydris grumbled. "I'm tired."

"Five fire breathing reptiles ... five guards ... That's one each," Nym said.

"We dive together. Make it quick. Don't let the *rokun* have a chance to fight back."

Tornyth grinned, feeling Et-hir's grip tighten. He waited for Sidrah's signal and dove. Being the smallest dragon, he was quicker. The ground sped up to meet him, and he only had seconds to see the face of the guard he was taking out. Whites of eyes widened as he grasped the armed man up, rose and dropped him from a height. The man fell screaming, and his body cracked as he hit the ground below.

The prisoners were yelling, writhing in their chains. He landed, tucked his wings in and let Et-hir off his back. She didn't wait to look back at him. She ran towards the prisoners, her hands flying as she yelled at them to be calm and that the dragons were freeing them.

Tornyth manifested back into Jodathyn and considered that perhaps falling from the skies to kill the guards hadn't been the most considerate plan where humans were concerned. Dragons were believed to be gone from Rama's shores for hundreds of years and for them to suddenly appear ... it would be a bit of a shock.

He glanced around at Will, who was staring gingerly at his hands, and Fydellah, whose deep bronze skin had paled.

"Well, I gotta say, dropping someone from a height is certainly dramatic," Nym said. "But Will ... you take vicious to a whole another level."

Will was still staring at his hands, which were covered in blood.

"Will," Jodathyn whispered, "what did you do?"

Will's deep brown eyes glanced up at him; they seemed glazed. "I tore a man in half."

Jodathyn blinked. "Oh, well, when Tornyth was still in visions, I think he impaled someone ..."

"A truth," Fydellah said, holding her stomach.

"We're at war," Tiernan said, jumping down from Roane's back. "Sometimes death is the only answer."

"A truth," Fydellah replied. She flipped her dark curly braid over her shoulder and sauntered over towards the prisoners. "Let's see if they have any water we can wash Will off with."

Sidrah had landed on the other side of the human prisoners with Kieryn. Jodathyn lifted his head to see that his brother was already soothing the worries of the common folk. He stood back and watched as Kieryn opened his arms wide and greeted his people as if they were old friends.

With Et-hir at his side, Kieryn soon had the prisoners, who ranged from the very old to the very young. They were shackled securely together so that Roane was tasked with breaking their bonds and Sidrah looking each human over to ensure they were healthy.

Lawman Floyde also watched at a careful distance. He walked to each of the dead men, checking them over for any weapons. Laying anything he found in neat piles, he then moved over to the provisions and began sorting.

Fydellah took Will to where she had found a canteen of water. He observed Will's closed-off features as he washed off his bloodied hands.

Tiernan, who had been watching Lawman Floyde closely, seemed satisfied that he wasn't up to anything drastic and grabbed another canteen of water. He drank deeply and then seemed to notice Jodathyn watching him. Capping the canteen, he strode over, holding it out.

"Your Highness, drink."

Jodathyn took the canteen and glanced around. "Is there enough for everyone?"

Tiernan nodded. "You were up early this morning. Vision?"

Taking a sip from the canteen to appease Tiernan, Jodathyn wiped his mouth. He took only a mouthful of water. Others could use it more than him. "How did you know?"

"I had time to learn your quirks when I guarded you," Tiernan replied. Jodathyn handed the canteen back. "In truth, it wasn't difficult to surmise you saw something last night."

Jodathyn brushed his hands through his hair, glancing towards Sidrah and Roane. "How can I face battle with only snippets of knowledge? Nothing I've seen has use or purpose."

"Faith," Tiernan replied. "Most of us go into battle blind. All anyone can do is press forward even when the future is uncertain."

"Perhaps being blind to the future is better for everyone." Jodathyn's shoulders drooped. "How do you live with such uncertainty?"

"The life of a soldier is not for everyone," Tiernan said. "I live each day as a gift."

"The vision started at Curran's grave. I gather you knew him," Jodathyn said.

"I knew him well," Tiernan replied. He averted his gaze. "He would have been proud to be able to serve you."

Jodathyn shook his head. "From there, Wind Song showed me where prisoners were held. There was talk about the white dragon—me ... and a great battle. I saw Mandros fall in a vision."

"Did you see his death?" Tiernan asked, his lips downturning. "Or did you see something that suggested he might?"

"I heard his roar of pain as Galgothmeg and another attacked him ..."

"Well, this we do know," Tiernan said. "Nothing is certain. Did you tell Mandros?"

"Yes." Jodathyn sighed. "He didn't seem overly concerned."

"He has a great deal many advisers a lot wiser and older than I," Tiernan said. "He may also know more than he has told you."

Jodathyn suppressed the urge to scream. "It drives me insane ... not knowing."

"Come what may, Your Highness," Tiernan said, lifting his hand to rest it upon Jodathyn's shoulder, "we will face the future together."

They decided to camp the night with the humans, escorting them as far as they could towards Kudah. When the weakest among them could no longer move, Sidrah ordered them to stop and make camp.

Jodathyn was thankful. He had decided to accompany the humans on foot, with Et-hir by his side. Fydellah and Will had done the same, planning to conserve their energy for the flight back to Torryn.

Jodathyn wasn't sure what he should be expecting in Torryn. He could only imagine the size of the camp with the number of humans that were amassing for war.

Most humans retired early for the night; Tiernan stood guard at one end. Lawman Floyde, obviously feeling obligated, guarded the other end.

Kieryn wrapped himself in his cloak and leaned against a lonely tree. His eyes were shut, and Jodathyn had no wish to disturb his brother.

At his side, Et-hir nestled closely against his chest. Her fingers gripped his shirt loosely. Her soft, sighing breaths calmed his racing heart. He let his fingers run down her hair and pressed a chaste kiss to her brow. Breathing in deeply, he tried to memorise the warm press of her body.

"I can feel her heart," Tornyth whispered. *"She's at peace."*

In the dim moonlight, Jodathyn fiddled with the golden ring that was supposed to protect his mind. He stared at the piece of jewellery, tempted to take it off. The very idea of having something of Vadroil's on his physical body made him uneasy. If he understood Zapyr's words correctly, the ring was only added protection. They had said Kieryn was safe from him. Surely it wouldn't hurt to remove it while both Roane and Sidrah were nearby.

Tugging the ring off, Jodathyn closed his fist around it. He surrendered to sleep, confident that Tiernan would wake him if there was any dire need.

"My son."

Jodathyn swallowed a lump in his throat and turned around to see who spoke to him.

Broad shouldered and tall, the stranger beckoned to him. "Come."

"Who are you?"

The stranger smiled. "Dragons have a strict hierarchy. Mandros has deceived you. I am one who has greater claim to you."

"I trust Mandros."

The stranger laughed. "Yet he did not allow me an opportunity to relinquish my claim over you. He took you for himself. It's greed, mynrell.*"*

Jodathyn felt a slither of unease snake up his spine, hearing the stranger call him the term of endearment. Although the man had made no effort to threaten him, he felt cautious. He blinked furiously, trying to bid his physical body to wake up.

"You suggest Mandros has been dishonest."

"Did he tell you how the war began between humans and dragons?"

"Vadroil."

The stranger tilted his head back and laughed. "Ironic from a dragon who abandoned his own aluel *and his nestmates."*

"Fine, tell me your story."

"I once had a dragon-mate. My ketur and five healthy mynrell. All male. In those ancient days, Ramyr was still a collection of self-governing towns. The humans near my cave invaded my home while I was out hunting and when I came back, I found my family slaughtered. My sons were not of age to manifest and protect themselves. Do you understand what I am saying to you? My little children—slaughtered. Like pigs. Their bellies opened for the birds of prey to feast upon them. That's what I came home to. That's what I can never forgive.

"It became quite apparent that the plague that was humankind needed to be wiped out. If they wanted me to be a monster, I would be a monster. I hunted them, and then I turned my attention to building an army of dragons. Dragons that sympathised with humans were put down. We took their young under our wing. The only way for our kind to survive was to weaponise our population. I found a way to increase our half-blooded side. I found a way to control those of human blood.

"My aim was to kill every single human living in this land. Dragon land. And to keep our half-blooded brethren under control."

"What does this have to do with Mandros?"

"Mandros fled his destiny and joined those who opposed me."

"Doesn't sound at all a terrible thing for him to have done."

"No?"

Jodathyn shook his head.

"Tell me, why is it your brother sits upon the throne?"

"He is the rightful king."

"No. He is not," the stranger said. "That is not our way. It's the most powerful heir that inherits. He has no dragon. You're the Dragon King."

Jodathyn shook his head again. "My nephew is the Dragon King. I am his herald."

"Why settle?"

"Why cause unnecessary dissent? We're at war."

"You could avoid war. Give yourself to me. Let me be your herald, and you'll be the king of the new Ramyr."

"I cannot."

The stranger's face twisted in fury. His human form rippled; dark scales pressed against his human flesh.

Jodathyn held himself still, waiting for the inevitable onslaught. Claws curled around his belly and drew him backwards. He let out a startled shout of surprise, taking in the furious look that crossed the stranger's face as he was pulled forcibly out of the vision and into another.

He was in his dragon form, dizzy and disorientated. The ground beneath his claws was hot and barren. Great spires of rock towered towards the midday sun. In the distance, he could hear the crashing of waves and taste the sea salt in the air.

A female dragon he had seen once before, one with blind eyes, looked past him. She lifted her head towards the sky, her nostrils flaring as if to take in the arid smell of dust and salt.

"Winter's Dragon was too much of a temptation for my mate to let go," the female dragon said. "He was always destined for great things, and life with him was never going to be an easy one."

"Why have you called for me, Mashikah?"

Another dragon, older than he had seen before, appeared. His hide and face were littered with many ancient scars. His wings were wrinkled from lack of use, yet his eyes still burned with an ancient power. It was he that had pulled him out of his vision and into this one.

"You are the all-seeing one, Gahryk. When you speak, you cause such a ruckus," Mashikah replied.

"Galgothmeg is not the only Artrothian dragon that would see the white dragon crushed before him."

"Can he be saved?" Mashikah asked. "Or is Mandros wasting his time?"

The ancient one chuckled. "The future is not fixed. I've just pulled him from a vision with a great one."

"You speak in riddles, old scales."

"An ancient threat believed to be dead has risen."

"Artroth ... yes ... we know."

The old dragon hummed. "Mandros' war party will not be enough."

"I'll send another," Mashikah replied.

"Send all ..." Gahryk smirked and coughed. "Well, except the aged, frail and blind."

Mashikah scoffed. "We have no young here ... We'll meet Artrothian forces fang to fang, and though I be the Lady of Mercy, they will find none."

Tornyth crept forward, belly to the ground, until he was almost snout to snout with Gahryk, the one Mashikah had said was the all-seeing one.

"Oh, great one," Tornyth whispered, "do you sense me?"

"I sense you, little lizard. I am the one who pulled you here and out of trouble."

"Please," Tornyth said, "please tell me how to thwart Mandros' fate?"

Two large, piercing eyes stared down at Tornyth. "One thing is clear. You are destined to be bathed in your blood thrice in your lifetime. Twice that has happened."

"I don't understand."

"You've met the one that even Galgothmeg answers to. He hates hard, and you have denied him."

"He's going to kill me," Tornyth muttered.

Gahryk's scaled face twisted into a feral smile. "Beware the knife in the dark. He approaches. May the moon give you her light in your darkest hour. Though bones may shatter, fly hard and fast with news to your aluel."

CHAPTER TWENTY-SIX

Jodathyn

The Hills of Paruhulise

Overhead, a full moon, shrouded by clouds, looked down upon Jodathyn. He was sure that Gahryk's choice to include the lines about the moon had been deliberate. Many dragons were in the habit of speaking in riddles. Gahryk's combination of a prayer and a warning was baffling. Images from his vision, of the terrible dragon's words, whirled in his mind. He had more questions now than he had answers.

Dread curled in his belly. It was quiet. Too quiet. The ancient one said he was coming, and he didn't want to face the stranger in the waking world. He sucked in a deep breath and gently extracted himself from Et-hir's embrace. She hummed in her sleep, her hands seeking out the warmth of his body.

"I have found you."

Jodathyn lay gasping on the ground, his heart hammering in his chest. The insidious voice was back. He glimpsed the world through the voice's eyes and saw the night sky and the rolling green hills. His blood sang of a victory that was not his ... and a thirst for dragon flesh.

"Foolish hatchling. You revealed your location to me."

"Sidrah!" Ramming the ring onto his finger, Jodathyn sat upright with a cry.

Sidrah's dark body lifted from where she was slumbering. Roused by his shout, Tiernan's head shot up.

"The enemy is upon us," Jodathyn projected forward, hoping that he was able to reach Roane as well. They didn't need panicking humans to complicate matters.

"Are you sure?"

"He told me he found me."

"Everyone, up!" Roane roared.

At the olive-green dragon's command, confused humans bolted upright. Tiernan was already striding towards Jodathyn. Kieryn was stumbling to his feet.

"Quick! Humans, take the supplies you can and get to cover," Roane barked. Dazed and confused by the sudden wakeup call in the middle of the night, the humans stared at Roane. "Move, quick, as fast as your legs can carry you! If you see movement in the sky, lie low on the ground."

Humans began to scatter, their frightened voices rising into a din. Captain Tiernan and Lawman Floyde moved forward to help. Jodathyn swallowed, watching as desperate hands groped for supplies.

"With your permission, Your Majesty," Floyde said, "I would like to go with the people and escort them to safety."

Kieryn considered him in the dark. "Go in peace."

"Our humans on the backs of Rigyl and Vydris. Tornyth, your back remains free ..." At Sidrah's command, both Will and Fydellah manifested. Rigyl lowered himself for Kieryn and Tiernan, his tail swishing side to side.

Jodathyn wondered how much he had gleaned from his thoughts. Taking no chances, Nym clambered onto Vydris' back.

"I'll go with you," Et-hir whispered.

"Whoever it is is after me." Jodathyn shook his head. "Please go with Vydris. We don't have much time. Please, Ettie ..."

Still looking unsure, Et-hir spun on her heels and ran towards Vydris. Lowering her hand, Nym helped to haul Et-hir up beside her.

Jodathyn felt it. The one who had been attacking him was getting closer. He glumly looked down at the innocent gold ring on his finger. His experiment with it had been foolish. Manifesting into Tornyth, he raised his snout to the sky. He was being hunted. Being with people put them in danger.

By this stage, the humans had melted into the darkness, running as fast as their two legs could take them. Tornyth looked to Sidrah for instructions. "I'll fly with you as the front guard. Roane will take the rear. Tornyth, at the first sign of trouble, fly north towards the ruins of Torryn."

"Mandros is on his way," Roane said.

"Thank the Otherworlds," Kieryn muttered.

In any other circumstances, Tornyth knew he would have enjoyed night flying. The wind was cold. Her soft, feather-like fingers brushed his scales, warning him of an enemy that was near. He shivered and glanced over to Sidrah; he knew she heard the same message.

"Keep vigilant," Sidrah said. "Your white scales make you the easiest target."

Tornyth's stomach churned. "He's close."

"So is *Aluel*," Sidrah replied. She grinned at him, flashing her fangs. She was trying to relax him. "This is not my first skirmish, little brother."

"Tornyth, fly!" Tiernan bellowed.

Tornyth sensed the presence the moment that Tiernan screamed his warning. A huge shadow, larger than Mandros, loomed above him. Blinking, he stared up in horror at the large dragon hovering over them. He recognised the dark blue scales and red horns from the cave paintings back on Torqui. The enemy dragon was flanked by two large Grey Shadows.

Tornyth froze.

"Impossible. It cannot be ..." Sidrah murmured.

"Look at you." The dragon spoke, dragging his tongue along his teeth. "Helpless little worm. And Sidrah the Most Noble. Mandros' favourite."

"Move!" Sidrah cried as their hunter spiralled into a dive.

Thankful for Deovyn's drills and coaching, Tornyth took off at speed only to find himself intercepted by another pair of Grey Shadows. He inhaled, spewing fire into their faces. One tumbled from the sky, shrieking as it was consumed by dragon fire.

The other escaped and lunged forward to dig his fangs into Tornyth's hind leg. Rigyl came to his rescue, jumping onto the creature's back. Tiernan was standing on the very tip of Rigyl's nose and thrust his sword through the skull of the dragon. The Grey Shadow jerked and released Tornyth's rump.

Ears ringing with the confusion of the attack, he faintly heard Et-hir screaming for him. As hard as it was, he knew he could not respond. They needed to press on, and he needed to make sure everyone survived.

"Mandros!"

"I'm close."

"Get the king to safety!" Tornyth bellowed at Rigyl. For a split second, he thought Will's dragon would protest. But he knew that Rigyl understood that Kieryn's life was paramount. Their job was to protect the king at all costs.

"Vydris, go!" Tornyth yelled. He caught sight of Vydris' scales to his far right. He glanced frantically around for Sidrah and Roane. They had killed one Grey Shadow, and they were both fighting the dark blue dragon with the red horns. If he could find a way to bite him with ice-fire ... "I'm right behind you!"

Vydris had opted to skim low over the ground. Dipping to follow her path, Rigyl roared at him to do the same thing. Still flying at height, he caught sight of the incoming Grey Shadows first.

Rigyl had no time to react to his bellowed warning. The Grey Shadows coordinated their attack and rammed into him. Wanting to protect the king and Tiernan, Rigyl attempted to bank, only to find himself pushed off balance.

Unable to hold on, Tiernan and the king toppled from Rigyl's back. Tornyth roared in horror and dove. He hit the first Grey Shadow, chomping down on the creature's wing. His ice power flowed through him, and the enemy dragon screamed in agony. Wrenching his head around, he let the Grey Shadow fall. His wing frozen, the enemy dragon fell from the sky and hit the ground with a thud. Punching his claws through the eye sockets of the second Grey Shadow, Rigyl let the creature twitch convulsively in his grasp.

Knowing Rigyl had the situation under control, Tornyth landed with a thump. He scouted the area and saw Tiernan lying face down on the grass. After charging over, he picked up the motionless captain in his front claws and looked again.

He spotted Kieryn dragging himself along the ground, one of his legs broken. He hobbled towards him, Captain Tiernan tucked under his belly.

"There you are, brother," Kieryn gasped, lifting his head up despite the pain. To protect the king, Tornyth stood over him. "Tiernan ..."

A thundering roar of fury heralded Mandros' entry into the fray. The large emerald dragon had not come alone. The horrible red eyes of the great enemy looked up, assessing Mandros and the three dragons that were at his side. Mandros didn't hesitate. He ploughed forward, pulling the enemy off Sidrah's back. His dragons followed him in his attack.

The dark dragon glared and turned tail and fled. Two dragons pursued him.

Tornyth shifted his weight, peering in the darkness to study the injuries on Sidrah's back. She landed painfully, stumbling, and Mandros was immediately at her side. Tornyth was thankful to know he wasn't the only one the green dragon fussed over.

"Tor!" Lifting his head, he noticed Vydris had her claws on the ground. Et-hir jumped from her back and was running towards him, tripping on her skirt. "Are you hurt?"

Twisting his nose around, he surveyed the damage to his hind quarters. The bite was deep, oozing black blood, but not life-threatening. He shuffled over so that the puncture marks were less visible to her. "I've been bitten. It doesn't look too bad."

Kieryn, who had dragged himself closer to Tiernan to check him over, glanced up at him. The king's jaw was tightly clenched. In the dark, his eyes looked glassy. Tornyth could see the bone protruding from his ripped pants, and he winced in sympathy.

"Humans need help!" Tornyth cried out.

As Sidrah took some lurching steps forward, a familiar dark red dragon landed beside Tornyth. "Heal yourself first, Sidrah. I'll see what I can do."

Sidrah wearily nodded. "Thank you, Edisyn."

Edisyn turned his appraising stare first to Tiernan's still form. The Captain of the King's Guard emitted a low moan as the dragon above him tapped him with his snout. His eyes fluttered open, widening, taking in the king's concerned expression.

"Stay still, Captain," Kieryn said. "That's an order."

Tiernan groaned and closed his eyes.

"Nasty hit to the head ... dislocated shoulder." Edisyn looked to the king's broken leg. "Best to leave limbs for a healer."

"We can wait, can't we, Tiernan?" Kieryn closed his eyes in tired defeat.

"*Ri rshon hanoch*!" Tiernan cursed.

Resolving himself to wait, Tornyth lay down on his side to take some pressure off his back end. Using his curled hind leg, Et-hir climb up to get a better look. Her slim fingers prodded his damaged scales.

He closed his eyes, and he started to drift off. It was Kieryn's voice that startled him back to consciousness.

"Tiernan first, Lady Sidrah. I've just a broken leg. Can't have my captain with an addled brain."

Tiernan muttered something that sounded distinctively uncomplimentary, and Tornyth battled to open his eyes. Sidrah was standing over the humans. Tiernan's pinched expression relaxed under her power, and he slumped into unconsciousness. As she turned her attention to Kieryn, Tornyth lifted his head to survey the dragons.

Mandros had come to stand over him. Roane was with Vydris and Rigyl, speaking in low tones. At Vydris' side, Nym stood patting her foreleg, intently listening to Roane. Edisyn along with two others stood at a respectful distance.

Tornyth heard Kieryn's soft intake of breath as his bones fused together. When the king spoke, it was without pain. "I take it from your reactions that the dragon who attacked us is known to you?"

"I thought I killed him over a millennia ago," Mandros rumbled.

"It's him," Tornyth said. "Isn't it? It's really him. Vadroil is alive."

He sensed the uncomfortable shuffle of the others at his outburst and cursed his loose tongue. He should have been more subtle.

"I am as baffled as you, *sudunyn.*" Sidrah loomed over him, and he felt the wash of her power against the bite on his leg. "Next time, it's good practice to manifest back into your human form if you are injured."

"I don't understand."

"Listen carefully, *mynrell,*" Mandros said above him. "If you die as a dragon ..."

There was something in the way that Mandros couldn't finish his statement that sent a shiver of dread up his spine.

"You are lost to us," Sidrah said. "At the time of death of our human hearts, the dragon will manifest, and all is not lost. It gives healers more time to help you."

"If your dragon dies, you're beyond the help of the healers. Both your human and dragon are dead." Roane looked at each of the young dragons in turn. "Remember that. We should all rest here until sunrise."

At dawn Mandros roused the camp. Even though Sidrah's healing magic was a marvel and Jodathyn felt no discomfort, the green dragon insisted that he did not manifest into Tornyth for the flight back. When Jodathyn opened his mouth to argue, Mandros stared at him with a stern, unblinking gaze. It would be quicker, the green dragon said, over the distance they needed to travel for the inexperienced dragons to take a break today.

After flying for an hour, Jodathyn was glad he hadn't put up much a fight. Mandros had wanted him to go over everything he had seen in his vision in as much detail as he could. He had the feeling the green dragon was looking to make sense of what happened.

"Gahryk, the all-seeing one," Jodathyn murmured. He tightened his grip around Et-hir's waist. "I felt weary of him."

"Many are," Mandros replied. "Sometimes he is a help, sometimes a hinderance. Once he was a dragon who was well respected in Artroth, until one day he saw something that made him leave Artroth's shores. He's ancient and cantankerous ... and has little patience for the current politics and humans."

"That's a shame."

"He's been fading for centuries," Mandros said. "But his tongue and his wit are twisted as ever. He won't hurt you."

"Could this all-seeing one help us?" Kieryn asked. He sat behind Jodathyn, and his voice carried easily. "Or will he side with Artroth?"

"Sometimes I wonder if he is seeing this world or the Otherworld. He has no love for Artroth," Mandros replied. "Gahryk takes no sides."

"It is said that Gahryk is waiting for the rise of the white dragon before he gives up the ghost and dies," Edisyn said. He exchanged an amused glance with a speckled brown dragon on his left-hand side. "He's been waiting since the rise of Lady Torqui."

"Three thousand years, they say," the brown dragon replied.

"I hope I'm worth the wait," Jodathyn muttered.

"I'm sure you are," Et-hir whispered. She leaned back into Jodathyn's chest and looked up at him adoringly. He kissed the end of her nose and held her closer.

"Do you have any other questions about what you saw?" Mandros asked, his voice cutting through Jodathyn's moment of peace.

"I have a few." Jodathyn pressed his hands down on the warm scales of Mandros' shoulder. "Mashikah is your mate? Where is she?"

"She is. She's keeping the isle of dragons safe from Artroth."

"I've seen her twice now," Jodathyn whispered. "She doesn't like me. And she's planning on coming with more dragons."

"Welcome news," Edisyn murmured.

"She doesn't like the idea of another dragon born of winter in the family," Sidrah interrupted. "*Lullah* will not harm you, if that is what you fear."

"Mashikah, dear Mashikah, was once a powerful battle dragon in her own right. As a dragon born of winter, she was hunted by Vadroil and her family massacred when she was young. She is concerned about sheltering another Vadroil is after." Mandros' voice was low. He looked straight ahead.

"My presence is a danger to everyone," Jodathyn said.

"We're in danger with or without your presence," Sidrah replied. "Don't let it bother you. What will be, will be."

"Vadroil told me of how humans destroyed his family. He said you were lying to me."

Mandros scoffed. "While the death of his mate and his five very young children is a tragedy that should never have happened, it was the result of centuries of poor treatment of *vehyl* at the claws of the Artrothian emperor. Did he tell you how he built his army to destroy the free dragons of Rama and her people?

I myself was born of a dragon father, pure of blood, and a slave woman. It was intended that dragon young like me would be Grey Shadows, his personal soldiers with no mind of their own. I am called 'traitor' in Artroth because I fought him."

"He called me his son," Jodathyn whispered. "He said you stole me from him."

"How can one steal something with a soul?" Mandros snarled. "He wants ownership. He doesn't want to be an *aluel*."

Jodathyn lay down, pressing his cheek against Mandros' neck. He had learned from his time as a dragon different ways dragons communicated with their bodies. Mandros wasn't angry with him, nor was he irritated. There was a fury that ran deep within the green dragon that he buried. Vadroil was the cause of his anger. "There's so much I don't understand, *Aluel*."

"You will learn in time," Mandros replied. "There's so much to teach you."

Jodathyn looked down at the world below. Rama in all her glory was there for him to see. There was a part of him that never wanted the flight to end and another that was desperate to put his feet on the ground.

The great mountains of the Stonethaw Ranges came into view first. They sped forward until he caught a glimpse of the ancient capital of Rama. The ruins of Torryn spread for miles, and among the great boulders and columns, he could see activity of humans and a few dragons moving.

"We've set our council hidden in the mountains," Mandros told the humans. "I'll take you there."

CHAPTER TWENTY-SEVEN
Orion

The Ruins of Torryn

Prince Carvelle's moods had been swinging like a pendulum, and it was taking all of Orion's patience to keep the young boy distracted. The girl, Larelle, watched the prince pine and throw tantrums from a safe distance. Even the queen didn't know what she could do to calm Carvelle.

Deovyn and Zapyr had left earlier that morning to organise the camp, taking Theo with them so he might have chance to train and prepare with humans. This left Rhox and Orion in charge. By the time mid-morning came around, Rhox retreated into his own mind and curled up to sunbake in his patch of sun. From the determined way the young bronze dragon ignored Prince Carvelle, he wanted to be alone.

When Mandros and Sidrah were spotted, Orion was relieved. Hopefully with the return of his father, Prince Carvelle would be more settled.

Hand in hand with the prince, Orion watched the dragons land. When Jodathyn swiftly dismounted, Orion could tell something was wrong. He was perplexed when Jodathyn turned his gaze up at the king and lifted his hand as if to assist his brother. King Kieryn shook his head and slipped from Mandros' back.

He knew he wasn't the only one to feel the unease of the group. Queen Odelle was watching her husband's face closely. "Kieryn? What has happened?"

"We are well," the king replied. He glanced towards Jodathyn, eyes sweeping over his brother.

Prince Carvelle dropped Orion's hand like a hot poker to rush at his father. He came to a skidding halt halfway between his parents, his nose scrunching up in confusion.

"You're all worried," the prince declared. "Uncle had a disturbing vision. Are you well now, Uncle?"

"I am well," Jodathyn replied. He glanced over to Rhox, his dark grey eyes failing to mask his anxiety. "Perhaps, Lord Mandros, we should ..."

"Of course," Mandros interrupted. He nodded his great head and pierced Rhox with a commanding stare. "There has been a development. The hiding of the vulnerable is now a very delicate task. Are you up to the job, Rhox?"

"Of course, grandsire," Rhox answered, shifting his weight. His wings fluttered uneasily in the breeze.

"If the battle looks to be lost, you take the queen and the little children and you get them as far into Sion as you can. Do not look back."

Rhox seemed perplexed by the command. "I thought the idea was to shield them here under illusion?"

"He's been spotted," Mandros said. "Vadroil is alive."

At the emerald dragon's announcement, Orion felt his insides melt in fear. He glanced between the others. The stiffness in Nym's shoulders, the stoic stillness of Tiernan and the flaring nostrils of Sidrah.

"Alive?" Rhox echoed. "But *Aluel* assured me he was dead … Oh no!" The bronze dragon hunched his shoulders, his great head lowered to the ground. His long, scaly tail tucked in around his body. "No, no, no, no, no!"

"What is it?" Jodathyn asked, striding forward. His master reached out and touched Rhox's side with his palm. "Whatever it is, tell us."

"What have I done?" Rhox cried, lifting his snout. His voice rose into a wail. "What have I done?"

"What is it?" Jodathyn pressed. "You can tell me."

Rhox tilted to stare down at Jodathyn as he blew out hot air from his nostrils. "I'm the dragon of illusion."

"Yes, I know," Jodathyn said.

"They used me!"

"That isn't a surprise," Sidrah replied.

"They turned me into a Grey Shadow and used me to mask Vadroil," Rhox cried. "Whoever was killed on the battlefield that day wasn't Vadroil. Now he has returned … He's coming back."

Mandros' large eyes closed as if he was in pain.

"And we will meet him head-on," Jodathyn vowed.

"I'll do everything possible, grandsire," Rhox said, rolling back his scaled shoulders to sit upright.

Mandros opened his eyes, regarding Rhox solemnly. "I wish I didn't have to ask this of you. But we need you here."

"I'm so sorry," Rhox said. "When *Aluel* said Vadroil was dead, I hoped …"

Mandros shook his head. "I am thankful that we have this second chance. I am so sorry that we lost you …"

Rhox sat on his haunches at the edge of the human encampment and looked over the grassy fields of Torryn. Orion stood by his side, painfully aware that Zapyr had dismissed them from the mountain caves to rest in the hopes that he might find a way to support the brooding bronze dragon. He glanced up at his brother and wondered if he was also suspicious of his father's motives.

"I miss being human," Rhox said. He lifted his snout, and the air about them shimmered. Before him Orion could see a powerfully set man astride a black horse. A younger man with dark curls thundered after him on a large, young bay stallion. They galloped across the grassy plains before disappearing into nothingness. Rhox sighed.

Orion looked away; he didn't want to be found staring. "What do you miss about it?"

"You must know *Aluel* was the first King's Guardsman, a fierce warrior and horseman. He taught me everything I know. I miss the feel of a sword in my hand and a horse between my thighs."

"My father was a warrior too," Orion replied.

Rhox looked over his horseman's lock. He lifted a lazy claw and right before Orion's eyes, he could see his parents. His father, tall and proud in his full-dress armour, and his mother, her red Sionian scarf twisted into her dark hair.

"How?"

Rhox looked at him balefully as the phantoms of Orion's parents faded away.

"You must miss them. They were simple to conjure; they're never far from your mind. The day that Phill Maysden's son walks into the Other-world with his lock on the right side of his temple will be a proud one for him."

Lifting his hand, Orion touched his temple, feeling a little self-conscious.

"Yes, I know about the right-hand side," Rhox continued. "Theo silver-ear says I should request a story from Prince Carvelle about you."

Orion groaned. "To save you time, I shot someone in the face."

Rhox snorted back a laugh. "Doesn't surprise me in the least ... I was nineteen ..."

The sudden change of topic had Orion baffled for a heartbeat. When he considered what Rhox had been through, it became apparent what the comment meant. "You were young when you were ..."

"Killed," Rhox interrupted, "I know. Grandsire didn't want Deo or I anywhere near the Battle of Haven Bay. I argued that I was ready. It was the first time *Aluel* took my side. And I got myself killed."

Orion shifted uncomfortably.

"Just don't be surprised if he doesn't want you in the air during ..." Rhox's words hung in the air between them. He turned his snout downwards and clawed at the earth under his feet. Orion had noticed, when he was bored or frustrated, the bronze dragon's habit of destroying things around him.

Stepping away slightly, Orion tilted his head and studied a figure coming quickly in their direction.

"Hey! Orion! Theo said you were about."

Orion couldn't help but grin as he spotted Tad astride one of his father's famous stallions racing towards them. He lifted his head in greeting, taking note of his friend's leather armour.

"Friend of yours?" Rhox rumbled.

Tad pulled on the reins, bringing his stallion as close as he dared to the dragon.

"Tad, this is Rhox," Orion said. "Rhox, Tad. We grew up together in Silverdyne."

Rhox's nostrils flared as he scented the pawing stallion. "Nice animal."

Running his hand down the quivering neck of the stallion, Tad turned his gaze back towards the bronze dragon. "Father has me exercising the horses to keep me out of trouble. I told him the ride from Silverdyne to Torryn was enough. He set a brutal pace to get here."

Orion burst out laughing. "How did that go down?"

"Not well." Tad grinned.

"What's the morale like in the human side of camp?"

Tad's expression hardened. "I hear a rumour you aren't exactly human anymore."

Orion winced.

"All this time, and you never told me!" Tad cried. "I'm insulted! Could you imagine the adventures we could have gone on?"

Rhox's brow furrowed. "His dragon burst out during a battle, *vehyl*. Not something to crow about."

"It's okay." Orion laid a palm on Rhox's warm scales. "Tad and I often tease one another. He means nothing by it."

Exhaling, Rhox slumped on the ground. He glanced up at the twitching stallion, watching as his ears swivelled. "I see *Aluel* has cast a wide net and is keeping the animals in camp calm."

Orion blinked.

"Did you honestly think, *sudunyn,* that horses are naturally calm around dragonkind?"

"*Aluel* is keeping *all* the animals calm?" Orion couldn't believe it. He could barely hold three horses. The moment he had sought to control the Grey Shadow during the attack on the road to Silverdyne, their horses had bolted.

"Power is like a muscle. The more you train it and use it, the stronger it is," Rhox replied. "Give you a thousand years or so, and *Aluel* thinks you'll outshine him."

"A thousand years!" Tad chuckled. "What will I do in the Otherworld without you?"

"His human part will be there," Rhox said.

Orion nudged his dragon brother. "He's playing again. Is that ... a dragon?"

Lifting his head, Rhox looked in the direction Orion was pointing. The bronze dragon squinted his eyes against the glare of the sun. "A stranger ... I think ... small, red ... male. He's struggling."

"Get help." Orion didn't waste any more time. He manifested and sprung into the air. He loved the way his powerful muscles bunched and propelled forward. Streaking through the sky, Orion approached the red dragon.

Whoever he was, he was hurt. Claw marks ran down his back and down his nose. His head was half bowed as he flapped about clumsily.

"Land!" Ayrdonyth called out. He had no way of knowing who the young dragon was, if he was friend or foe. Until his identity had been established, he couldn't in good conscience allow him into camp.

The stranger's large green eyes full of misery looked up at him. The relief was very visible on his triangular face.

Seeing that the red dragon was weak, Ayrdonyth approached and helped him to land. By the time they came to the ground, the red dragon panting, Mandros and Sidrah were only a short distance away.

"Ayr ... get back!" Sidrah commanded.

Ayrdonyth hurried to obey but turned where he was still in earshot. His dragon side was curious. It was something he couldn't contain.

"Great ones!" the red dragon cried. "Please don't eat me."

"We're not here to eat you," Mandros rumbled. "Tell us who you are."

"A few days ago, I was a human. Galgothmeg stole me from the citadel ... now I'm stuck in dragon scales, a slave to the dark one. I've escaped. Please! Help me!"

"You will not be stuck for long," Sidrah rumbled.

"The dark one helped you to manifest?" Mandros asked.

"I didn't want to!" the red dragon cried. He pushed his belly low to the ground. "I went to sleep and woke up like this."

Sidrah turned toward Mandros. Curious, Ayrdonyth stepped forward, trying to pick up their words. Mandros glanced at him briefly, a small smile of acknowledgement on his lips.

"*Aluel*, Vadroil does not help young ones to manifest ..." Sidrah seemed confused by Vadroil's motives.

"We now have four that you have helped," Ayrdonyth said. "That means there are more like us. Why wouldn't Vadroil use all the resources at his disposal?"

"Vadroil's style is to create Grey Shadows," Mandros replied. "This is unprecedented."

Sidrah shook her head. "He didn't even teach him to fly well ... What use is he in battle?"

"Perhaps I was too small for his liking, oh glorious lady," the red dragon said.

"Give us your dragon name, young one."

"The dark one simply called me Tygunyr."

"*Sharp blade.*" Mandros sighed. "Come, let's find you somewhere to rest your weary wings."

"Please, milord," Tygunyr cried. "I have news, and I have flown so hard to reach you!"

Mandros seemed amused by Tygunyr's enthusiasm. "Speak."

"He has a great host of human soldiers coming. Ships from Artroth have made their way into the remote regions of the Clearwater."

Mandros shifted. His amber eyes slid towards Sidrah to see how she was taking the information. But Tygunyr was not finished.

"I heard talk ... Dragons supporting the dragon Flame and Fury have been intercepted. They're not coming."

Mandros' noble face froze. Then very slowly, he turned towards Ayrdonyth. "Go and get King Kieryn, Roane, Curarfur and Zapyr. We have a war council to convene."

The red dragon slid along the ground on his belly. "They could be here in a matter of days. I flew as fast as I could."

Mandros touched Tygunyr's shoulder with his nose. "Be at peace, my son. You have done well, indeed."

Deciding it was best to find those Mandros wanted in his war council immediately, Ayrdonyth spread his wings and took off. It was a little troubling that the dreaded Vadroil was also searching for new dragons and forcing them to manifest. He couldn't help but wonder if Tygunyr's experience was as painful as his own. He shivered in sympathy.

CHAPTER TWENTY-EIGHT

Jodathyn

The Ruins of Torryn

While Kieryn and Mandros spent the next few days in closed meetings with their generals, Jodathyn was given the task of watching Carvelle or raising morale in the human camp. It involved being seen in both human and dragon forms and pretending to be unaffected by the tense atmosphere. His time as Son of the Crown made him quite practiced at pretending that nothing was wrong.

Day by day their human army numbers steadily grew. There had been talk of a dragon called Tygunyr in the camp who had escaped Vadroil. As of yet, Jodathyn hadn't met him. He hoped to ask the other new dragon questions about Vadroil.

When he attempted to seek him out, Sidrah admonished him and told him to let the new dragon settle in before he bothered him like an overeager hatchling. He bristled at that comment. Sidrah did not notice. She was preoccupied with whatever news she heard from Vadroil's camp.

According to Orion, Zapyr was volatile, which led to the newest King's Guardsman avoiding the golden dragon. Jodathyn heard Orion grumbling to Theo that Zapyr had lectured him severely about the dangers of approaching an unknown dragon.

The rumours of Galgothmeg and Vadroil were also increased alarmingly. Jodathyn found himself often at the edge of the encampment, his chin tilted to the sky, waiting for the promised dragon reinforcements. They never came.

Early one afternoon, Jodathyn found himself yet again standing sentry at the edge of camp, and he heard the first rumours of the enemy closing in. Shivers of dread snaked up his spine. He expected Mandros to be the one to contact him and confirm what he already knew deep within his bones, but it was Orion.

"Tomorrow," Orion whispered behind him. "The battle for Rama begins."

Jodathyn stiffly nodded his head. He didn't turn to look at Orion. "Our orders?"

"I'll be with cavalry," Orion said. Jodathyn could hear the frustration in his voice. "*Rshon Aluel* doesn't want me announcing my presence unless absolutely necessary."

"And I?"

"Fly at Deovyn and Zapyr's sides." Orion huffed. "Vadroil knows of your existence; Lord Mandros was concerned that Vadroil would be able to sense you even in your human form."

"I'm safer among the dragons ..." Jodathyn grimaced. He internally winced at the look of envy that crossed Orion's face.

"Prince Carvelle wants to see you before he goes into hiding," Orion replied.

Jodathyn's shoulders slumped. He didn't know how, but he needed to put on a brave face for the sake of his nephew. "Yes, of course. Where is he?"

"In the King's Guard tent."

Jodathyn turned upon his heel and faced Orion. He briefly smiled at his servant, sure that the nerves that were ravaging his gut were plain to see. Striding through the camp, he was aware of Orion trailing him at a respectful distance. He didn't look to his left or right as the troops about him all murmured their greetings. He could see it in their eyes that they were all nervous.

Jael met him by the King's Guard tent. In the last few days, he had kept nearby, a source to speak to if he felt he needed to loosen his tongue. The healer grasped his hand in a firm grip and patted his shoulder. Jodathyn swallowed.

"You both have plenty of courage," Jael said. "Remember that in the fray."

Orion nodded at the advice. "I've been stationed with the Silverdyne Cavalry."

"As it should be," Jael replied. "Both Captain Tiernan and Lord Zapyr have agreed on this point. Come, the prince is waiting for you."

Jael opened the flap to the King's Guard tent, and Jodathyn entered. Carvelle was sitting on a makeshift bunk, swinging his legs back and forth. The smile on his little face didn't quite reach his eyes as he looked up to greet them.

"Uncle!" Carvelle cried. He jumped from the bunk and threw his arms around Jodathyn's legs. "I don't want you to go to war!"

"Carvelle," Jodathyn said, kneeling before his nephew. "In life there are many duties that one must fulfil."

Pressing his small nose into Jodathyn's chest, Carvelle shook his head. "I've heard what is said about the camp. They say you're not a man yet. You shouldn't have to fight! And they're afraid."

"I'm a dragon," Jodathyn replied, brushing his fingers through Carvelle's hair. "There's no victory without sacrifice."

There wasn't much more that he could say to soothe his nephew's worries. Jodathyn stayed sitting cross-legged, holding the prince until the little one wiggled out of his hold. Lifting a shaking hand to wipe away his tears, Carvelle murmured, "I need to be with Papa."

Orion held out his hand. "I can take you back up the mountain."

Jodathyn felt a sense of helplessness, watching his nephew leaving with Orion hand in hand. He remained sitting in the middle of the tent, feeling lost.

It was Carew that tapped him on the shoulder. "Follow me."

Confused, Jodathyn left the tent with the young King's Guardsman. He must have been in the tent for quite some time. The afternoon was cooling off, and the sky was a dark blue

"Whatever may come," Carew said as they moved through the camp, "we're ready."

"I have faith in my brother's forces," Jodathyn replied. "Where are you taking me?"

Carew sent him a sideways glance. "Tomorrow brings us war ... but tonight is for friends."

"Friends?"

Humming, Carew continued to lead him through the camp. Most of the troops were busy with evening meals and making final preparations for the morning. A few lifted their heads curiously as they passed, but everyone moved in silence. It was the atmosphere of a coming storm.

It was to a campfire that Carew led him. Will and Fydellah were already sitting around the fire. A few younger guardsmen were also with them.

"Come, join our merry company and take your mind off things." Grasping Jodathyn's elbow, Carew escorted Jodathyn to his own log and plonked him down.

Another guardsman handed Jodathyn a water canteen. He didn't wear the black and silver of the King's Guard, but he thought his face may have been familiar.

"Want to keep our minds clear for the morrow," Carew said, leaning over to whisper in Jodathyn's ear. "My father is a big believer in sobriety before a skirmish."

Jodathyn tilted his head back and was grateful for the water. For a long moment, everyone eyed each other, and then Fydellah cleared her throat and grabbed some rations. "We should eat something," she said, throwing a hunk of bread at Will and then Carew.

Grinning at her, Carew broke the bread and shared it with Jodathyn. He accepted it with a small smile.

"Here he is," Will said, plucking small portions of his bread before putting them in his mouth. A self-satisfied smile curled on his lips.

Confused, Jodathyn looked around and spotted Et-hir and Ruevyn.

"Are you sure about this, my lord?" Ruevyn asked, looking first at Will, then Carew and the guardsmen.

"Quite sure," Will said. "Jod could do with the company, and Carew doesn't normally bite."

Confident of her own welcome, Et-hir placed herself beside Jodathyn. Smiling, Carew abandoned his own seat and indicated to Ruevyn he should sit. Ruevyn stared at the blond guardsman.

"Sorry about arresting you the first time we met," Carew said with a cheeky grin.

Will burst into laughter at the incredulous look that crossed Ruevyn's face. Unsure, Ruevyn slowly lowered himself next to Jodathyn.

"So, what have you been up to?" Jodathyn asked.

Ruevyn shrugged. "The usual. Sharpening, polishing … sorting blades of death."

Leaning forward, Jodathyn stared down at the dry husk of bread he had been given. He twirled it about in his fingers. "I know …" he whispered.

Ruevyn looked up at him sharply.

"I'm sorry for your loss."

The farmer's eyes narrowed and glared at Will, who held up his hands in surrender. "I figured you deserved a friend that understood what you were going through."

Ruevyn swallowed thickly. "We'll talk more after tomorrow."

"And if there is nothing after tomorrow?"

"Then we can collect apples in the Otherworld and peg them at unsuspecting passersby for eternity."

Fydellah snorted back a laugh as Et-hir's fingers sought his own. They sat next to their campfire as the sky continued to darken. Nym and Theo joined them. Then Orion, who had spent some time with Zapyr and Rhox.

When the moon was high, Captain Tiernan came to the fireside and ushered them to their beds. The captain's gaze lingered on Carew, who saluted him. For once his cheeky grin was missing from his lips.

"Get off him!"

Jodathyn's eyes snapped open in the darkness, awoken by a shout. Even in his half-aware state, he recognised the voice belonging to Will. His body stiffened, realising he was being straddled by a shadowed figure, his hips pinned to his sleeping pallet. A blade swiped down.

Roaring, Jodathyn lunged forward, grasping a bony wrist and twisting. The intruder screamed in pain, and Jodathyn used both hands to throw him backwards into Will's grasp. At his side, Et-hir fell out of bed with a strangled cry.

Both Orion and Nym had rolled to their feet, weapons in hands. But it was Ruevyn who surged across the distance of the tent and punched the intruder in the face. With a moan, Jodathyn's would-be attacker slumped, and Orion kicked the weapon from loose fingers.

"Get guards," Nym croaked, pointing to Theo. "Quick."

Et-hir stood, staring in shock, her fingers curling around Jodathyn's arm. Theo darted out of the tent.

Will's wide eyes speared the intruder and then Jodathyn. The lord drew in a shaky breath and wiped a hand down his face. "Sorry ... I heard his evil thoughts and yelled."

"You saved my life," Jodathyn croaked, hardly daring to believe that an assassin had made it into his tent. It was foolish to attack him when he was surrounded by so many people.

"Forgive me!" the figure cried. "I have a message."

Jodathyn wrapped his arms around Et-hir's waist, tugging her close as he stared down at the boy who had tried to murder him. Seeing him crumpled on the floor, he guessed the boy was younger than Orion. Flaming red hair framed his pale face, and bright green eyes widened, a tactic used to make himself look less threatening.

"A truth," Fydellah said, stepping forward. She glanced to Will, and he nodded. Her face hardened as she regarded the top of his bowed head. "How old are you?"

"Fifteen summers."

"Your name?"

"Filyx."

"You're Tygunyr," Orion said. He circled around the would be assassin. "I recognise your voice when we met as dragons."

Filyx cringed, hunching his shoulders as if he thought he might be struck. Jodathyn's brow furrowed.

"This boy is the dragon who escaped from Vadroil." Orion shook his head.

"Vadroil sent us a mole," Jodathyn said, his stomach churned at the thought of Vadroil's agent in their camp. "What is your message?"

"Vadroil is coming with a great host."

"We already know that," Nym grumbled.

Frowning, Fydellah circled the intruder. "I sense that's not the whole truth."

"I swear, milady," the intruder cried. "I mean no actual harm. I was forced to do this. I was hoping to be caught so you might save me!"

"Three lies."

"What's happening in here?" Theo had returned with a stern-faced King's Guardsman.

"Guardsman Lyntton, this boy came into our tent with the intention of stabbing Prince Jodathyn," Orion said. He stooped to pick up the weapon and handed it to the older guardsman.

Jodathyn swallowed an impatient sigh as more King's Guardsmen entered their tent.

"No!" cried the intruder. "That's not true!"

"Lies," Fydellah hissed.

Guardsman Lyntton turned to sweep his eyes over Jodathyn. "Your Highness, are you unharmed?"

Jodathyn nodded. "Could you remove him?"

Lyntton nodded and moved through the tent. When he reached the wretched boy, he forced him to his feet. "Get me some rope," he said, turning towards his companions.

A man with severe burns to the face nodded grimly and left.

Lyntton ran his large hands down the boy's trousers, finding another dagger tucked into his boot. When he searched his jerkin, he found a piece of parchment.

Curious, Ruevyn stepped forward and snatched it up. "It's old … hard to make out," the farmer grunted.

Jodathyn held his hand out for the parchment. It was crinkled with age. He squinted in the dim lighting. He could see that the paper was illustrated with a man lying in a puddle of blood. A horse stood vigil over the body. Ignoring the picture, Jodathyn read the words, "*Rokun* will kill a king of Pallarus blood." This had been a prediction the great lords liked to mumble about a dragon, namely himself. "There's a picture of a dead man, presumably a king."

"That's you," the boy spat. "*Rokun*. Dragon spawn."

Folding the parchment, Jodathyn glanced up at him, doing his best to seem unconcerned. "You've mistranslated it, I'm afraid," he replied. "The word for dragon is *rshon*. *Rokun* is the word for an evil human."

"Your Highness, if I may?" Guardsman Lyntton held out his hand for the parchment. Seeing no reason to deny him, Jodathyn handed it over.

Lyntton thrust the prisoner at Orion while he unfolded the parchment. Two of his counterparts stepped into the tent and took the prisoner from a befuddled Orion. Jodathyn watched, caught somewhere between concerned and amused, as Guardsman Lyntton paled. The veteran of the King's Guard cleared his throat and shoved the parchment into his shirt pocket.

"We'll take him," Lyntton said.

"Not yet," Fydellah replied. "I want to know what the message is …"

The intruder must have known he was caught in his own web of deceit. He hung like a limp doll in the guardsmen's grip. Then slowly he lifted his chin, his green eyes alight with hatred and pain. The corners of his lips curled, and he nodded in Jodathyn's direction.

"Lord Vadroil bid me to cut out your beating heart as a gift for Mandros, the dragon of Flame and Fury."

There was a long pause. Then Fydellah strode across to Orion and snatched the dagger from his hand. She tilted her head as she regarded the would-be assassin. "You are too far gone for us to save," she said. Before any of the King's Guardsmen could stop her, she thrust the dagger into the boy's heart. She wrenched it back out as the guardsmen released him, and he fell like a dead weight.

"Who's going to tell the king?" Will asked weakly. His eyes slid over to Fydellah, who was cleaning the blade. She tilted her chin and smiled up at him.

"Not at this hour." Jodathyn shook his head. "After the battle. There's nothing more to be done tonight."

"I will be speaking with Captain Tiernan," Guardsman Lyntton said. "He will seek out His Majesty. The king must know."

"I can go," Orion said.

"Get your rest," Lyntton replied, bending down to grasp the dead boy's boots. "Let your elders worry about this mess tonight."

Et-hir's hands tugged Jodathyn back onto the bunk beside her. Where the tips of her fingers touched, a pleasant warmth lingered. "You heard the guardsman. Time to sleep."

After narrowly escaping an assassination attempt, Jodathyn didn't think sleep would be possible. But at dawn he was woken to the clattering of men and weapons that echoed through the camp.

Huddled, wrapped up in his cloak, Et-hir peered up into his face. He wondered how long she had been awake, watching him. He pressed his lips against her brow, and he reached over to shake Ruevyn.

The farmer had insisted on sleeping at his back to protect him. It brought a sense of nostalgia, as they used to sleep in the same position as children to guard each other from the violent men at Aviah Valley. Ruevyn's eyes snapped open.

"Up!" Orion cried, dashing into the tent. "Armour on! The enemy has been spotted."

Studying Orion's calm mask, Jodathyn rolled to his feet and offered his hand to Et-hir. Kieryn's newest guardsman looked older this morning, alert and already dressed for battle.

Jodathyn turned to Ruevyn, who was frowning. "Let me help you with your armour."

"Jod ... you don't have to."

"I insist. It'll be quicker, and you'll be available to help others."

Orion nodded in approval, stepping up to Will, whose hands were trembling so badly he was struggling to tie the laces of his shirt. The young horseman smacked Will's hands out of the way and laced the shirt. He then stepped around Will and proceeded to dress him in the hauberk and mail shirt the lord had taken from the stores. Defeated, Will stood like a stiff wooden doll.

"Come, brother, I'll help you," Nym said softly, tugging on Theo's arm.

Jodathyn finished with Ruevyn's bracers, his eyes memorising the faces of his friends. They made an odd bunch, he decided. But he loved each of them in their own way. He couldn't imagine living life without them ...

Captain Tiernan charged into the tent, Carew at his shoulder. "Join the horsemen, Guardsman Orion."

Orion nodded and saluted.

"You're the best friend a thief could ask for." Theo gripped Orion's shoulder, frowned and then let his arm hang loosely at his side.

"You're no longer a thief," Orion replied. "Don't let anyone tell you anything different."

"It's been an honour, Guardsman Orion," Jodathyn said, holding out his hand to stall Orion. "I am glad that I get to call you friend."

"The honour has been mine, Your Highness." Orion saluted Jodathyn. He glanced once more at Tiernan before stepping from the tent.

"Your Highness, Lord Mandros awaits you and Lady Et-hir. The rest of you, stay close to Guardsman Carew and those he points out. He will protect you as much as he can in the melee."

"Yes, captain." Carew saluted. And Tiernan's eyes softened for a moment.

Will cleared his throat. "Well, farewell then." He exited, grasping Jodathyn's hand as he passed. Theo and Fydellah nodded their heads. But Nym ... As she drew level, she threw her arms around Jodathyn's neck.

"Stay safe, palace brat!" she cried. "You better come back in one piece, lizard breath!"

"Thank you, for everything," Jodathyn muttered into her shoulder. His arms tightened their grip around her. He released her, and she fled the tent.

"Good luck, my friend," Ruevyn said.

"Don't die!" Jodathyn blurted.

Ruevyn snorted back a laugh, grasping the sides of Jodathyn's face and drawing their foreheads together. "Well, if I do, promise me this, Jodathyn Pallarus. Fight for the children like us, the slaves, the orphans, and the unloved."

"We'll do this together."

"Your Highness." Tiernan cleared his throat. "The king ..."

Jodathyn took Et-hir's hand and exited the tent, blinking into the golden dawn light. Steering Et-hir towards the edge of the camp so that he might have room to manifest without causing chaos, Jodathyn drew her close to him.

She had been silent for most of the morning. Last night they had a 'lively discussion', which Nym called an argument. Et-hir was not impressed that Kieryn had asked her to stay at Odelle's and Carvelle's side. She had fought valiantly, determined she would fly upon Jodathyn's back into battle.

"You won't be left unarmed," Guardsman Carew said, interjecting himself into their discussion. "You are Jodathyn's intended; a princess-in-waiting. If the king should fall, the duty to protect Carvelle and defend the country falls to the queen and other royal relatives. You are the last line of defence."

Et-hir had fallen silent, and she said no more on the matter. Jodathyn knew that she didn't understand or like the honour Kieryn had asked of her. He had no words of assurance, no way to make her or himself feel any better.

He pressed his trembling lips against hers. She sighed into his kiss, her body melting into his embrace. Jodathyn opened his eyes to drink in the sight of her dark lashes brushing her glowing copper skin in the morning light. It wasn't lost on him that this might be the last time he held her in his arms.

Jodathyn pulled away, knowing that they had delayed for long enough. He manifested into his dragon form and gently lifted Et-hir in his scaled grasp and placed her onto his back. Once he was sure she was settled, he spread his wings to find his brother.

It was a short flight. He found Kieryn at the separate area from where Rhox, Odelle and the children had been staying. The king seemed to have aged a few years overnight. He was dressed in his armour, his eyes alight with fiery retribution for anyone who dared to cross him.

"Listen, Jodathyn," Kieryn said, striding over to place his palms against his scales. "If anything were to happen to me in battle … it's you. You'll look after Carvelle for me. Love him as your own and teach him how to be a good king. A better king than his father."

"Kieryn …"

"Thank you for all you have done. Stay safe. I must go." The king withdrew his hand and turned towards Et-hir, who had slipped from Tornyth's back. He took her slender hands in his own and pressed a brotherly kiss on her cheek. "Stay safe, my dear."

"Don't die, my king."

Tornyth felt ridiculous. All around him were men and women willing to lay their lives down for the realm. He knew once the day was over, many would have stepped from the mortal realm into the Otherworld.

"Jodathyn …" Kieryn lowered his voice. "Tornyth … it is my duty to fight beside my people. If I don't lead Rama into battle, then who will?"

Gylleah stepped forward, her silver scales winking in the morning sun. "It's time," she said. "I'll take you to your men, *vehyl pallu*."

Kieryn nodded and smiled once more in Tornyth's direction.

And then it was just Et-hir and a few dragons.

"It's a short walk to the queen," Et-hir said. She pressed her lips to his scales, and Tornyth could feel the dampness of her tears. "I can go from here. But come back to me ..."

"I love you, Ettie," Tornyth rumbled.

Et-hir nodded glumly, her head downcast. Saddened, Tornyth watched the little human that he had learnt to love above all others leave him behind. He didn't blink until she disappeared from view. Surrounded by his dragon brethren, Tornyth had never felt so alone.

CHAPTER TWENTY-NINE
Orion

The Ruins of Torryn

Zoryn, the grey stallion who Orion had stolen from the king's stables, was waiting for him when he reached the place where the horses were kept. When the horse saw him, he pawed the ground. Stroking the grey stallion's velvet nose, Orion murmured soft reassurances. His power mingled with another's and for the first time, Orion felt the touch of Zapyr's beast-magic.

Orion swiftly saddled Zoryn and mounted, his heart thudding in his chest. He nudged the animal through the ranks of the horsemen of Silverdyne. He tightened his grip on his reins and resisted the urge to look at the faces about him.

A young horseman reached out, touching his black and silver cloak. It came as a shock to Orion that he didn't recognise Tad.

"May fortune favour you on the field, brother," Tad said.

Words stuck in Orion's throat, but he swallowed past them. "Remember your training. I'll see you after the battle."

"Let your arrows strike true," Tad replied.

"I'd prefer to be flying," Orion muttered.

"You two!" Orion and Tad's heads shot up, and they found themselves looking into Spearmaster Natayn's stern scowl. "Stop gossiping and keep your wits about you."

Orion schooled his face to something that resembled stoic concentration. Tad, however, snickered as his father started shouting orders at men on his other side.

"At least we aren't the only ones afraid."

Not daring to look in his friend's direction in case he dissolved into undignified, nervous giggles, Orion stood in his stirrups to look up ahead. "I can see the king's banner from here. The right flank is in position."

Tad moved his stallion closer. "And we're ready too. No mercy."

"No mercy," Orion echoed.

Their generals hoped to encircle the enemy before eliminating escape routes. Once enemy forces were trapped, their ranks would move to constrict the battlefield, allowing for complete annihilation of the invaders.

Their battle lines bordered on the less traditional. Foot soldiers stood at the very front. Orion knew even though his view was obstructed that they were spaced evenly apart, each man given a long pike. Instead of perfectly straight lines, the foot soldiers' ranks would form a convex line.

The mounted troops such as himself would remain in reserve, waiting for the signal.

Orion inhaled deeply and let his fingers relax on his reins. A calm mind would serve him well in what was to come.

Moments before the warning roar rippled through the air, Orion sensed a malevolent force coming their way. His eyes flickered towards Tad as he realised his beast magic was stirring, warning him of what was to come. Mouth dry, he ran his hand down Zoryn's neck and let his own beast magic calm his racing heart. He could only hope that the battle was theirs today. It was best for the country for one swift battle instead of a long, drawn-out war. Today's blood bath was necessary for tomorrow's peace.

"Eyes forward, Guardsman Maysden," Tad said, flashing Orion a cheeky smile. "Which one is your dragon father?"

"He's gold … He's in the second wave." Orion returned his eyes forward, knowing he would not see Zapyr entering the fray just yet.

"I'll keep an eye out for your white dragon and your gold then," Tad said. "I'll let you know if there's anything of note."

Orion nodded his head. "Concentrate on the enemy before you, Tad."

"Yes, sir."

"Foot soldiers … enemy cavalry."

The news began to trickle down through the ranks. Overhead, the two opposing sides of dragons clashed.

"Hold," Orion's power whispered to his mount. He had some experience with hearing a dragon upon dragon when he saw Tornyth take on a Grey Shadow. He inched his stallion forward, raising his eyes at the same time to see the mass of scales, tooth and claw that was dragon battle.

The faint cries of enemy soldiers charging caught Orion's ears. He knew that the front rows of their foot soldiers would be lowering their pikes and surging towards the enemy. He almost retched as he heard the enemy colliding with the points of the spearheads. The sounds of impaling flesh and the screams of the dying would haunt him.

"Easy …" Tad murmured. "Not long now …"

Orion notched his arrow, squeezing his thighs to keep himself in the saddle. He kept his eyes forward.

"Retreat!" His heart thudded in his chest as he heard the decided upon signal that was designed to confuse the enemy. The lines of their foot soldiers would be moving backwards now, their lines forming a concave shape. From the sound of the roaring enemy, they were pouring forward, sure of their easy victory.

In these tense moments, their foot soldiers were vulnerable, and still the cavalry held until the right moment.

It was then the dragons dropped their first surprise on the enemy below. Orion caught sight of the white underbelly of Tornyth flying low. He registered the heavy boulder he was carrying moments before he dropped it directly onto the enemy lines.

Orion flinched as the boulder plummeted down upon the unsuspecting men. He had never considered the type of carnage a dropped projectile might have. Tornyth had chosen a reasonably sized piece of rock that crushed a decent number of men in one foul swoop. In the chaos, he couldn't count how many lives the rock took. Beside him, Tad barked with laughter.

Before the enemy could reform their lines, Deovyn swooped with his own rock. Another three dragons followed suit. Over the sound of breaking and shattering bones, Orion could hear the yelled commands for his company to prepare to move forward.

With an encouraging nod, Tad kicked his horse's side. "Couldn't the dragons just cook the enemy? They breathe fire."

"No," Orion replied. This was something he had discussed with Zapyr. "Fire spreads quickly, causing mass casualties on both sides."

There was another shout from the officers, and their sedate pace increased into a galloping charge. Horses, men and weapons surged towards the enemy. All around him the roar of the Silverdyne horsemen filled his ears.

"*Araae helphelwyn. Terini gorthorawyn!*" Orion's voice mixed with the men about him. His stallion leaped forward, and they raced around their foot soldiers in an unyielding crush of men, horses and steel. He turned his head to regard the enemy lines.

When their foot soldiers had begun their retreat, the enemy had been foolish to eagerly follow them. They were in peril, and yet they continued to hack needlessly forward into their front lines in what could only be described as a triumphant bloodlust.

Orion was happy to see their foot soldiers were holding up remarkably well, holding the line while the two flanks of cavalry shot out from behind. One to encircle the enemy on the left and one on the right.

The horses continued to thunder forward, rounding the field of battle so they met the second cohort coming from the opposite direction. Now they could take them from behind.

Orion caught sight of the king; his face was taut in grim determination. Tiernan was at his side, along with four senior King's Guardsmen.

The cavalry slowed as they came together, closing the gap to begin constricting the enemy into a small area. The space for escape was rapidly closing, and still none of the enemy captains had the wits to see the danger until one man looked up.

Orion let his arrow fly; he didn't think about it. A split second later, his arrow pierced through the man's throat. He reeled backwards onto the ground, his own men trampling over him. Killing those with rank, leaving the enemy lines confused, would sway the battle into their favour quicker.

"My turn!" Tad cried, letting loose one of his own arrows. He hit his mark, spearing an enemy soldier through the eye.

Orion felt the stirring of heat that he knew was his dragon churning in his belly. Ayrdonyth wanted out. The dragon inside him was roaring. His fingers trembled with the effort to keep himself under control.

Orion's eyes travelled down, staring at the blood streams forming beneath his stallion's hooves. His stomach churned, but he gritted his teeth and shot another three arrows in quick succession. Each found their mark.

Horses and men surged forwards, further constricting the enemy's movements. Orion found himself pushed along with the majority of the horsemen. He had his bow notched and ready and wherever he had a clean shot, he took it.

Tad laughed every time Orion's arrows imbedded into the skulls of his victims. His long, dark hair and face were spattered with blood. "Bows away! Swords out!"

The time for long range weapons was over. The battlefield was a press of friend and foe alike. Orion tucked his bow away and had his sword grasped in his dominant hand in moments.

The grin on Tad's face had fallen. He looked ashen as they turned back to the battle.

Many of the horsemen and guardsmen he had spoken to in the last few nights had surmised the enemy would lose their courage to fight when they realised they were trapped. They couldn't have been more wrong. The enemy turned upon the Ramian forces, determined to have victory.

On his right side, Orion caught sight of a horseman dragged from his saddle. Enemy soldiers hacked him with their long-handled axes. He turned his head away from the horrific distraction and went to turn back for the unfortunate man when Tad grabbed his reins.

"Eyes forward!" Tad yelled.

"The sky is on fire!"

Both Tad and Orion looked up in horror at the shout. It was true. Great globes of fire tore through the skies. Orion had been so occupied with the enemy on the ground, he forgot about the dragons. The burning balls began tearing through the ranks and wings of dragons. He gasped in horror as a silver battle dragon fell from the sky, and with her, the ball of fire.

"Gylleah!" The silver dragon's name burst from his lips even as he tried to rein in his panicking stallion.

The ground trembled as Gylleah hit the ground, and flames licked the blood-soaked grass.

Tad looked at him, face pale and lips quivering.

"Courage," Orion cried. "Courage, my friend. You've got plenty of it."

CHAPTER THIRTY
Tornyth

The Ruins of Torryn

Tornyth cursed that his dragon sight and hearing were sharper than his human half. The clamouring of the humans as they fought and died was a deafening echo in his mind. The first wave of dragons clashed, and he couldn't help but suck in a horrified gasp at the number of Grey Shadows that filled the sky.

Wedged between his two brothers, Deovyn and Zapyr, he wondered what was going through their minds.

"Brace yourself, *sudunyn*," Zapyr said. "After the Grey Shadows comes the Artrothian dragons."

"They like to send in their mindless slaves first," Deovyn continued. There was a bitter tone in his voice.

Tornyth shivered. They sent in the Grey Shadows to take the first initial heavy losses. War was a game of strategy. But that didn't stop him from disliking how callous the tactic seemed. Not long ago, it could have been

Rhox up there fighting them with no connection to who he was or why he was fighting. This brought a fresh wave of horror.

Zapyr's azure gaze held his. The golden dragon seemed to understand where his mind was taking him. Rhox had been held prisoner for so long, he wondered how his brother wasn't driven mad with the fear of what had become of him.

Raking his claws against the hard earth, Zapyr lifted his head to the sky. He spotted the Artrothian dragons before Tornyth. "Live Valiantly, *sudunyn*," he said, launching himself up.

"Die Honourably," Deovyn and Tornyth echoed.

Like a golden arrow, Zapyr was gone. Deovyn watched him for a heartbeat and then nodded towards Tornyth. "Stay close."

Tornyth's nostrils flared as he heard the cries of their *vehyl* as the lines began to retreat as planned. An idea tickled the back of his mind. He eyed some of the large pieces of ruins. It would be a shame to desecrate the old city. But ...

"Deovyn," Tornyth said, "what will happen if we drop something heavy from the sky on humans?"

Deovyn's large tawny eyes widened. He looked at Tornyth as if he were seeing him for the very first time. Then a slow, almost cruel smile parted his lips. "I'm always up for experimentation. Choose your weapon!"

Tornyth's wings fluttered with nerves. He glanced towards the ruins and picked out a rock. Deovyn had already selected his, clawing at it as if to assess its merits as a deadly projectile.

"What are you two doing?" From up above, Tornyth heard the annoyed roar of Zapyr, who had wheeled around.

"Tornyth, choose and go!" Deovyn snapped.

Tornyth grasped at the nearest rock. The weight was heavy and pulled him down, but he spread his wings and struggled to get airborne. He would have to fly low.

"Tornyth ..." Zapyr wasn't impressed.

"Cover us!" Deovyn grunted. "We're experimenting!"

Ignoring Zapyr's incredulous snarls, Tornyth moved as quickly as he could across the fields. He became aware of larger dragons circling above him, picking off any Grey Shadow that became a threat while his claws were full.

There wasn't too much time to think of the consequences of his actions. As soon as he hovered over the enemy soldiers, he released his burden. The rock plummeted as Zapyr growled, "Go! Up!"

Tornyth didn't watch his rock fall. He turned his snout upwards and shot into the air. The heavy thud and crunch told him his rock hit humans. There was a second thud and then cries of horror from below.

"Fantastic result!" Deovyn cried. "Get your breath, brother, and then we're into the fray."

Tornyth rolled his shoulders, daring to glance down. Gylleah, Edisyn and Curarfur had followed their lead and dropped their own missiles on the unsuspecting *rokun*. The ground was running red with blood.

Frantic, Tornyth looked around for his friends.

"No time for that." Sidrah bumped into him to get his attention. "Stay with us, *sudunyn*. Deo and Zapyr, we need to goad the dragon battle away from the humans ..."

Deovyn nodded his head in understanding and dipped. Tornyth followed while Zapyr roared his understanding and shadowed them.

It wasn't long before Tornyth's white scales got them unwanted attention. A large Artrothian dragon raised his head. He was the colour of smoke, with large orange eyes. A snarl formed on his scarred face.

"Hang back!" Deovyn cried and nipped Tornyth's tail. "Moroth! The Grey Doom!"

Zapyr had also seen the enemy dragon. He veered upwards; a threatening growl rumbled from his throat. He dove between Deovyn and Tornyth, his claws and talons outstretched.

The one Deovyn called the Grey Doom widened his snarl at seeing Zapyr, as if he was venomously amused by the golden dragon. Zapyr didn't give him any time to talk. Their bodies crashed together, his teeth snapping, attempting to catch the grey's neck.

"Move," Deovyn cried. "Zapyr can look after himself!"

Tornyth followed as Deovyn banked. Seconds later Sidrah and a brown speckled female joined Zapyr in his attack of the smoky-coloured foe.

"Who is he?"

"Danger," Deovyn answered. "He'll kill you just to hurt *Aluel*."

Deovyn gracefully swooped around another pair of battling dragons. On his way past, he grabbed the enemy's wing and snapped it. He moved on before the enemy could lash out.

As the foe turned his head to follow Deovyn, Tornyth came up on his other side and tore his opposite wing.

This was the strategy that Deovyn had stressed to him. They were smaller dragons. It wasn't their job to clash with larger, more powerful dragons, rather it was better they became a hindrance. A small dragon was agile and could easily goad larger, infuriated dragons into the deadly clutches of one of their own. Or they could cause injury and disappear before a larger dragon could react.

"Deo, left!" Tornyth cried.

Deovyn was already alerted to Curarfur struggling with a pair of Grey Shadows. He tucked his wings into a tight dive, speeding forward with deadly intent. He flew past the teal dragon, raking his claws through the

Grey Shadow's back. The enemy dragon let go with a shriek, his snapping jaws only finding air where Deovyn had been. Deovyn flipped over and slashed its throat with his sharp claws. Thick black blood spurted from the gaping wound.

Free of the first annoyance, Curarfur dealt with the remaining Grey Shadow with ease. Tornyth raked his claws along its back for good measure.

Before Curarfur could lift his snout to bellow his thanks, Deovyn was speeding towards another dragon needing help. Tornyth tucked in his wings and followed in his brother's deadly wake.

"Your turn!" Deovyn yelled.

Tornyth plummeted into a dive. At the last possible moment he spread his wings, his claws finding the sensitive eyes of a Grey Shadow. Plunging his hands forward, he could feel the thick gore on his claws. He closed his fist, feeling his foe's body trembling in his grasp. He let go, watching as the Grey Shadow tumbled from the sky. He heard Deovyn's growling laughter as he too dispatched another Grey Shadow.

An agonised cry turned Tornyth's attention to a battle dragon falling from the sky, her body broken. A gasp caught in his throat as he recognised the distinctive silver scales of Gylleah. He could only watch helplessly as she fell, her body engulfed in flames.

Below, humans were panicking as the grass around them caught fire.

More fire balls lit the sky.

"Gylleah!"

"Leave her, Tor, she's dead!" Deovyn snapped. "Our energy is to go to the living."

Tornyth lifted his snout and looked around to search for where the fire had come from. He spotted the dragon Moroth on the ground. He was forming a flaming ball between his claws. Once formed, he tossed it into the sky.

"Edisyn! With Tornyth!" Deovyn cried.

Another ball of fire was tossed into the sky.

"Deo!" Tornyth cried.

Edisyn, the dark red battle dragon who he had worked with during the battle for Pallaryn, came alongside him. With a sharp movement of his head, he intercepted Tornyth. His eyes did not move from Gylleah's slumped body. He rumbled and flashed his fangs. A ripple of horror wound up Tornyth's spine, recalling that Gylleah had been his mate.

"Too dangerous for you to follow," Edisyn said. His deep rumble held a quiver.

A cry lodged in Tornyth's throat as Deovyn raced after the flaming ball of fire. His brother's wings spread wide as he slipped between one of their dragons and flames. Deovyn's claws gestured. The wind curled about his brother, grasped the flames and tossed them to the side.

The dragon on the ground released another flaming ball in the opposite direction, and Deovyn surged forward.

Tornyth wondered for how long his brother could use his wind power to protect their own. He wouldn't be able to save them all. Even as the ball of flames hit the ground, the *vehyl* screamed.

The best they could hope for was someone killing the flame-throwing dragon quickly. He was tempted to link minds with Mandros to make the suggestion but decided against it. He was sure his *aluel* would have thought of it. It wouldn't do to disturb him.

His thoughts had been shared with a human on the ground. A soldier on the back of familiar black mare broke from the ranks. For a long moment, all he could do was watch in disbelief as the human proffered a long spear out in front of him and charged Moroth, the Grey Doom.

The horseman thundered forward, never wavering. All around him seemed to stand still. Then the spear hit the dragon's side and sheered off.

"Rue!" Tornyth screamed, watching the rider tumble from the impact of his spear hitting the dragon's side. The helmet upon Ruevyn's head rolled away.

He didn't care for Edisyn's yells for him to stop. He dived, even as Moroth shook his head and turned towards the human annoyance. The large Artrothian dragon swiped out with his foreleg, killing the limping black mare.

Tornyth dashed low along the ground, growling and rumbling as he saw Ruevyn desperately searching for a weapon as Moroth lumbered towards him.

A cry behind told him that Edisyn had been intercepted. He pressed forward.

"No!" he cried as Moroth stood, a looming shadow over his most cherished friend.

The enemy dragon lifted his head, a cruel smile spreading his scaly lips as he regarded Tornyth. He could see the disdain in his foe's eyes as he took in his small size and white scales.

"So the rumours are true." Unlike the voices of the Grey Shadows, Moroth's voice was refined.

"Let him go," Tornyth demanded, setting his claws on the ground. Zapyr's whisper that a downed dragon was a dead dragon tickled the back of his mind. But he didn't care. Ruevyn was in trouble.

"What's a human life to you?"

Breathing heavily, Tornyth glared at Moroth. "Let. Him. Go."

"Oh, I see. You're a shield." Moroth's smile widened. He nodded at Ruevyn. "The human is your pet."

"He's my friend," Tornyth snapped.

"Humans are never friends to dragonkind," Moroth replied. He stepped forward and placed his claw over Ruevyn's body.

Tornyth flinched as Ruevyn cried out in pain. He could tell by the unnatural twist of his friend's leg that it was broken. "He's my brother."

"Dragons aren't brethren to *rokun*."

"That's where you are wrong!" Tornyth snapped.

Moroth, the Grey Doom, tilted his head, his eyes gleaming. "It's your polluted *rokun* bloodline that ruins you. A shame ..."

Lowering his head, Tornyth growled. "I am warning you ..."

"You're warning me?" Moroth laughed. He smiled, flashing his fangs and pressing his claw to the ground. Ruevyn screamed. "I don't think you are in the position to negotiate."

"Fly," Ruevyn gasped, even as ribbons of blood dribbled down his chin.

"The *rokun* has it right. I'll tell you what: surrender to me, and I'll let him go."

Tornyth paused, taking in the suffering etched on Ruevyn's face.

"No!" Ruevyn said, finally finding the strength to make his lips work. "No. If I die, my suffering will only be moments ... Jod ... if you give yourself to him you will suffer for centuries. I love you too much for that!"

Love.

The word punctured Tornyth's heart like a spear being driven through his chest. The human was right. He loved him as a brother. He couldn't simply watch him die under the claws of an enemy dragon.

"No!" Tornyth snarled. "I can't lose you!"

Moroth laughed.

"I'd spill my blood one thousand and one times for the Apple Tree Prince," Ruevyn said, using all his strength to press himself into the drag-on's claw.

"I can save you!" Tornyth cried.

Ruevyn looked over to him, a small smile forming on his pale lips. "Death is a gateway ... Life a poor reflection of the Otherworld."

Tornyth felt each thumping beat of his heart.

Ruevyn looked up into Moroth's face. "I'll go willingly to death's embrace."

Moroth didn't look at Tornyth as he pressed down and crushed Ruevyn under his weight. Ruevyn's screams were cut off abruptly, leaving only Tornyth roaring in pain and anger.

A smirk plastered on his scaly face, Moroth swiped Ruevyn's lifeless body to the side. His luminous eyes were alight with hatred as he looked at Tornyth. "Now, little one, you're mine!"

Tornyth's nostrils flared. He didn't want to take flight and back away; he wanted to stand his ground. He knew even if he took off now, he couldn't get far before he was captured and killed. Growling, he stepped forward and spewed fire into the larger dragon's face.

The fire didn't touch him. "Fool! Where there is smoke there is fire. It can't harm me!"

"Fool!" came another voice. "Touch Mandros' son, and you face me!"

Tornyth had to jump out of the way as a large female dragon landed. Cloudy, sightless eyes seemed to pin Moroth where he stood sure of his triumph.

"Mashikah, darling ..."

Mashikah rumbled, stepping in front of Tornyth. He stumbled to the side so that she wouldn't step on him. "I might be blind ... but I can still rip your smug face off!"

Moroth laughed, but Mashikah lunged and caught the side of his face with her teeth. Another three dragons landed, causing Tornyth to jump. One large female attacked Moroth's opposite side.

Edisyn pushed Tornyth out of the way. He tilted his head, rumbling in fury as he stared at Moroth, the one responsible for his mate's death. "Up, boy! Not your fight." The dark red dragon lurched forward, his teeth grazing the underside of Moroth's neck. He latched on and wrestled the grey dragon to the ground.

Tornyth had no choice to obey, watching in disbelief as more dragons he had not met attacked Moroth. He wanted to circle around and make sure the mysterious Mashikah, Mandros' mate, was okay. The reinforcements were expected days ago. What had happened? Why were they so delayed?

"What did you think you were doing?" Deovyn cried. Tornyth noticed his gaze looked down upon his *lullah* and the other dragons. Tornyth winced as Edisyn successfully ripped out Moroth's throat, black dragon blood spurting over the ground. "This isn't a game!"

Tornyth had no answer for his brother. "When did the reinforcements arrive?"

"While you were playing around with Moroth!" Deovyn snapped.

"I wasn't playing!" Tornyth snarled. "He killed Ruevyn. He *killed* my friend!"

"Reinforcements will take out the dragons ... We're going to finish the enemy humans."

"Galgothmeg ... Vadroil ..."

"We leave the likes of them to *Aluel* and Roane." Deovyn indicated with his snout, and he spotted his *aluel* along with some of their largest battle dragons fighting the enemy of old.

"Come!"

Unaware of Tornyth's scrutiny, Mandros continued to fight Vadroil tooth and claw. He could see the green dragon's side was slick with his blood. Vadroil had only eyes for him. They had an ancient enmity between them ... One of them was going to die today.

"Vadroil needs to perish."

"In time. Come," Deovyn replied.

Above them Vadroil snarled and lunged, piercing Mandros' neck with his fangs. The dark blue dragon brought his claws to Mandros' panting side to rip out his scales. Wrenching away, Mandros allowed Vadroil take a clawful of his flesh and freed himself.

Tornyth opened his mouth as larger dragons began to swarm around Vadroil to help the dreaded general. Roane was busy with Galgothmeg … he would never make it in time. Both of the ancient dragons' claws were slick with one another's blood. The olive-green general was fatiguing.

A cry from up above and a dark blue streak heralded the arrival of Rigyl. The younger dragon landed on Galgothmeg's back, clamping his front claws over the red dragon's face. Galgothmeg tried to shake him off, but Rigyl held on firm.

In his frenzied state, believing he was victorious, Vadroil lifted his head and bellowed. Anger boiled in Tornyth's belly. So many good people and dragons had given their lives to defeat their enemies. Heat burst through him, and ignoring Deovyn's cries of disbelief, he shot forwards. He tucked his wings in close to his body and spiralled up as quickly as he could.

Vadroil had lifted his chin; the soft skin of his throat was exposed. The great dragon never saw him coming. The impact of his teeth slamming into Vadroil sent a painful shudder through his body. In seconds his mouth was filling with blood. He relished the cry of shock coming from Vadroil and clamped his teeth down harder and squeezed.

"Stop beating your wings!" Vadroil's command rung in Tornyth's mind. *"Fall from the sky."*

His body pressed so close to that of his enemy, Tornyth felt the rhythm of his wings falter.

"That's it. Fall to your doom."

Tornyth struggled against the voice within his head, refusing to give it any sway over his own thoughts. He held on tight, his eyes briefly searching the sky for Mandros. He could see a blur of emerald to his side. It was for him, and all dragons and *vehyl* that had suffered under Artroth that he was fighting for. *"You misread the situation, Vadroil. I'm your doombringer. It's over."*

The sound of the enemy's roars turned into shrieks of fury as Mandros' dragons flew in to join the fray. The sky around him echoed with the sound of teeth gnashing and dragon bodies colliding. While Vadroil's dragons were working to free their leader, Mandros roared in fury.

The heat of Tornyth's power turned to a coldness that slithered through his veins. His teeth ached with the pain. The blood in his mouth cooled, freezing on his teeth. Vadroil shrieked in anguish ... His wings trembled as he failed to pump them up and down to keep them in the air. The temperature dropped.

Vadroil attempted to shake his head to dislodge Tornyth, but he tightened his grip and held on. He squeezed on the older dragon's neck, satisfied with the strange gargling sound that tore through him.

The dark dragon's long claws found Tornyth's underbelly, his eyes bulging with hatred. Powerful talons dug into Tornyth's side, puncturing his scales. Tornyth refused to let go. He bit down harder as his own blood dripped from his wound.

"Not our tiny *sudunyn,* you bastard!" Sidrah forced her way through the lines of Vadroil's generals and pounced on Vadroil's back, wrenching him backwards. Tornyth wouldn't let go. All he knew was Vadroil had to die. It had to end now.

Deovyn clawed at Vadroil's face. "Let go, Tor ... Zapyr, catch him!"

Ice-fire power flowed through him. Small crystals of ice formed along Vadroil's dark blue scales. The malevolent light in his eyes dimmed as he shrieked in horror. The great dragon's body convulsed as his outstretched wings locked into place, held by sheets of ice.

Dazed from the fight, Tornyth released Vadroil and flapped uselessly like a lame duck. Unable to move, Vadroil fell from the sky.

Golden claws grasped his shoulders and his rump. Zapyr was strong enough to bear his weight, but his brother gasped, "Manifest back into your human heart ... quick!"

Through the fog of his own confusion, he did so. Pain tore through his belly and jaw as his brother lay his human body gently on the ground.

"Ice-fire," Jodathyn muttered. "It burns."

CHAPTER THIRTY-ONE
Orion

The Ruins of Torryn

The ground was on fire. Orion clutched his reins and ran his hands down the side of his stallion. He let his power flow and felt the horse's muscles spasming in response. Glancing up, he tried to catch Tad's eyes only to find his friend was nowhere to be seen. All around him was a crush of men, horses and weapons.

Orion tightened his grip on his sword and nudged his stallion further. There would be no finding Tad until this mess was over. He swung his sword, cutting down the enemy as he inched forward. He didn't let his mind linger on the dead piling up on the battlefield.

"Keep moving," he murmured to himself. He swung his sword again.

The ground quaked as another fireball fell from the sky. It was uncomfortably hot.

In the back of his mind, he felt the heavy presence of Zapyr. The golden dragon was checking his status. He could feel his *Rshon Aluel's* fatigue, the tear of claws against his side. The melee in the air was fierce.

"Find a more defensible position." Zapyr's words echoed through his mind. *"Get away from the fire."*

He lifted his eyes and spotted the king. Enemy soldiers clawed at his cloak as they attempted to pull him from his horse. Tiernan dismounted at one side, cutting down as many of the enemy as he could. The king's face was spattered with blood as he raised his sword. But as they killed the enemy before them, more rose up.

"The king," Orion replied, unsure whether Zapyr would hear him.

"Get him and yourself out quickly."

Orion nudged his horse and pushed through the ranks. He swung his blade, taking the head clean off a foe who was reaching forward.

"Remove your cloak!" Orion screamed. "They'll pull you to the ground!"

The king spared him a glance. "Maysden." His shaking fingers reached around to unclasp his cloak.

"We have to stop these fire balls," Orion panted. He glanced down to Captain Tiernan, whose face was pale and streaked with sweat.

"Kelvie gone ..." Tiernan said. "Couldn't stop him."

Orion nodded his head and swung his sword, decapitating another enemy soldier.

Tiernan's face paled only seconds before an anguished cry left his lips. "Carew!"

Whipping around, Orion caught sight of Carew clutching a bloodied lump to his chest. Nym was at his side, supporting him. His right arm, hand still holding his sword, lay severed on the ground. Carew's mouth twisted into an ugly scowl. His knees buckled as he dropped to the ground. Groping for his weapon, he grasped the handle like it was a lifeline. He stumbled forward, swinging his sword with his left hand, while his bloody stump bled over himself and Nym.

Carew wouldn't last long in the press of human bodies. He would soon bleed to death. Orion swung down from the horse, pushing the reins into Tiernan's hands. "Get him to Jael!"

Tiernan looked up at the king and then back to his son, his face etched with a father's despair.

"Up, Tiernan!" the king barked. "Get your boy."

Tiernan nodded, looking very much like a broken man. He swung himself into the saddle, screaming Carew's name. It was Nym who looked up at him.

Behind her, Lyntton and another guardsman guarded Theo, who was clutching at his face, rivulets of blood dripping down his fingers.

"Make space!" Orion cried, and he manifested on the spot. He grabbed the king around his middle and placed him on his back. His sudden change pressed the enemy back, and Tiernan urged the horse forward and reached Nym's side. He offered his hand and lifted both Carew and Nym into the saddle.

Ayrdonyth roared, lowered his head and advanced. "Theo, get on!"

The thief looked at him in disbelief. "Lyn ..."

"Can look after myself, boy!" Lyntton yelled. "This is your only chance."

Grasping on to Ayrdonyth's horns, Theo swung up to hold on to the side of the dragon's face. The common fighting folk around him surged forward in their panic. Hands grasped on his scales, weighing him down.

Growling, Tiernan dismounted and pushed past the men, parting them with curt orders for them to move. Lyntton and a few other surviving King's Guardsmen came to assist.

Tiernan never saw the enemy blade.

One moment the captain was at Ayrdonyth's side bellowing orders, and the next his eyes widened, the wind knocked out of his lungs. Carew was screaming, the thought of losing his father far more traumatic than that of his limb.

Tiernan's shaking hands went to his stomach, touching the tip of the pike that had impaled him. His lips quivered, and he rallied what little strength he had. He turned to Lyntton. "Get my boy to Jael."

Ayrdonyth inhaled, blowing hot air through the milling soldiers to clear a path for the horse. Lyntton turned and vaulted into the saddle, ignoring the screams of Carew.

Sinking to his knees, Tiernan watched the grey stallion disappear until the light in his eyes faded and he slumped, his duty over.

"Back!" Ayrdonyth snarled. The King's Guardsmen around him moved away, and Ayrdonyth swiped his tail around to make more space. With one last parting look to the captain, he took to the air.

From the sky, the battlefield was a mess of fire, blood and bodies. His stomach churned as he shifted positions to check his surroundings. He could feel poor Theo's shivering in shock and fright on his back. The thief was not made for war. His friend was for creation and things of beauty. He needed to keep him safe.

"Ayr ..." Theo's voice trembled as his hands grasped at his scales. "There're more dragons coming."

Ayrdonyth looked up and saw it was true. He lifted his snout and sniffed. *"Rshon Aluel ..."*

"They're friendly," came Zapyr's clipped reply. *"Keep your head low."*

Theo was tapping the base of his neck. "There ..."

"Ayrdonyth, take us to the ruins." The king's voice sounded weary. "We can regroup there."

Ayrdonyth flew low under the main battle and did as the king had asked of him. At the ruins he let Theo and the king slide off his back. Blood continued to pour from Theo's face.

The king lay a gloved hand on his shoulder, making the thief jump. "Come, Master Torkelle. Let's get that looked at."

"I'm returning to the battlefield," Ayrdonyth said.

The king looked up at him. "As you will, Ayrdonyth."

Ayrdonyth returned to the air, a plan already formulating in his mind. He quickly spotted two large dragons, one he presumed was Galgothmeg and the other Vadroil. Recoiling at the horrid sound the great dragons made as they fought, Ayrdonyth shot up.

When he had eavesdropped on Zapyr and Rhox's conversation, his *Rshon Aluel* had doubted the enemy knew about his power. He summoned all of his courage and darted into the midst of a group of circling Grey Shadows.

"I release you!" His power sung. The enemy didn't know of his power, and it was time to reveal it to them. *"I release you to take your revenge on your masters."*

At first, nothing happened. The Grey Shadows seemed to watch with unsure, haunted eyes. And then the scales began to fall. The weaker ones fell from the skies, but the stronger dragons steadied themselves, shaking their heads in confusion.

"Galgothmeg ..." Ayrdonyth said. He pointed with his wing.

His human father had always told him that evil deeds would eventually find wrongdoers. The confused and frightened Grey Shadows shook off their dull scales. Unlike Galgothmeg, he released the command holding them in the sky. He let them clear their heads to think for themselves.

It would be their choice.

And he wasn't disappointed.

Snarling, saliva dripping from her jaws, the first large Grey Shadow headed towards Galgothmeg. Ayrdonyth could only assume that after many long years of captivity, she no longer worried about whether she lived or died.

The others, another five in total, followed.

Ayrdonyth didn't wait. He flew towards more Grey Shadows and released them. They too converged onto Galgothmeg. Overwhelmed by a flurry of Grey Shadows, there was no escape for Galgothmeg. Every part of his body with bitten and scratched and torn by those he had imprisoned.

The battle would be over for Galgothmeg soon ... The freed Grey Shadows would make sure of it.

Ayrdonyth forced himself to watch the spectacle.

Surprised by the aggression and the ferocity of the attack, Galgothmeg, the dragon of Death and Despair, had very little opportunity to defend himself. The freed Grey Shadows ripped him into pieces, circling him in a frenzy. The red dragon bellowed, calling for help from his Artrothian allies. None answered his summons.

It was a terrible cry from above that made him turn from the sight of Galgothmeg's death. He caught sight of a small white dragon holding on to the torn throat of Vadroil. Mandros was intercepted by two enemy dragons, preventing him from helping.

The fighting around Tornyth, Mandros and Vadroil was fierce.

In horror Ayrdonyth watched as Vadroil and Tornyth plummeted to the ground. He burst forward to see if there was anything he could do to help.

Deovyn dove with him to try and shake the great dragon from Tornyth.

Ayrdonyth bit back a cry of anguish ... Then the white dragon let go, his wings desperately trying to keep himself in the air.

He never saw what direction Zapyr came from. His *Rshon Aluel* neatly caught the white dragon and just before they hit the ground, the white dragon melted away, revealing the bloodied form of Jodathyn.

Ayrdonyth's claws hit the ground beside his *Rshon Aluel*. The gold dragon fussed over Jodathyn. Peering at the slumped form of his friend, he could see Jodathyn's hands were clutching at his belly.

"Get a healer!" Zapyr barked.

Ayrdonyth looked up at the sky. The two healers he knew, Sidrah and Curarfur, were both fighting furiously. He looked back at Jodathyn and along the ground to where Vadroil lay still. The evil lump was still breathing. How he longed to rip his throat out.

"Ayr, now ... healer!"

Jael Aryk was his only chance.

CHAPTER THIRTY-TWO

Kieryn

The Ruins of Torryn

Sheltered by the ruins of Torryn, Kieryn looked out over the battlefield. Soon after they had forced their way through the ranks, the dragons started taking his forces to safety. Then the dragons commenced the annihilation of the enemy.

Today was not a day to show mercy. Every enemy had to be put to death lest Artroth decide Rama was still theirs for the taking.

Studying the once serene fields, he felt it would be a betrayal to turn away. Many had fallen this day for the safety of his kingdom. His eyes swept over the bodies of human and dragon alike. The battle had been swift and brutal.

Behind him he could hear the soft groans of Carew as he lay bloodied and injured in Jael's care. While he had been weak and dazed by blood loss, he didn't register the horrific injury to his arm. But once Jael had started healing him, it began to sink in. That along with the death of his father.

Nothing Nym could say could quieten Carew's broken sobs as he realised his right arm was gone. He begged Jael to put it back, but the healer could only calmly reply it was not possible.

"You should have left me to die," Carew said, looking up into the healer's face. "It's over ... I'll never wear the black and silver again. You should have left me on the field with Father."

The pain that crossed Guardsman Lyntton's expression as he smoothed back Carew's matted hair was enough to make Kieryn's stomach cramp.

"Carew, lie still," Jael said as Carew's sobs racked his whole body. The young guardsman's cries turned to screams of anguish. Kieryn swept past Nym, who was watching frozen like a stone statue. He took hold of Carew's left hand, interlocking their fingers. Tortured blue eyes looked up at him, and all Kieryn could do was murmur soft reassurances. When Carew had sufficiently calmed, Jael held a cup to his lips, and the young guardsman slipped swiftly into a state of unconsciousness.

Flexing his fingers, Kieryn released Carew's hand and stood. Nearby, Nym was watching, tears running down her face. "He can longer serve you, can he?"

"No," Kieryn admitted. His King's Guardsmen were his elite. A man with a severe injury was not permitted to serve him in the ranks of the King's Guard. "The crown will ensure he'll be looked after."

"Along with his brothers-in-arms." Lyntton brushed his hand through Carew's hair.

"He's a guardsman," Nym said. "That's all he has ever wanted."

Kieryn knew this was true. "Tiernan's other sons live in a summer house near the Arelle Forest. The Candydes know how to look after one another. Perhaps they too are here. I never asked Tiernan ..."

Nym frowned at him. But he did not know what else he could do. If he could, he would scour the battlefield for Carew's arm, but that was a foolish fantasy. If he could have taken Tiernan's injury away, he would have. But they were living in reality.

"Jael! Jael!"

Kieryn tilted his head up, recognising the young dragon that was Master Maysden. He still marvelled anytime a dragon spoke that he could hear their human voices, albeit they were deeper.

He lifted his hand to greet the blue-grey dragon.

"Jael!" Ayrdonyth cried. His nostrils flared as he looked at him. There was something panicked in the way he moved. "Jael!"

"I'm here!" Jael stumbled from Carew's side, wiping his hands on his uniform trousers. "What's the fuss about?"

"Jodathyn! Hurry!"

The way his brother's name burst from Ayrdonyth's mouth sent a shiver of horror up Kieryn's spine. Ayrdonyth flattened himself against the ground.

Jael darted forwards. "How bad?"

The young dragon didn't answer the question.

"I'm coming, dragon," Kieryn said.

Nodding as if he had expected it, Ayrdonyth offered his claw palm side up for him to stand on. He knew that his guardsman wrapped in dragon scales would not bring him any harm, so he stepped forward and let the dragon place him on his shoulder.

Ayrdonyth skimmed low over the battlefield, and Kieryn resisted the urge to cover his nose and mouth from the smells of death and horror.

"How bad?" Jael asked again.

Ayrdonyth seemed to consider his words. "He doesn't have long ..."

It was a reflex to open his mouth and demand from his man what had happened, to ask why Jodathyn hadn't been protected. But he bit his tongue. Upsetting the young dragon would not help him or his brother. Later there would be time to speak with Mandros about the matter.

He spotted Mandros first, his great wings unfurled out to give shade. He could see the emerald dragon was also injured, his own sides wet with blood. Nearby the great golden bulk that was Lord Zapyr paced back and forth. Above their heads dragons still battled, which gave reason to why they hadn't been able to call for their healers.

Before Ayrdonyth's claws could properly touch the ground, Kieryn jumped from the dragon's back. He ran forwards and spotted a bloody lump.

"Thrice bathed in his royal blood ..." The words stuck in his throat. Jodathyn's skin was grey. His eyes fluttered as his fingers twitched.

"I want to climb the apple tree," Jodathyn muttered, his voice coming out slurred. "I hurt ..."

Lowering himself to the ground, Mandros breathed over the prone form of Jodathyn's body. "Keep your eyes open. Fight for me."

Jodathyn lifted a hand, blindly reaching up to stroke Mandros' scales. "It's strange," he said. Kieryn's heart constricted as his brother's face screwed up with pain. "You're more my father than my father ... My body is cold."

Kieryn drew closer. Jael seemed to come out of his shock and sunk to his knees at Jodathyn's side.

"Illeanah ... you look so beautiful ..." Jodathyn sighed. "Rue ... Donatein."

Jael brushed Jodathyn's bloodied hair away from his face. "Stay with me. I'm going to take a look at your wound."

A sudden seriousness washed over Jodathyn's features. "I'm dying."

"Hush, now. I'll do everything I can do to help you."

Jael's fingers ghosted over the terrible opening at Jodathyn's belly, his face taut with concentration as he attempted to heal the damage. He could see the beads of sweat forming on his medic's forehead as he clamped his eyes shut. He had seen Jael work many times, seen the miracles that his healer was capable of. But he had never seen him heal such a catastrophic injury.

"Don't let go, Jod," Kieryn whispered. "Carvelle needs you ... I need you."

Jodathyn's head lolled to the side. His stormy grey eyes seemed to look past him. His brother's lips twitched, and then he sighed as his eyes slid shut.

Clenching his teeth, Jael screamed, and Kieryn could feel the gooseflesh rising on his skin as the healer attempted to pulse more magic into Jodathyn. The wave of power washed over him, and then all was still.

Jael remained kneeling, his fingers on Jodathyn's belly and his eyes squeezed shut. "Don't go ... don't go ..."

It was over for Jodathyn.

A dark shape that lay nearby started laughing. Mandros lifted his head, his lips peeling back into a snarl.

"Don't you understand, oh great one?" Mandros said. "The white dragon was your doom. Fire isn't the only thing that burns. Ice has paralysed you and cooled your blood. His *vehyl* body may die, but his dragon will rise."

"I killed another one of yours," Vadroil slurred. "Tore your heart out as I promised."

Kieryn had heard enough. He unsheathed his sword and rushed forward.

"No!" Mandros barked.

The dark shape shifted as the wind touched his wings The fragile bones shattered like brittle shards.

"This man," Mandros said, "is Kieryn Pallarus, High King of Rama. The *vehyl* strength of my bloodline. The father of the rising dragon king. My legacy lives on ... Yours is ashes in the wind."

A cry to Kieryn's side left him dumbfounded. A small soldier with a long pike ran at Vadroil. Before he could register that the voice was female, the point was rammed into Vadroil's eye.

The dark dragon's body shuddered as the soldier took off her helmet. "I'm the white dragon's heart."

"Et-hir."

Dressed in a soldier's uniform, Et-hir looked sad and weary. She stumbled, looking at her hands and then to the pike protruding out of Vadroil's eye. Kieryn dashed forward, clasping her elbows as she collapsed. Jodathyn would have him look after the woman he had come to love, and he would.

She was sobbing, Kieryn realised. He helped her to Jodathyn's side and lowered her so they were both able to say their goodbyes.

Jael's eyes were still closed, sweat dripping from his forehead from the exertion.

Very slowly, Kieryn leaned over and took Jodathyn's hands in his own. "I'm sorry, little brother."

"His dragon hasn't manifested," Mandros mumbled to himself.

"Not dead yet. Not letting him go!" Jael snarled between his clenched teeth.

There was a resounding thump as Sidrah and then Curarfur were able to land. Jael was the only one who didn't look up. With a quick flick of her head, Sidrah ushered Mandros and the pacing Zapyr out of the way and stood behind the struggling medic. Curarfur came to stand beside her. Still Jael took no notice of the dragons. Kieryn could see the muscles in his jawline tighten.

Kieryn tried to concentrate and witness the moment the dragons' power joined with Jael, but it was so seamless he wasn't sure when Jael's power began and where it ended. For a long moment, nothing happened. Then before their eyes, Jodathyn took a deep, shaky breath, and his skin immediately took on a healthier hue. Jodathyn's grey eyes blinked open. The expression on his face was one of tired confusion.

Kieryn had been so caught up looking into his brother's face that he missed the moment the wound on his belly fused together.

Jodathyn licked his lips. "Hello," he whispered, looking up at Et-hir. His eyes closed. His breathing evened out as he began to snore softly.

"Hello?" Et-hir laughed between her tears. "Is that all he has to say to me?"

"He'll be groggy for some time," Sidrah warned.

"I'll take him back to camp," Deovyn offered. The small russet dragon came to stand next to his large golden brother. "You'll want to check on Rhox and Ayr, and Sidrah will be busy."

"This is the third time you have brought Jodathyn back from the brink of death, Jael Healing Hands," Mandros said. "Three is a significant number."

Jael stood, brushing his hands down his trousers. "It is as you say, lord dragon. Once from poisoning, once from near drowning and now once from a battle wound."

"I dare say you'll find your power only increasing," Mandros said.

Jael bowed stiffly. He glanced towards the battlefield. "Forgive me, lord. I have work to do."

CHAPTER THIRTY-THREE
Orion

The Ruins of Torryn

Skin still burning from the power coursing through his veins, Orion looked back along the makeshift beds of the injured. Jodathyn lay still, his chest rising and falling with soft breaths of one who had no idea of what a fuss he had caused. Nearby, Nym moved between Carew and Jod, watching both of them with a concerned look on her face.

From underneath his bandage, Theo observed her. His friend was now blind in one eye, and Orion was resolved to find leftover leather to create a more comfortable patch. Theo's remaining eye seemed haunted by all he had seen. He was doing his best to keep himself together, which meant he was singing under his breath.

Galgothmeg, Galgothmeg,
You're going to die.
Let me tell you why.

Galgothmeg, Galgothmeg,
You're going to fall.
Don't you hear our call?

"Dumping dragon dung!" Nym exclaimed after a while. "Must you sing? You sound like a warbling tomcat."

Stepping around Theo, who was sitting on the floor with his legs outstretched, Nym touched Jodathyn's arm lightly. When Jodathyn didn't respond to her touch, she lost her temper and shook him.

"Wake up!" Nym snapped. "You're cold as ice. I'd much prefer you wake up."

"The singing is soothing him," Theo said. "And he is Winter's Dragon. Perhaps that is why he is so cold."

Nym didn't answer. Instead, she grasped Jodathyn's shoulders and shook. Jodathyn's body flopped like a rag doll. "Wake up! Wake up, you scaly little upstart!"

"Mandros wasn't concerned," Orion added.

Nym's hands fell to her side. "I still don't like it."

"Mandros did say Tornyth burned Vadroil with ice."

"Ice-fire!" Theo chuckled. "I like it."

"The dragons wouldn't have left him with us if they were afraid for him." Et-hir entered the area, carrying a small bowl of water. She regarded Jodathyn's sleeping form with a frown and then made her way to Carew.

"Sir Carew," Et-hir whispered. "I brought you some water to wash if you like."

Carew turned over, his face pinched with torment. He regarded her for a long moment, then nodded. Nym hurried over to help him sit but he waved her away.

"Let me help," Nym said.

"I am not a babe," Carew snapped. "I can wash myself."

Nym stepped back as if she had been struck. Grumbling to himself, Carew was too deep in his misery to register that he had hurt Nym.

"And I'm not your ma to kiss and coddle you at the teat."

Carew's jaw tightened, his gaze firmly fixed on the nothingness before him.

Nym's hands balled into fists at her side.

Et-hir set the bowl down and took Nym's elbow. "Come now. Let's give the boys some privacy."

Head bowed, Carew sat forlornly looking at the water. He swore viciously, then slumped back down on his bunk, his back to Theo and Orion.

Orion turned his attention away from him and stared out at the camp.

"Will you be alright for a little while?" Orion asked, turning to look at Theo. "I'm going to see if Curarfur and Sidrah need anything."

Theo frowned at him. "You're going down there?"

Orion nodded. "I won't be long."

Theo glanced back at Jodathyn and Carew, then waved him away. Grateful to be able to leave the oppressiveness of the medic tents, Orion quickly stepped out into the camp. He wandered aimlessly for a little while before changing directions and heading out to the fields.

He was stopped by Will and Fydellah. Will looked defeated. He walked with his shoulders hunched over. Gone was the confident lordling before the battle. Under his left eye there was a faint line of a scar. He had not escaped the battle unscathed. Fydellah's eyes looked haunted. When she locked gazes with Orion, she immediately turned her face away. Her message was clear. She was not ready to talk. Orion could respect that.

"Carew could do with some company," Orion whispered as they passed.

Will looked at him, raising his eyebrows. "I'll do what I can."

Orion didn't pause to find out if Will had any thoughts about him visiting the battlefield. It had been a day, and he hadn't found Tad. There were men everywhere, busy with dozens of tasks that needed to be done before they could leave Torryn.

Hesitating at the edge of the battlefield, Orion observed as healers and men shifted through the corpses. They had started sorting them into friend, foe, human, dragon and animal. There was also a pile of weaponry to be sorted. Knowing Tad, he was among the weapons, looking for something sharp to inherit.

He walked forward, nodding to those who were working away. He rounded the weapons and was disappointed that Tad was nowhere to be seen.

He didn't want to return to the tents of healing, so he decided he might as well find a senior guardsman and work alongside them to help. Many hands made light work after all.

Working mechanically, he stripped bodies of weapons and sorted them. He did this without looking too closely into faces or thinking whether or not it was his blade or arrow that had finished them off. It wasn't too bad if he didn't think of the corpses as human.

After an hour of sorting, he found himself working alongside Lyntton. His fellow King's Guardsman raised his eyebrow at him but didn't say a word, for which Orion was grateful.

Keep moving, Orion told himself. *Keep making yourself useful.*

His hand reached out and turned a body over. Instantly recognising the still form of Spearmaster Natayn, he felt his breath catch in his throat. The Spearmaster was one of his father's dearest friends. He was Tad's father. Quickly he swallowed the bile, smothering his cry of despair. He blinked past the tears that gathered and clenched his fists. What was he going to tell Tad?

Then the ground was pulled out from underneath him. Natayn had been sheltering a smaller warrior. A young man with dark hair like his and his mother's Sionian skin tone.

A scream startled him. And it was even more shocking to realise it was a scream from his own lungs. He tried to reel backwards to get away from Tad's unseeing eyes, but there was no escaping them.

Gloved hands grabbed him, spinning him and pressing him into a hard, warm chest. "Otherworlds!" Orion screamed.

His knees buckled underneath him. More boots came in his direction, and he tried to flinch out of the strong arms holding him up.

"Ain't he a bit green for this job?"

"Battle shock," another voice said above him. "He's not the first one."

The arms tightened around him. "I'm in charge of the new recruits ... I'll take him back to camp. Come on, guardsman, one step in front of the other."

Orion came back to himself sitting wedged between Will and Fydellah. He blinked and let his fingers curl in the long grass, pulling it up by the roots.

"You back with us?" Will Hartcurt didn't look at him. He didn't have to, Orion knew. The lord could read people's minds. "I'm good with secrets."

Stretching forwards, Fydellah grabbed a dandelion. She brought it to her lips and blew. "I wish for this to be over."

Will grunted in agreement and glanced sidelong at Orion. "We dragons need to look out for one another, I think."

Fydellah sighed heavily and lay down in the grass. She stared up unblinking at the clouds, resting her hands on her belly. "This dragon would like them to hurry up and burn the fields."

"They're looking for anything of use," Orion said, surprised at how hoarse his voice felt. "And survivors."

"Hope is fading." Will breathed in through his nose and held it. He stood and offered Orion his hand. "Let's get you back to camp. There's word that Jodathyn is worried about you."

"Jodathyn is awake?" Orion lifted his head. "How long have I been out of it?"

"A while," Fydellah said.

Will wiggled his fingers. "Come on, horse boy. Sitting here worrying about what people think about you won't help."

"It might," Orion grumbled.

"A lie," Fydellah replied, but this time there was a teasing tilt to her smile.

Taking the offered hand, Orion let himself be hauled to his feet. "What happened to you two in battle? I didn't see you in the confusion."

Will grinned at him sheepishly. "We took to the skies when the ground became a furnace. Fydellah began ferrying out as many wounded as she could."

"A backbreaking and thankless task," Fydellah said.

Orion looked up at her in a new light. "Not to the soldiers you pulled out of danger."

"I tried to fly above the dragon battle, reading minds and intentions and relaying what I could to whoever I thought was one of ours." Will stared up into the wide-open sky.

"I'm glad you are both well," Orion said. He rubbed his forehead, feeling a headache starting to pound in his skull. "I'm not sure I can show my face."

Will shrugged his shoulders, his eyes swivelling to stare out on the horizon. "There are many in camp close to the brink, Orion. And you're not the only one to have a moment."

A moment? Otherworlds! Orion didn't want to know what Zapyr's reaction might be if he found out how poorly he had taken the carnage of the battlefield. His cheeks flared at the mere thought of the golden dragon knowing his weakness.

They reached the edge of the camp that faced away from the battlefield. Orion didn't want to question how they had dragged him that distance in the state he was in. He swallowed and looked around at the troops. No one was paying him any mind.

"Do you think we can walk for just a little longer before I have to ..."

"We can walk," Will said, "if you think it will help."

Orion nodded and trained his eyes forward. Will and Fydellah kept step with him even though he knew they had better things to do. Neither of them said a word.

"Will," Orion said, keeping his voice steady. "Might I hold one of your daggers?"

He wasn't entirely sure how Will's gifting worked. But he tried to project his thoughts forward. A tall shadow of a man had been following them since they passed the supply carts. He felt tendrils of unease and tried to tell himself that it was his imagination. The fact that he left his weapons behind in the tent with Theo made him nervous. Captain Tiernan would have his hide if he found out. And then he remembered the captain was no more ...

Slipping a dagger from his side, Will handed it to Orion. He wondered if his anxiety was rubbing off on Will. He could see the nervous twitch of the lord's fingers. "Nothing like the Silverdyne make I'm sure you are used to."

Orion took the dagger with a smile and lowered his voice. "We're alone. We can talk openly."

He had heard that Fydellah could hear whether or not someone spoke lies. She lifted her head to gaze at him, then winked before ducking into a narrow gap between two tents. Orion slowed and let Will step ahead of him, his fingers tightening on the handle of the dagger.

Orion was prepared for the hand that reached out and grabbed him. He spun, the dagger pressing against the soft skin of a man's throat.

The stranger was tall, once handsome, with dark hair framing his face. He looked worn and haggard. Orion was sure half the men in the camp looked like walking ghosts. He opened his mouth to ask the stranger who he was and what his business was, but Will's surprised yell stopped him.

"Thylyssa!" Will's eyes hardened; he stepped forward to study the man's face. "I must say, my lord, you look a little worse for wear."

Orion had no idea who Thylyssa was, but he kept his hand steady and pressed his dagger closer to the man's throat. From Fydellah and Will's reaction, the man was an enemy.

"What are you doing here?" Will demanded.

"Taking back what's mine," Thylyssa rasped. "If I can't use you ... Pallarus can't."

There were three types of enemies. The first was cold, calculating and patient. Another group relied on physical prowess. And then there was the third group, men who hid behind a cloak of power and acts of intimidation. Thylyssa was of the latter.

Even though he was a head taller, Thylyssa didn't pose a problem. There was a madness in his eyes, something wild and feral. So when Thylyssa lunged with his own dagger, Orion swiftly lowered his weapon and swung it into the man's gut.

Fydellah swore at the blood congealing around them.

"Murderer!" someone screamed.

Orion lifted his head, a faint buzzing sound running through his brain. It felt like the ground was swaying beneath his boots. He widened his stance to stop himself from toppling over. "I'm Orion Beast-Whisperer ... Send for Lord Zapyr; he'll vouch for me."

"And Jael ..." Will muttered.

"Will," Fydellah whispered. She thought she was being quiet so Orion wouldn't hear. She failed. "Thylyssa is dead. There's nought Jael can do for him."

Orion wrenched his hand back and stepped away from the body. The ground beneath him ran red. "I *don't* need a healer."

Roane landed nearby, looking from Will to the dead lord at their feet. Zapyr was behind him, closely followed by Rhox.

Rumbling, Zapyr's head swayed back and forth as he regarded the corpse. "Can you read anything off him?"

"No," Roane said. "He's very dead."

"Nice aim, *sudunyn*!" Rhox said, laughter in his voice.

Will gave the lord a swift kick with his boot, which made Fydellah gasp in horror. "Will!"

"He was my slave master," Will said. "I for one am happy he's dead."

"Do you think he had anything nefarious planned?" Rhox peered around his father's flank.

"Does it matter?" Orion asked. He crossed his arms against his chest. "The threat was terminated."

Zapyr's brow furrowed. "Double the patrols. I have a hatchling to look after."

Roane nodded grimly as Zapyr's clawed hands plucked Orion up. "Sidrah is currently patrolling the skies. Curarfur is available, napping in the mountains."

"I do *not* need a healer!"

CHAPTER THIRTY-FOUR

Jodathyn

The Ruins of Torryn

Something wet and cold slid down Jodathyn's chest. He moaned in disgust and blinked his eyes open. He had been in middle of a pleasant dream, flying and playing with two ancient dragons. He had recognised Mandros' *aluel* but not the large emerald-green female dragon at his side. From the air, Rama had looked different. Many of the villages and towns did not exist. He was much smaller than the ancient ones, and he had little hope of catching them as they dodged among the clouds.

At first, he was confused, opening his eyes and seeing Et-hir's face. He had expected something more reptilian. He was a dragon, wasn't he?

Et-hir didn't say anything, only brushed his wet curls from his forehead. He lay still, blinking up at her. She smiled and returned to wiping his bare chest with a lightly scented cloth.

"Ettie?"

"Do you think you can sit up? I'll help you wash your hair."

"You were on the battlefield," Jodathyn said, his voice coming out a croak. "You could have died."

From the infuriated look that crossed Et-hir's beautiful face, it had been the wrong thing to say. Still, she said nothing but laid her fingers on a new scar low on Jodathyn's belly. He wriggled to sit up and looked at it, his lips curling in disgust. It was star shaped, large and puckered.

"You did die," Et-hir finally whispered. "You foolish man, you died!"

Jodathyn's brow wrinkled in confusion. "But I'm here."

"Much to everyone's shock," Theo muttered. Jodathyn turned his face down to see that Theo was sitting on the ground, his knees drawn up to his chest. He schooled his face to not register his surprise when he realised Theo was missing an eye. He let his gaze wander about the tent, releasing a breath of relief when he spotted Carew and a few other guardsmen he had gotten to know.

"Nym!" Jodathyn cried.

"Getting you something to drink, you lounging lizard."

Water did sound good. His mouth felt like it was stuffed full of sawdust. He groaned and licked his dry, chapped lips.

"Orion!"

Nym came into view, rolling her eyes, and passed him a cup of water. "Went for a walk."

"Kieryn?"

"Still king."

"Let him orientate himself," Carew muttered from his bunk. He lay with his back to Jodathyn.

Drinking deeply from the cup, Jodathyn tried to take another look at his belly without looking too distressed. He set the cup down, his finger automatically coming to where Vadroil had pierced his side.

"It didn't heal."

"Of course it didn't heal." An old woman bustled into the tent. Her long grey hair was held up in a messy bun on the top of her head, which flopped side to side as she hobbled forward. Jodathyn noticed she moved about with the help of a cane. "You, young sir, were very lucky to have some very gifted healers."

"Jodathyn," Et-hir murmured at his elbow. "This is Ninah. She's been looking after you."

"Nice to meet you, ma'am," Jodathyn said with an incline of his head.

"Bah, nonsense," Ninah said. "Young men like you don't like healers."

"Well, I'm grateful nonetheless," Jodathyn insisted.

"Be careful, war-worm," Nym cautioned. "Ninah chased your brother from the tent. She's not afraid to use her cane."

With his back still to the rest of the tent, Carew's shoulders shook with a chuckle. His movements caught Ninah's attention. She took a few steps in his direction, lifted her cane and prodded him in the middle of the back. "Now you," she said, "need to get out of your bunk, eat something and have a wash. My pigsty smells better than you."

Jodathyn watched as Ninah, despite her stern words, helped Carew to sit. The guardsman kept his back to the rest of the tent and made a bit of a fuss when Ninah unbuttoned his shirt for him. There was something not quite right with the way Carew miserably tried to fend off the old woman, so Jodathyn lay back down on his bunk and let his recent memories wash over him.

"Tiernan ..." Jodathyn whispered, wincing as Carew flinched at his father's name. "I walked the Otherworld."

Memories of faces, of soft touches and whispered words, spun in his mind. In the Otherworld, there had been no more fear. No more pain. Only a peace that he could not dare to hope to understand.

He touched his cheek where he had felt a young Donatein's bearded kiss. It had been him that waited in the Otherworld, not his father, and he wasn't disappointed.

Ruevyn had been there, standing alongside Illeanah, the image foreign but somehow right. Valt and Voran had gripped his hand, Valt hushing him as he tried to apologise for his death. Jodathyn insanely noticed that he was wearing supple leather gloves that he had been so fond of in life. Curran watched a small Meena playing with his faithful hounds.

Tiernan had been among them, standing tall to attention. His expressive blue eyes watched him in confusion. "You walk among us, but you're not quite one of us."

"A vision," Jodathyn replied. "Somehow I've pulled you into a dream."

Tiernan shook his head. "This isn't a dream. I'm gone."

"Gone where?"

Tiernan's stern face softened. "I've passed from the mortal realm, Your Highness."

The words should have cut him. Pain should have followed the simple declaration, and yet there was none.

Through those who had been near and dear to him, another dark-haired man walked. Keen eyes observed him, his noble face lighting up with pleased curiosity. *Arturyn.* Jodathyn could only wait as the great king approached him. Jodathyn knew the human form of Mandros did not *know* him, but certainly he knew *who* he was.

"Your Majesty," Jodathyn said, bowing at the waist.

"None of that." The voice even sounded like Mandros. "I am your *aluel,* am I not?"

Jodathyn nodded, finding he was tongue-tied, overwhelmed at meeting the human heart of Mandros.

"Tell me, what has happened that you find yourself here so young?"

"You don't know?" Jodathyn murmured.

"The lives of the living are not for the dead."

"I'm dead?"

"Almost. Only those still living have the ability to bleed in the Otherworld."

Jodathyn felt a sharp tugging on his belly. He looked down. His wound was still dripping blood. Rivets of glistening red were left in its wake. The sight should be horrifying, but it left him with a sense of satisfaction.

"I've done it! Vadroil is dead ..."

Donatein was at his back, and then Tiernan's hands were on his shoulders.

"Come, my son. Go home and live," Donatein said.

The tugging on his belly increased.

"The best revenge is living a life worthy of the honourable man you've become." Tiernan's voice was low. "Tell Carew to fight for a life he can be proud of. He's young and talented. It's not over for him. Tell my sons to fight for one another."

He had tried to protest. But the world faded to a blanket of black.

Nym snapped her fingers in front of Jodathyn's face. "Did you just go back to the Otherworld?"

A smile curled on Jodathyn's face. "Maybe."

"Carvelle wants to see you," Et-hir said.

Jodathyn nodded and swung his feet off the edge of the bed. He stood, thrusting his feet into his boots, which had been unlaced and left beside his bedside. As he laced them up, Carew finally turned over to look at him.

"Might I bother the white dragon for a flight?" Carew asked. Ninah's aged face lit up. Behind the guardsman's back, she nodded her head. "It might help keep my mind busy."

It took all of Jodathyn's firm resolve not to react to the now apparent injury Carew had suffered. The pinched look on Nym's face was practically begging him to do something.

"Of course," Jodathyn agreed. He fumbled around for a shirt, so that he might hide his shock at Carew's stump. "Get dressed."

"Perhaps, young dragon, you might take an old healer to visit the queen?" Ninah asked. "Her Majesty said I might be the royal midwife, and I'll like to hold her to that promise."

When they arrived to the place where Rhox had kept the vulnerable under an illusion, Tornyth found Carvelle entertaining the large blind female dragon that he knew was Mandros' mate, Mashikah. Carew slipped from his back and started a lonely walk through the mountains. Tornyth felt a twinge of sadness for the young King's Guardsman and wondered if Captain Tiernan knew what had happened to him.

Very carefully he lifted the old healer from his back and set her down on her feet. She looked up at him, patted his snout and told him he was a good lad before tottering towards the cave system to look for the queen. Tornyth watched her, his tail swishing to the side. She had no ill intentions towards the queen, but he was on high alert. The young babe was beginning to grow quickly. It was his job to protect her.

"Winter's Dragon." Mashikah turned her head in his direction. "There are some dragons that a young one shouldn't meddle with. Moroth was one of them."

"Lady Mashikah," Tornyth said with bow of his head. What could one say to that admonishment? He dipped his head, feeling foolish. "Thank you for your intervention. Might I ask what happened to your contingent of dragons? I looked for you every evening ... I was worried."

Mashikah lifted her snout and sniffed at him. "Worried? For an old, blind dragon?"

"My lady, you must have some strong battle-fire in you if you challenged Moroth. And you are Mandros' mate and Deovyn, Sidrah and Zapyr's *lullah*."

"Yes," Mashikah said, "I fear we are family now."

"I don't mind at all."

Mashikah harrumphed. "If you must know, Ice Fire, Vadroil sent some of his dragons to delay us. It didn't work. We were victorious."

"I am glad," Tornyth replied.

Mashikah nudged him. "So am I. Mandros would have been devastated to lose you."

He lowered himself to his belly as Carvelle eyed him cautiously. His nephew seemed somewhat subdued. "Uncle? They said you were badly hurt ..."

"I am well, Carvelle."

Carvelle scrambled to his feet, and now assured that his uncle was in one piece, ran to him. Tornyth returned back to his human self as the prince hit him, his arms out wide.

"There're rumours an assassin attacked you the night before," Carvelle said.

"Oh, erm ..."

"Yes, I heard the same rumours."

Jodathyn turned upon his heel and standing before him was Kieryn, looking tired, dirty and somehow more magnificent than ever. With him stood his queen, Odelle. With the way she moved, he could now see the small bump where the unborn princess was growing.

"Your Majesty, there was a situation, and it was dealt with."

"In the spirit of honesty, there is something I need to tell you, brother, before you hear it from another source." Kieryn moved forward and slapped Jodathyn on the shoulder. He took out the parchment that had been found on the would-be assassin. "Father wasn't killed in a hunting accident."

Jodathyn's stomach clamped. "He was murdered? This is Father?"

"Aye."

"Oh." Jodathyn felt nothing when he heard the news. He gazed into the pinched expression on Kieryn's face. His brother had known better man than he had. "I'm sorry you had to find out this way."

Kieryn scoffed. "I should have realised it earlier. I was so intent on finding Carvelle, I didn't see this page."

Jodathyn's eyebrows rose.

"It's a sketch from your mother's journal," Kieryn said gruffly. "She kept detailed illustrations of what her gifts showed her. All her predictions and visions."

"All these years you've had something of my mother's?"

"I never intended to keep it from you," Kieryn replied. "When we return to Pallaryn I will find some less distressing work of hers for you. A boy ought to know his mother ... however much I disliked her."

"Truly?"

"Truly." Kieryn's grip on his shoulder tightened. "There is a beautiful sketch of Tornyth and Carvelle. Your mother labelled it, 'My son and his child'. I can't help but think she would be disappointed with the truth."

"If what Mandros said is true, Carvelle and I are bonded. Our dragons at least," Jodathyn said. "She's not wrong. You're *vehyl aluel*, and I am *Rshon Aluel*."

Kieryn smiled and turned to look back at Carvelle, who was watching their conversation with intense concentration. "Then my son is indeed blessed."

"The assassin in your tent, white scales, may not be an isolated case," Mashikah said. She raised her sightless eyes skywards. "The one called Will was attacked not long ago, Zapyr's new human, Orion, dispatched the fiend before he could be questioned. Best be on your guard."

"Can you tell us anything more, Lady Mashikah?" Kieryn asked, stepping away from Jodathyn.

"Royal dragons can attract the unsavoury types. General Roane is investigating further. It is an excellent opportunity to train up young Rigyl," Mashikah replied. "Go on with your lives."

Kieryn exhaled heavily and glanced back at Jodathyn and then to Odelle, who had been content to listen and watch. He held out his hand to his wife, and she stepped forward, placing her slim hand in his.

"What now?" Jodathyn shifted. He knew part of the answer. *Home.* But what type of home would they be returning to?

"We'll honour those we can ... burn the rest," Odelle said.

Jodathyn made a face.

"It is necessary if we don't want to spread disease," Mashikah replied. It was almost like she could sense Jodathyn's expressions. "Rhox has made a friend."

Jodathyn looked up. Rhox was sitting with Guardsman Carew. They seemed to be in deep discussion. As they watched, Carew mounted the bronze dragon, and they took to the skies.

"Good," Carvelle said with a nod. "They'll be good for each other."

The fields of Torryn were burning. It was impossible to separate those who had fought for Rama into the regions and decide what funeral rites were acceptable. In the end they had laid their fallen in neat rows. Kieryn stood before the surviving troops, uttering a solemn prayer as dragons dropped wildflowers and greenery from above. It had been an effective way to do a mass Shredding of the Flowers ceremony.

Captain Tiernan's body had been found. They laid him on a pyre in the front of his troops. A pair of King's Guardsmen assisted Carew to the edge of the field, and Jodathyn could feel his eyes mist up as he watched Carew mourn his father.

Jodathyn found his feet walking forward, and he sunk down onto the soft earth beside Carew.

"Wake up, Pa," Carew mumbled, his body half draped over the pyre. "Please. Wake up. I cannot do this without you ... I can't."

"You can," Jodathyn replied. The young guardsman started when he lightly touched his shoulder. "I have a message for you." And at Carew's nod, he told him of what he saw and heard in the Otherworld.

Carew stood then, looking down at his father's body. He saluted with his left hand and stepped back to join the ranks.

Jodathyn returned to Kieryn's side.

Then as one, the dragons burned the dead. Human alongside the dragons. Jodathyn stood for a long time watching, Et-hir beside him. He could hear the soft sounds of a Sionian prayer on her lips. But his heart was too heavy to catch her words to translate.

As the morning turned into afternoon, he turned to leave. He decided he would walk among the common men one last time. As a royalborn, he would leave for Pallaryn in the first wave. Kieryn was keen to have his family returned behind the palace's walls.

There would still be much to do for the men left behind. Nym and Theo had volunteered to help with the pack down of tents and supplies. They would return to the capital at a later date. Jodathyn would wait for that day.

"You haven't asked the king for anything," Theo had said to his sister the night before. "I'll return to stone masonry; what about you?"

"I was thinking I would ask for a ship," Nym replied.

Theo had laughed. And Jodathyn had to wonder how serious Nym was about her request. When he was new to his dragon kin, he had listened to what Mandros had to say. He remembered Nym being told that she would have another adventure on the seas.

The flight to return to Pallaryn was a solemn one. Kieryn flew ahead on the back of Mandros. The two kings to enter the capital as one. Tornyth flew slightly behind with Odelle, Carvelle and Et-hir.

Then, behind him, Mashikah, Zapyr, Deovyn and Sidrah.

Their dragon host and those who were needed in Pallaryn flew behind them.

To his dying day, Jodathyn would never forget the roar of victory from Mandros as they flew over the citadel. He didn't know what he was expecting. The city was no longer burning and smoking. Those left behind to pick up their lives were working in the streets. At Mandros' trumpeting call, they lifted their faces. Many still with fear. It would be a long time before the people of Pallaryn could feel they could return to their normal lives.

Mandros landed on the crumbling wall of the palace, and Kieryn dismounted. Tornyth followed and watched in silence as the others made room for themselves. For a long moment, Kieryn and Mandros stood facing each other.

"There are no words, Lord Mandros, to thank you," Kieryn said.

Mandros swayed his head back and forth. "Your council has fallen, *vehyl pallu*. It is time to raise up the next generation and train them to be your supporting force. The fight isn't over."

"The young dragons ..."

"Are the first of what I hope will be many more," Mandros said. "These four are referred to in the dragon tales as the Fulfilment. Each is equipped with the skills and fortitude to help you root out Vadroil's corruption once and for all.

Rigyl has such a wide net to read minds, and Vydris and her truth discernment. They're a formidable pair. Ayrdonyth will always be your soldier. He has great capacity with his powers that he still has time to unearth. And Tornyth ... your shield. Tornyth, Winter's Dragon, Ice Fire, is the one to train up the young Carvelle and his own daughters. He will strengthen the Pallarus bloodline."

Kieryn nodded and reached out his hand to touch Mandros' scales. "I'll look after each of them, I swear it."

"Good." Mandros smiled. "You know how to communicate with me."

Kieryn's eyes slid to Tornyth.

"Yes, your brother can call me at a great distance. He's a noisy little thing. Come here, Tornyth, Winter's Dragon. Let me take a look at you."

"I guess this is goodbye," Tornyth mumbled.

"What's this? Such a long face, *mynrell*," Mandros replied. He reached forward and bumped their snouts together. "No. Just goodbye. We dragons are going to be busy finding suitable cave systems to live."

Tornyth's eyes lit up. "You're staying in Rama?"

"Well, of course," Sidrah said from behind. "There's a baby princess to bless come summer."

Mandros shook his head and turned his large amber eyes towards Tornyth. "Rama is home to many mountain ranges. Why do you think the first dragons came here?"

"I for one am looking forward to plumper, juicier fish," Zapyr continued.

Tornyth tilted his head to the side. "You never taught me to hunt."

"It's time to rest, but soon we'll come and teach the four of you what you need to know as dragons."

"Come winter, I'll teach you to fly through the wild winter storms out at sea," Zapyr promised.

"Or racing through the mountain ranges …" Deovyn said. "And how to battle with snow."

"You are a menace, Deo," Sidrah commented.

When Jodathyn finally made it to his chambers, Myrus was waiting for him. The lad had taken initiative and cleaned his chambers and his servants' rooms from top to bottom. There was no sign of the damage that had been left behind.

"So, do I have the job?" the boy asked when Jodathyn's jaw hit the ground. "I straightened your woman's chambers as well. I found her some pretty gowns and a maid."

"How old are you?"

"Ten summers, Your Highness."

Jodathyn considered Myrus for a long moment. "The rebuild of Pallaryn will be hard work."

Adjusting his jerkin, Myrus straightened his posture. "I'm not afraid of hard work."

Jodathyn glided towards his desk. One of the only journals not damaged was the red leather book gifted to him by the king of Sion, the one he had told Et-hir he had been too frightened to write in. He swept his eyes over Myrus, who was looking up at him hopefully. Originally, he didn't like the idea of taking a child as his servant. But Myrus was right; his options in life were few. Finding himself employment was the boy's best chance at life.

"I made a promise, Myrus. I promised someone very dear to me that I would look after the orphans and unloved. Would you like to be my page and assist me?"

"Your Highness, I don't have the skills ..."

Jodathyn's fingers ran along the leather binding. "A boy like you has the brains to learn."

In the following days, Jodathyn meticulously collected the names and information of families that had been split up. He sifted through parchments of notes trying to reconnect as many Ramian families as he could. At his side, Myrus sat practising, writing names and numbers in his journal. In the evenings, Jodathyn taught him herb lore, music and history.

Et-hir's experiences with organising large trades and merchant documents came in useful in his endeavour. The number of orphans saddened him.

One evening Jodathyn was quite frustrated with the number of orphans who had been identified. It had become customary for the king and queen, along with Et-hir, to join him in an evening drink. Tonight, he voiced his concerns out loud.

"Maybe you should ask your brother for help," Et-hir said, turning to smile sweetly at Kieryn.

"Absolutely right, my dear," Odelle replied. "I have the perfect building we can purchase to house and educate so many vulnerable children. The crown ought to support the next generation, shouldn't it, husband?"

"The only appropriate response, brother, is 'of course, my dear'," Kieryn said, raising his goblet.

The next morning, the queen summoned Jodathyn and Et-hir and escorted them through the citadel and to a brothel. Much to Jodathyn's astonishment, it was here she introduced them to a woman with a head full of blond curls: Madam Nurlah.

Odelle reminded Madam Nurlah she had once been a midwife and soon convinced her it was a much better idea to help them with the children in a paid position. As a patron of the orphanage, the queen had also employed Nurlah's girls to help look after the children. The whores' children got an education as well.

Madam Nurlah was paid handsomely for the building, and Jodathyn started immediately collecting the lost children of the citadel, regardless if they had lost their parents in the reign of Galgothmeg or not.

Within a week, Kieryn had some fine tutors for the new establishment. Rumour on the street was the pay was exceedingly good. The king also provided a weekly delivery of food and money for clothing. Over the first season of opening, Kieryn had names of trades and businesses looking for apprentices for the older children.

Under Jael and Lyntton, new men were brought into the ranks of palace guards and King's Guard. The city was vulnerable from the coup and the time of unsettled administration, and it required a small influx of lawmen. All ranks of men under Jael and Lyntton were also rostered to help with the clean-up and the physical rebuild of the city.

Jodathyn was a little disappointed when Theo returned to Pallaryn without Nym. She went with Carew to his family estate to help him recover and meet his brothers. Theo told him this with a wink. True to his word, Kieryn found Theo a new master to finish his stone masonry apprenticeship. The ex-thief spent countless hours sketching new designs and joining the labour crews removing rubble.

Kieryn didn't immediately convene a new council. Many of the great houses no longer stood, and the king made it quite clear that ancient bloodlines were no guarantee that they would be called upon to serve. A place at the king's side was no longer a position held by hereditary right, but an earned privilege.

The first family to fall from grace was house Hartcurt. The lands were immediately passed to Will. Likewise, Fydellah's family estate was taken from them and passed to her. Fydellah refused to return home and let her mother stay on the property. The sister that had betrayed her was tried for the act of selling Fydellah into slavery.

Many had seen the return of dragons as the doom of Rama. When the white dragon stirred, it was the beginning of a new dawn. From all accounts from the trackers Mandros sent out, without Vadroil and his supporters, it was only a matter of time before the old way of the Artrothian Empire died out. The dragons of Artroth had lost their final hold on the other races that lived on the island. Soon they would be just a bad memory on the wind.

The Wind Song spoke of the endurance of Rama, of a white dragon who would continue to heal the land for centuries to come. Under the claws of the Herald of the Dragon King, the kingdom would flourish. And during the reign of the coming Dragon King himself, the blessings of Rama would spread to neighbouring lands.

Rama's story would stand the test of time.

Chapter Thirty-Five

Jodathyn

Twelve Years Later - The Fields of Adavan, High Autumn Feast

The scent of autumn fruits and festival wines was heavy in the air. Jodathyn lifted his goblet to taste the strong flavour of the king's wine. He hummed in pleasure; it had been a particularly good year for the harvest.

Completely at ease within the king's pavilion, he unclasped his cloak and tossed it to the side. His manservant, Myrus, stepped forward and folded it neatly over his arm and refilled his goblet.

It was a marvel how much his dragon part could now effortlessly heat his human body. A gift his wife greatly appreciated in the winter seasons. Unnaturally warm, he rolled up his sleeves so the intricate dragon tattoo on his forearm was clearly on display and reclined back on the plush velvet cushions.

Hearing the strands of an old traditional dancing tune, Jodathyn turned his gaze to the crowd. He flexed his fingers and breathed a sigh of relief that

Carvelle was spinning Larelle among the dancers. The ill-fated autumn festival made him nervous. He wasn't the only one; the King's Guard under Jael's command was especially diligent.

"Hail, Prince Jodathyn of house Pallarus."

Jodathyn turned his eyes away from the festivities and towards his brother, King Kieryn, the High King of Rama. The toast hadn't come as a surprise to him. Every year, as those closest to house Pallarus gathered in the king's pavilion, his brother made a toast to acknowledge his part in the Battle for Torryn. Over the years he had learnt to accept the praise with a dignified nod of the head.

Jodathyn caught Kieryn's amused smirk as the king glanced over the revellers looking for the inevitable signs of trouble. Jodathyn was no fool. He knew exactly who Kieryn was looking for. He was relaxed, which could only mean he was moments away from being clambered on by his three exuberant daughters.

Too comfortable to move from his position to look for his children, Jodathyn lazed back, enjoying his last moments of peace. He knew that there were several guardsmen on the lookout for his girls. He had overheard Captain Jael drilling his men that morning.

"Perhaps someone should seek out Prince Jodathyn's three princesses," Guardsman Orion suggested, giving Jodathyn a playful nudge with the toe of his boot.

"I'll hear from them soon enough," Jodathyn said, waving the comment aside.

"Prince Jodathyn spotted the twins only ten minutes back," Will said. Handsome as ever, he leaned over and plucked a bunch of grapes from a platter. He pulled them off one by one, testing the plump purple globes between his two fingers. "That, and I sense they are dancing nearby."

Grinning at the western lord, Jodathyn reclined further. Will's incredible tracking abilities had become invaluable since the twins had learned to run.

"Perhaps you should be dancing too, Lord Will," Jodathyn said, a sly smirk on his lips.

Will glanced over at him, looking politely confused.

"Courage, man," Jael scolded Will lightly. "If you can face battlefield, then you can ask a certain pretty lady to dance."

"Really?" Will asked the tent. "Am I that obvious?"

"Yes," Orion answered.

"Come now, my lords, it's no easy thing for a woman to court a dragon." Et-hir swept into the tent so that Jodathyn set down his goblet to admire her in her Sionian gown of rich red silk. Her small daughters had woven matching ribbons into her long, dark hair that were held into place with delicate honeybee clasps, which had been a wedding gift from the king of Sion in honour of their union. In one graceful movement, she joined Jodathyn on his cushions and laid her head in his lap.

"You are rumbling again, my love," Et-hir told him.

"Eight years of marriage, my dear," Jodathyn replied, "and my dragon still sings every time he sees you."

Will downed his goblet and stood. "Well, if you two are going to be making eyes at one another ..."

Orion waited until Will was out of earshot, then gestured to Myrus. "If you can get Fydellah and Will to have a romantic moment together, I would be most grateful."

"Orion!" Et-hir gasped.

Orion grinned, his cheeks blushing furiously. "Well, you listen to their dragons pining! It's *distracting*."

Jodathyn laughed into his goblet. "Go have fun, Myrus. Let's see if you have any more luck than poor Orion Maysden."

Myrus bowed, a grin spreading on his face. He practically skipped from the tent, and a small white dog, a gift from Jodathyn, bounded after him.

Across the field, Jodathyn spied Nym and her brothers. Pleased that they made it to the celebrations, he lifted his hand in greeting. Still with her short haircut and trousers, Nym sauntered towards the king's pavilion. At her side he realised she had with her Carew, which was not a shock.

After the Battle for Torryn, Nym had asked for a ship and a crew. Soon after, without a word of what her plans had been, she disappeared, Carew one-hand with her. Theo had spent months worrying for them.

Then one clear summer's afternoon, the pair rode into Pallaryn unannounced, accompanied by a stranger. At the time, Theo had been working at the palace on some of the stone work and had raced to the palace gates to meet her.

Jodathyn would never forget the look of pure disbelief and delight on Theo's face as he gazed upon the stranger, who twitched nervously. Pale eyes pierced Theo, the expression on his face somewhat slack.

"Ryn, you remember our brother, Theo?" When Nym spoke to the stranger, it was with an unusual tenderness.

"Theo?" the stranger repeated. His voice was cracked and slurred. "He got only one eye."

"Ryn, this is Jod," Nym continued, as if she were speaking to a small child. "He's my friend."

"What's happened to him?" Theo asked.

"He's nervous ..." Nym's hands fell to her side.

"Of everything," Carew added in an undertone.

After his reintroduction to Ramian life, Ryn followed Nym wherever she went. He spoke little and only to those he seemed to trust. A broad-shouldered giant, Ryn seemed to enjoy working on Nym's ships.

Delighted to see Jodathyn, Ryn lifted his hands and waved a greeting. He stepped over Jodathyn's three young hunting dogs, bobbing his head in the king's direction before picking up the first wriggling dog.

Both Nym and Theo paused by the entryway and bowed politely in Kieryn's direction before entering. Nym attempted to give Ryn a warning look, but her brother seemed oblivious to her irritation. Instead, Ryn sat by Jodathyn's left-hand side uninvited and scooped up the remaining dogs.

"You said not to treat the palace brat like a prince," Ryn said, shrugging his shoulders.

"Blessed High Autumn to you, brother Ryn," Jodathyn said, lifting his goblet. He smirked in Nym's direction.

Theo stepped past his siblings to give Orion a friendly clap on the shoulder and a nod to Jael. Under his arm, Jodathyn spied a neatly rolled parchment, a clear indication that Theo was working on a new design.

Unlike his siblings, Theo had little love of the sea and had continued to stonemason apprenticeship under the king's benefactors. His artistry was now on display through the rebuild of Pallaryn for generations to come. Many of Theo's sketches included the story of the battle of Pallaryn and Torryn. In some cheeky corners, there were also hints of other parts of their stories. Such as the drunken night they had spent at the abandoned house before Galgothmeg. Jodathyn had also heard it rumoured there was a relief of him somewhere in the citadel bathing and being discovered by his now dear wife Et-hir. The cheeky stonemason wouldn't confirm the rumours.

Seeming nervous of his welcome, Carew one-hand stood rigidly eyeing Jael and Orion. It was no secret in Pallaryn that Carew never recovered from the realisation that even as skilled as he was with one hand, he would never be the swordsman that he once was.

"Guardsman Carew, please join us," Kieryn said.

"I am no longer a guardsman, Your Majesty," Carew said stiffly.

"Bah, always one of my men," Kieryn said, lifting a goblet. "Come, have a drink with us."

"I have thought your proposal over, Your Majesty," Carew murmured. He looked about the tent, his eyes brushing over Orion.

"And what do you think, guardsman?" Kieryn asked.

"I'll be honoured to accept as long as you are happy for me to serve in this manner."

"Excellent," Jodathyn said, draining his goblet. "Be prepared to be exhausted."

Jael raised his eyebrows.

"Carew has agreed to be the princesses' swordmaster," Jodathyn said. "Kieryn's dear daughter Princess Nia shouldn't give him much of a bother … It's my three he'll have to worry about."

Theo's eyebrows shot even higher at the news. "You're coming back to Pallaryn? With Nym?"

Carew exchanged a glance with Nym and nodded. "We have discussed it and decided it would be for the best."

"Where's chaos?" Ryn asked between mouthfuls of food.

"I'm not sure," Jodathyn said. "Is anyone watching my daughters?"

"I'm off duty," Jael grunted.

"Jasmeena was shadowing Carvelle and Larelle earlier," Kieryn said.

Jasmeena, Jodathyn's eldest, a girl of six summers, simply adored her older and wiser cousin and his special friend. She had the uncanny ability to make friends with anyone. Even Ryn was not immune to her charms. Indeed, it was a favourite pastime of Jasmeena's to sit upon the tall man's shoulders and have him gallop around the palace grounds. From Jodathyn she inherited her quick intelligence and was reading texts well above her peers.

Jodathyn looked around, dreading catching sight of his twins. While they were only four summers old, they knew how to get into all kinds of mischief. Et-hir claimed that their prolific climbing and scrapes were heredity traits from his side of the family, for both Alina and Estah were fearless climbers. On more than one occasion, he had to scale the stables to pluck his daughters off the roof. He may have occasionally been 'oblivious' to his daughters' antics until Jael eventually volunteered to bring them down.

Jodathyn caught sight of them running to and fro between the revellers, barefoot and their hair undone and wild.

Spotting her father watching her, Alina streaked across the path of a dozen adults. Estah followed in her wake. Although he had plenty of warning of his progeny approaching, Alina still managed to barrel into his ribs, knocking the air out of his lungs. Sedately, Estah clambered into Jodathyn's lap.

With a wide, toothy grin, Alina grabbed Jodathyn firmly around the neck, smashing their foreheads together. He winced and brought his arms around their slim waists. Estah clung to her father's middle.

"I love your cuddles," Jodathyn said as he kissed the top of their heads.

Nothing in all of Rama could hold the twins' attention for long. They jumped from Jodathyn's lap and grabbed each other's hand and ran haphazardly through the crowd, narrowly missing at least two servers.

"When they hold hands, they're invincible," Ryn commented.

Jodathyn opened his mouth to reply when they both did a spectacular nosedive into the grass. Wincing, he hurriedly looked the other way. It was best not to let the twins know that Papa saw their fall; he had learnt that from experience.

"They're up and running," Odelle said.

"Alina! Watch that pole," Et-hir cried just as the elder but smaller twin ran straight into a pole.

"It's always Alina," Kieryn said with a shake of his head.

Orion and Theo both choked back laughs.

"She's up," Nym said. She glanced up at Carew. "Good luck teaching that one."

Carvelle entered the tent, tugging Larelle with him. He flopped down onto cushions beside his mother. Jodathyn looked his nephew over. Eighteen summers old. Time had flown. Looking at Carvelle now, it seemed impossible that he had been only a little older when he had rescued him from kidnappers, which resulted in battles. The contemplative expression on Kieryn's face told him his brother was thinking the same thing.

Soon it would be time for him to take on more responsibility as the first dragon king in centuries. Kieryn had spoken to him at length last week of what he was hoping for Carvelle.

Lifting his goblet to his lips, he watched as Larelle demurely knelt to sit nearby Carvelle. He hid his smirk, his eyes seeking out Odelle and then Kieryn. The young ones thought that their blossoming interest in one another had gone unnoticed. The queen had been the first one to comment two years ago.

Prancing in the tent closely behind Carvelle, Princess Nia and his own daughter, Jasmeena, entered.

"I caught Carvelle kissing Lar ... elllle!" Nia said, skipping to her mother's side. Odelle hushed her daughter with a half-hearted stare, while Carvelle flushed and blustered at his infatuation with Larelle being so casually mentioned.

"Serves the little bugger right," Nym muttered. "The amount of times he embarrassed his elders ..."

Jodathyn coughed on his wine and wheezed.

"Lord Will is a mind reader, princess," Et-hir said. "We all know."

Carvelle groaned, relaxing back into the cushions.

Jodathyn, however, was watching his eldest. She sidled up to Kieryn with a smile he was sure was supposed to be innocent but had a distinctively sly edge to it.

"Dance with me!" she demanded, holding out her little hand.

Kieryn looked down at her.

"Jas ..." Jodathyn growled.

"You simply must, King Uncle," Jasmeena continued after rolling her eyes in Jodathyn's direction.

Kieryn regarded her and then slowly placed his goblet down with a clink. He removed his robes and pulled up his sleeves, all the while his dark eyes never leaving the expectant face of his niece. "Do you think you can keep up with the High King of Rama, Princess Jasmeena?"

Jasmeena thrust out her chin. "I know I can."

Jodathyn watched on as Kieryn led his eldest daughter to the dance floor. He couldn't help but smile at the unusual choice of a white dress she had chosen in honour of his winter scales. She had tied ribbons of red and orange around her waist as compromise.

"Where do you suppose we'll find her shoes?" Nym remarked, noticing her bare feet.

"Oh, honestly!" Et-hir cried. "Why do I bother with shoes for my girls' feet!"

"Up a tree!" Ryn boomed.

"The stream," Orion replied with a sage nod.

"Back home under her bed," Theo suggested.

"Or the queen has learnt from past experiences," Odelle said, holding up a pair of white slippers. "And rescued the shoes before it was too late."

Et-hir watched out for the girls, standing to see if she could get a better look. Jodathyn stood, swiftly taking her about the waist and dropping them both down onto the cushions. Yelping in surprise, Et-hir let him drag her down with him but battered away his hands.

"Come enjoy the peace, milady," Jodathyn rumbled, his voice lowering.

"I should really check on the twins."

Jodathyn kissed her neck, delighting at the goose flesh that rose along her skin. "We have all the King's Guard watching."

"And who is watching that they don't devour a platter of sweets?"

Jodathyn ran his hand down his wife's side, his fingers lingering on her waist. The red Sionian silk suited her very well. He lifted his fingers to adjust a few of the golden bee clasps in her hair.

"Don't go siring any more twins," Carvelle muttered.

"Carvelle!" Odelle cried, but she laughed.

"The kingdom wouldn't be able to handle another set of Pallarus twins," Carew added.

Et-hir pulled herself out of Jodathyn's lap. "I'm going to look for your children," she said.

Jodathyn smirked up at her. "They're yours as well if I recall correctly."

Busy watching his wife's silhouette, Jodathyn didn't hear his nephew trying to call him. That was until Carvelle picked up a nut and threw it at him.

"Yes, nephew of mine."

"I want to go with you to Apple Tree House."

"Only if your father permits it," Jodathyn answered. His eyes still hadn't left Et-hir's back.

"I need your help in convincing him, *Rshon Aluel*," Carvelle muttered almost mutinously.

"Using my dragon title isn't going to help your case, *mynrell*."

"I want to see the school built in Master Kelvie's honour," Carvelle protested. "What do we have now? One hundred and fifty orphans?"

"I hear they call him Papa Prince," Ryn muttered, grabbing another pastry.

"Please, Mother, help me convince Papa to let me fly out with Uncle."

"Zahayn the Green needs to mind his uncle," Kieryn said, stepping back into the tent, looking a little puffed. Jasmeena followed in his wake, looking victorious. "For the love of the Otherworld, no flying through thunderstorms."

"I can accompany them if you wish, Sire," Orion looked devilishly amused. "I am well equipped to keep the young prince in line."

"Father," Jasmeena said, plucking at his shirt. "When will I manifest into a dragon like you?"

"When your dragon is ready, dear one," Jodathyn murmured. He pressed his brow closer to hers. "You have much to learn before then."

"Dragons!"

At the cry of the crowds, Jodathyn's head whipped round. He sprung to his feet, leaving the pavilion behind him. He heard Carvelle's whoop as he manifested into his large green dragon beside him, and then they were leaving the human revellers behind on the ground.

He found Mandros immediately. His *aluel* looked him over, his scaled lips quirking into a dragon smile as he caught sight of the young green dragon beside Tornyth. "He is growing well, *mynrell*."

"I'm bigger than Tornyth and Deovyn now!" Carvelle's dragon, Zahayn, crowed.

"Thank the Ancient One's Talons for that," Sidrah commented from nearby. "Without the suppression herbs, the new generation of dragons has a chance to grow large."

Zahayn wasn't paying attention. He took after Deovyn, playfully snarling and nipping.

"Where's Ayrdonyth?" Zapyr demanded impatiently, his great golden head looking this way and that.

"Right behind you!" Ayrdonyth tapped Zapyr's back spines and then spun into a hurtling dive. With a roar of delight, Zapyr pursued him.

"Why, hello to you too, *sudunyn*," Tornyth muttered. He turned to Sidrah. "I highly suspect Rigyl and Vydris may have sneaked away for some quiet time."

Behind him, Roane chuckled, and Tornyth knew his assumption had been correct.

"Where's Carew?" Rhox bumped Tornyth's side impatiently. "Is he here?"

"Down below."

The bronze dragon nodded his thanks and dove into a steep dive. Since the ending of the great battle of Torryn, Rhox and Carew had forged a close friendship. He had heard Zapyr muttering that the Candyde boys fed Rhox too much rich meat when he visited them at the summer home in Arelle.

"Rich meat makes for slow flying," Zapyr was fond of saying to Rhox.

"I enjoyed every minute of consuming it," Rhox would answer.

Tornyth dipped into a steep dive and landed safely on the ground. He shielded his three daughters, who all came running to greet him and their dragon family. He nuzzled them each in turn, and they predictably climbed up his sinewy neck to sit astride him, unafraid.

That was what he wished for them. A childhood of freedom, exploration and the chance to face the world, unafraid of their futures. He was Tornyth, Winter's Dragon, Ice Fire, Father of New Era and Father to the Fatherless. His childhood might have been a cruel and twisted fate. But he had endured. And from his endurance, he had built a new legacy. Through himself and his children, he could change the world.

Destiny had never looked so sweet.

Thank you for taking the time to read my work. If you enjoyed my book, why not leave a review on Amazon or Goodreads and help an author out?

 amazon.com/author/kjburrage

 goodreads.com/author/show/22623993.K_J_Burrage

Acknowledgments

Jodathyn's journey has been a long one.

The first drafts of his story began when I was still in high school, circa 2000. Although there have been many versions of the story, this is the one I like best. In the very first draft, there were no dragons and Carvelle was gruesomely murdered. The plot has morphed over time, but the idea of who Jodathyn was at his core never wavered.

I wanted so badly to write a story where the main character was sensitive, kind-hearted, with dreams of grandeur. I wanted to showcase a tale where someone like this demonstrated that they too were capable of great things. Why? Because this is what I wanted to believe for myself. That even as a shy introvert, I too was capable of greatness. I wanted Jodathyn to come to not only accept but embrace who he was as a man. This is demonstrated through the progression of the titles in this series.

Son of the Crown – in this story Jodathyn is weighed down by the horrible title he was given at birth. He lets this have control over him.

Prince of Scales – Jodathyn takes on a new title. He's learning about himself, and he makes some mistakes along the way.

Herald of the Dragon King – Jodathyn embraces his destiny, and he steps forward into his future even though he is afraid.

Like Jodathyn, I didn't make my journey alone. And while I can only hope to show a portion of courage that my main character has developed, I want to acknowledge those who took the journey with me.

Janine Burger - the best beta reader in the world. She started reading her big sister's stuff when she was eight years old. She's read so many versions of this story and is still with me. Janine, I hope that Orion surviving made you happy and me killing Tiernan didn't make you too miserable.

Jacki Stevenson - my mum and first editor. She has marked and corrected so many of my kiddy scribbles. That took effort and dedication, Mum.

Glenn Stevenson - a dad who believes I am capable. He might not have any idea what I'm talking about, but he doesn't mind talking about writing.

Shelley Cooper and Peej Caskey - my cheerleaders on the sidelines. I appreciate everything.

Kaye Burrage - my mother-in-law who has beta read for me and has done what she can as I muddle my way through publishing.

Stephanie Harding and Ronda Jenkins - another pair of beta readers, family members and cheerleaders.

Thanks also goes to my editor Katie Wolf for helping me to get this trilogy past the finishing line and Miblart for the fantastic artwork on the covers.

About KJ Burrage

KJ Burrage currently calls tropical North Queensland, Australia, home. She has been developing her craft since she was ten years old. Alas, the original floppy discs from 1995 have disappeared!

She lives with her three young daughters, an exuberant pug-cross and a cheeky blue parrot.

Growing up she had grand visions of becoming CS Lewis. When she grew up a little more, she decided she was going to be JRR Tolkien. Now, she's learnt to be proud of her own voice and the pen name KJ Burrage is perfect for her.

She has a Bachelor Degree in Primary Education with a major in literacy and worked as a primary school teacher. She has also been a co-owner of a laser engraving business.

Life can be unpredictable (and unfair). After the sudden and tragic death of her husband, she returned to her passion of the written word.

You can read more at www.kjburrage.com.

facebook.com/profile.php?id=100071328683512

instagram.com/kjburrage_author/

tiktok.com/@kjburrage_writes

goodreads.com/author/show/22623993.K_J_Burrage

amazon.com/author/kjburrage

https://twitter.com/KJBurrage

Language Guide

Aluel (AY-l-ool) – Father

Araae helphelwyn. Terini gorthorawyn (AH-ay HEL-fel-win TE-ree-ne GOR-thor- A-win) – Famous words of the King's Guard. Live Valiantly. Die Honourably.

Brigyn (BRIG-n) - Winter

Elt (EL-t) – My

Kairn (K-AIR-n) – Two meanings – a) bastard/ illegitimate or b) mongrel

Ketur (KET – er) – Beloved (used for life mate only)

Lyron finyr (LIE – ron finn – near) – Lyron means either scaled or armoured. Finyr means overlord.

Pallu (PAL – loo) – Two meanings a) sovereign can be king or queen b) wind – out of interests Pallarus means a)Sovereign over seas or b) Sea Wind.

Mynrell (MIN-rell) – has many meanings son, daughter, heir, fosterling, adopted. All the same and all equal. Dragon use only.

Ri Rshon hanoch (RI R-ish-on HAN-ock) – Considered coarse language – Old Dragon's Genitals

Rokun (ROO-k-un) – Word for a human not worthy of dragon respect. Also used for a wicked person.

Rshon Aluel (R-ish-on AY-l-ool) – Dragon Father. The title given to an older male dragon who adopts a vulnerable dragon. Note dragon adoption does not supersede human parentage. A dragon would refer to their acquired heir's father as Vehyl-Aluel (human father) or Vehyl-Lullah (human mother)

Rshon mahthyt (R-ish-on MA-th-at) – Dragon Dung

Sudunah (SUE-dun-ah) - Sister

Sudunyn (SUE-dun-en) - Brother

Terini (TE-ree-ne) - Die

Vehyl (V-hay-el) – Word for a human that is worthy of dragon respect. Often used affectionately.

Wirahli Sais-levly – (WER-ah-lee S-ace - LEV-lee) Enslaved Flying Lizard. This is what is tattooed upon Jodathyn's skin and what Mandros' will not speak.

Extra words and dragon concepts

Aluel veh desn (AY – 1 -ool V-ay DES -n) – An honourable dragon term meaning father-by-heart. This term is for a man or dragon who has chosen to care for a younger, vulnerable person or dragon. In the case of Donatein he could not foster or adopt Jodathyn but he choose with his heart to love and care for Jodathyn as if he was his own.

Ayraelth (AIR - ay - leth) - Dragon Friend. Word only used to describe a close human/dragon friendship

E vydel el taldyn (EH VI-del EL TAL-din) – I love you fiercely

Elt rshon desn tollah hy el (ELT R-ish-on DEZ-n TOL-ah HI EL)

– My dragon heart beats for you

Character Guide

Humans (Vehyl)

Alina (Ay – lean -ah) – one of Jodathyn's predicted daughters

Addryn (ADD – rin) – the newborn son of Guardsman Tryst and Hallea

Carew Candyde – (CA – roo CAN – dy – d) – Guardsman of the King's Guard

Carvelle Pallarus – (CA – vell PA – la – rus) – the Crown Prince of Rama, the son of Kieryn and the nephew of Jodathyn

Estah (Es – ta) – one of Jodathyn's predicted daughters

Et-hir – (ET - her) – A Sionian barmaid in Kudah

Filyx Ostyn – (FEE – lix OH-stin) – Kamoore's young servant

Floyde (Lawman) – (FL – oy – d) – A lawman in Kudah

Fydellah Nahilya – (FI – del –ah NA – hil – ya) – An ex-slave, she was once a free woman

Hallea (HAL – leah) – the wife of Guardsman Tryst

Jael Aryk (JAY – el AY – rick) – Guardsman of the King's Guard and Troop Medic and Healer

Jasmeena (Jaz – mean – ah) – one of Jodathyn's predicted daughters

Jodathyn Pallarus - (JOD – ath – en PA – la – rus) – the Son of the Crown, the brother to the High King of Rama

Kamoore (Lord) – **(KA – more)** – A great lord of the King's council

Kieryn Pallarus (KEER – ren PA – la – rus) – the High King of Rama

Kya (KI-ah) – An old woman in Kudah

Larelle (LA - rell) – an orphan found need Habron, believed to be an ex-slave

Lyntton Pressun (LIN-Ton PRESS-sun) – A King's Guardsman

Myrus (MY – rus) – a child that Tornyth rescues during the battle for Pallaryn

Natayn Vyron (NAY -tian VY – ron) – the Spearmaster of Silverdyne

Ninah (Nee - nah) – An old healer in Habron

Nurlah (NUR - lah) – A madam of a brothel in Pallaryn

Nym Torkelle (N-im Tor-kel) – A rescued thief

Odelle Pallarus (O – Del Pa-la-rus) – the Queen of Rama, Kieryn's wife

Orion Maysden (O – ri -an Mays-den) – Jodathyn's servant, a horse-man of Silverdyne

Ruevyn Kelvie (ROO -Ven Kel-vee) – A childhood friend of Jodathyn

Solan (Lord) (SO-Lan) – A great lord of the King's council

Swyft (Magistrate) (SW - ift) – The magistrate of Kudah

Tad Vyron (TAD VY-ron) – a childhood friend of Orion's in Silver-dyne the son of Natayn the Spearmaster

Theo Torkelle (TH -e-o Tok-kel) – A rescued thief

Thylyssa (THIGH – lis - sah) – A great lord who had been banished from court

Tiernan Candyde (TIER-nan Can-dy-d) – Captian of the King's Guard

Voran Axtin (VOR-an AX – tin) – Jodathyn's ex-personal guard

Will (Willyrd) Hartcurt (WIL – lard HART –curt) – A young lord at court with a bad reputation

Yanna Vyron (Yah – nah Vy-ron) – the wife of Natayn, the mother of Tad

Dragon (Rshon)

Averyn (AV – er – in) – The orange battle dragon killed in action, believed to be a close friend of Mandros and second father to Sidrah, Zapyr and Deovyn

Ayrdonyth (AIR – doh – neath) – a new manifested dragon

Curarfur (CUR – ah – fur) – A blue battle dragon under Mandros' command with healing power

Deovyn (DEE- o -vin) – a russet dragon called the Small and Mighty, the son of Mandros. His human name was Jodathyn (JOD-ath-en)

Edisyn (ED – I – sin) – a dark red battle dragon who works alongside Tornyth. Life mate to Gylleah

Galgothmeg (GAL – goth – meg) – A red dragon known as Death and Despair

Gylleah (GUY - lee - ah) – A silver battle dragon, who fights along Tornyth. Life mate to Edisyn

Mashikah (MA - shis - car) – A sightless dragon, Mandros mate and mother to Sidrah, Zapyr and Deovyn

Mandros (MAND - roz) – An emerald dragon with many titles, including Flame and Fury, Deliverer, Father of this Land, the Green

Moroth (MOORE – oth) – a dragon known as the Grey Doom. Has power over fire and is a known enemy of Mandros.

Rhox (ROX) – a young bronze battle dragon, son of Zapyr. Sometimes call the illusionist

Rigyl (RI – gelle) – a newly manifested dragon

Roane (ROW - n) – an olive green dragon, known to be a trusted general and friend to Mandros

Salvea (SAL - vay) – a purple female battle dragon, her name is mentioned within the story

Sidrah (SID - rah) – a black dragon called Noble and Honourable, the daughter of Mandros. Her human name was Arturah (AR-tor-ah)

Tornyth (TOR- n -eth) – Winter's Dragon

Tygunyr (TIE – gah – ner) – a young battle dragon who escapes the evil one and has a message

Vydris (VI – driss) – a newly manifested dragon

Zapyr (ZAP - ear) – a gold dragon called Splendid, the son of Mandros. His human name was Kyran (KI-ran)

Support Animals

Zarine (ZA – reen) – A stolen mare

Zoryn (ZOR-en) – the grey stallion Orion had stolen. Named by Prince Carvelle

Zyan (ZI-an) – Voran Axtins red stallion named by Prince Carvelle.

Deceased Characters and Historical Figures

Ammerie (AM – ma – ree) – Jodathyn's late mother

Arturah (AR – tor - ah) – The human name of Sidrah, daughter of Arturyn

Arturyn Pallarus (AH – tur – en PA – la – rus) – The first King of Rama

Bear (B – air) – Jodathyn's dog

Curran Norrys (CAR –ran NOR-ris) – the barkeep in Kudah who protects Jodathyn and Nym. An ex-guard.

Donatein Manideep (DON – a – teen MAND – i – deep) – Jodathyn's oldest manservant

Edd Ryfern (ED RIGH – f - urn) – A King's Guardsman

Elyssa (E – lis - sah) – Ruevyn's love interest

Frayn (Lord) (FR – ain) – A great lord of the King's council

Hadryn Pallarus (HAD – ren PA – la – rus) – the late King of Rama. The father of Kieryn and Jodathyn

Hallidyn Whitoak (Lord) (HAL – i – din WIT – oak) – A great lord of the King's council. The King's favourite Lord

Illeanah Whitoak (Lady) (ILL– len – nah WIT – oak) – Hallidyn Whitoak's daughter and childhood friend of Jodathyn

Jodathyn (JOD – ath – en) – The human name of Deovyn, son of Arturyn

Kyran (KI - ran) – The human name of Zapyr, the son of Arturyn

Parrie (Par - re) – Jodathyn's dog

Soren Monster-Blade (SOR – en) – A human counterpart to Vadroil

Tomas Hartcurt (TO-mas HART-curt) – Will's elder brother

Tryst (TR -ist) – A King's Guardsmen

Tyr (TEAR) – The brother of Et-hir believed to be deceased

Vadroil (VAD – roy – el) – a dragon of myth and legend who

Valt Axtin (V – al – t AX – tin) – Jodathyn's personal guard

Location Guide

Arimac (ARA – mac)

Astyan (AST-yan)

Adavan Fields (AD-a-van)

Androssah (AN-dr-os-a)

Arah (AH-rah)

Arelle Forest (AH-el)

Arimac (A-ri-mac)

Artroth (ART-r-oth)

Aviah Valley (AY-vee-ah)

Belrah (BEL-rah)

Corlyn (COR-lin)

Farholm (FAH-hol-m)

Habron (HA-bron)

Halbeth (HAL-beth)

Haven Bay (HAY-ven)

Kudah (KOO-dah)

Korkalie (KOR-ka-lee)

Malara Gorge (MA-la-rah)

Myryn (MY-rin)

Paldera (PAL-deer-ah)

Pallaryn (PA-la-ren)

Paruhulise (PA-roo-hool – ees)

Paru (PA-roo)

Pyth (Pith)

Rama (RAH-ma)

Sant Burgundy (S-an-t BUR-gun-dee)

Silverdyne (SIL-va di-n)

Sion (SI-on)

Stonethaw (STONE-thaw)

Tannryn (TAN-rin)

Thrangul (THR-an-gool)

Torryn (TOR-ren)

Torqui (TOR-key)

Yanyima (YAN-yim-ah)

www.ingramcontent.com/pod-product-compliance
Lightning Source LLC
Chambersburg PA
CBHW060814120726
47909CB00006B/1921